Mrs Sidhu's JUST Desserts

Suk Pannu has written for some of Britain's best-loved Asian shows including *Goodness Gracious Me* and five series of the award-winning *The Kumars at No 42*. He has also contributed to radio shows like *The News Quiz* and Armando Iannucci's *Charm Offensive*, and he has had several successful series and pilots of his own.

Suk Pannu grew up along the M4, the draughty corridor that connects London to Slough. The son of immigrants, his upbringing was filled with discipline, love and aunties. At an early age, he got his head stuck into books and escaped into other worlds. He has long believed that one of his aunties would be the perfect crime solver.

BBC Radio 4's production of *Mrs Sidhu Investigates* charmed audiences and won praise from across the national media. The show was pick of the week/day in every national daily and Sunday paper, and earned the top spot on Radio 4's *Pick of the Week*.

X @sukpannu
@suk.pannu

Also by Suk Pannu

Mrs Sidhu's Dead and Scone

Mrs Sidhu's JUST Desserts

SUK PANNU

HEMLOCK PRESS

Hemlock Press
An imprint of HarperCollins*Publishers* Ltd
1 London Bridge Street,
London SE1 9GF

www.harpercollins.co.uk

HarperCollins*Publishers*
Macken House, 39/40 Mayor Street Upper,
Dublin 1, D01 C9W8, Ireland

First published by HarperCollins*Publishers* Ltd 2026

1

Copyright © Suk Pannu 2026

Suk Pannu asserts the moral right to
be identified as the author of this work

A catalogue record for this book is available from the British Library

ISBN: 978-0-00-856297-7 (HB)

This novel is entirely a work of fiction.
The names, characters and incidents portrayed in it are
the work of the author's imagination. Any resemblance to
actual persons, living or dead, events or localities is
entirely coincidental.

Typeset in Sabon LT Std by Palimpsest Book Production Ltd,
Falkirk, Stirlingshire

Printed and bound in the UK using 100% renewable electricity
at CPI Group (UK) Ltd

All rights reserved. No part of this publication may be
reproduced, stored in a retrieval system, or transmitted,
in any form or by any means, electronic, mechanical,
photocopying, recording or otherwise, without the prior written
permission of the publishers.

Without limiting the exclusive rights of any author, contributor or the publisher of this publication, any unauthorised use of this publication to train generative artificial intelligence (AI) technologies is expressly prohibited. HarperCollins also exercise their rights under Article 4(3) of the Digital Single Market Directive 2019/790 and expressly reserve this publication from the text and data mining exception.

To my Mum. Where it all started.

PART I

Every caterer loses a waitress once in a while. Three chief reasons:

1. Pay
2. Conditions
3. Murder

Life With a Knife, Mrs Sidhu's Memoirs

PROLOGUE

There were selfies and there were selfies to die for. This would be the latter.

For two hours Daisy drifted between the knots of excited people. She handed out wine and elegant plates of canapés. Her feet ached and the tray was wearing her arm out. Her chest and throat were stinging as the cold she was carrying around did its worst to her immune system. So it was nice when someone talked to her.

He had eyes the faded blue of an over-washed jumper, but still he was all coiled excitement. *La Scaletta* was in the building, the man said. It was the first time the painting had been shown in a decade. He bit down on a pastry and his faint smile seemed to betray a secret.

Daisy lingered, and the man opened up to her about the painting. She found that people often did, when you were young and pretty and not very important. Daisy had heard of the painting before, had studied it at school, but she listened all the same. Then he excused himself, slipping through the door with the keypad, as if a new destiny awaited him on the other side.

Nothing else remarkable would have happened if the door had been closed properly, but as Daisy went to turn away, either to return to the throngs with her tray, or to the kitchen to restock, she realised the door remained ajar the smallest crack. It was swollen and must have stuck as it closed behind him.

Her hand touched the handle.

Maybe the virus had addled her judgement. Maybe it was everything that was to come, and the idea that Daisy was on the cusp of becoming someone else. University was a week away, and she could barely wait to get there and show who she really was. Maybe it was the animation in the man's eyes, and wanting some piece of that for herself.

Daisy took two quick looks around. The other waiters had scuttled off for a fag break in the car park. Even Mrs Sidhu was looking the other way.

History of Art, Module 2, Modernism in Europe. She could hear Mr Samuels droning on as if he was right here. 'Gaston Lefevre was one of the early pointillist painters. He shared a studio with Seurat. Of course, his best-regarded painting by far is *The Bathing Pool*, also known as *La Scaletta*.'

Daisy had loved the picture from the instant she saw it, first on the overhead projector in the cramped classroom, then later running her finger over the satin-slick picture in the textbook. All that colour, all those dots, and when you added up the dots and the colours it made this transcendent picture of a woman ascending steps from a swirling pool of water. She was a goddess.

In secret moments, Daisy thought that was what university would be like. It would be showing her real self and everyone would have to look. Now the actual painting was here, in the building. She grabbed her phone from her pocket. Breaking in for a selfie with *La Scaletta*; now that was a cool story for freshers' week. With a shove, she slipped through the door.

She was in a corridor lit with bare bulbs and lined with bare brick. It smelled of river damp. At the end was a second door. That one was open too. She hesitated again, but she had come this far. She pulled at the handle and stepped inside, into the light.

What she saw next forced a gasp from her mouth. Fear froze her chest. She trembled and backed away. There was still time for her to leave, before she was seen. Except then the thing that had threatened to happen all evening, happened. The thing Daisy had been fighting as she smiled and circulated, and kept her face as far from her serving tray as possible. Before she could stop herself, Daisy coughed.

After that, she saw things in flashes and bursts, like a broken video transmission. There was the nice young man, with the washed-out eyes like they'd been through the laundry with the wrong detergent, but there was something so different about him. Mum always told her to use the right detergent or her dresses would fade. The man looked at her in the very strangest way as he approached, as if she wasn't there at all, as if she wasn't even human. Daisy hastened to run, but couldn't. A shadow arced across her vision. She felt a thud, and the world tilted, and when she touched her head, her hand came away red.

She heard a whimper. It must have come from her own

throat. She missed her mum, she wished she was here. Or Mrs Sidhu, who was the next best thing.

Now everything was colour. This was her time, she was the goddess emerging from that pool of water, maybe. Except she was still in the pool, and the water was red and spreading out all around her. Perhaps if she just took another step out of it she could get away. She could ascend those steps to heaven, like the girl in the painting. She could make her mum proud. She wished for her mum again, because she was cold and the light was fading, like the over-washed jumper, like the nice man's eyes.

I

Two Weeks Earlier

Until that day, life had been rolling along very nicely for Mrs Sidhu. It was difficult to know exactly when the wheels fell off. When they did, they would fall off one by one like those clown cars at the circus.

For now, the morning sun shone brightly on number 21 Jubilee Drive, Slough. It burst through the curtains of the bedroom.

Mrs Sidhu yawned and stretched. She lay at the centre of a swirl of bedcovers like a breached whale wrapped in sea foam. A stretch and her spine snicked into line. A smile tickled her lips. She had every expectation this day would go as perfectly as the one before.

A chime sounded. Mrs Sidhu lifted her phone from the bedside table, knocking to one side a stack of brochures. Brochures, she thought with a guilty swallow. She should have read them by now. She read the email instead.

Dear Mrs Sidhu,

I am seeking a caterer and the job is rather unusual. My employer, Hector Keys, would like you to make a sample dish at his house for two people. The dish can be of your own choosing, but as he will already have had dinner perhaps a sweet would be appropriate.

May I check your availability for tonight, and also for the night of the 17th?

Yours sincerely
Ivor Langtree (he/him)
Assistant to Hector Keys
The Keys Foundation
@keysfoundation

She typed out a reply with her thumb.

Dear Mr Longtrees,

I have catered a number of high end events partyand other gala type of things not just birthdays and funerals in Slough if you see my drift.

My collndar is very booked up in this time, but I am available tonight for sure. Please send me address and time.

Yours infinitely
Mrs Sidhu (Mrs/ Mrs)
Sidhu's Fine Catering
Slough and Environs (including Eton, Windsor and The Royal County of Berkshire)

[sent from my mobile device]

Mrs Sidhu sent her email, and an instant later, she winced. The autocorrect had done the usual opposite of correcting. She should have checked the spelling. She pinched up her eyes. Should have checked the grammar too. Still, it was sent now. There was no point dwelling on it. There was nothing to worry about.

She gave an easy sigh and let her head drop back onto her pillow. Despite her slapdash approach to business emails, Mrs Sidhu had every expectation of getting the job. She had sweated it out to build a decent reputation and now the hard work was paying off. For the last three months things had been going that way. She was on a roll, she was on fire, she was rolling sixes.

Rolls, though, have a habit of bumping into things, fires have a way of burning down their surroundings, and dice are only fast friends of the fates.

She yawned and allowed the phone to slip out of her fingers. It landed on the shagpile carpet with a thud. The bedroom was unreconstructed Seventies without any hint of playful irony. It simply hadn't been redecorated since the Seventies, and now Mrs Sidhu lived in a time warp. She slept in a land that knew disco. There was no time in her life to update it, and besides it had suited her husband's tastes, who too had been unreconstructed Seventies and even prone to a bit of disco if the right playlist came on the radio.

He had gone to the great glitter-ball in the sky, catapulted up there by the racking throes of a major coronary (his third and final one, thank you for asking). The debts he had left behind had pushed Mrs Sidhu to dance to her own tune and start her catering business. Initially it was a case of 'Staying Alive'. Recently, though, things had been easing, and it was more of a case of 'Good Times'. As she had reflected several times already this morning, it was going very nicely, thank you.

A few hours later, washed and dressed, Mrs Sidhu eased open a thirteen-inch sandwich tin and teased out a sponge cake. This one was perfect. They didn't always come away clean, and that meant starting again, but for three months Mrs Sidhu's life had been a well-greased cake tin – nothing stuck to the sides, and everything smelled delicious.

New Mrs Sidhu forged forward like a cruise ship. If she had searched her memory, she would have seen that her run of luck stretched back to her parting ways with Mr Varma, her former boss. She had shaken him off, ended their very unequal business partnership. One in which she did the work and he reaped the rewards.

Now the rewards were all hers. She had expanded her business and pulled in a lot more customers from outside her home town of Slough. These new customers paid plenty, but were also more demanding. There was nothing wrong with that. Hard work was what had got her here. She rose each day at five, as every good chef should, and attended to her prep work for a series of private catering jobs from Windsor to Eton, from Staines to Stoke Poges. When the private jobs took a dip, she had a bedrock of cafes and restaurants that relied on her to supply cakes, tray bakes, savouries and fancies.

Her recent success was because of her new motto. It was stuck to her bathroom mirror with a Post-it note, and it had stayed up no matter how steamy it got in there. It expressed in three words on crinkly paper what volumes could not. 'CRIME DOESN'T PAY' it said in blue-black biro. Blue-black was the most serious of biro inks in Mrs Sidhu's opinion.

Just sometimes, her eyes would stray to the headlines in the *Slough and District Chronicle*, especially when DCI Burton was featured. Burton's reputation had been rocketing since they last met. At these times distant yearning would sound through her, like a dog hearing the whistle of a previous owner.

At these times she would shiver and pull her cardigan tighter around her, she would watch her son, Tez, snoring in his bed, she would hold a photo of her departed husband to her chest until the whistle was silenced. She told herself, very properly, that solving crimes was not her job. Cooking mouth-drooling food was her job.

Today, this flawless cake was destined to be the top layer of an Empress sponge, an invention of her own, with a few tweaks to the classic Victoria sponge recipe. If Victoria was the Queen of England, she was also Empress of India, so why not a few touches of the subcontinent? Earl Grey tea was folded into the sponge mix, mango jam used instead of strawberry, buttercream icing made from cane sugar. Each touch elevated it a notch higher. She printed out the description on a card for the cafe owner to put out in front of the cake.

The phone pinged. That would be the veritable Ivor Langtree and she would be confirming the appointment. Mrs Sidhu wiped her hands on her apron and picked up the phone.

Dear Mrs Sidhu,
    Could you please meet Hector and Tani Keys at their home in Bowler's Green this evening at 8pm. We think it

would be retrospectively ironic to produce something like a traditional suet pudding. Bring your ingredients and equipment with you. A kitchen will be provided. Your fee will be £1,000, in cash. Hopefully, that will be adequate.

The address is Peety Lodge, Digbourne Lane, Bowler's Green, Berkshire.

Yours sincerely
Ivor Langtree (he/him)
Assistant to Hector Keys
The Keys Foundation
@keysfoundation

Her jaw hung loose. She read the email again. A thousand pounds, for a suet pudding? They could eat it as ironically as they wanted – this was going to be a cake walk. She chuckled at her own joke.

When she looked back on it, she would wonder if she should have asked more questions. A thousand pounds for a pudding, surely it was too good to be true.

The problem was she had stopped asking questions a while ago. New-found success and easy living had trained her out of the habit. It seemed to her that it was no more than she deserved. Life was going her way.

As she teased the tin away from the second Empress sponge cake layer, the metal side tore a lump the size of her fist away from the sponge's edge. Hands on hips, head shaking slowly, she blew a raspberry through her lips. Now when was the last time that had happened?

2

A broken sponge was not the worst start to the day, but when things are going well, the smallest of mishaps can have a disturbing effect. Mrs Sidhu spent the rest of the morning in a jittery state, which was not like her at all. Plus, something about its happening just when she got that email disquieted Mrs Sidhu. She often had these unplaceable feelings, and made connections that other people didn't.

No, it wouldn't do to start thinking like that, she told herself. She wiped her hands and made for the living room, a cup of tea in one hand and a plate of pani puree in the other. The spicy Indian snack was a favourite teatime treat. Paper-thin balls of deep-fried gram flour, filled with soft potato cubes shot through with tangy tamarind sauce.

She eased into her favourite armchair. Her usual pleasure was to read up on local news in the *Slough and District Chronicle*. Not today. Today, awaiting her was a stack of brochures and a weighty decision to be made.

Mrs Sidhu deserved a holiday. Starting the catering

business had been achingly hard work, and she finally had the income to take some time off. So why was she having such trouble deciding where to go?

She picked up the first brochure. Lush photographs caught the aquamarine of swimming pools and sandy beaches, the sunlight streaming in through hotel bedroom windows. It looked idyllic. Yet a voice in her head grumbled. 'But sand gets into your toes, you can never get them clean. As for swimming pools, you can't even swim.'

With a sigh, she closed that one and moved to the next. This displayed ancient stone churches and wine glasses tilting in the late evening sun of a Tuscan vineyard: winding roads, hilltop villages. The voice spoke up again. 'Winding roads? You'll get carsick. Hilltop villages? Vertigo. Those vineyard tours are a con, they're trying to get you to buy a case of priced-up plonk. And as for stone churches, what's the big deal? There's a temple right here in Slough, if you could be bothered to bow your head to someone more mighty than you.'

She slapped the brochure down. 'Oh shut up, will you?'

The voice in her head was not her own. It was the voice of her deceased husband, and it was a replay of the conversation they always had when discussing holidays. A conversation that almost inevitably led to a stalemate and a day trip to Bekonscot Model Village (a private obsession of her late husband) or a cream tea at a National Trust property. Mrs Sidhu was as fond of a National Trust cream tea as the next person, but sometimes she yearned for more.

'You all right, Mum?' Tez said.

Putting aside the matter of choice, there was another difficult matter and it was entering the room right now, her own son.

Two and a bit years ago, when her husband passed, her twenty-five-year-old, perennially unemployed son, Tez, had moved in. Apparently this was to 'look after' her. She quickly discovered that 'looking after' her meant sleeping late, occupying the sofa, going out until all hours and returning when his instincts told him food would be on the table.

As if to make her point, he was carrying a plate of pani puree and a hot cup of tea and dumped them on the coffee table before dumping himself on the sofa opposite his mum. 'So you chosen yet?' He grinned before taking a bite of the snack and a glug of the tea. 'Or is Dad still bugging you?'

'What makes you say that?'

Tez peered at the cover of the brochure in her hand. 'I know you're talking to Dad, because otherwise you just told a "Tuscany by Road" leaflet to shut up.'

'Oh, you heard that.'

'It can't be that hard.' Tez plucked up the brochures. 'Just get on and choose so we can get the packing right.'

How should she break it to him? He was flicking through a brochure for all-inclusive resorts in Majorca, grinning. In the end, she ripped the Band-Aid off in one swift move. 'I'm sorry, Tez, but you can't come along. I need time alone.'

'I don't mind,' Tez said.

'It's not that I don't want you with me,' she continued. 'It's that . . .' She had talked herself into a cul-de-sac. The painful truth was that she needed a break from Tez as much as the work. '. . . Sometimes I just like to be on my own.'

'I don't mind at all,' Tez repeated.

'I know it's a disappointment . . .'

It took a moment for Mrs Sidhu's ears to catch up with her mouth. 'Oh.' Her voice faltered. 'You don't want to come?'

Mrs Sidhu rubbed at her wrist. It was one thing when she wanted to go on holiday without Tez, but now that Tez wanted the same thing she felt as if she was owed an explanation.

Tez drew his eyebrows together. 'To be honest I feel like we could do with a break from each other.'

'Oh,' Mrs Sidhu said.

'I love living here with you, but you're always cooking or watching TV or shouting at holiday brochures. I wouldn't mind the place to myself for a week.' Tez turned concerned brown eyes on her. 'I hope that's not a disappointment.'

Mrs Sidhu swallowed. 'Of course not.'

'Great.' Tez let out a relieved breath. 'And I mean, I'm grown up, I don't want a holiday with my mum.'

'Quite.' Mrs Sidhu tossed the brochure aside. 'Anyway, I can't choose right now, I've got a job.'

A frown wrinkled Tez's brow. 'You said no more jobs. You need a rest. You promised you'd go on holiday.'

'Tez, it's just come in. And it's a thousand pounds for one cake, tonight. I'm taking the job. And maybe I'll get an upgrade on my hotel room.'

'You need to book one first,' Tez grumbled, and pouted. 'Just as long as you're going.'

Mrs Sidhu eyed him curiously. 'You definitely don't want to come.'

Tez shrugged. 'I'll be fine here.'

They each took another pani puree, filled it with sauce

and threw it back whole. And Mrs Sidhu observed Tez carefully from the corner of her eye.

Mrs Sidhu drove, and she drove hard and fast. Her green Nissan Micra complained and grumbled. Tough, she was in a bad mood too.

As the journey unwound, it eased the bitterness from this morning's encounter. The sour taste of Tez's rejection of going on holiday with her, even though she had been about to reject him, had stung.

Her eyebrows drew together in thought. Tez said he was concerned for her. Any mother would readily believe a son was concerned for her well-being, would get carried along on the tide of warm feeling. Not this mother. As an unofficial aunty to a swarm of nephews and nieces she had an instinct for these things. Tez was up to something and he needed her to be away. For a chest-constricting moment her head filled with visions of him throwing a party in her house. Her tension soon eased. She smiled and shook her head. Tez barely had any friends.

As she left the limits of Slough the concrete warehouses gave way to green verges and put thoughts of Tez out of her mind. Tuscany, she decided. And the money from this job would pay for some add-ons, like a vineyard tour. Or a sea-view room, she also decided, in a beach resort.

Mrs Sidhu swerved off the M4 a couple of junctions early. Berkshire's great, thundering motorway was, as usual, too impolite for her tastes. It was a classless intruder, a brusque commuter, too busy to take notice of the fields and hills either side. And years of domestic service had taught her the back entrance was far more revealing than the front. She eased her old Nissan Micra off the A-roads and out into the green lungs of the countryside.

It was evening and the late-summer sky was fading to deep blue. Below her was the Thames. On the other side, cupped in the valley like a silver coin in the palm of a hand, was the small town of Digbourne. On the near side, the village of Bowler's Green. They were connected by an ancient bridge, which she could see now, breaking the sunlit reflection of the river. The car plunged down the hill into Bowler's Green.

At last she turned through the gates of Peety Lodge and squeaked to a halt. He was waiting for her outside.

3

'Ivor Langtree.' He extended a limp hand. Ivor was a reedy man in his mid-twenties, tall and spare. He wore a linen suit which hung off him like a tent, and he was so thin that when a gust of wind caught his straw-blond hair, Mrs Sidhu was alarmed he would blow away.

'You're Mr Keys's assistant, the one who sent me the email. It's an unusual request.'

Ivor's lips twisted into a narrow smile. 'Uncle Hector gives the orders and we underlings do his bidding. Don't ask questions is the motto around here.'

'Mr Keys is your uncle?' Personal assistant to your uncle. That was a cushy number, she thought. Tez would call Ivor a nepo baby.

Her eyes took in the house for the first time. Peety Lodge was an imposing place. Tall, elaborate chimneys stared down to lichen-etched walls. It swept on to large grounds with trimmed lawns.

'It's an Arts and Crafts house,' Ivor said, answering the unasked question and leaving her less the wiser. 'One of the finest products of the movement, if you like that kind of thing.'

'Must be nice living here with your uncle and aunt.'

'Must be. But I live down in the village. They kicked me out of the big house.'

'Why was that?'

Ivor coughed. 'No reason.' Then his face twisted. 'Well, apparently, Little Ivy's got to toughen up, got to learn the realities of life.'

Mrs Sidhu listened and opened the boot of her car.

'Let me tell you, little Ivy's seen some pretty tough stuff. Little Ivy's mixed it up with the big boys, he's seen the underbelly of life. Oxford wasn't exactly a stroll in the park.' Then he added as an afterthought, 'Whatever Uncle Hector thinks, I'm not afraid of hard work.'

'Oh, good, I'm glad to hear it.' She swung a box from the boot of the car, which she held out for Ivor. 'Could you?'

It took a moment for Ivor to realise she meant him to carry it and he took the box with an ill grace. Mrs Sidhu heaved the rest of her supplies from the boot and they crunched up the gravel drive together. It was a short walk, made longer by Ivor's foot-dragging gait. Mrs Sidhu's arms were soon hurting.

'You remind me a little bit of my son.' She considered her own statement. 'He didn't go to Oxford, of course. And he doesn't know anything about art either. And he doesn't live in a lovely village.'

A frown marked Ivor's forehead. 'So in what way does he remind you of me?'

It dawned on Mrs Sidhu that she couldn't actually say the reason Ivor reminded her of Tez, because it would be frankly insulting. She settled for, 'He is also of medium height.'

If Ivor was nonplussed, he didn't show it. 'Did you know that I only got into my second-choice postgrad course? Did that happen to your son?'

'It didn't. That must have been quite a hardship for you.'

At the point where Mrs Sidhu's arms were about to fall off, Ivor stopped walking.

'It wasn't exactly ideal. Did I burst into tears?' He paused, his eyes watering. 'Well, I had a little moment. One isn't made of stone, you know. But –' Ivor raised his eyes to the sky – 'I picked myself up and made the best of it. And things worked out there for me.' His eyes misted. 'I had a wonderful experience.'

There seemed to be light at the end of the tunnel, and Mrs Sidhu allowed herself a relieved smile. 'That's great. So a happy ending after all. Shall we find Mr Keys?'

Ivor stood his ground. 'If only it were a happy ending,' he said. 'I was getting along marvellously in Paris, but then Uncle Hector saw fit to haul me back here – to learn the practicalities of life, stop wasting time and money on my education, he said. I mean, it's only my third postgrad degree.'

'Uncles, it's always the way. They always have money on their minds, in my opinion.'

Ivor dropped his voice, and his tone became menacing. 'Let me tell you something. My education was not wasted and I'm going to prove it very soon.' A momentary wind caught his hair and he narrowed his lips in a sly smile. 'Little Ivy's got plans, and Uncle Hector is fairly warned. He'd better play the game.'

The sharp tone of voice, filled with knives, made her bristle, but as the wind dropped the moment passed and Ivor fell again into his foot-dragging stride. He led her into the house and the kitchen, walking away with a droop to his shoulders.

Mrs Sidhu dismissed the threatening words. Ivor Langtree was as harmless as a fly. In fact, the only truly remarkable things about him were his eyes. They looked faded, as if they had been through the wash one too many times.

Cooking would have been easier in her own kitchen. In the client's home she had to make do with domestic equipment and cramped work spaces. On the plus side, the view across the back garden was much better than hers. Instead of foot-high weeds, a trimmed lawn ran down to the river where water lapped at a boathouse.

She murmured a prayer and wiped a bead of sweat from her brow. Summer was departing as slowly as an unwelcome relative, an Indian uncle who had cleared out the booze cabinet, belched his way through dinner, and was now tarrying at the door and hoping to stay the night.

For Mrs Sidhu, summer could not end soon enough – heat was no friend to the menopausal chef. She turned to her work.

The pudding steamed and the aroma of strawberry jam and suet rose from the salver. Mrs Sidhu breathed it in, took up the cake slice and steadied her hand. With careful movements, she cut the roly-poly and tipped the first slice onto an ivory-white plate. The pudding was soft, and it could tear at any moment, but the first transfer was successful. There it was, the thousand-pound pudding.

Soon a row of single portions were laid on the counter in warmed bowls. Fresh Devon custard was running from her ladle and formed a pool around each, a vanilla sea breaking against a fragrant desert island framed in a perfect white-china horizon. She just hoped it was worth it.

Mrs Sidhu knew she was a good chef, but short of covering it in gold, there was very little she could do to a jam roly-poly to up the value. It was the simplest and most traditional of English puddings. Now it was delivery time and a chance to meet her clients. What kind of people paid a thousand pounds for one bowl of pudding?

4

Everything was white: white walls, white furniture, white bookshelves, white carpet.

She approached the living room, tray loaded with pudding portions, but held herself back at the door. Though it was open, some kind of meeting was in progress. To Mrs Sidhu's relief, the group inside the room were engrossed in their own business. It gave her time to observe her mysterious clients.

In the heart of the room, holding court, were a couple that could only be Hector and Tani Keys. They were seated on a low white sofa. They were both in their fifties. He had spiked silver hair over a swept brow and neon-pink spectacles. She had a hard bonnet of dyed blonde over dark glasses, and was half-turned towards him, a long leg folded over her thigh. To one side, sat Ivor, twirling a pen with a notepad on one knee. He gazed out of the window, contriving to look bored and annoyed at the same time. In a row behind them on chairs, were a handful of people. They perused thoughtfully and appreciatively but otherwise remained silent. They fell into the category of 'flunkies'.

She took a step forward and was halted by Tani's raised hand.

As Mrs Sidhu watched, silence fell on the room. Two men wearing grey overalls entered. In white-gloved hands, they carried between them a painting. It was small, about a foot and a half long and a foot high. It was made up of dark rectangles.

The group observed the little painting without discussion.

Tani lit a cigarette and watched Hector through the dark lenses. Hector stroked pink lips with small fingers. At last, he emitted a strange noise, like the cooing of a pigeon. 'Ooooh.'

Tani nodded to the two men who took the painting away. 'Make a note, Ivy. Stan Obard's *A Night Song*, it's a yes.'

Ivor made a mark in his notebook. The two overalled men returned shortly, carrying between them a photograph.

'Next is *Art Rocks*, by Petra,' Ivor said, checking his notes. 'This is a photograph, naturally – the actual piece stands four feet tall and is made of iron-rich rocks collected in Australia. It's the last entry for the opening-night show.'

Mrs Sidhu watched in fascination as Hector whined low and long before nodding again.

This time Tani flexed her long fingers. 'If you say so, Hector.'

At this point, a woman entered. She was in her forties, attractive with a low dark fringe bobbing over serious brown eyes. Tani stood. 'Ah, Hector, Ivy. You haven't met our new gallery director yet. Please meet Jenny Leblanc.'

Jenny stepped forward. The effect on Ivor was electric.

He dropped his notebook, apologised, then scrambled to pick it up and in the process upset a vase of flowers.

'I'm so sorry,' he said.

Hector squawked at the sudden disturbance, and Tani eyed Ivor with maternal concern. 'Ivy, are you all right?' Eventually it was all sorted out and Jenny Leblanc shook hands with Hector. When she moved to Ivor, he spoke first. 'Ivor Langtree, assistant. Um, I'm very pleased to meet you.'

'We're very lucky,' Tani drawled. 'Jenny has come from the Louvre with excellent references and at short notice. Jenny, we're making our last selection.'

Jenny turned to look at the photograph. She tapped a finger to her cheek and assessed the work with a professional intensity. 'I'm worried that the work is immature, that this artist isn't ready for such a major exhibition,' she said. 'She's barely out of art school. I would vote no.'

Tani's eyebrows arched. Hector sat in cold silence. Tani reached for his hand, but he snatched it away. He cleared his throat.

'I have to disagree.' Hector spoke in a rich voice, tinged with an accent Mrs Sidhu couldn't place. These were the first words he had spoken since she had entered the room, and came almost as a surprise after his birdlike noises.

'I take the point about youth and immaturity,' he continued. 'But I have seen a great many young artists. In Petra, what I see is potential. In my opinion Petra is going to be the next Ned Barrow.'

This attracted sighs and gasps from the others. This Ned Barrow must be a big deal, thought Mrs Sidhu.

Jenny's demure features wrinkled in surprise. 'Are you sure?'

Hector blinked through his pink frames as if he didn't

understand the question. 'I rarely joke about art. But of course, I am just one vote.' He cast his gaze around the room to see who might vote against him. All hands leapt up.

'So that's a yes for *Art Rocks* by Petra,' said Ivor.

For some reason, Jenny sent him a look of pained hurt. Ivor focused on his shoes and blushed.

Hector smiled. 'So it's in the show, Jenny?'

Jenny blushed. 'Of course, it's your choice. I didn't mean to . . . After all, you are Hector Keys. I should have thought.'

Hector nodded graciously.

Mrs Sidhu cleared her throat. She had been standing with her tray of puddings throughout this performance. Now, for the first time, everyone in the room seemed to notice her. A sweat broke out across her back.

Tani's dark glasses turned on Mrs Sidhu. 'Who's this?'

Hector gestured airily. 'Ah, this is Mrs Sidhu,' he smiled. 'She has brought some food for us to savour. Let's eat before it gets cold.'

Colder, thought Mrs Sidhu.

'What happened to Maurice?' Tani asked.

'I wanted to try something new. Something fresh. Mrs Sidhu is from Slough.'

A stir went around the room. Her face flushed. They were all looking at her, as if she was a rare specimen. She was searching for somewhere to put down her tray when the weight was suddenly lifted from her hands. The two overalled men took it between them and carried it before Hector. Hector held it up to eye level, and examined the puddings from all angles.

'Aren't you going to try it?' she asked.

The idea seemed new to both of them. Tani stubbed out her cigarette and passed a bowl to Hector. Finally, he took the spoon, and like Arthur grasping Excalibur, pulled it from the suet and custard and held it aloft.

Mrs Sidhu tensed and patted a napkin to her forehead. As Hector piled the spoon high with jam, suet sponge and custard, Tani did the same. Mrs Sidhu's heart beat slightly faster than usual.

Hector, with great deliberation, inserted the spoon, compressed his lips and drew it back out clean. He chewed, he munched, he swallowed. Slowly he smiled and having taken a second spoonful, he handed the bowl back to Mrs Sidhu.

'Mmmm, yes,' said Hector excitedly. 'A monument to traditionalism with brutalist irony.'

'Yes,' said Tani, flat-voiced. 'Substance and form guided by colour.'

This was the signal for the others in the room to dig in. The tray was passed around and for the next few moments Mrs Sidhu heard the music of spoons on porcelain and her own heart thumping. Heads nodded with approval, lips were licked in satisfaction and Mrs Sidhu's heart rate returned to something almost approaching normal.

'Thank you for coming at such short notice. It was quite delicious, Mrs Sidhu.' The guests had left. Hector led Mrs Sidhu through the corridors of the house, which were lined with paintings. 'Now I have a treat for you.'

'There was a mention of a cash fee,' Mrs Sidhu said.

'Of course, of course.' Hector patted his pockets absently.

'Let's see now, where did I put it? I know, it's in a drawer in the vestibule.'

'Oh, shall we?' Mrs Sidhu said.

'In time, but first, I can't let you leave without seeing our art collection. You must be straining at the leash.'

'That's most kind.' Mrs Sidhu's feet hurt, her back hurt and her fingers hurt. The only thing she was straining for was to sink into a hot bath, count her money and book her holiday. 'But don't feel you have to,' she said.

'No, I insist, and I will take you personally.'

The house smelled of wax polish and cigarettes. It was large and twisted in on itself like a geometric puzzle.

As Hector strode forward, Mrs Sidhu scurried after him. His bowl of pudding was still in her hand. 'You're sure you're not going to have any more?' He had only had two spoonfuls. Was there something wrong with it?

The nerves of Hector's reaction were combined with the nerves of carrying a custard-thick plate, heightened by the presence of valuable art. The walls were decked with abstract oil paintings, the console tables held fragile ceramics. None of them, thought Mrs Sidhu, would be enhanced by custard spatters.

They stopped at a painting. Hector admired it and let out an airy sigh. Mrs Sidhu did the same. 'Seurat. Pointillism is so complex, simple, superficial. Yet it's so deep, don't you think?'

Mrs Sidhu decided it was best if she thought the same as her client. 'Oh, yes, my favourite.'

Hector nodded before they moved on once more, and Mrs Sidhu noticed a space between two paintings.

'Now, I must disappoint you here. No doubt you were

expecting to see the legendary *La Scaletta*, Lefevre's masterpiece.'

Mrs Sidhu's feet throbbed. 'Of course, what a blow. That's also my favourite.'

They moved on. The door was in sight now, thank the heavens. Hector spoke in a lowered voice. 'It has been moved for its own safety.'

'Safety?' she stopped.

'A twelve-million-pound painting needs special precautions, especially in the light of recent events.' Hector carried on towards the door and she scurried to catch up. He said no more on the subject, but Mrs Sidhu couldn't help marvelling at the sum of money or the reference to 'recent events'.

Fortunately, her aching feet were finally at the front door. Hector opened it, and Mrs Sidhu shuffled uncomfortably on the spot, prompting a confused look from Hector.

'The fee?' she said.

'Of course.' Hector threw his hands up in the air, sending the spiked tips of his hair bouncing. There was an antique sideboard by the door, and he went through the drawers, throwing out envelopes and old receipts. 'Ah, here it is.' He pushed a roll of notes into her hand. 'And a little something extra. Thank you again – the pudding was delicious. It took me back to my childhood. We will be in touch soon.' Hector closed the door behind her.

Mrs Sidhu bounced the roll of cash in her hand. Now, that was the kind of easy-money gig she wouldn't mind doing again.

She stood on the doorstep clutching the roll of banknotes and a bowl of pudding, barely touched. She marvelled at both and stuffed the money into her pocket, wondering instead about what a rented villa all to herself might feel like, and what Tuscan wine would taste like straight from the vine. A small part of her mind wondered what he meant by being 'in touch soon', but only a small part.

5

The answer to what Hector meant came the next day in yet another email from Ivor.

Dear Mrs Sidhu,
    I am delighted to tell you that in view of your successful trial last night Hector Keys has selected you as the caterer for the opening of the Pump House Gallery.
    The Pump House will be the cutting-edge space to house the Keyses' extensive art collection. We would be delighted if you could provide finger food for the opening. We will provide wine. The opening is on the evening of Saturday the 17th and we expect 100 guests. Details of our budget will follow.
    If you have any questions, please do not hesitate to ask myself or gallery director Jenny Leblanc (copied in). More details to follow on your acceptance. Hector himself has asked me to convey personally to you that he expects great things.

Yours sincerely
Ivor Langtree (he/him)
Assistant to Hector Keys
The Keys Foundation
@keysfoundation
cc
Jenny Leblanc
Gallery Director
The Pump House Gallery
Jenny.Leblanc@PumpHouseBerks.org

Another email pinged in a moment later with a breathtaking figure for the budget. It was followed by a humble apology. 'We do hope this will be sufficient.'

She realised she was holding her breath and let it fall out in one big exhalation. Once again, Mrs Sidhu found herself reading an email from Ivor Langtree twice.

A voice in her head whined that it was too good to be true. Even with staff and equipment hire it was a huge profit, an obscene profit. She should confess immediately that it was too much.

She clenched her jaw shut. She needed another voice, someone who worried less about morals.

'This is very impressive this, Mrs Sidhu.' Mr Varma tapped the printout of the email twice for emphasis. 'Very impressive indeed. And all you had to do was cook one pudding?'

'For a thousand pounds,' Mrs Sidhu said. 'It was the strangest job of my life. But it turned out to be a test. This is the real job.'

'How much are they offering for this one?'

Mrs Sidhu showed him the follow-up email. He licked

his lips. Mr Varma was in his late fifties. He was a small man, of restless energy and cheap suits. Cheap everything, now she came to think of it. The King of Slough's cash-and-carry scene was prone to special offers and deals of all kinds.

They were in his office, which perched on top of his flagship cash-and-carry store. It occupied a battered and torn square of broken tarmac on an industrial estate sandwiched between Slough and the M4 motorway. On one side a tyre and exhaust centre plied a busy trade; on the other a windowless, bright-blue warehouse which sold storage cubes for Berkshire's hoarders. Mrs Sidhu had read that when the owners defaulted on the rent, the contents of the cube were auctioned off. On at least one occasion the contents included nothing but stacks of old newspapers and magazines of almost no value. On another, the lucky buyer uncovered a collection of art photographs worth thousands of pounds.

Varma's office overlooked a broad square of cracked tarmac, divided into parking spaces by fading white lines.

'So you think it's on the level? You think I should take it?' She twined and twisted her fingers. 'I'd value your advice.'

Varma had been her husband's oldest friend. Together they had built their businesses, advising each other, supporting each other. When her husband needed a best man, he called on Varma. When Varma needed a bank loan, Mr Sidhu stood as his guarantor. In the long run Varma's business had prospered and her husband's had failed. When her husband died, Varma was the one who had covered the debts left behind. He had, for a time, become her boss. They fought. He took advantage of her work ethic, forcing her to cook endless aubergine bhajis. For her part she may have got distracted by a murder to the point where she allowed herself to stretch hygiene regulations. It was an uncomfortable thought, and she pushed it to one side. They had parted ways and since then their relationship had improved; now she came to him with all her important decisions just as her husband had. Varma might be a cheapskate but he was the closest connection she had to big business. There was also a little part of her that wanted him to see how well she was doing without him.

Varma mused, sniffing sharply. 'What were you thinking of doing?' he asked.

'I was thinking,' Mrs Sidhu said, finger on chin, 'onion bhajis, and some of my cakes and tray bakes, maybe some Indian sweets.'

He chuckled. 'They don't want your onion bhajis and your tray bakes, Mrs Sidhu.' He waved his arms excitedly. 'You can't just scatter a few samosas and a couple of ludoos around the place. This is an art gallery.' Varma's cupped fingers grasped empty air, his eyes turned to the ceiling. 'An ART GALLERY,' he repeated, all in caps. 'They expect . . .' He broke off, his empty hands fell to his desk. It seemed he could not even imagine what they expected. He tapped the email again. 'They expect great things, says so right here.'

Her chest tightened. 'Where?' Mrs Sidhu put her spectacles on and peered at the email over his shoulder.

'Right here.' He tapped at the page once more, testily. 'You really have to read your communiqués more carefully.'

'Great things? What's that supposed to mean?' She wrung her hands. 'Salmon blinis?'

'Salmon blinis?' Varma spluttered. 'Can you hear yourself? Can you hear the condescending laughter from the art aficionados? Mrs Sidhu, I beg you, go big or go home.' He spun his chair dramatically, sighed and looked out onto the car park. 'They're paying top dollar.' Again the tapping of the email was playing on Mrs Sidhu's nerves. 'You need something extraordinary to pull this off.'

She twisted her fingers once more. 'So you think I shouldn't do it?'

He spun back round to face her. 'Mrs Sidhu, have I taught you nothing? Don't you see this opportunity for what it is?'

'A chance to grow as a chef, as a caterer and even as a culinary artist.'

Varma waved all that away like a bad smell. 'It's a chance to make a lot of money for doing virtually nothing! That's what art's all about. Think like an artist. You throw a load of paint at a canvas, suddenly it's worth a couple of million. It's the biggest racket in the book.'

Mrs Sidhu didn't know much about art, but she was pretty sure that's not what it was about. She thanked him, nonetheless. 'You're right that I should take the job, for whatever reason.' She clapped her hands together. 'I'll simply have to delay my holiday.'

'Your holiday?' A change came over Varma as he read the email again with a worried frown. 'I see now, Mrs Sidhu, that this event is on the seventeenth. You're supposed to be away for that whole week. It's your holiday week.' Varma was pacing around his office now, arms behind his back, head slunk. 'If you stay it means you'll be here, in Slough, for the week following the seventeenth.'

Mrs Sidhu's head tilted to one side. 'How do you know about my holiday?'

Varma became vague. 'You must have mentioned it.'

She had no memory of mentioning it to anyone but Tez.

'The main thing is,' Varma continued hastily, 'that you need a holiday. Look at you – pale, exhausted, worn out, old.' He stopped his relentless pacing and sat at his desk, staring at Mrs Sidhu and fiddling with his pen. He cleared his throat. 'It's just that everyone was so relieved when they heard you were going away.'

Her eyes opened wide. 'They were? Who's everyone?'

Varma brushed forwards. 'We are all relieved for your health and well-being. The more I think about it, Mrs Sidhu, the more I think this job is not for you. Frou-frou snacks for posh snobs, an ART GALLERY!' He said it with all caps again, but this time added a sneer around the word. 'I mean, what do you want with that?'

Mrs Sidhu blinked. A moment ago she had a clear decision. 'But you just told me it was a chance to make a lot of money.'

A pinch of perspiration broke out on Varma's face. 'Did I? Doesn't sound like me.' He took an imitation silk handkerchief from his breast pocket and wiped the very real sweat on his brow.

Mrs Sidhu clenched her fists in a moment of decision. 'Thank you for your kind advice, Mr Varma, and for your concern about my health and well-being. But I think I'll take your advice.' She considered this. 'I mean, your first advice not your second. When a challenge is presented, Mrs Sidhu always accepts. I'm taking the job.' Her fingers fumbled on the phone keyboard as she poked out a reply. She needed to strike an aloof tone. It never pays to look over-keen.

Dear messes Langtree.

You have caught me at an opportune mum aunt. I have nothing pending in my shed yule on or in the enver ons of the 17th. Therefore, I am grudgingly able to offer my services for said fee.

Yours infinitely
Sidhu (Mrs.)
Sidhu's Fine Catering
Slough and Environs

PS can I just check that was the correct fee and not a typo?

The reply came back immediately. It was not a typo.

6

'We expect great things.'

That had been ten days ago. Now each word sounded like a gong in her head, a bell at a funeral procession.

Mrs Sidhu had a piece of paper in front of her. Elbows propped on the kitchen counter, she stared at it. It was blank, white and featureless. It was as empty as the sky that extended without end over Jubilee Drive.

She clicked her tongue on the roof of her mouth. Mrs Sidhu was stuck. How had it come to this? Things had been going so well.

Eleven days ago came the job at the Keyses' house followed by the offer of the gallery-opening job. The next day she had run into Mrs Prakesh at the market.

'Mrs Prakesh, how nice to see you.'

Mrs Prakesh had smiled her thin-lipped grin, and asked with a twist of her head how things had been going since Varma sacked her. She frowned in a pretence of sympathy, as if Mrs Sidhu had a terrible illness, an illness called 'unemployment'. Mrs Sidhu picked up a handful of okra and stuffed it nonchalantly into a brown paper bag. She was able to reassure Mrs Prakesh, and wipe the smug smile from her face, that she was doing very well. In fact, she had just secured a job at – and here she paused for a breath and to scrumple up the paper bag dramatically – an art gallery. The effect on Mrs Prakesh was like salt on a slug.

'So you won't be going on holiday on the seventeenth?' she asked.

Should Mrs Sidhu feel disturbed that everyone knew about her holiday? Idle gossip, of which Mrs Sidhu disapproved, was an epidemic in Slough. 'If it's any of your business, no. I'll be too busy serving finger foods to the arts elite,' she said, with a narrow smile.

Mrs Prakesh had wrinkled up like a prune and slithered off down the aisle.

Mrs Sidhu sighed deeply; it was a happy memory. That had been ten days ago. Ten days in which she had nothing but time. No demands, no directives from her new employers, just a free hand to do whatever she wanted. She had even palmed off her regular baking orders to other suppliers, just so she could concentrate on this job.

So.

What should she do? Her nails rattled a rhythm on the kitchen counter. She looked at the calendar, where the 17th was ringed in red. Today was the 14th so she still had four days, which was plenty if she just made a decision now. She opened her cookery books and magazines and set out to find what she should cook next. It could be anything, but it could not be any old thing.

Colourful photos flitted past as her fingers flipped the pages. Meringues, pastas, casseroles and cakes. Mrs Sidhu clicked her tongue on her palate. She actually felt like cooking a vegetable dish and she was just circling around the thought that perhaps that dish was an aubergine bhaji. She slammed the cookbook shut to exorcise the thought. Aubergine bhaji was the exact dish that Varma had forced her to cook endless amounts of. She was never going back to that hellscape.

She scratched her side. Her hair was wild, her dressing gown was stained. She sniffed herself. She smelled bad. She had not had her customary daily shower or bath in three days.

The good news was that Tez was helping. 'I have this theory about modern art,' Tez said. 'You know how you tell what's what with modern art?' He furrowed his brows seriously; it was clear he was about to deliver the killer blow. 'Boobs.'

She dragged her head up from the counter. 'Tez, this is not helping.'

'Hear me out to the end. If the boobs are normal, it's smut. But if the boobs are upside down, or they've put them on a metal dog or something, it's art. That's how you tell.' She stifled a groan, but Tez was not finished. He laid a compassionate hand on her shoulder. 'What you need to do is find the "boobs" within your cooking and put them on a metal dog, or upside down.' Tez, seemingly assured that he had helped, wandered away to solve deeper problems of space and time.

Action was what she needed. Action would force the issue. She reached the kitchen counter in short strides. It took her three goes to light the ring. Her fingers were shaking.

She picked a sauté pan at random from the rack,

slammed it down on the range and upped the gas. The pan reverberated, ringing out into the silence that had filled the kitchen for ten days like a suffocating blanket.

Mrs Sidhu favoured aluminium over non-stick and the light metal was soon heated. It smoked with aromas of past dishes cooked, dishes that had come to mind so easily. Perhaps there was an idea somewhere in the corner of her consciousness, but if there was, it would not come out of the shadows. She flipped the cooker knob and the flame futtered out, taking with it any remaining confidence that she was about to have a breakthrough.

What had she done?

A panicked film spooled across her mind. She would run back to Varma, she would beg him to take her on again, she would accept her place as a lowly producer of cook-chill foods that would rest in the fridge of a corner shop until the sell-by date (and a bit longer if the cabinet belonged to Varma) until being disposed of in a landfill.

No, she took herself in hand, she was not going back. The problem was that she wasn't going forward either. She returned to the kitchen table and the piece of paper. It had not miraculously filled itself with ideas. Perhaps she could force one. She wrote across the top, 'Menu for Art Gallery Opening'. It looked good. She scratched in two underlines. Now it looked too important.

Perhaps the piece of paper itself was the problem: too smooth, too regimented. She screwed it up and threw it away. From the recycle bin she plucked out an old envelope. This was better. She began writing easily and freely on the rough, brown paper, finding after half an hour of this concentrated effort that she had produced three doodles. One of a dog, one of a bird and one abstract circular shape, possibly a plate. The crumpled envelope bounced around the rim of the recycling bin before joining the blank sheet of paper.

The sound of laser-gun fire and explosions interrupted her thoughts. In the living room, Tez was hunched on the sofa with a game controller, spitting death at hordes of space zombies. Now there was a mind that could handle huge amounts of nothing. His mind was a powerhouse of nothingness. For the first time in her life, she envied him.

Aware, somehow, through base animal intelligence that his mum was glaring at the back of his neck, Tez yawned, scratched and paused his game. 'What's for dinner?' he said.

More choices. She spoke through clenched teeth. 'I don't know! Just tell me what you want!'

Tez jerked round in his seat. She had spoken with too much force. She apologised and asked again, calmly. 'You've got all the choice in the world. I'll cook you anything you want, anything you can think of, no time, no expense spared.' She sat back, arms crossed. That was laying it on a bit thick, but he had asked for it. Now let him break his spirits on the rocks of indecision.

With no pause whatsoever Tez spoke. 'Chana dhal, rice with peas, chicken, two rotis, mango pickle.'

Mrs Sidhu sighed. What it was to know your own mind, but then it was easier if that mind was small; less space for the ideas to hide. Still, at least she had something to do. She started slicing onions, soaking chana, defrosting chicken. And slowly, that gave Mrs Sidhu the glimmerings of an idea. She rushed back to the recycle bin. For a moment she could not choose which balled-up piece of paper to grab. Laser paper or envelope? There was more space on the laser paper and it already had the title. The envelope seemed more friendly but was filled with doodles. She dithered like this for a few moments, eventually deciding to start afresh on a torn piece of cardboard from a cereal packet, and was just heading back to the kitchen counter when the phone rang, completely wiping the idea from her mind. It was a wrong number and she wrung the phone like a chicken's neck.

The phone responded by flashing up the last email from Ivor. She must have left it open. She read it again, and slowly a new thought formed in her mind. Not a menu idea, as such. A spark of hope flashed inside her. Maybe this Jenny Leblanc could answer some questions.

She knocked the cornflake off her chin, showered, put on her best Marks & Spencer's slacks/cardigan combo and scooped her bag and her car key up from the hall table. It was time to seek inspiration, and she knew exactly where to find it.

7

The Pump House, paradoxically, was neither a house nor had any pumps in it.

Small groups milled around the entrance, and Mrs Sidhu hesitated to enter. It was such a lovely morning, and suddenly she wished she had taken her holiday and that all this worry about what to cook would just go away. Without thinking, she allowed herself to be carried along by the buffeting currents of the people around her and found herself at the back of a tour group.

The tour guide was a large woman draped in purple chiffon, a grimacing smile and a lot of perfume. She carried a bright umbrella which she used to point at things. Her name badge said 'GERTIE' in large letters and she spoke in a loud, deep voice.

'Gather in, dearest ones. The Pump House was originally a pumping station. It was opened in 1876 to move water from the Thames to be treated at a nearby waterworks.' She rolled her large shoulders and stabbed the umbrella in the general direction, forcing an American couple to duck. 'Now defunct. It has been converted into a modern art space by the Keys Foundation which will soon open to the public, housing their extensive art collection. A Japanese architect has reworked the building, inspired by the water setting.'

Mrs Sidhu took a closer look at the building. Much of the original brick building had been dismantled and replaced by glass and steel and there was indeed something liquid and clear about the design.

'Still pumping plenty of sewage though.' The man standing next to her sniffed. He had one eye larger than the other, and wore a frayed waistcoat. His air was one of someone who fully expected everyone to share his disapproval. 'The Keys collection,' he snorted. 'Just a few knick-knacks, hardly a true collection.'

Gertie aimed her umbrella and her grimacing smile at him, though it was uncertain which was more terrifying. 'Ludo, dear, I'm working. Do toddle along.'

Ludo grumbled something obscene but did as he was told, shuffling away from the gallery back towards the village.

Gertie took up her story again. 'The most significant of the works being shown here will be *La Scaletta*. You've heard of it, no doubt.'

There was a gasp from the tour group, one of whom spoke up. 'Will we be able to see it today?' When Gertie gave a sad shake of her head, everyone groaned in disappointment.

Twelve million pounds, Mrs Sidhu thought, and something Varma said about art being a racket came back to her. Who worked out what such a thing was worth?

'Security has been increased around the great work. As

you know the painting, in its relatively short history, has been stolen four times. The fourth occasion was during the war, and in the chaos it remained hidden and unrecognised until Hector Keys came along.' Now Gertie beckoned the group closer, though most stayed outside the radius of her umbrella. 'Come closer, dear ones, for I can disclose that there was a recent attempt to steal the painting from the very home of the Keyses. That's right, an art heist right here in Bowler's Green.' Hands leapt to mouths and Mrs Sidhu could feel the electric current of scandal and intrigue running through the tour group. Gertie pulled back her shoulders.

'I shouldn't have told you that, but it happens that I am personally acquainted with the Keyses. So please do keep that between ourselves.'

Some of that electric current jolted up Mrs Sidhu's spine. She had to admit this was intriguing. It must have been what Hector Keys had meant by 'recent events' and the reason it had been moved from his house for safekeeping.

Something here, though, struck her as odd. Mrs Sidhu kept up with the *Slough and District Chronicle*, especially the crime pages. An attempted art heist was a big story and she couldn't believe she hadn't read about it. She shivered with the thrill. It must have been hushed up.

'I've got permission from Hector Keys himself to go inside but we need to be careful. As you know the gallery opens in three days with a private function.'

Three days to opening. Now a new electricity ran up Mrs Sidhu's spine, as with a dull shock she remembered why she was here. She had a job to do. She was supposed to be looking for inspiration, she was supposed to be looking for Jenny Leblanc. The tour group entered the building, but Mrs Sidhu dithered for a moment. Perhaps her search for Ms Leblanc could wait a little longer. She tagged along behind the tour group, unable to help herself. It was such a fascinating tour.

Mrs Sidhu edged into the Pump House gallery like a crab walking into a seafood restaurant, hoping to go unnoticed.

Discreet lights picked out artworks. Freshly painted white walls displayed paintings. Glass mounts cradled eggshell-thin ceramics. Everywhere the eye fell there was an object of beauty. The fear that she might break something was followed by the teeth-on-edge horror that she might just do that.

This was a concern that didn't afflict the gallery staff. Everywhere there was movement and action. Jumpsuited technicians unwrapped vases, carried paintings and hoisted sculptures into place.

The guttural sound of an engine made Mrs Sidhu jump and she had to skip smartly out of the path of a tractor. It swung round, shiny and new and bearing the Keys Foundation logo. She shrank back as it clanked past her. A strange metal contraption groaned and creaked, suspended from its forks.

'Please be careful.' Gertie continued her tour. 'As you can see, everything is being made ready for opening night. We are privileged to be allowed in, a special favour from the Keyses.' They followed the tractor to the back of the gallery where a pair of double doors opened on to a smaller gallery. 'This is Gallery 2, and I've brought you here because it is a special place. Here, Hector Keys has assembled three artists. Of course, Lefevre.' She pointed the tip of her umbrella to a space on the wall, like the space on the wall in the Keyses' house. 'That is where *La Scaletta* will hang.'

There was so much reverence for the gap, Mrs Sidhu honestly feared that some of the tour group were about to kneel in prayer. Gertie swung her aim to the left. 'Then flanking it on this side is Ned Barrow's contemporary masterpiece *The Knight*.' She pointed to the tractor. The driver threw a lever and the metal thing swung upwards to the ceiling. There, in the shadows, technicians on ladders were working with chains to secure it in place. It took Mrs Sidhu's eyes a moment to understand what she was looking at. Suspended above was an inverted medieval knight, arm held forward and in its chain-mailed fist a glittering glass sword. Her eye followed the gigantic steel body, the thrusting arm, the gripping fist and along and down to the thinning tapering glass blade to the tip. She swallowed but her mouth was dry, and as her gaze moved down the ever-reducing shape, her heart beat harder, faster as if it, and she, were accelerating at a dizzying rate.

'It's big,' said one of the tour group.

'A nod to the ancient Greeks. They deliberately made sculptures of the gods larger than life. Barrow has done the same here, to impressive effect. The entire sculpture will be filled with a black liquid, which Barrow uses in all his works. It's his homage to Damien Hirst who, as you know, preserved various animals in formaldehyde. Barrow calls it "the liquidus", a mixture of chemicals and oil. The liquid will be pumped in when the sculpture is in its final position. Empty, *The Knight* weighs over a tonne and special equipment is needed to lift it.' The tractor was moving away from the work, with a whine of motors. Mrs Sidhu was surprised to see the driver was not a grey-clad technician but a woman in a black skirt and silk blouse. 'As you can see, the gallery director Jenny Leblanc is involved even when it comes to hands-on work. Jenny waved cheerily at the group before zipping the little tractor outside through large double doors.

Gertie tipped her umbrella to the right. 'And finally the work of an unknown artist, a new discovery of Hector Keys. Little is known about her. She works completely anonymously and goes under the name Petra. An allusion to the material of choice.' Gertie's brolly was aimed at a pile of rocks. After the drama of *The Knight* it seemed very sedate, almost dull. While Mrs Sidhu doubted her own taste in art, she could see the disappointed faces of the tour group too.

'I know what you're thinking, but Hector Keys can spot a rising star. Would you bet against the famous Hector Keys, the man with the golden eye?' Gertie asked. There was laughter from around her. Had she heard right? Had Gertie said 'eye' not 'eyes'? When she had met Hector Keys she was sure he'd had two. Perhaps one of them was glass. She filed it away. The tour, anyway, was moving on. Mrs Sidhu thought about staying, but with a stone in her heart she knew she had work to do. She threw one last glance at *The Knight* and stifled a shudder. It creeped her out.

She moved away from Gallery 2, drifting into the centre of the main gallery. She thought again about the attempted theft of *La Scaletta*. Mr Keys had said it was worth twelve million, so it was obvious why he moved it out of the house to somewhere more secure. Yet, there was something odd about it.

She stood perfectly still like this for some time, retreating into a state she called Aloneness, a state where she could be on her own even in the midst of all these people busily doing their jobs. Aloneness was different to loneliness. Loneliness made her feel breathless, crushed her chest with grief. Whereas Aloneness filled her lungs with the oxygen of thought. She was so still she could have passed for one of the sculptures, until she felt a touch.

It was a light hand on her arm, and a gentle voice. 'Are you all right?' it asked.

It took Mrs Sidhu a moment to recollect where she was. She was looking into serious brown eyes.

'I'm Jenny Leblanc, the gallery director. Can I help you at all? It's just that we need to hang some work and you're in the way.' Jenny waited impatiently with a step ladder. Behind her two technicians were carrying a crate.

'Jenny Leblanc,' Mrs Sidhu said with relief. 'You're just the woman I wanted to see.'

8

There was a limited amount you could learn from talking to legs. These legs were standing on a stepladder; they were clothed in a calf-length skirt and for a woman of forty or more were shapely and strong. 'Someone actually tried to steal *La Scaletta*? It's the first I've heard of it.' Jenny Leblanc's voice came from above. 'Is that what you wanted to see me about?' She spoke with a tightness in the chest, which comes from physical exertion.

'Oh, no, no. It's just odd, isn't it?'

'I suppose,' said Jenny. 'I mean, there are the pranks going around, but that's just what they are.'

'Pranks?' Mrs Sidhu asked.

The legs began to descend the ladder. 'I'm sorry, everything's in chaos.' Jenny Leblanc was, like her legs, shapely and strong. It was the same Jenny from Hector's selection committee, the same serious face, the bobbed brown hair. There was a French lilt to her voice and up close, Mrs Sidhu caught the whiff of expensive perfume. Incongruously, in one hand she carried a screwdriver.

'They've got me doing everything including hanging the work. We're desperately getting ready for Saturday night.'

Mrs Sidhu had the same tightness in her chest, but for other reasons. 'You mentioned pranks.'

Jenny retrieved a piece of paper from her pocket. 'Someone has been sending these to everyone in the village.'

Mrs Sidhu unfolded and read it:

DEAR RESIDENT,
   'LA SCALETTA' WILL BE STOLEN AT PRECISELY 7PM, FROM THE PUMP HOUSE GALLERY, ON OPENING NIGHT. YOU HAVE BEEN WARNED.

'Just a silly prank, I'm sure.' Jenny screwed the page up and threw it into a dustbin, where it rattled around the rim before disappearing inside. 'People like the Keyses attract this sort of thing.'

'Why would anyone send something like that?'

'It's ironic that some of the most expensive artworks in the world are in the hands of the banks, investors, moneyed collectors, the tasteless and the soulless, when they were produced by penniless artists. Not exactly justice. But beautiful things don't always attract beautiful souls.'

'Are the Keyses moneyed and tasteless and soulless?'

Jenny tapped her chin. 'No. Hector's a very successful dealer and collector. But I don't exactly agree with all his choices.'

Mrs Sidhu recalled Jenny and Hector crossing swords over the Petra artwork. 'You don't get along with Hector?'

'I'm very new here. I'm still getting used to him. Like I say, who am I to disagree? He's got the Eye.' When Mrs Sidhu looked helpless once again, Jenny explained. 'People in the art world say you either have "an eye" or you don't. It's a way of saying you have taste, that you can tell good work from bad. Hector's uncovered so many great artists, he's got the reputation. It means a lot in our world. Strange I never heard about the attempted theft, though.'

'Could Ivor have sent them? He seems so disgruntled.'

There was a strange, cool look in those eyes, like the sea on a sunny day when a cloud comes over. 'I wouldn't know. I barely know Ivor at all.' She recovered her poise. 'He seems pretty harmless to me. But as you can see I'm quite distracted. So what's this about?' Jenny asked. 'Unless you're investigating an attempted art theft?' She smirked, meaning it as a joke.

'Absolutely not!' Mrs Sidhu's firm tone of voice was to remind herself of her vow.

It startled Jenny. She could not have known Mrs Sidhu's past involvements with crime and after an awkward silence she changed the subject. 'How's the catering for opening night coming along?' Jenny asked.

'The menu, vis-à-vis the dishes, is currently in flux.' She fidgeted, rubbing the top button on her cardigan, and quelled a warble in her voice. 'Many factors are in play, and I don't want to bore you with them.' Then she waved an airy hand as if the 'many factors' were beneath even Mrs Sidhu's contempt, let alone someone of Jenny's exalted position.

Jenny took one leg of the stepladder in her hand. 'Could you?' She motioned towards the other leg.

It took a moment for the penny to drop. 'Oh, of course.' Mrs Sidhu grabbed the other side of the stepladder and they dragged it, squealing, to the next position.

'OK, just here.' She motioned to the two technicians.

They had been disassembling a crate. Inside, like a Russian doll, was another crate, and that crate was suspended on springs.

Mrs Sidhu's eyebrows rose above her brown eyes. 'My word,' she said.

'It's to protect the work from vibration in transit,' said Jenny.

Within the inner crate was a small painting. The technicians, handling it as gently as a newborn, brought it up to Jenny and held it to the wall. Jenny put the screwdriver between her teeth and climbed once more. 'Mmm, what were you saying?'

'It was about Hector and Tani Keys. Do you know anything about their tastes?' Mrs Sidhu asked.

'As I said, I'm new, so I'm only really finding out by trial and error, but I'd say they were quite eclectic.'

'Eclectic?' Mrs Sidhu nodded enthusiastically. This was promising. Mrs Sidhu was a woman of education, even if it was a self-taught one, and she kept abreast of words like eclectic. It meant they liked lots of different things. 'Give me a hint.'

The stepladder creaked as Jenny descended again with her screwdriver.

'They collect a lot of modern pieces, installation works like *The Knight*.' Jenny lowered her voice as if sharing a scandalous secret. 'But they've also acquired some early-twentieth-century pieces too, like *La Scaletta*.'

Mrs Sidhu nodded and said in a weak voice, 'That is fascinating. But my concern was more their taste in food. I haven't been able to raise either of them on the phone, nor Ivor, and they gave me a very open brief.'

'Can't help you there, I'm afraid, Mrs Sidhu.'

'Jenny!' The voice that called out from across the room was languid and familiar. Tani Keys wore large dark glasses and was walking while waving. 'Oh, Jenny, this won't do. We need a complete re-hang.'

'Of course, you could just ask Tani,' Jenny whispered.

Tani stood at the other end of the gallery clutching an espresso and yawning languidly. One look at her glacial face, bug-eyed under the sunglasses, froze any suggestion in Mrs Sidhu's mind of a warm chit-chat.

'Does she ever take those dark glasses off?' Mrs Sidhu asked.

Jenny's bobbed hair shook from side to side. 'It's her trademark.'

Mrs Sidhu swallowed. 'I'll see how I get along on my own.'

'Good call. Sadly, I don't have that luxury.' Jenny took a breath, glanced at the ceiling for a pause, and reset herself. 'If you'll excuse me, Mrs Sidhu.'

Jenny fixed a smile on her face, turned to face Tani Keys. 'Wonderful idea. It may be a little late in the day for a *complete* rehang. Let's see what we can do.'

Jenny turned quickly back to Mrs Sidhu and pressed her forearm. 'No one will worry about the food, they'll be thinking about the art. So see this as an opportunity to express yourself. Just do what you want to do.'

Jenny strode over and led her to the far end of the gallery. Mrs Sidhu smiled a little wanly.

When Jenny was gone, she went to the bin, retrieved the screwed-up threat note and put it in her pocket.

She needed a place to think.

9

As Mrs Sidhu dragged out a chair in the cafe, she was aware of the man with the tight jeans and the cowboy smile watching her. He was either a lover or a salesman and she had no time for either.

Jenny's words should have reassured her, but they had the opposite effect. She had wasted another morning and she still had no idea what to cook. She took solace in a little caffeine and sugar.

After the cold, empty expanses of the Pump House, the Greenview Cafe was a welcome touch of cosiness. The smell of fresh pastries and the hiss of the Gaggia met her as the door swung closed behind her. As advertised, it looked over the square of lawn that Bowler's Green was named for.

The waitress was a severe-looking ginger-haired girl whose badge declared her to be Poppy. She gave her order at the counter – a breakfast tea and an almond slice – and took herself to a window table. She dragged out a chair and thumped herself down. She hitched her sleeve over the heel of her hand and cleared a circle in the steamed window.

Low clouds made a ceiling of grey over the green and some overnight rain had given the grass a lush sheen. A boy played with his dog, throwing a stick for it over and over again.

What had she learned from her trip to the gallery? She did have two interesting new facts to play with.

Fact 1: Someone tried to steal *La Scaletta*.

Fact 2: Someone was threatening to steal it again.

She uncurled the screwed-up flyer from her pocket and read again. It did read like a prank. None of that was her business of course, and none of it helped her decide what to make for the gallery opening. Mrs Sidhu had made a vow, a vow written in blue-black biro (the most serious of biros) on a yellow sticky note (the most urgent of colours). She screwed up the threatening flyer again and tucked it back away.

Her shoulders sagged. This was not like her. She had no right to feel this way. She had a well-paid job. She had as much leeway as she wanted, freedom to express herself. It was almost too good to be true. Some more tea, some sugar, and something was bound to come to her.

She bit down on the almond slice. Sometimes it was nice to eat food someone else had made. Jam oozed over her tongue, almond flakes speckled her lips. Washing it down with tea, some strength returned to her.

She pulled out the piece of torn card that she had ripped from the cereal box that morning. Its reverse side was grey and as unmarked as the sky outside. She put a pencil down beside it. She must have sat there for some time, tea going cold, fingers twirling her hair, because she never heard him coming up behind her.

'It has a name.' The voice was deep and slow. 'It's called the blank-canvas problem.'

Mrs Sidhu jumped in surprise at hearing a male voice so unexpectedly close. Her panicked elbow nudged the pencil. She heard a sad rattle as it rolled off the table and hit the floor. She had lost track of the man whose eyes had been following her since she came in.

He was smiling, friendly, offering a hand to shake. 'Ben Trimble.' It was the cowboy. His hand was large, dry and warm. He was in his late fifties, still boyish. The hair was still black with silver here and there, a peppered moustache, and an impish smile which crawled up one side of his face higher than the other, offering a punchline to the laughter in his eyes. He could have been a cowboy too, if the accent had been Texas instead of Berkshire. 'I thought I knew everyone around here. What a nice surprise to be wrong.'

He rescued her pencil from the floor and tapped the piece of card. 'The blank-canvas problem. Or in your case –' he lifted the grey card and looked on the reverse – 'the blank-box-of-Cornflakes problem.'

Her neck flushed. She snatched her pencil back. 'I'm doing fine,' she said. The pencil hovered over the piece of card.

'Mind if I sit?' Without waiting for a reply, he dragged a chair over. His too-tight jeans creaked as he sat. 'It's a problem every artist faces. Maybe every human being. What do you do when you've got all the choice in the world?' He stroked his chin. 'It's the first challenge all my students face. May I ask what exactly you're trying to create?'

Mrs Sidhu's throat felt like there was a knot in it. 'Food.' She coughed the word out, and immediately felt like a monosyllabic dunce. For no reason she wiped her lips again, checking no almond flakes still clung there.

'I see, some kind of still life maybe?' He twinkled and tugged his moustache, mock serious. 'One of those people who likes apples and oranges, some grapes or maybe even a dead pheasant.' He smiled, eyes taking her in. 'You don't look the type.'

Mrs Sidhu pulled her cardigan together by the lapels. 'I am not trying to draw anything. I am a chef and I'm catering at the opening night of the Pump House. I'm making a menu plan and I want to surprise everyone.' She snatched her piece of card back.

He leaned back in his seat and chuckled. 'If the surprise is that you don't have a clue what to make, I think it's out of the bag. But you're in luck. I can help. You've come to an art teacher.'

She felt her shoulders tense. 'You think I'm stupid.' She wanted to add that *he* had come to *her*. Apparently only to mock her predicament.

'I didn't say that.'

The heat rose in her face. 'No, no, please, I'd love to hear what an art teacher has to say on the subject of food to a professional caterer with thousands of hours of experience.'

'I know you're being sarcastic, but I'm going to tell you anyway.' Despite her protests, Ben gently took the card and the pencil from her. 'There is a theory.' He waggled the pencil. 'It's called the theory of creative constraints. It's not really my theory, but it works and most of all, it's the opposite of what you'd think.'

Ben began writing on the card.

'Art, creativity, is about opening up to your subconscious. But that's not so easy. We've got all this potential inside us that can become formless and confusing when we ask the question, "What shall I do now?"

'You see, choice is the problem. If we narrow it down it can help. Most people think that great art is being allowed the freedom to express yourself limitlessly.' He circled his arms around the universe. 'But that kind of thing can drive you mad.' That wolfish smile broke out again. 'People have cut their own ears off for less. So why not limit yourself?'

He wrote something on the card and handed it back. She recited out loud in a monotone. '"Opening night menu for the Pump House Gallery. Everything will be orange."' She sighed and started to object. 'I don't think you're taking me seriously, Mr Trimble, and I have very little time.' She meant that to end the conversation.

'Imagine you did this. Can you think of any orange foods? Name some.'

Her jaw tightened. She tossed the card onto the table and crossed her arms, determined not to play along with such a simple-minded game. 'Oranges, of course, and everything can be orange if you add orange food dye.'

He picked up the card and added, 'No artificial colouring allowed.' Then he slid it back to her. 'Come on, it's just a game, play with me.'

His moustache and his tight jeans didn't seem to be going away. She sighed and propped her chin on her hand. 'Lentil dhal fritters. Carrot halwa. Mandarin sorbet.' She was slowly sitting upright. 'That's actually not a bad start.' She hastily covered her enthusiasm. 'But there's a lot more to it than that.'

'At least it's a start. Now you've got the broad strokes, go on and fill in the detail. The point is, you've got yourself going.' Ben folded his hands behind his head, leaning back in his chair and offering a winning smile. 'Creative constraints win the day once again.'

She suppressed returning his grin. She was just beginning to think maybe he wasn't so bad, when a gaggle of well-preserved older women entered the cafe. 'Oh, he's here! Hi, Ben!' They were suddenly all around Ben, talking excitedly. Each trying to gain his attention.

A wry grimace wrinkled Ben's cheeks. 'My eleven o'clock class. Excuse me.' He put a business card on the table. 'Art can be in everyone's life. If you want lessons, I teach every day of the week.' She watched him stride out, chatting with each of the women in turn. A salesman *and* a lover, she thought.

When the ginger-haired waitress came with the bill, Mrs Sidhu was still watching Ben and his middle-aged groupies leaving. 'I'd watch out for Ben, always works his magic with the biddies.' She pointed at the business card and frowned. 'That's why all his classes are full.'

'I wouldn't call them biddies exactly.' She tipped the girl well, who gave her an odd look. It was only when she was climbing into her dented Nissan Micra that she caught sight of herself in the rear-view mirror. Tucking a greying hair behind her ear, her heart sank. 'Biddies. Oh my word, she meant me.' Well, Ben Trimble would not be working his magic on her. Nonetheless, she carefully pushed his card deep into her cardigan pocket.

10

Mrs Sidhu was cooking again, as evidenced by the scattering of open ingredient jars on the kitchen counter. It was vexing to admit it, but Ben Trimble's advice had unlocked the frozen gears of her mind. Now, her fingers fell on all the right spices and herbs.

While her mind had worked on the practicalities of the limitations, her subconscious had found the answer, and the answer was in the very first time she had met Hector Keys.

The next three days were happy ones, for as anyone knows, when you are immersed in your work, you are happy. She rushed to her many different suppliers, selecting the freshest of ingredients and the finest of herbs and spices. Then she set to work.

Her kitchen resembled a laboratory, dishes arrayed in organised rows like test tubes, each sizzling and bubbling with a different concoction. Each one spilling out scented fumes.

This was her chance to shine, and she would have to

take it. If she was going to be a great artist, she had to think like a great artist. Ambition, daring, nerveless cool. She would be like her culinary heroes. Steely in resolve, light in execution.

She had dumped 'the orange menu' idea. As Ben had said, it was a starting point, merely a stepping stone to greatness.

This was her concept: Just Desserts. It was inspired by the one thing she knew about Hector Keys. He had a sweet tooth. He had insisted on a pudding as her trial dish, and she would take her lead from that.

Sweet things have a place in our senses that reach back to the first cave dweller risking his neck to climb up to the bees' nest, to reach in for the chewy, sticky nectar and barely waiting to slither down the tree to gulp it down before chewing and spitting the wax to the ground. It was worth every sore, every sting and burning bite.

A few thousand years of civilisation had changed only the sophistication of the final product. The smiling visage of sugar, fat and flour had been turned to a thousand faces, but embodied the same soul. A hungry arm probing a dangerous black hole in search of the purest hit.

Just Desserts would be the biggest culinary risk she had taken in her life. It made her sweat to think about it. A menu made entirely to resemble desserts. All the finger foods would be made to look like puddings, but real art always had a twist, and it was this: they would be savouries.

From her knife flowed idea after idea: mini quiches made to look like tarte au citron, smoked salmon blinis built like a Victoria sponge, stuffed mushroom mince pies, arancini bon-bons, fried onion ring doughnuts, pigs in blanket chocolate truffles. The flexibility and scope of 'Just Desserts' was boundless and in each bite was the surprise pairing of sweet look and salty taste.

She worked with total concentration for the remaining four days and by mid-afternoon on opening night she was surrounded by catering containers, hands greased, apron stained. Which is when her phone rang with disastrous news.

Daisy Carr was at death's door.

When it came to waitresses, Daisy Carr was 'a find' and she was Mrs Sidhu's find. She was the kind of girl who everyone loved.

Mrs Sidhu knew she only had her for a short time. Daisy had a university place secured, and she was raising money to help pay her fees with some waiting work. She was intelligent, responsible, well spoken, she had good posture and in black and white she looked so classy she could have passed for French. Not only that, but she had even studied art at A level, so she could talk knowledgeably with the guests and clients.

'I'm so sorry, Mrs Sidhu, but I've got a terrible cold.' Mrs Sidhu could hear it in her voice as soon as she started speaking and with dread she realised what this meant.

Mrs Sidhu mastered her rising panic. 'It doesn't sound that bad.' The fact was it sounded terrible. She kept her voice as calm as she could, sympathetic, motherly, caring. 'I can barely tell.'

'I'm running a temperature, and I can hardly see straight.' Her voice was thick with mucus. She sounded a little woozy. She sneezed.

'You know what my mother always said to me when I got a cold? She said sweat it out. That's the thing to do with a bad cold, sweat it out. And what better place to sweat it out than in the furnace of a catering job?'

'I suppose so.' She heard the rustle of linen and realised Daisy was still in bed. 'It's just I don't want to be ill for the beginning of university.' Daisy let loose a racking wet cough.

Mrs Sidhu swallowed. 'There you see, the bad stuff is coming out. I can hear you're getting better already.' She winced and told herself it wasn't a lie. Daisy sounded better than, say, a terminally ill lung patient. 'And it's an art gallery. You love art. Did you know there's a painting called *La Scaletta* there?'

'Really?' That perked up her interest, until she let loose a groan. 'But I feel awful. Mum says I should rest.'

Mrs Sidhu drew in a sharp breath. Without Daisy, she was sunk. Her other waiters were from the temp agency, unknown quantities. Daisy was the lynchpin. It was time to pull out the big guns. 'Freshers' week will go a little better with an extra two hundred pounds in your pocket.'

'Two hundred pounds?' Daisy gasped.

'That's your bonus payment and a little going-away gift from me.'

Mrs Sidhu suffered the agony of waiting. For moments there was only the sound of adenoidal breathing. Eventually Daisy spoke.

'OK, I'll do it.'

Mrs Sidhu put her phone away and whispered a prayer of thanks, then another, asking forgiveness from the gods of catering. She was ready.

11

The first time Mrs Sidhu had entered the Pump House Gallery, it was with a shy trepidation, a hesitant step and an eye on the door as if she wanted to leave again as soon as possible. Things couldn't be more different the second time.

She entered at the head of her waiters. She was dressed for battle, in clean chef's whites, her badge of office. Tonight she was the creator, and everyone should know it. Behind her the waiters fanned out, carrying trays of buffet food and wine. Within moments they were merged with the guests. This left Mrs Sidhu a breathing space to step back. The opening stages of any catering event are when most is happening. Someone had to make sure the waiters were supplied with plates and glasses. After taking a moment to check their work, Mrs Sidhu retired to the prep area to do just that.

She was using Jenny Leblanc's office as a kitchen cum workspace. Jenny had been very kind about it. 'Is everything all right in here? Do you have enough room?' she had asked. Mrs Sidhu thanked her for the use of her workspace. The walls were a testament to a glowing career in art; lined with art books, folders from important conferences, Jenny's degree certificates, she even had a poster of the Louvre. It had half a dozen signatures. 'A leaving gift from my old colleagues,' she had said.

Mrs Sidhu let out a slow breath. 'When I heard you worked at the Louvre, I couldn't help wondering how you could leave Paris for a little village in Berkshire.'

Jenny hesitated before replying. 'Personal reasons.' She had cleared her desk and helped push it to one side along the wall, like a counter.

There was a jarring note in the room: a blinking black-and-white display carried a feed watching over *La Scaletta* in Gallery 2. 'They've made me head of security too,' Jenny said. 'As if I don't have enough to do.' Before Mrs Sidhu could ask any more questions, Jenny had been called away by the demanding tones of Tani out in the gallery.

Now, looking at the poster, Mrs Sidhu couldn't help but be impressed again by Jenny and also by the Keyses. Personal reasons or not, the Pump House must be something special to have lured her away from one of the world's most prestigious galleries.

Now, here were waiters returning with empty trays and Mrs Sidhu was unstacking wine glasses at speed from the delivery crates when she came across the rogue.

These crates resembled the old-fashioned milk crates that she remembered as a child. Except instead of milk bottles, a wine glass nestled in each square, its delicate stem protected from its neighbours by the plastic walls. The glasses she had hired were a little different to the ones she normally used. To fit well in an art gallery, she felt they needed to be a little . . . well, a little artistic. She had chosen ones with a long stem and a tulip shape to the bottom, simplicity over fussiness. Yet somehow a rogue glass had sneaked into the mix.

Snatching glasses and pouring wine mechanically, Mrs Sidhu's hand stopped as soon as she felt it on her fingers. The rogue glass had a squat stem with a fussy straw-twist design – she could feel the rippled edges. She compressed her lips. There was always one. All the other glasses had plain stems, to echo the clean lines of the gallery.

No matter. She put the odd-man-out carefully to one side on her catering trolley so it wouldn't get mixed in with the other glasses.

Having another thought, she hopped lightly to the pile of side plates and checked through those too. Again these had plain, undecorated rims. She favoured minimalism; let the food do the talking not some fancy piece of crockery.

'Aha,' she exclaimed. 'Another rogue.' She'd had a feeling there would be one. This plate had a decorated rim. With satisfaction she put the rogue plate next to the rogue glass on her trolley, out of bounds from the waiters. No mistakes, not tonight. Job done, she loaded the trolley with canapés and strode out into the gallery.

Something was wrong. Mrs Sidhu knew it as soon as she hit the gallery floor.

Mrs Sidhu's eyes searched the faces and the plates of the assembled crowd.

Everything seemed normal. The gallery floor teemed with a hundred elegantly dressed guests, talking, looking at paintings, reacting with surprise at meeting with old friends or simply swaying to the gentle classical music oozing from the hidden speakers. Among them some familiar faces. The tour guide woman enthused, Tani wandered the floor coolly in her dark glasses, and the rude man with the waistcoat was casting sour glances at the artworks. That's when she saw it.

What they were not doing was eating. Her stomach fluttered. Not eating? Was there something wrong with her food? She took a few paces into the crowd and tried presenting her tray to a cluster of couples. 'No, thanks' was all the reply she got. She tried again, with a man standing alone admiring an abstract sculpture. He waved her away, and stole a glance at his watch.

Her shoulders slumped. All the time and care she had put into her 'Just Desserts' menu and no one was even trying them.

'Is that Mrs Sidhu?' The deep voice was instantly recognisable as was the peppered moustache, the jeans and the kind of baggy blazer worn by teachers the world over. She stifled a groan. It looked as if everyone had turned up to see the show, including Ben Trimble. He squeezed through the crowd. 'It is you.'

Mrs Sidhu blushed. Her mismatched plate and glass weren't the only rogues in the gallery tonight. She pushed her trolley faster, as if she hadn't seen or heard him.

Ben wove his way around in front of her. 'I couldn't resist coming, if only to see your culinary efforts.'

Her jaw clenched, duty bound she stopped, offering up the canapés with a thin smile.

He cast his eyes over the selection. 'Not seeing much orange on the menu.' Ben picked out an arancini bon-bon.

'But I see you got over your chef's block.' He munched. 'Very successfully, yum. Was it my advice?'

'You're here,' she said through a false smile. 'Lovely.'

'Of course I'm here. Biggest art event in Bowler's Green in years.' Ben plucked a handful of canapés from the tray and shoved a couple in his jacket pockets for luck. 'What? You've never heard the expression "starving artist"?'

She said she had never heard the term starving art teacher.

He seemed hurt by this. 'Oh, you're one of those. The ones who say, "those who can do, those who can't teach."'

She bit her lip. 'I didn't say that.'

'Sounded like it. And I'm a really good teacher. And, hey, it's a gig economy.' He munched on another canapé, his eyebrows lifting in surprise. 'These are really great. Love this idea, savoury but looks sweet. What's this one?'

The tension in her shoulders eased. 'You really like them?' She went through each one describing how she had constructed, for instance, a quiche to resemble a tarte au citron. Ben tried each one. He was glowing about the visual impact, the flavours, the aroma. When he'd finished she shrugged. 'I can't understand why no one's eating.' A shiver of doubt passed through her. 'Unless you're just flattering me.'

Ben grinned. 'You've clearly never met an artist. Flattery is not in the DNA – we're brutal with ourselves and with each other.'

'So why is no one eating them?'

'That's easy,' said Ben. 'They're waiting for the big surprise.' Ben unfolded a piece of paper. 'You haven't seen these notes everyone's been sent? It's all happening at seven o'clock, if you believe it.'

She had been working so hard the last few days she had completely forgotten about the threatening notes.

'I saw that, but everyone thinks it's a prank.' Despite her burning desire to get away from Ben, Mrs Sidhu felt that crumpled-up ball of paper pushing into her side. Why hadn't she thrown it away? When had she stuffed it into her chef's whites? There was a familiar stirring in her stomach, a stirring that almost always led her into trouble. Mrs Sidhu stopped and turned to face Ben. 'Do you honestly think that someone in the village sent those threats?' she asked.

He jabbed an accusing finger at her. 'Aha! I knew it. You can't resist a bit of scandal.' He broke out that lopsided smile under his salt-and-pepper moustache. Ben took a step closer. She could feel his breath on her.

She coloured again, raising her tray so it took the space between them. Mrs Sidhu turned away. 'I must keep moving, so many people.' She thrust her chin towards a group of women. 'Why don't you go and talk to your harem?'

'Harem?' Ben's face reddened. For once his lopsided smile deserted him. 'Now listen. I don't know what you've heard but I'm a—'

Whatever Ben was about to say was lost as her phone buzzed. She checked the text. It was from Jenny Leblanc. 'Please could you take a plate of food and some wine to Hector? He's locked in Gallery 2, the keycode to the access door is 3762.'

'Sorry, another time,' Mrs Sidhu said. 'I've got an urgent mission.' She showed him the text.

'Don't let me keep you.' His voice was cold. 'But you've got a rare privilege, a private audience with one of the greatest works of twentieth-century art. Try and enjoy it. If you know how.'

Her face flushed hot as Ben pushed his way through the crowd. She shouldn't have said that to him, it was so unlike her. This whole job had made her so nervous. Maybe she needed a quick break, a reset.

The ladies' loos were a haven of quiet. Gentle music exuded from hidden speakers, and a scent of ginger-lily pervaded the place. For a moment she thought she was alone. She closed her eyes and ran the cold tap at a marble washstand. She splashed water onto her face, mopped her neck with a flannel until it cooled. She must have stood there for some minutes before she opened her eyes. That was when she saw her.

Tani was at the far end of the room, where it turned a corner obscured by a pot plant. She too was running a tap, splashing water. Moving closer, she watched fascinated as Tani removed her dark glasses. She had to stifle a gasp at the sight that was behind them. Tani's eyes were bruises, red aching wounds. Eyes closed she pushed at the swollen, dark skin around them.

Mrs Sidhu let out a gasp.

Tani's eyes flashed open. The whites were shot through with red, her pupils pinpoints. She quickly put her glasses back on and turned to face her, blank-faced. 'Didn't see you there.' She stretched a wrist to her mouth, yawning in a bored way.

Mrs Sidhu averted her eyes. 'I just came in,' she lied.

Tani straightened her dress, applied some lipstick. 'Did you get the message? Taking some food to Hector.'

Mrs Sidhu nodded. 'Yes.'

'Well, then. He'll be waiting.' Tani sashayed out.

12

The side entrance to Gallery 2 was through a door with a keypad. She punched in the code and shunted the trolley through the door.

The smell of damp and mildew greeted her. The humidity must have swelled the door stuck as she went to close it. She grunted, pulling it behind her hard until the lock clicked.

The trolley wheels crunched over broken concrete, as she rolled alongside a thick pipe that lined the wall on one side. She shivered. Of course, they were close to the river here, and the Pump House had originally been just that. This must be an original part of the building.

Ben's parting shot had stung. She knew how to enjoy herself. It was just that she was working. Tonight meant a lot to her, nothing was allowed to go wrong.

At the end of the corridor was a bare brick wall, and next to it a nondescript door. She knocked, gently. The door opened a cautious crack.

She saw the pink neon rims first. His eyes found her

through the spectacles perched on his nose. 'Excellent, it's you.' Hector beckoned her in.

She swallowed but her mouth was dry. She checked her trolley one last time. A light selection of canapés paired with a sweet wine, perfect for Hector's palate. Let's hope it would live up to his expectations. She could at least have one happy customer tonight. The most important one, the client, Mr Golden Eye. 'I've brought you some food,' she said and he closed the door behind her.

'I'm sorry about all the security. Taking no chances.' He seemed uneasy, his hair running in several different directions as if he had been tugging at it. He had a sheaf of pages in one hand, which he used to fan his face. 'I am a little nervous for my opening speech.' He ushered her a couple of paces into the room.

As Mrs Sidhu approached, Hector checked his watch. Without thinking she did the same.

'A quarter to. Fifteen minutes to the curtain,' he said.

It was indeed fifteen minutes to the appointed hour, she would remember that later. He folded up his notes and put them in his jacket pocket to take the food and wine from Mrs Sidhu's trolley.

'Oh, not that one. It's a rogue glass, and should never have got into circulation.'

Hector smiled indulgently. 'Perfectionist, I admire that.' He took the plain-stemmed glass that Mrs Sidhu offered, and a canapé on a plain plate. 'Now, close your eyes please.'

She did as he asked.

'You must have a moment with *La Scaletta*, it's the least you deserve. I will withdraw with my food, let you take it in alone.' Footsteps and Hector's voice faded as he walked away to the opposite end of the room.

Mrs Sidhu's arms hung limp at her sides. She played along, though she would much rather have been watching Hector's reaction to her food. She screwed her eyes shut until Hector called out, his voice coming from a distant corner. Her stomach knotted. Was his mouth full, was he eating? She would say that the painting was nice, her stock response, and then scuttle over to hear his thoughts on her canapé concept. That was her intention. Until she opened her eyes.

Time stopped. 'It's . . .' The words she wanted to say simply weren't there. She was left open-mouthed and empty-headed. The painting was about two and a half feet square. It was a woman, naked, climbing the steps out of a pool, half-in, half-out of the water and it was made up entirely of tiny, coloured dots. That's what pointillism meant – Mrs Sidhu had looked that up – but she wasn't ready for the dizzying effect. Every nuance of light and reflection had been captured by the simple technique. In it and through it she dreamed even though she was awake.

Hector returned, purring his admiration. 'It is my most precious possession, my first addition to the Keys collection, Tani's family's collection. It was what brought our lives together.'

'I don't understand. You married, but you both had the name Keys?'

Hector's pink face broke into a shy smile. 'Actually, I took her name. It was already established in the art world, and convention be damned.' He adjusted the neon pink frames and turned back to the painting. He was talking now in an excited way, the white tips of his hair quivering. '*La Scaletta*. In Italian, it refers to the set of steps, the ladder she's climbing. The painting is actually called *The Bathing Pool* but when it was shown in Italy, it picked up the nickname and it stuck. They say it's a privilege to be in the room with a true masterpiece.' He stood next to her, admiring it for a minute.

An age seemed to pass. 'It appears to glow from within,' she managed after a while.

'Lefevre was a genius, and a pure one. One of the early pointillists, he painted light.'

Hypnotised, she took a step closer, to touch such a thing, to touch the heavens. Hector held out an arm. 'Please don't get too close, you'll trigger the alarm.'

He looked again at his watch and coughed. 'Ten minutes until the doors open, I must get ready.' He wiped his mouth once more and put the plate down.

A small wave of worry lapped at her on seeing a half-eaten canapé. 'Full already?' she said.

'Please don't be concerned. I have butterflies for obvious reasons. But I will not let that go to waste, I'm keeping it here to finish after my speech.'

Mrs Sidhu felt a little better. 'You're sure you like it?'

'It's excellent.' He choked a little as he spoke and Mrs Sidhu took a step forward.

'Are you all right? Did some go down the wrong way?'

'No, just my stomach feels a little off. I'm sure it's nerves.' He checked his watch once more, a man clearly on a timetable. 'Not long before those doors open. May I ask you to leave? I must rehearse my speech.'

Mrs Sidhu quickly cleared the tray and backed out of the room with her trolley.

Mrs Sidhu left Hector rehearsing his words in a mumble. She rolled her trolley along the damp corridor, following the old pipework. A strange warmth spread through her body at the thought that she'd had what none of them could dream of; a moment almost alone with something that touched heaven.

As she got to the end of the corridor, she was still dazed by . . . dazed by what? By the light, Lefevre's extraordinary capture of the light. She struggled with the outer door, finally barging it open.

As she rammed the trolley through, she heard the twitter of excited conversation and then an exclamation. 'Oh, great, I'm famished.'

She reached for the handle behind her, and felt the door lock click into place.

The group descended on her trolley, hands reaching for the remaining food on it. She beamed; thank goodness people were eating again. 'Help yourselves to anything else except—' Before she could complete her sentence, she was interrupted.

'Can I take my break now, Mrs Sidhu?' Daisy sniffed, wiped her nose, then quickly hand-gelled.

'Oh, yes, but wait a minute.' Mrs Sidhu turned her back to the room and fished around in her apron pocket.

'Daisy, you're the best. Thank you, I know I said two hundred.' Mrs Sidhu finally found what she was rummaging in her pocket for. She stuffed a roll of notes into her hand. 'But you've been a hero. There's an extra fifty in there.'

Daisy grinned. 'Thank you!' She gave Mrs Sidhu a warm hug.

'Just promise me you'll spend it on your studies.'

Daisy put her hand to her heart. 'Textbooks, I swear. Well maybe textbooks and some new earrings.' She giggled.

'Go and take that break, you've earned it.'

'Now, where was I?' Mrs Sidhu turned back to pick up

with whoever it was she had been talking to. She had quite forgotten who it was. Anyway, they all were gone, having plucked her trolley clean like a swarm of locusts. She turned back only to find Daisy gone too.

As she passed, she noticed the service door was ajar. She was sure she had felt the snick of the lock when she had closed it. She sighed. Everything had to be done twice these days. She bumped it shut with a sway of her hip and made sure she heard the lock click. The last thing she needed was to be responsible for a security breach.

It wasn't until she was halfway across the main gallery that she noticed the rogue glass and plate were gone from her trolley. That was what she'd meant to say to the hungry crowd, don't take that plate and glass. She spun around, but they had all dispersed. Never mind, she told herself, she was fussing too much. People were enjoying her food, she thought with a warm glow, that was enough. She should go back and restock.

It was when Mrs Sidhu rolled her trolley into Jenny's office that she sensed something was wrong.

13

Mrs Sidhu checked the room. Uneasiness chilled her insides. Something was out of kilter.

She scanned the room again. No one else was there. Everything seemed in place. In place, that is, for a busy catering station at a large event. Empty plates were stacked in the corner, wine glasses on the desk, some with pools of white or red still in them. Outside, in the main gallery, she could hear the throng of chatter and excitement dying down.

She glanced at the clock on the wall. Five to seven. Almost time for Hector's speech. She should go, she would miss the big moment. She went to the door and snapped the light switch off. It was in the dark that she saw it.

All along, the light had been blinding her eyes with details that were not important. Nothing was out of place but something was missing. What she had failed to notice in the light she could see in the dark. With the lights off, the room should have been flooded in blue glow from the security monitor, like her living room TV at night. Instead there was only mute blackness.

She snapped the light switch back on. Then she saw it, the wires cut through, showing their bare copper insides.

Something was very wrong.

She checked her watch. It was two minutes to seven o'clock.

14

In the main gallery, as the clock turned to seven, conversation died back. The guests began to make their way to the front, Mrs Sidhu found herself part of a gathering mass of bodies pressing forwards to the doors of Gallery 2.

The clock hit seven o'clock. All chatter stopped, music rose up from the perfectly tuned speakers around the room.

Right on cue, the double doors to Gallery 2 hissed open, sliding sideways like theatre curtains. Murmurs spread through the party.

'Is this a joke?'

'Some kind of publicity stunt?'

'I think it's part of the artwork.'

Mrs Sidhu stood on tiptoe but could barely see. 'What's going on?' she asked Ben, who stood a head taller. But Ben seemed to have lost the power of his voice. His cocksure smile had been replaced with a ghost-faced blankness. Mrs Sidhu waved her hand in front of him, but he was a statue carved from ice.

A scream sounded out, Tani's voice, she was sure. What could make Tani Keys screech like that?

Mrs Sidhu used her elbows. 'Caterer coming through.' That way she pushed herself to the front. She wished she hadn't. She froze as time broke like shattered ice. Images flashed through her brain like disconnected snapshots with no order or relative importance to sort them.

She heard screams.

She saw blood.

Then, the crumpled form of Hector Keys. Tani shook him. His head lolled in her arms like a puppet's. Jenny stood beside them, hands covering her mouth.

Then the sight beside them shot splinters through Mrs Sidhu's heart.

Daisy Carr lay alone, curled into a ball like a sleeping cat. Blood pumped from her crushed head. One arm was cradled to her chest, the other stretched out with a pointing finger. The finger seemed to Mrs Sidhu to be pointed directly at her.

15

When the call came, DCI Burton was watching *Strictly* with a supermarket curry on his lap.

The dance reality show was a private pleasure that he would never admit to, certainly not around Newton police station, and certainly not to his friends. Though who was he kidding? What friends? There were precious few of those left. The ones who hadn't taken his wife's side in the divorce were dying or retiring, fizzling out their lives in seaside towns.

It was ironic that, in the divorce, she had cited a lack of common interests. *Strictly Come Dancing* was one of the shows that he had sternly refused to watch with her. Yet, here he was.

Still, he felt he had properly put it all behind him, and it was paying off. DCI Burton had invested all that energy into his job, he was on a roll of solved cases, and he had the newspaper cuttings and the commendation letters to prove it.

The phone call interrupted Claudia Winkleman summing-up and he was tempted to leave it. Until he saw the number. Saturday night, he was off shift and the station was calling him. He hit mute on the remote and Claudia mouthed silent words from a silent smile. She reminded him of his ex. Is that why he watched it?

'DCI Burton,' he said into the phone. He listened while he exchanged slippers for shoes. By the time the call finished, he had his coat on and was on his way to the front door. He returned, momentarily hit record on the PVR. He still couldn't get the hang of streaming. He'd have been happier still with a VCR, but even he knew those days were gone.

He plunged one last forkful of curry into his mouth and turned to the door. It was going to be a long night.

'So this is modern art.' Burton was looking at a pile of rocks. Each one was fist-sized and piled up roughly like a flat-topped pyramid.

Sergeant Dove gestured towards the body of a young woman. 'Daisy Carr, waitress. There was a "do" here tonight.'

'I gathered.' It was hard to miss the abandoned half-empty wine glasses. He stepped over blood, and a splatter of red wine. His nostrils burned. 'What's that smell? It's like someone got drunk in a chemical factory.'

Dove pointed up. 'It's called *The Knight*. Ned Barrow, a colossal commentary on the death of heroism apparently.' Dove was holding the gallery catalogue. 'He uses a mixture of embalming fluid, alcohol and oil to fill his sculptures.'

'Nice little cocktail.' Burton turned his attention to the body. His stomach lurched. Bodies were not DCI Burton's speciality. He dealt with them routinely, with as little fuss as possible, but the details he left to the professionals. In fact the very professionals whose noses were better attuned to the smell of embalming fluid.

The girl was young and pretty, like a lot of bodies Burton had seen. It didn't make it any easier to bear. If they'd had a kid, she'd have been around that age. She was curled up, as if she was asleep. Her phone was in her right hand. Trying to call for help, maybe. No, the way she was holding it was wrong, the position of her thumb.

Burton crouched beside her, as if he could offer assistance or comfort. 'She's been struck on the front of the head with something hard.' Her other arm stretched out, pointing, accusing. He followed the direction to empty space.

He was grateful when crime scene officers covered Daisy Carr's body with a white shroud. He took a strong mint from his inside pocket and sucked on it, felt the cold spread across his tongue.

'It's a tragedy.' He took some of the flint edge off his voice. He was thinking ahead. He would have to interview relatives, and the mother, and decide what he could possibly say to her. The coroners took the body away. He sucked down the rest of the mint, his stomach easing.

He turned slowly around, hand on chin. 'Show me that catalogue, Dove.' Burton riffled through the pages until he found the one he wanted, then walked back to the rock sculpture. 'Think I know what the murder weapon is.' He tapped the photograph in the catalogue. 'This sculpture has a missing rock. Look at the photo in the book – it should be a pyramid.'

Dove took the guide. 'Oh, yes, sir. I can see that now. I'll make sure the searchers are aware.'

'OK, what's this all about, Dove? Why is this waitress

dead in the middle of an art gallery?' He motioned for Sergeant Dove to move forward.

Dove was a portly, shambolic man in the middle of life who sweated when nervous – and Burton unfailingly made him nervous. He cleared his throat and read from his notebook. 'Daisy Carr's the murder victim, sir. The other victim is Hector Keys. He's an art dealer and collector. He also was in the gallery when what happened, um, happened.' He snapped his notebook shut in an official and conclusive manner.

Burton looked around. There was no sign of another body. He waited, silently eyeing Sergeant Dove. This silent observation started to take its toll on the sergeant. A man of open pores, he began to sweat, despite the strictly regulated temperature in the gallery.

Burton's nose wrinkled. He could smell the overpowering aftershave evaporating off the man over the embalming fluid and the iron-rich smell of blood. Perhaps he should be grateful for that. Dove fidgeted under his superior's gaze and seemed to be trying not to emit any more smells. He gave his notebook another snap, but it was far less confident than the first one.

Burton's shoulders slumped. He was tired of waiting. 'So where is he?'

'Sorry, sir?'

Burton felt his chest tighten. 'Where is Hector Keys? Where's his body?' Burton tried, but failed, to keep the impatience out of his voice. He shouldn't be so hard on Dove but something about the shuffling, slovenly sergeant never failed to irritate him.

Maybe it was having his quiet evening at home shattered by a sudden phone call, but he knew that was a lie. He tried to tell himself that he was genuinely upset that he had been called away to work in the middle of a microwave chicken korma, a can of supermarket lager and what passed for Saturday night TV these days. Even he knew it was hollow. None of that was Dove's fault. That was down to a failed, childless, petless marriage which itself was down to a life with little or no time devoted to anything but dead bodies. Lo and behold, here was another one.

The words seemed to have a motivational effect on Dove. He raised his index finger as if he now understood everything. 'He's not dead, sir. He was unconscious, he's recovering outside.'

'I'll want to talk to him.'

'He has a bump on the head. Paramedics are working on him now, probably going to hospital.'

'Tell me when he comes round.' Burton yawned and lumbered towards the double doors. Maybe there was some coffee out there. Another exclamation from Dove stopped him.

'It's not just that, or the body, sir. There's another reason we're here. Follow me, please.'

He followed Dove across the gallery towards the back wall where the sergeant pointed. Burton's eyebrows crawled up his forehead.

16

I'm responsible for this, Mrs Sidhu thought.

Mrs Sidhu kept special words for special things. In her mind, she capitalised those special words so as to underline their importance. Nightwater was one such word, Mrs Sidhu's term for water at night. That might sound less profound than it was. There was a feeling that went with Nightwater – a dread, a claustrophobic combination of cold, constriction and the sucking sensation of not being able to breathe. Just seeing a river at night filled her with horror. It was as if it would reach out and take her, or she would experience a kind of vertigo, an irresistible urge to throw herself in and sink into the dark depths. Despite this revulsion she was heading to the river right now with only one thought on her mind. To get there before she threw up.

She clutched her stomach, shivered as she stepped out of the gallery and followed the smell of damp, just as she had followed it in the service corridor earlier, downhill, alongside the outside wall of the Pump House.

It was a crisp night, stars were coming out, and Mrs Sidhu was glad she was sensibly dressed in chef's whites. They offered some protection from the cold. She pulled her tunic tighter. The cold she was feeling came from within. She couldn't get Daisy's pointing finger out of her mind.

Most of the assembled guests wore thin evening wear. For the women, expensive-looking black, strapless dresses for the most part. Some of the men had donated their jackets to some of the women. Tani Keys's pale shoulders quaked as she was led to a chauffeur-driven Mercedes. Whether her tremors were from the chill in the air or the sight of her husband on the floor, it was difficult to tell. As she climbed in, her face had caught the moonlight, white and expressionless, a long cigarette hanging from long fingers.

The people of the gallery, once ordered to leave the space indoors, had divided naturally into two: the guests and the workers. Separated as they were by money, they were unified in their shock. That shock was now turning to leg-twitching tedium as all waited for the police to finish their business, taking statements, names and addresses. She had given her statement already, such as it was. 'I was standing there, I didn't see anything much,' was about the size of it. Now she had made up flasks of coffee, which she had given to her waiters to serve. Her waiters. There was one missing. Her stomach roiled again.

Ben had comforted a group of women, all in their little black dresses. The same ones, Mrs Sidhu thought, who had dragged him away at the cafe. His eleven o'clock art class. Or were they comforting him? They pressed themselves on him, taking and giving hugs in turn. Rather them than her, she told herself.

The wall of the gallery stopped but the path continued. The noise of her steps on concrete underfoot turned to hollow thuds on wood. She was in an open space behind the gallery. Somewhere, out in the dark, Mrs Sidhu could sense the movement of Nightwater. The river was out there, beyond the lawn.

She kept moving forwards, leaving the gallery behind her, stroking her belly until she was some distance from the others. It wasn't horror or sadness or even the sight of blood (Mrs Sidhu was a robust woman) that was crushing her insides. It was her old friend guilt pressing down on her guts, poking at her spleen, shoving on her diaphragm, rearranging her organs like the trick shuffle of a card sharp. Guilt because she couldn't shake the feeling that she could have done something. If she had been paying attention, if she had thought more about the threats to her client than her precious menu idea. Just Desserts, who was she kidding? She was no artist, she was a widow turned caterer, and this place, made of glass and steel and strange dreams, made no sense to her. She was way out on a branch without the evolutionary instinct to sustain her grip on it.

There was that green peal in her guts again, like a stomach flu. Daisy Carr had flu. On any other night she would have been home, tucked up with a Lemsip and a hot water bottle. But oh, no, Mrs Sidhu simply *had* to have her.

She followed the sound of the river; she could hear it now as it gurgled and sucked at the banks. She gasped, stopping suddenly and pulling up short as she almost walked into someone. For a moment, in the half-light shed by the gallery, her pupils large with wonder, she thought she was looking at a familiar face. As her eyes adjusted, the reason came to her. It was a monumental metal statue of Hector Keys himself, looking down on her with hollow eyes, pointing an accusing finger. Her stomach lurched at the realisation. She stumbled on until she finally found it. There was a boardwalk and boat jetty, built into the back of the gallery. The water was unlit and black, lapping at wooden pillars.

Nightwater, she hated it. The idea that water was down there, beneath her feet, unseen, made her shiver. She imagined herself sucked under, into darkness, thrown and tumbled until she didn't know what was up and what was down. She had read that scuba divers could become disorientated in the depths, losing track of which way was up to safety, and would swim down to their deaths instead.

Into the river, she released all the tension she was carrying along with the contents of her stomach. She coughed it all up, and spat out the brackish bile. The river, down there unseen, carried it away, sucking and bubbling on its mysterious path. For that she was grateful.

That was when she saw the woman running. She was all in black and her soft footsteps bounced on the wooden boards, carrying their hastening vibrations to Mrs Sidhu's own feet. The pattern though, was irregular. When Mrs Sidhu saw the reason, her jaw dropped.

17

DCI Burton rested his rheumy, cow-like gaze on a flat, white piece of blank wall. He clicked his tongue against the roof of his mouth. 'What am I looking at, Dove? Is this another one these conceptual works?' he added suspiciously.

Dove lurched forward. 'According to, well, according to everyone here, this space was occupied by a painting shortly before Mr Keys died.'

The skin on the back of Burton's neck tingled. He rubbed at it with thick, red fingers. 'There was a painting?'

Dove checked the gallery guide again. '"Gaston Lefevre's pointillist masterpiece *The Bathing Pool* but most people call it *La Scaletta*,"' he quoted, then closed the guide. 'It's got a woman climbing some steps after bathing, you see.' Dove tapped his chin for a moment. 'I suppose she's got a downstairs bathroom, sir,' he said. 'Maybe that's a clue.'

Burton fought the temptation to shake Dove physically until he spoke sense. Instead, his thick fingers rubbed the back of his neck. 'What's the painting worth?'

'Latest insurance estimate was twelve million pounds, sir.'

Burton exhaled a low whistle. 'That's some serious motive.' His eyes scanned the room, first drawing his gaze back towards where Daisy Carr had lain. 'My guess is she sneaked in here for a selfie with the famous painting.'

'We'll check her phone, see if she caught anything else.'

'My second guess is she didn't. Because the phone's still here. The person who did this is careful.'

He spun round to take in the open space through the large double doors. It was all laid out so that everyone would see the painting, framed by *The Knight* and *Art Rocks* artworks. Daisy's body had lain between them, her left arm pointing towards the area under *The Knight* which hung ten feet off the ground. Burton went and stood under the tip of the sword. He reached up. Burton was a tall man but his arm stopped a couple of feet short.

He walked it through. 'So they knocked Keys out, they planned for that. But the waitress comes in and catches them in the middle of stealing the painting. They grab the first thing that comes to hand.' Burton pointed over to the rock pyramid. 'And strike her on the front of the head. She stumbles, falls, dies.' He rubbed his lower lip, deep in thought.

'Looks that way, sir,' Dove said. 'The whole place was locked up tight before that, with Mr Keys personally guarding the piece.'

Burton scanned the room, first drawing his eyes back towards where Hector had lain, then on into the open space through the large double doors. 'So this is Gallery 2.' He pointed through the doorway. 'That's Gallery 1, the main gallery, where all the guests were gathered waiting for the big speech. What happened when the doors opened?'

'Utter shock.'

The new voice came from behind him. It wasn't Dove's. It was female for a start, with a gentle continental lilt. She was standing in the doorway, wearing a black evening dress. Not that it mattered, but she was attractive, in a serious sort of way. Burton opened his mouth; he wanted to tell her that she was trespassing on a crime scene, but he heard the quake in her voice, saw the trembling lip, the wet in her eyes.

'Jenny Leblanc,' she said. 'I'm the gallery director and I'm very much afraid that I'm responsible for this.' She collapsed into tears.

18

Mrs Sidhu gasped. This was too much. The woman in black was not just running. Every third step was a whirl, a pirouette or a balletic leap. She was dancing, and with each spring she held something aloft. It was square and about two and a half feet wide, and it was hauntingly familiar to Mrs Sidhu. The woman in black was escaping with *La Scaletta* and she was coming towards Mrs Sidhu like a balletic steam train. This wasn't just a robbery, it was an act of mockery. And still the woman in black came.

Mrs Sidhu froze. She was standing on a narrow raft made of wooden planks. Moonlight glinted from the water, only inches away on either side of her. This was a situation a caterer would rarely find themselves in; there was very little in the manuals about it.

She took a deep breath. Then she thought of Daisy's murder, and balled up her little fists.

They say a lioness will protect her young. As an Indian aunty, Mrs Sidhu had taken an unspoken vow to protect all the young. Sometimes it took a strong word or a wagged finger, and sometimes it meant avenging yourself on black-clad dancing art-heisters. It was water to the left, it was water to the right. The only way past was through her. Bring it on.

She bent her knees into a low crouch, put her arms out wide and let out a hot-blooded roar. Let's see what the black-clad figure did now.

Mrs Sidhu's throat went dry. What she did was keep on coming. In fact, to Mrs Sidhu's concern, the patter of flying feet only increased in intensity. As she doubled her pace, the moonlight found her face and Mrs Sidhu could see the bizarre horror of the woman's outfit. Behind her, wings were folded against the onrush of air. You would say they were angel's wings, but this was no angel. Wherever this one came from, it was not the heavens. The mask itself was a skull, with a shining smile all picked out in white sequins. She let out a low moan. The masked woman bore down on Mrs Sidhu like the Angel of Death itself.

19

Burton offered Jenny Leblanc a tissue from the recesses of his pocket.

She took it gratefully. 'Sorry, I'm not usually emotional.'

'Death affects us all in different ways. You can't underestimate what it'll do to you.'

Jenny sniffed. 'You seem fine.'

'Let's just say it's not my first rodeo.' Burton noticed her shiver. That backless dress was very strappy and sophisticated but he saw the goosebumps on her skin. He gave her his jacket, and she pulled it across her shoulders. 'Thank you,' she whispered.

Burton tried not to be distracted by her smile, which was, like everything about her, understated and quietly charming. That, he told himself, was purely a professional observation. He had a job to do. He straightened up. 'You said you were responsible for all this. I find that hard to believe.'

'I'm as responsible as the thieves. I've been receiving these all week.' She slipped him a piece of paper. 'Everyone in the village got them. But I dismissed them as a prank.' She held her head. 'What an idiot.'

Burton read the note. It was printed on A4 paper in black ink. He blinked. 'They actually told everyone what they were going to do and at exactly what time?' He shook his head in disbelief. 'Don't beat yourself up, Ms Leblanc, I would have thought it was a prank too.' He handed the page to Dove, who slipped it into an evidence bag. 'We've got your statement. For the time being, go home to Mr Leblanc, or Ms Leblanc, and try not to think about it.'

'Oh, there's no Mr or Ms Leblanc. It's just me.'

Burton's neck reddened. 'My mistake.' Why was he glad?

'And home right now is a cold empty hotel room. I've only just moved over from France.'

Why was he fishing so ham-fistedly for the answer he so clearly wanted? Even Dove was smirking. Burton fumbled for a card. 'If you remember anything, that's my direct line.'

Her fingers brushed his as she took the card. 'Thank you, Chief Inspector Burton. You've been so kind.'

She exited the way she had come in, leaving a faint aroma of perfume. Burton recognised it. He had bought his ex-wife Channel No 5 for her fortieth birthday. It had cost him an eye watering amount for a small bottle.

He stood for a moment with his hand still outstretched, feeling like a fool.

'She was nice.' Dove burst in on his thoughts like a tractor bursting into a chamber concert.

The blood-red blush on Burton's neck spread up his face. He put his hands in his pockets and turned on his sergeant. 'Why don't you check out that door she just came through, and why didn't we know about it?' he barked.

Dove pouted. 'I knew about it, sir. It's a service entrance, connects to an old corridor. The other end comes out in Gallery 1. It's got a keypad, and only the staff had the code.'

'Is there an exit through there?' When Dove shook his head, Burton pushed harder. 'Then how did they get the painting out?'

'Not clear, sir.'

'"Not clear, sir,"' Burton mimicked, watching Dove break into a sweat. His mercy deserted him this time. 'All right, so how do we even know the painting was in here?'

Dove gulped. 'Technicians unpacked it and brought it in. After that the place was sealed until Hector Keys entered this evening.'

Burton bared his teeth. 'So? What's the timeline, sergeant? They could have been lying in wait for Keys. Knocked him out the second he walked in.'

'No, sir. We have a statement from a witness who saw the painting in here just before the robbery.'

Dove's fingers raced through the pages of his notebook.

'How did they knock him out?' Burton was in Dove's face now.

'Not clear—' Dove broke off. 'We're looking into it. He has a bump on his head, but not big. He's still not conscious.'

Burton exhaled slowly. Then he caught himself. 'No one leaves,' he said. The growing look of fear in Dove's eyes turned Burton's heart cold. 'We've already let people leave? Someone could have just stuffed it in the boot of their car.'

Dove quailed. 'Not exactly. They would have had to carry it through the guests, sir. Would have been noticed. And the fact is, sir, you and I got here very quickly. I guess we were both off duty and neither of us had Saturday night plans. By the time we had enough officers here to manage the crowd a lot of people had left.' Dove grabbed a printout, triumphant. 'But we do have a full guest list, sir.'

Burton digested three points. First, Dove was right; officers were still just arriving to help, but he had been first on the scene so it was his problem. Second, a twelve-million-pound painting had gone and the clock was ticking. Third, and most disturbing, he and Dove had parallel social lives.

'I want a watch put on ports and airports. No one from this party leaves the country. And shut this place down now. Nobody else leaves. And get uniforms checking the perimeter.'

Dove passed the instructions on to a uniformed officer. Burton pulled at his lip. 'Did you say who that witness was? The one who last saw the painting?'

'I didn't. It looks like she's the caterer, sir. The gallery manager, Ms Leblanc, the woman who you . . . who was in here a minute ago, she said she asked her to come in here and she took her trolley with her.'

'Did she now.' Burton cast his eyes around the gallery, his breathing picking up pace. He saw a plate with half-eaten food and a half-drunk glass of wine. 'He was drugged. Hector Keys was drugged. Collect up that plate and any other food Keys might have eaten. Get it to the lab. And find the caterer's trolley, it might not be too late.'

Dove was clearly struggling to follow. 'Don't you see?' Burton said. 'Keys was drugged with the food, the painting was stolen and the caterer had a trolley, which might just hold a painting.' Burton slapped his hands together. 'Where's this caterer now?'

Dove blew through his lips. 'Somewhere out there.' He pointed through the giant wall of glass that formed the front of the building, to where two hundred or so people were being kettled in a car park by a barely adequate number of officers.

'Shall I find her, sir?'

'Don't bother, I'll do it myself. Get the message out, don't let the caterer leave. Detain on sight.'

Burton made his way on spidered legs to the main entrance. He grabbed a uniformed officer. 'I'm looking for the caterer, is she still here?' The officer looked nonplussed. 'She's a suspect,' Burton added.

The officer seemed to remember something and pointed to the back of the building. 'There's a path, she went down there.' Burton read a fingerpost, chiselled artfully to read 'Marina'.

'There's a marina?' Burton said. 'Oh, no. There's a marina.' He ran.

20

The thought crossed Mrs Sidhu's mind that she could run backwards, along the narrow jetty, and find an escape that way. Most caterers would have done just that. Not Mrs Sidhu, though, her spirit had been forged in the fires of a hotter kitchen. She braced herself for impact and closed her eyes. Let her come. She roared again, adding some choice obscenities which she had no idea lurked inside her.

She waited, and nothing. She waited some more. Still nothing. No pain, no sudden strike to her arms and shoulders. She heard a voice, a familiar male voice, shout, 'Stop, police!' Then she felt a brush of wind against her hair and heard a heavy thud. When she opened her eyes, the space in front of her was empty. Her brace, timed to anticipate the impact, now carried her stumbling forward. She turned, and there was the woman in the skull mask, still running. She must have jumped right over her. The last she saw, as she teetered to her side, was the masked demon's flying feet jumping onto a waiting boat, and as she did she reached down and picked something up. Mrs Sidhu could have sworn it was a camera on a tripod.

Now more feet were thundering along the jetty. Heavy, men's feet, police feet. Mrs Sidhu, however, had no time to take this in. The vibrations underfoot were enough to upset her already shaky balance. Suddenly, the stars and moon were in front of her. She hit the river, and instantly the cold of the water soaked through the thick cotton of her chef's whites. Her apron wrapped itself around her face. As she sank among the stinking green weeds she had only one thought.

This was, without doubt, the worst catering job Mrs Sidhu had ever had.

21

Burton clattered down the wooden walkway. He saw them at the end of the jetty. One figure in black lycra and a woman in chef's whites; that second one had to be the caterer – his chief suspect. A diminutive Indian woman who was bellowing, arms wide, at the top of her voice. 'Come on, you dirty slag!' The words were unexpected, but the voice was woefully familiar.

For a brief moment, Burton stood bewildered. What would Mrs Sidhu be doing killing people and stealing paintings? The moment passed, it was an idiotic thought. The woman in black was the thief, he could even see the painting she was carrying. Mrs Sidhu was the only thing standing between her and her escape.

'Police, you're under arrest!' he cried out. He cursed himself for not bringing any other officers with him. Another mistake.

The woman in black turned to look at him. He squinted, hardly believing what he was seeing. Were those feathers? And a skull mask! He measured the distance from his position to theirs. It was too late to stop a collision between them. Then the incredible happened.

The masked dancer actually sped up. Her pounding footsteps accelerated into the rhythm of a gymnast running at a vault. She was within a yard of Mrs Sidhu when her feet left the ground. Her body took to the air, rotating, spinning, completely inverting, until her feet landed on the other side. She had somersaulted over Mrs Sidhu.

Burton had only a moment before his heart fell to his stomach. Because then he saw the wobble. Not in the gymnast. The lycra-clad woman was already running, feet flying like a sprinter's, bouncing along the boards, up a gangway, jumping for a boat. It was Mrs Sidhu. 'No, no, no!' he shouted. He watched powerless as she staggered to the edge of the dock, lost her footing and fell backwards into the water.

He reached for his phone, but he knew there was no time to call for backup when an outboard engine sputtered to life, blowing smoke and churning the water.

Burton scrambled to remember anything Mrs Sidhu had ever said about knowing how to swim, swimming lessons, going swimming. Nothing came. Not so much as a hot-tub spa day.

Twin engines at the back of the motorboat tore up the water into twin storms.

Burton reached the place where Mrs Sidhu had gone in. Ripples were spreading from her impact with the water. He hesitated. Time slowed for Burton. The boat was already moving, with a murderer and a twelve-million-pound painting on board. Burton looked from the water to the boat, with only a split-second to make a decision.

22

The water was a crypt of ice crushing Mrs Sidhu's lungs. Her legs went down first, she was a tombstone, sinking fast. Instinctively she made to swim. Nothing moved. The cold water was slowing her thinking. A tiny portion of her mind was laughing that people did this for their health. She kicked her feet, trying to get them to rise, but she carried on sinking. And there was another problem.

Her impact with the water had instantly expelled all the air in her lungs. She'd had no time to fill them before she fell. They felt like two empty carrier bags, crumpling in on themselves. The tissues on the inside were burning as oxygen depleted and carbon dioxide built up. She would soon have to suck in a breath, and that breath would be pure liquid, it would be the breath of death.

With the last of her air she kicked herself in the direction of the jetty.

Sharp exhale, slow inhale, cold water entered her mouth. She tried to choke it out, but it was futile because once expelled, the next in-breath just brought more in. It was life's final joke on her body. It would kill itself trying to save itself. There were lights glimmering above her now. This was it. Goodnight, namaste and sat-sri-akal, time to go. She was at the bottom now, down among the tin cans, the shopping trolleys and the bike tyres. A shadow moved over her and the light was gone.

PART II

In every dish, the ingredient people crave most is love. The sad thing is, it's an ingredient absent from so many lives.

Life With a Knife, Mrs Sidhu's Memoirs

23

When Mrs Sidhu swished the bedroom curtain open the next morning, she was determined that this would be a normal day. The sun washed over her through the glass yet she shivered, as if all the icy river water she had swallowed was still gushing around her veins.

The digital clock on her bedside table shone a set of numbers unfamiliar to her waking eyes. Her eyebrows furrowed. 'Tez, why did you let me sleep in till ten o'clock?' There was no answer. Probably he was still asleep himself.

She got up quietly. What was there to get up for anyway? It was an off day, a rest day, a paperwork day. Especially after last night.

The memory of sitting on the dock, water streaming off her, was still there. She could still taste the weeds in her mouth and every inch of her was slimed with mud. Her breathing had just been returning to normal when she'd felt a hand on her shoulder.

She found herself looking into a concerned pair of cow-like eyes, eyes she knew of old, and heard a familiar voice speak. '"Come on, you dirty slag"?' said her old friend Detective Chief Inspector Burton. 'Not the sort of language I expect from you.'

She and DCI Burton had met before. His was the voice she had heard before she fell in. They were old friends and adversaries. Burton maintained that Mrs Sidhu had been a pain in the backside during several of his investigations. Mrs Sidhu maintained the same but with the names reversed. They had often crossed words over a dead body, but never like this, where Mrs Sidhu was almost the corpse.

Burton was similarly covered in water and mud. He was the one who had pulled her out. Eventually someone brought them towels and blankets, wrapped them around their shoulders. 'I was improvising,' Mrs Sidhu said. 'I've never tried to stop an art-heister before, so I don't know the normal form of address.'

That was it for conversation. At Newton police station there was a change of clothes, a warm interview room, and questions and statements. The facts had been simple. The painting was stolen by an acrobatic woman, disguised as the Angel of Death, who escaped in a motorboat. If that sounded simple.

She shivered at the memory and turned away from the bedroom window. She pulled on her scruffy old dressing gown. Correction, her husband's scruffy old dressing gown. It still had a little of his smell on it, she kidded herself. She padded down the stairs. The boiler was thundering and the radiators were creaking into life.

Burton thought Hector had been drugged with her food. The food she had carried in to him. They were still waiting for the test results to come back and she could only pray they were clear. If they weren't she could add that to the weight of blame pressing down on her. It was a feather compared to the rest.

The last time she saw Daisy Carr alive was when she had given her the cash bonus. Then there was that moment of distraction and that had left the door ajar. 'I was sure I hadn't. But I had. It could only have been for a minute, maybe two,' she had pleaded, clasping her hands together. Burton put a steady hand on her shoulder. 'It's not your fault,' he said. 'She went in for a selfie.' Of all things, a selfie, for her new university friends.

After that, Mrs Sidhu had gone home, showered the slime from her body, collapsed into bed and fallen into black sleep.

Now, as she descended the stairs, there was a dream still fading from her mind as they did every morning, melting like snow in the spring. Yet this one was still there, hard and crystalline, as if it had found some shade from the sun.

Downstairs, in the kitchen, she did what she always did after a job. She powered up her ancient laptop. While it whirred and clicked she made pathili wali chai, 'thinking tea'. She scratched a match on the side of its box and used its yellow flame to spark the gas stove to life. With automatic movements she filled a saucepan with fresh water from the tap, tore open a PG tips teabag and scattered the black leaves onto the water's surface. With the flat of her knife she cracked open two cardamons, added those to the pan followed by a couple of cloves.

The water in the pan steamed and roared while she opened her paperwork drawer and pulled out all the crumpled, folded and creased pieces of paper within. She grabbed a biro out of the jar, then two more until she found one that actually worked, and started going through the receipts and invoices for the Keys job. But the memory of the dream would not leave her. It was abnormal.

Not that any of her dreams had ever been normal. She had dreamed about being a cream cake and what it's like to be eaten. She had dreamed about being inside out, and about being a spoon too. That's what dreams were like, weird and disturbing in confusing ways. But even normally abnormal dreams were normal. In all her slumbers she had never once before dreamed of being inside a painting.

In this new abnormal dream, *La Scaletta* had come alive. She flew through its bronzed and blue points of colour bathed with light while some reptilian thing chased her on burning wings.

She shuddered and pulled the dressing gown tight around her. What was it Jenny had said? 'Beautiful things don't always attract beautiful souls.' She scuttled back to the saucepan just as the water was starting to bubble and added milk and far too much sugar. Sated for the moment, the frothing mass settled back down.

In the dream she had fallen, shrieking, but instead of burning she was drowning. There was so much light that she was swallowed up by it, submerged by it, the light forcing its way into her mouth and down her throat. And then she had woken, choking, dying.

The froth bubbled up in the pan. She let it rise to the lip, then snapped the heat off. She poured it from the pan, foaming into her favourite mug: 'Keep Calm and Curry On'. The smell of cardamon and cloves followed her around the house as she drank it. Through the window she watched the dew steam off the plastic chairs on the back lawn.

She drifted into a state of Aloneness, a condition that she was prone to. Aloneness was that feeling she got at midnight standing under a streetlight in the rain, as goosebumps prickled her skin. In Aloneness, sometimes thoughts carried her down into a deeper stream of consciousness, like a subterranean river. In Aloneness she could think clearly.

There were things that to Mrs Sidhu's mind didn't add up about the previous evening. First, there was the delay. Between the doors opening and the masked thief trying to escape, at least half an hour must have passed. Why would they wait so long to flee the scene?

Then there was the curious lycra-clad figure who took the painting. The memory of the skull mask made her shudder once more. She could have sworn that the woman was dancing. Could that explain the delay? She was actually waiting for an audience. What sort of thief announced themselves well in advance, then hung around waiting for an audience before making an acrobatic and dramatic getaway?

So that was two interesting things that didn't add up.

She felt a curious itching in the tips of her fingers, and found herself reaching for a marker pen and the chunky block of sticky notes. She stopped herself, put the marker pen down, pushed the chunky pad block away. She was not going to make a crime board, because that would mean she was investigating, and the last sticky note she had written told her 'CRIME DOESN'T PAY'. What paid was invoicing.

Steeling herself against temptation, she went back to her paperwork. The item on top was the crockery hire invoice. Counting the breakages was the most tedious part of the job, so she liked to get it done first. Mrs Sidhu cast her mind back to the previous night. She had shown Burton

Hector's leftover canapé and wine, and the forensics team took them away for testing, so that would account for one glass and plate. The rest of the crockery she and her remaining waiters had numbly collected up. It was all in her car still, waiting to go through the dishwasher.

She had already heaved the crates onto the kitchen counter when she heard the front door open. 'Tez, is that you? I thought you were still in bed. My word, you're up and about early. I haven't checked today, but has hell frozen over?' She spoke in a distracted way, her attention focused on the boxes of glasses and plates. Her fingers riffled through them, looking for something. Something that she wasn't finding.

'I went out for supplies.' He put a shopping bag down as he entered. 'How are you getting on with holiday planning? You've done the gallery job. Take the rest of the week off. You could get a last minute deal if you hurry.'

'Everyone is very keen I take a holiday. First you, then Varma, even Mrs Prakesh is on at me. If I didn't know better, I'd think something was going on.'

There was an awkward pause before Tez burst out in hollow laughter. 'Good one, Mum.'

On another day she would have noticed, on another day she would have pinned Tez down and got the truth out of him. On another day her mind wouldn't have been whirring and spinning on a different axis.

The glasses were in crates, with a square for each one to nestle in. She noticed instantly that one of the squares was empty.

A grain of sand shifted in Mrs Sidhu's mind, loosening one more.

The skin on the back of her arms tingled. She checked every glass in the top crate, then heaved it to the floor and checked the next until she had checked them all. She checked the plates too.

When she got to the end of her search the conclusion was clear. Every wine stem was smooth, every plate was undecorated. Only two items unaccounted for and they were the ones on her trolley, the rogue plate and glass. Of course, they might be at the gallery still, they could have been missed in the chaos.

'I got you the paper.' There was an edge to Tez's voice. 'I know how you like the morning paper.' The *Slough and District Chronicle* made a thud as it hit the counter, interrupting Mrs Sidhu's train of thought. She peered at the front page.

'Top Cop Saves Old Woman in £12m Art Heist,' the headline blared.

Her lips pressed against her teeth. 'Old!' she hissed. She read the article with growing exasperation. It described a daring heist, an intrepid cop and a bungling chef who got in the way allowing the thief to get away. It also went on to describe the villain as 'ruthless' for the murder of a waitress. That part, at least, she could agree with. She slapped the paper down. 'Well, Tez, you can't always believe what you read in the papers.'

On page two, Daisy looked up at her from the newsprint. Mrs Sidhu's throat pulled tight. 'She went in there to get a selfie, Tez. Something to show her friends in her new life.' She stopped herself. Any more and she would do what she had resisted so far. She wasn't going to cry.

Tez's eyes bulged. 'Why did you get involved?'

'Because I was there. It's what you're supposed to do.'

'No, no, you're not.' He slapped at the paper. 'And how many times have I told you to get swimming lessons?'

The only answer she could dredge up was an apologetic shrug.

'Just get some before you book that holiday,' he said. 'I don't want to read about some lifeguard giving you mouth to mouth.'

All the emotions she had walled up from last night suddenly broke in her. She slapped her hand down on the kitchen counter. It stung her palm and made Tez jump. 'I'll take my holiday when I please, thank you, and I can tell you one thing, I'm not taking any holidays while Daisy Carr's killer is walking free. She was one of us.' Her voice cracked. 'She was one of mine,' she said quietly. 'Understood?'

Tez nodded silently.

'And maybe you should be looking at the back of the paper, not the front. At the job ads, Tez.'

Tez shifted from foot to foot, suddenly uneasy. 'I'll get a job, don't you worry.'

'I hope so.' Mrs Sidhu grabbed her bag and car keys. 'In the meantime I have one for you. It's your turn to do the washing-up.'

Tez looked at the empty sink. 'There isn't any.'

Mrs Sidhu pointed at the plastic crates stuffed with dirty plates and glasses. 'That lot. Load it into the dishwasher. Let's call it rent.' She turned a beady eye on him as she departed. 'And don't break anything.'

'Where are you going?' Tez shouted after her.

She might have said, 'To round up the last of it.' But it was hard to tell.

24

Mrs Sidhu slowed the car as she passed the Pump House. The street was empty, but she spied a few cars and vans in the car park. Someone was at the gallery.

She pulled into a side street, a short one that led directly to the river. She didn't want to be seen, to have to talk to someone. She just wanted a look, that was all. If she could see what she wanted to see, she could turn back around to Slough and forget about the whole thing.

The wind was making choppy patterns on the water. A swan drifted by, buffeted but contriving to look untroubled. No one really knew what was going on with swans, Mrs Sidhu thought, they didn't give much away. You saw them hooting, gathering to migrate, and yet you saw them on the river year round. You could never quite trust them.

The gallery had large windows, so it should be easy to see inside. Mrs Sidhu put up a hand to shade the reflections and looked in. Her nose pressed against the glass, tingling from the cold.

Looking up, Mrs Sidhu saw workers dismantling

artworks and taking paintings down. They paid her no mind at all. She squinted as hard as she could, into the distance beyond Gallery 1, through the open doors into Gallery 2. Police tape blocked off the entrance.

Her eyes scanned back across into Gallery 1. There was her catering trolley. She squinted her eyes trying to get a clear look, but something blurred her view. She cursed, only to realise that Jenny was eyeing her curiously from the other side of the glass. Mrs Sidhu smiled wanly.

Minutes later Jenny Leblanc appeared at the door and let Mrs Sidhu in. 'We can move things in Gallery 1,' she said, 'but Gallery 2 is still out of bounds. Chief Inspector Burton is so kind but there's a limit.'

'He is kind, isn't he?' Mrs Sidhu eyed Jenny's small, elegant frame, her simple make-up, the whiff of Channel and the softest French purr in her voice. She wondered if lots of men were kind to her. Burton, in her opinion, would be completely defenceless. 'He's a true gentleman.'

'Exactly. And we've got so much to do. Some of these pieces have to be in New York for Thursday. Because of the theft, some collectors and galleries are demanding their works back early.'

Mrs Sidhu allowed herself to be led in; there was no getting away from it now.

'God knows if we'll get it all packed in time. I've got insurers calling round the clock and I've had police all over the building. The whole opening has been such a mess.'

Mrs Sidhu scuttled along beside her. Knowing nothing of the demands of running a gallery she fumbled for something to get the conversation going.

She ran her eye down Jenny. She made the best of what

she had. Her clothes, her shoes were good brands, but not exceptional. In all, her whole outfit cost less than the Keyses' haircuts. 'Must be strange, being surrounded by all these multi million pound artworks and not being able to afford any of them.'

'I count myself the lucky one. I get to work with them, see them up close.' Her eyes misted. 'I can become intimate with them.' She blushed. 'Sorry, bit melodramatic. But when you feel strongly about art, it can be that way,' she said.

'Working for the Keyses isn't a picnic. Especially after the Louvre.'

'I don't see it that way. For me this job was a fresh start.' Jenny laughed, tilted her chin. 'So how can I help? Did you leave some equipment behind?'

'In a manner of speaking.' How could she ask this without seeming petty? 'I left my trolley.'

Jenny took Mrs Sidhu to her office. 'Help yourself. Things are still a bit of a mess,' she said. Most of the catering equipment had been cleared, but the police left their own kind of mess when they searched. Books had been taken down, a folder lay on the desk and even her diploma certificates were askew.

Mrs Sidhu moved over to her trolley. She could see that it was empty. 'And I am missing one plate and one glass. Did the police take anything from here?'

'Some food. There were the plate and glass that Hector was eating from.'

'I've accounted for those.'

'Jenny was examining the cut wires from the security monitor, stroking the copper strands. 'And they were interested in this.'

'Did you see who cut those?' Mrs Sidhu asked. Of course, Jenny herself could easily have done it.

Jenny hesitated. 'No.' Perhaps she had the same suspicion about Mrs Sidhu. She turned a curious gaze on her. 'Did you?'

Mrs Sidhu shook her head. 'They had already been cut when I came in here.' She turned and made urgent strides out into Gallery 1, casting her eyes around. She stopped at the entrance to Gallery 2. The doors were open but police tape was strung across the entrance. A uniformed officer stood guard, standing alert as they approached.

'This part is still a crime scene, I'm afraid,' Jenny explained.

Mrs Sidhu looked over the tape. Daisy's body was gone, thank goodness. Hector's half-finished savoury tarte tatin was gone, as was his wine. White wine, she remembered, but there was a red wine splash on the floor. That was odd. Could one of the guests have spilled it in the panic after the doors opened?

However, there was no rogue plate or glass. She turned around, scanning the rest of Gallery 2 until her eyes settled on the outer door of the service entrance. 'Can we go in there?'

Jenny pursed her lips. 'There's no police tape, so I suppose so.' The uniformed officer nodded.

'Is it really that important?' Jenny asked. 'I imagine it's usual to break a plate or two.' Puzzled lines creased her brow.

Mrs Sidhu bit her lip. She was going to have to tell a small untruth. 'Not at all, it's just that the hire company are ruthless, and they have a form that demands I answer certain questions about the circumstances of the breakage.' Mrs Sidhu licked her lips, then quickly moved on.

If Jenny wondered what Mrs Sidhu might want with the broken fragments of a plate and a glass, she also decided not to let it show. She pushed in the code and held the door open. Mrs Sidhu stepped out into the damp corridor, Jenny following closely behind her, and ran her hand along the thick pipe. About two or three yards along, she felt a sharp prick on her finger. She pulled it away, sucking at the drop of blood forming on the tip of her index finger.

Jenny switched her phone torch on, shining it over Mrs Sidhu's shoulder.

'There we are.' Mrs Sidhu carefully pulled the pieces of crockery and glass from their resting place, the narrow gap between the wall and the pipe. There was the patterned edge on the plate and the spiral stem of the wine glass. The glass fragments were stained with red wine. 'This is them.'

'Are you sure?'

'I have an eye for these things.'

'What do you think it means?'

'There's red wine splattered inside Gallery 2 and I think it came from this glass. Someone broke this glass and a plate *inside* Gallery 2 and then hid them.' Mrs Sidhu pulled a plastic pot from her bag and put the pieces carefully into it. The police had evidence bags, Mrs Sidhu had Evidence Tupperware.

'Why would they do that?' Jenny asked.

Mrs Sidhu shrugged. 'Well, at least I've found them. It will put the crockery hire company's mind at rest.'

'You're very thorough.' Jenny's lips pinched together.

'And the hire company care that much about one plate and glass?' She looked dubious.

Mrs Sidhu half-turned towards Jenny. 'Catering is all about the details.' Like murder, she thought. She patted her bag, hearing the fragments shifting like loose slates. Jenny's eyes followed her out of the door.

25

DCI Burton rubbed the grit of a sleepless night from his eyes and stood up from his desk. He had sat there so long, he had to peel himself off the leather.

The search had continued through the night for any kind of clue as to how the painting had been stolen. He looked at the bottom of the empty paper cup. His fifth coffee had done little to stem the fuzzy feeling in his head. The sixth was a recipe for gut rot. It was time to call it a night, or call it a day might be a better term.

He stretched his neck and went to the window, where the sunrise was a distant memory, and people who had slept were arriving for work. There was a park opposite. A woman walked her dog, which met another dog pulling a man behind him. The two animals sniffed each other's bottoms, while the man and woman flirted in what looked like an awkward way. They exchanged coy smiles and tight laughter. Dogs had it so much easier when it came to romance.

'Sir!' Dove was out of breath, puffing from the exertion

of jogging from his desk to Burton's office. He leaned in through the door. 'Sir, we've finally got the CCTV footage from Gallery 2.'

Burton had no hopes it would show anything useful. This was too well thought through. His fears were confirmed by the dull look in Dove's eyes. 'Let's see it anyway.'

Dove carried a computer tablet in his hands. He tapped and clicked around until he had what he wanted, then handed it to his boss.

Burton bunched his jumper sleeve over his fist and wiped Dove's sweaty paw prints from the screen. The footage showed what he knew already. Mrs Sidhu came in, and Hector stepped away to eat his food while she looked at the painting. She left. The camera feed went dead.

He swore quietly. 'Is this the only CCTV camera covering the painting?'

'Yup.' Dove nodded. 'They had it installed especially.'

Burton fumbled, turning the device off. 'Have you seen the newspaper, sir?' Dove asked, handing him the *Chronicle*.

'"Top Cop Saves Old Woman in £12m Art Heist",' he read and suppressed a smirk. Mrs Sidhu would not like that. He continued: '"Art heisters kill one and injure another at the Pump House, the hot new gallery in Bowler's Green. Fortunately, Berkshire's top cop is on the case."' They had a photograph of him at the scene, commanding operations.

He had no time for the press on most occasions, but he had to admit they were glowing about his work these days. 'Never trust the press.' He thrust the *Chronicle* in Dove's chest.

'They got your good side, sir.'

'I have a bad side?' He looked again at the picture: he was slouching. Burton stood a little bit straighter.

'Looks like everyone's expecting a quick arrest,' Dove said. 'How did they do it, sir? How did they kill the cameras, in and out in ten minutes without a trace?' He looked to Burton who realised he was eyeing Berkshire's top cop with eyes filled with a shining hope.

Burton lifted his chin. It was his job to keep up morale. 'Don't fret, Dove. I'll get there, I always do.'

Burton retreated to the window with his doubts and wished he'd decided on that sixth coffee after all. Down below more cars arrived. The man and woman with the dogs parted company. The man seemed to shake his head, perhaps cursing himself for saying something stupid. The woman's eyes followed him for a bit. People do find love in the strangest places, but they were very good at screwing it up. A light cough reminded him that Dove was waiting for instructions.

Burton rolled his large shoulders, where a new tension was spreading from his neck down his back. He glanced again at the paper. 'Top cop,' he thought, then tried not to think about it. Pressure was the job. He had a dead woman and a missing painting to get to the bottom of. 'Now what about the boat the woman escaped on?' he asked.

'It belonged to the Keyses. We're sending officers out today for witnesses, narrowboat owners, houses that overlook the river. We won't have anything back on that till later.'

'What about the murder weapon? The rock?'

'Searched the gallery. Hasn't turned up.'

Burton puckered his lips, gently massaging the back of his neck. 'Must have taken it out with them.'

'Why, sir? It's incriminating. Better leaving it by the body than risk getting caught with it.'

'Perhaps they panicked after killing the girl.' It sounded hollow even in his own ears. This was a thoroughly planned job, maybe professional. Such people tended not to panic. Dreams of going home for a shower and an hour's sleep were evaporating. It didn't look as if he'd be seeing his bed for a while yet. He stared at his desk, where the screwed-up balls of paper made an almost laughable movie pastiche of a night's work and a complete lack of progress. 'The clock is ticking. No CCTV footage, no leads on the boat. Nothing from witnesses.'

Somewhere outside his office, fresh voices were exchanging greetings, putting on coffee and getting ready to start their day, fresh blood pumping into the veins of the station. It gave Burton an idea.

Dove lifted the meeting area table and jiggled backwards with tiny footsteps. 'How's that?' He put it down and rubbed at his back.

A digital projector and a laptop stood on the table. The latter projected an image onto the wall at the top of the room. The meeting area was the large space that stood in the open-plan part of the offices. Curious glances from day-shift officers were already being cast in their direction.

As Dove moved the table, Burton stood by the wall, where the whiteboard dominated. He had wiped it clean in a moment of annoyance, the few ideas that he and Dove had come up with in the night sending ants crawling over his tired brain. With the board clean, he could think again. And use the space to project a square of light. He unfurled a tape measure and held it against the wall. 'A bit more.' He strained, holding his breath, arms above his head, holding his thumb against the wall.

Dove inched the table back. As he did, the rectangle of light shining onto the wall expanded. When the edge between shadow and light hit Burton's thumb Dove put the table down again. The projector wobbled a little, shimmying the image on the wall for a moment until it steadied.

Burton beckoned the officers in the room forward, onto the chairs arranged in haphazard rows. There followed a movement of feet, a march of officers, coffees clutched in hands. When the seats had filled, he started.

'You'll all be aware that last night we had a robbery at a gallery. A painting known as *La Scaletta*. The thieves not only took the artwork, they also knocked out the owner and killed a waitress who happened on the scene. She was bashed over the head with a rock, we think taken from an installation piece nearby.' When the room drew a breath, and voices muttered to each other, Burton snapped the tape measure closed, silencing the noise.

He pointed at the projected rectangle on the wall. 'There it is full-size, ladies and gentlemen. *La Scaletta*. Gaston Lefevre's pointillist masterpiece formally known as *The Bathing Pool*. Painted in 1936. Stolen four, now five, times. Twelve million pounds' worth of painting. Gone in the ten minutes between the camera feeds being cut and the doors opening. We've been scratching our heads all night, but now you're all here bright and bushy, let's have some fresh ideas. How did they do it?'

He cast his eyes over the audience. The room was packed, there was a buzz of excitement. Members of the serious crime squad at Newton police station were supplemented by just about every officer at the station. He wondered if this was what it felt like on opening night for Hector Keys. Or should have done, had he not been unconscious for the vital moment.

He clapped his hands. 'That was not a rhetorical question. The thief or thieves got this out of the gallery somehow. I want to know how and what direction they took. I want this painting before they fence it, or get it out of the country.'

An officer raised his hand. 'They cut it out of the frame, rolled it up, and carried it out under a coat.'

Burton gave a sad shake of his head. 'The frame wasn't on the wall. We didn't find it, or any parts of it, anywhere in the gallery. The painting was moved in its frame, without anyone registering it.' He spanned his arms and mimed the act with the projection, turning back to face his audience, arms slightly wider than his shoulders, clutching the imaginary painting. 'Not so simple. It's two and a half feet square. Can't exactly slip it under your coat.'

'What about CCTV footage, sir?' asked another from the team.

'Useless. They cut the camera feed before the theft.'

'Did no one notice, sir? Someone must have been in charge of security.'

He thought back to Jenny Leblanc, her pale features, as she wrung her hands and blamed herself for the theft. 'It was opening night, they all had their hands full,' he said.

'How did they knock out the owner? Was he bashed over the head too?' That one came from a bright young uniform whose name Burton couldn't remember. He would get it later from Dove, and mark her down as a hopeful.

'Good question. He has a small head injury, but not

very big. He's still unconscious.' He checked this with Dove, who nodded. 'We think he was drugged. Waiting on the lab to get the results back. Again the element of planning here – this was no opportunist snatch and grab.'

'Where are the exits?' It was the same sharp, uniformed officer.

'The gallery has a set of double doors and there's an access door at the back which leads to a service corridor.'

'Then they must have taken the painting into the access corridor.'

Burton nodded briskly. 'Must have, but that has no exit to the outside. The only way out of there is another door that opens into Gallery 1. So the question remains, how did they get the painting out through a crowded gallery in its frame?' Eyes blinked in the sudden brightness. 'Any ideas?'

Another hand shot up. 'They left it in the corridor and it's still there.' This got some laughs.

'I wish. The corridor has been searched, and there's no sign of a painting. Forensics have been all over it. Anyone else?' Not a single hand raised itself in the crowd. Just nervous coughs, a couple of giggles and one almost silent breaking of wind. Burton shot Dove a glance, who blushed.

'But didn't you witness the thief jump onto a motorboat with it?' asked someone else. 'Does it matter how they got it out of the gallery?' Burton knew the officer was right, but it was a loose end.

As the room cleared, Burton put a hand on Dove's shoulder.

'I had an egg butty, sir.' Dove rubbed his stomach. 'Won't happen again.'

Burton narrowed his eyes. 'I don't care about the . . .

Look, get on to the river search officers, see if they've had any updates on the boat or the woman. Someone must remember a figure dressed like that coming or going.'

Dove made to move away and turned back. 'Oh, talking of women, *she's* in your office, sir.' Dove grinned. 'Maybe she's solved the case.'

Burton growled and strode into his office. 'Mrs Sidhu, charmed as ever. How can I help you?'

'I'm very much hoping that I can help you,' Mrs Sidhu said.

He slumped into his chair. 'Oh, good,' he said, his voice laced with sarcasm. 'Just what I need.' He started rummaging in his desk drawers – didn't he have a KitKat in there from last week? The week when he was being good and staying off the sugar. Oh, sugar, what a sweet, sweet word.

'You're in a bad mood,' Mrs Sidhu said.

'I've been up all night and I don't have any leads.' He spoke weakly, pushing around inside the drawer and only finding a stapler and a couple of old pens. 'Plus I'm famished.'

'Until now.' Mrs Sidhu pulled her Tupperware out of her bag and slid it towards him. 'I have something for you.' She tapped the lid.

Burton moaned with pleasure. 'You are a mind-reader, Mrs Sidhu.' He tore open the clips holding the lid down.

'Let's just say I have an instinct for these things.' She smiled.

Fingers fumbling, eyes gleaming, he got the lid off. He stopped, hands poised over the contents. 'What's this?' He almost yelled it.

'It's a lead. Isn't that what you've been waiting for?'

Tiredness and hunger were overwhelming Chief Inspector Burton's reserves of patience. They had been starved to death. He let his chin fall into his hands. 'Mrs Sidhu, do you by any chance know how to make an egg butty?'

'I can do a little better than that,' Mrs Sidhu said. 'Come with me.'

26

'I have to say, I saw your little slide show.' Mrs Sidhu tweaked the heat as the sauce bubbled in the pan. 'You've got quite a mystery on your hands.'

'I don't know how you even got into the station.' Burton's eyes narrowed. 'Unless you're bribing my sergeant with egg butties. If you are I'd like to point out the consequences. That meeting room will be out of bounds for days.'

'I don't do egg butties.' She smiled innocently. 'I'm not responsible for your sergeant's terrible diet. All I said to him was that I had urgent information about the robbery and he showed me to your office, which overlooks the meeting area.'

Burton seemed mollified.

'And where would you get the idea that I would bribe a police officer for information using food?' She ladled a creamy dollop of her chicken malabari on to jasmine rice and passed Burton the paper plate.

He took it gratefully, shovelling it into his mouth using

an inadequately tiny plastic fork. She breathed in fresh air. There was nothing like a little al fresco cookery to raise the spirits.

'I don't know what you're worried about.' She added another poppadom onto the pile at his elbow. 'Most of the details are in the newspapers. Look, you've made the press. Congratulations.'

'Hadn't noticed.' Burton looked more closely. 'Apparently I've got a good side.'

'Hadn't noticed,' Mrs Sidhu said with a grin. 'Which one is it?'

'At the moment I'm too emaciated to care.' Burton tossed the newspaper aside and focused on his food. 'Please don't show me that again until I've regained the half-stone I lost last night.'

They were sitting by the river at the back of the Pump House, with a good view of both the jetty where the thieves made their escape and the statue of Hector Keys. This was the ground zero of her guilt. She should have stopped the Angel of Death, should have made her pay for the blood she spilled.

She switched off the camping gas stove and the flame sputtered out. 'Aren't you worried?' She sidled up to the bench and sat beside him.

'Why would I be worried?' He raised an eyebrow.

'Like I said –' Mrs Sidhu tapped her spatula on the cooker – 'I saw your little talk. You've got an impossible crime.'

'That doesn't worry me. The crime isn't impossible. Do you know how I know that?' He pointed his tiny plastic fork at her. 'I know that,' he continued, 'because it happened. It's just that we don't know how they did it.

Now, I could sit around for hours like Sherlock Holmes, taking opium, playing violins, trying to work out how they did it from my armchair, or I can find the people who did it and just ask them.'

'What if you can't find them?'

'We always do.'

'What if they don't want to talk?'

'They always do.' Burton scraped the very last of the curry across the plate, lifted his head back and tipped it in.

Mrs Sidhu snatched the plate away. 'In all this excitement over the theft of a twelve-million-pound painting, I can't help thinking that people are forgetting something. This isn't a victimless crime. Daisy Carr is dead.'

This was why she wanted Burton here, why she had driven with him in convoy, starving, to the gallery. She wanted him to be present, right here where it happened, before delivering her devastating evidence. Or rather delivering it again, only this time Burton would have some food in him.

Mrs Sidhu had a philosophy on a comprehensive list of subjects in life. On the subject of bags, she believed there were two kinds of people: the compartment people and the bucket people. The compartment people wanted everything stowed away in pockets which they had already predetermined: keys in here, bus pass in there, purse in the other. These people did not want to waste time looking for things, thus they spent a great deal of their time making sure everything was in the right place and becoming very cross if it turned out not to be. The second type, the bucket people, wanted to get on with things and be able to chuck everything they owned into a void. Keys, credit cards, receipts, cash, breath mints, tissues, it all got tossed into the bottomless pit. These people did not want to waste valuable time sorting things out, thus they spent a lot of valuable time with hands plunged into open bags, sifting for what they wanted, becoming ever more cross that they could not find things when they needed them. Which is what Mrs Sidhu was doing now.

She had a large, brown, canvas bag with one pocket. Into it she threw everything. Which is why it took a few minutes of rummaging to find her Evidence Tupperware and wrench it out. With it came her laptop cable which was wound around her purse which in turn was caught up with her phone. 'What do you think of this?'

Burton stared at the contents of the bag, which had spilled onto the grass. 'It's a mess. Have you thought about a bag with pockets and compartments?' He helped her collect up the wayward items.

She sucked a breath in through her teeth. She didn't have time to explain her theory of bags, she seethed. 'I mean this.' She dumped the Evidence Tupperware on his lap. While Burton turned broken pieces of crockery over slowly in his hands she explained where she had found them and wrestled her belongings back into her bag.

'It's some broken glass and crockery. Why does it matter?'

She updated him with what she knew, that this plate and glass were on her trolley just minutes before the art heist. 'Daisy Carr never ate or drank on the job, and besides she had a rotten cold,' she finished.

'Someone else took this into Gallery 2, and broke it.'

'You think the thief decided to have a snack first?' Burton smiled without mirth.

'The question is, why would someone in a hurry to get away with a twelve-million-pound painting take the time to hide a broken glass and plate behind a pipe in the service corridor?' Mrs Sidhu waited for the answer, arms crossed.

Burton chuckled. 'Mrs Sidhu, you have the pieces of a plate and a standard-issue wine glass. Could have been there for months or years.'

Her chest tightened. 'So you don't think there's anything here?'

He smiled with a sad shake of the head. 'We are doing all we can to recover the stolen artwork and apprehend those responsible for Hector Keys's death.' Burton picked up the newspaper, maybe aware that he was sounding like a press release. 'When we do we'll have some answers.'

An electric buzz shook Burton's phone. He listened for a while, then covered it with a large hand. 'Must go. Hector Keys just woke up,' he said to Mrs Sidhu. 'Thanks for breakfast.'

Mrs Sidhu tried but couldn't hide her irritation. 'I'm not some crazy old cat lady, with her crazy bits of broken stuff.' She snatched her Tupperware back. 'Of course not.' Burton strode away his bulky torso carried on long spider's legs, barking commands down the phone.

Mrs Sidhu remained seated on the bench outside the Pump House for a long while after Burton had left, looking at Hector Keys's statue. Anger burned at her insides. Unlike Burton, she had slept, but not enough to make up for the intense pressure she had put herself under the last two weeks. She was an over-tightened spring unable to wind down.

She glared at the sad little fragments of glass and china.

They curled at the bottom of her plastic pot, somehow echoing Daisy's broken, prone form on the gallery floor.

This didn't end here.

Burton said Daisy was dead because she interrupted a robbery. She could agree with that, but it was too bland. There was . . . more.

Burton had left the newspaper behind. She smoothed it out, the headlines, the photographs, and with a sigh of revelation she saw what this was for DCI Burton. It was a career-defining moment. She had to forgive him for his focus on recovering the painting. If he had no time to think about Daisy, then it was her duty to do so, and to do that she had to think clearly.

She put the paper to one side, and placed the plastic pot on top. The question was, what did she have?

A noise was playing at the edge of her consciousness, like the distant buzz of machinery, and she couldn't shake it off.

She went back, touched the statue and blinked. It surprised her, how cold the metal was. Parts of her own face were reflected in it.

'He paints light.' That's what Hector had said about Lefevre, and suddenly she was in the realm of light again, flying through *La Scaletta*'s fields of colour. We are all made of light. Was that what the sculptor was saying?

She leaned in towards the bronze face, staring into the reflecting eyes, and seeing reflecting back just her own distorted, confused, bloated face. Like all artworks, on the surface it seemed clear, attractive and simple. And yet she had the feeling there was more to this than met the eye. However hard she tried, she couldn't rest her mind on what that might be.

She shook her head, trying to clear it. The pieces of the jigsaw would not fit together.

She walked to the jetty and traced her same steps from the night before, conjuring up the moment she saw the dancing apparition escaping with the painting, wearing the smiling mask of death.

She went back to the beginning again. Someone dropped the plate and glass, someone hid the pieces, which meant that person's presence in the gallery had to be kept a secret.

That person took the wine and plate, and walked through the same door that Mrs Sidhu had come out of.

She replayed that moment from the gallery opening in her mind.

She had closed the door behind her. There had been a pause, then she had turned away from her trolley and the door to give Daisy her money. In that pause anyone could have taken the plate and glass and entered through the door.

Her mental film continued. She had turned away, distracted by a sound, and when she turned back, Daisy was gone too.

It was only after that she had noticed the door was ajar. In those two turns the killer entered, shortly followed by poor Daisy.

Mrs Sidhu hadn't left it open, the other person had, and Daisy had followed. Now her heart fluttered at her ribcage, drumming ever faster.

Daisy Carr was dead because she saw the identity of that person. And that person had to be one of the gallery guests.

A shudder passed through her. She walked as fast as

she could away from the jetty. She looked up at the Pump House. It was as strange and exciting as the first time she had seen it. It was also completely beyond her experience. This whole place was. She needed a way in with these people.

After some shoving, Mrs Sidhu managed to get her Evidence Tupperware into her bag, where it instantly got bound up with the laptop cable and all the other things in there. Maybe she should switch to compartments, she reflected sadly.

She took a tour around the building. As she turned the corner, onto the side furthest from the jetty, Mrs Sidhu saw Ben Trimble entering a separate building. Lower and squatter than the Pump House but unmistakably the same modernist style. A plaque was attached to the wall: 'Educational Suite'.

This was her chance. Mrs Sidhu wrestled her phone out of her bag and checked the balance in her savings account. She watched the numbers for a little while, and stroked a finger across the screen at her holiday money. This would be a small investment in her personal growth, that was all. It was a holiday, just not very far from home.

27

Burton caught his face reflected in Tani Keys's sunglasses. He looked as bad as he felt.

'Chief Inspector, good of you to come.' She held the front door open, gesturing him inside with long flexible hands. 'Yes, Hector's awake. But he's very weak.'

Burton eased his bulk inside and instantly every muscle tightened. The old bull-in-a-china-shop fear crept into his mind. He had always tightened up in the houses of the well-heeled, living with a lifelong fear that he would knock over something precious. In the Keyses' house, his fear was trebled. Every surface seemed to be filled with fragile fripperies.

He kept his elbows tight to his sides as Tani led him through this terrifying maze, until with a breath of relief he found himself in a spacious living room. He took an awkward seat on a very stylish but uncomfortable sofa.

'Nina Linari, Italian designer,' Tani said.

Clearly the Italians had different-shaped backsides to him. Burton tried shifting around but it was no use.

Coffee was brought in and Burton gripped the tiny cup in large fingers, sipping as delicately as his frame would allow.

Tani snapped her espresso back in one tilt of the head, yawned and lit a cigarette. 'So, Chief Inspector, what about a progress report? Where is our painting?'

Burton checked his watch. 'It's been less than twenty-four hours since the theft. We are still gathering information.'

Tani drew in a long drag. 'Aren't the first twenty-four hours the most important? Didn't I read that somewhere?' She spread her long fingers wide.

'Indeed they are, Mrs Keys, but we do need to establish the facts. Mr Keys might have vital information, so I would like to talk to him.'

'The doctor says he's very weak. There's also the matter of our privacy.'

'The doctor is a fool.' Hector Keys dragged himself into the room using a walking frame. He was wearing silk pyjamas and had the newspaper tucked under his arm which he threw down onto the coffee table. 'I want to meet Berkshire's finest detective.'

'Hector, you should not be out of bed,' Tani said.

'Too late!' Hector beamed a wide smile. The effort, though, seemed to take the energy out of him. Tani rushed to help him onto another Italian masterpiece. 'Sorry about that. Still a bit unsteady on my feet.' He took a rasping breath. 'Now, I've read great things about you, Chief Inspector Burton. So what is the plan? *La Scaletta* is a masterpiece – it cannot be allowed to rest in the hands of criminals.'

'My plan depends on your memory, sir. As I explained to your wife, we're still trying to establish the facts.'

'There, you see,' Hector said, twisting towards Tani. 'This is how the police mind works, turning chaos into order. You should give the esteemed DCI more respect.'

Tani's shaded eyes looked blankly at Burton. 'I'd like to see a bit more progress at this stage, that's all.' A wisp of smoke curled from her nostrils.

'Your memory of what happened last night, sir?' Burton sat poised with pen and notebook.

Hector loosed a low, uncertain whine. 'Hmmm. It's all like a Dutch master painting. Dark and light, chiaroscuro – you understand, Chief Inspector?' Hector expanded his arms wide. 'Most of the evening is clear, brightly lit. I stayed with *La Scaletta* all night, guarding it personally. My only visitor was the caterer, Mrs Sidhu.'

'She left at six-fifty, is that right?'

'Yes, I remember because I needed to practise my speech. That's where things move into the shadows of the mind. It all becomes dimly lit and blurry.'

'Do try. Anything you can remember about who hit you on the head would help, sir.'

'My head?' He stroked his scalp, as if noticing the bruise for the first time. 'That's a curious thing. I have no memory of that. I would imagine being hit on the head, one would lose consciousness in an instant.'

'True,' Burton said.

'This was not like that. I began to feel weak and dizzy. My stomach was not all it should be. I thought to start with it was nerves.' He rubbed his belly. 'It still feels a bit off, as does my head.'

Burton was writing fast. 'That fits. I think you may have been drugged, sir. We're waiting on results from the lab. Did you eat anything other than the catering food?'

'No. I was unable to finish even that, I left it to finish later.'

Tani tilted her long neck. 'Doesn't that suggest the caterer is involved?'

'Don't be silly.' Hector shook his head, setting the points of his swept hair vibrating. 'Mrs Sidhu has no more motive to poison me than you do.'

Tani's face reddened. 'She was the one who brought you the food.' She flexed her fingers again like bird's claws.

Burton broke in quickly. 'I don't think that's likely. I happen to know Mrs Sidhu from –' Burton coughed – 'some police catering events. I'd vouch for her personally.'

Hector arched an eyebrow. 'Really? How interesting. Well, there you are, darling. She's in the clear.'

Burton continued, 'If you could return to the timeline, sir. In sequence as you remember it, if you don't mind. Who knew you'd asked for food?'

Hector ran his fingers through his spiked silver hair. 'Let me see. I felt hungry, so I phoned you, darling –' he nodded to Tani – 'to tell Mrs Sidhu to bring me some food and a little wine.'

Tani stuttered. 'I . . . I didn't actually handle the food. I was busy with some potential buyers and I just passed the message on to Jenny. Jenny Leblanc the gallery director. She and Hector disagreed on the gallery artworks. Perhaps she took it personally.'

'You can't imagine my gallery director was involved?' Hector said.

'What do we actually know about her, Hector? She's barely been here a week. Chief Inspector, could it be her?'

Burton chose not to answer directly. 'I'll speak to Ms Leblanc. See what she can remember.' He produced a sheet of paper in an evidence bag, which he handed to Hector. 'Ms Leblanc was kind enough to give me this. I'm told everyone in the village got one. She dismissed them as a prank. But you didn't, did you, sir?'

Hector giggled. 'Oh, Chief Inspector, I can see why you've earned such a glowing reputation. Yes, I was unsure. These threats were the reason that I took the extra precautions. Amongst other things.'

Tani interrupted sharply. 'I'm going to insist you get some rest now, Hector. You've got what you need, Chief Inspector, and my husband is still clearly suffering the after-effects of this poison.'

'Maybe it would be better if I talked to Mr Keys alone?' It was a power-play. It worked with the hoi polloi but with people like the Keyses it was an uncertain gambit.

Tani simply turned her dark glasses to the door. 'Better still if you talked to his doctor and our lawyers.' She ground out her cigarette. 'Shall I call them in?'

Burton wanted to know what Hector Keys meant by 'amongst other things' but he had dealt with Berkshire's elite before. The last thing he needed right now was a long meeting with a lawyer. He decided to back down, for now. 'Not necessary. But one last question, to both of you. Can you think of anyone who would do this to you?'

Hector opened his mouth. If he was about to say something it was interrupted by Tani. 'Absolutely not.' Tani bounced her hands on her thighs and stood. 'I'll show you out.'

Burton stopped when they were at the front door. 'By the way, we're still trying to catch up with Ivor Langtree. I understand he's your nephew. Is he here?'

'Ivor lives down in the village.'

'Yes, I have his address. He's also your husband's assistant. Is he at work today?'

'He hasn't come up here this morning. He might be at the gallery. After last night there's lots to do. Perhaps you'll catch up with him there when you question Jenny Leblanc.'

She bade him a curt farewell and closed the door. Burton scrunched across the gravel drive, turning back just once to see a curtain twitch. Now that was an interesting encounter. The answer to the question as to whether they could think who might want to do this was simple. They could have said, 'Who wouldn't want to steal a twelve-million-pound painting?' When Tani Keys gave an affirmative no that was as good as saying, 'Yes, but I won't tell you.' He filed that away at the back of his mind for later, when he had enough to push her harder.

For the time being he had a lead, and the guilty pleasure of interviewing Jenny Leblanc again to look forward to.

28

How did she get herself into these situations? These situations that forced her to tell untruths. She sometimes wondered if it said something deeper about her.

'Well, well, well. Look who's here,' Ben said.

They were in a teaching room attached to the Pump House. Flecks of paint, ink and clay marked the walls and floors and the smell of paint and turpentine permeated everywhere. Not being part of the main gallery, and having been locked up on the night of the art heist, they had quickly been cleared for use by the police.

'I'm surprised to see you here – are you applying to join my harem?'

Ben was dealing with an old man with striking features, who disappeared behind a screen as Mrs Sidhu reached them.

She felt the heat rising in her. 'I happen to need some art lessons, and I happened to remember that you give them.' Why did this man make her so angry?

She took a deep breath and hoisted a smile into place.

'Look, I apologise for what I said. But I don't want to get to know you, or understand anything else about you. I just happen to need art classes, and I need them today. Urgently.'

The teaching room was light and airy. It didn't feel like the classrooms Mrs Sidhu remembered from school. There were no desks, no blackboards, no periodic tables on the walls. There wasn't even a teacher's table. Instead there were easels scattered around and at the front there was a bed. It was unmade, and was so out of place in Mrs Sidhu's mind that she almost blanked it out. Perhaps it was modern art. Hadn't there been an artist who had put an unmade bed in a gallery? Maybe the students had to make it. If this art class was about making beds, then Mrs Sidhu was on for an A grade, that was a fact.

'Urgently? My, my, we have an emergency. Then I'm sure we can fit you in.'

She wasn't sure she liked the sly grin that upturned Ben's moustache.

'Why don't you take some materials and find an empty easel. We're doing life in here.'

The cramp in her shoulder eased. There, a little bit of courtesy was all it took. 'I love life, life is my thing. As long as it's a bowl of fruit or something. I like bowls of fruit.'

The man with striking features appeared from behind the screen wearing a silk gown. He tugged at the sash and allowed it to fall to the ground. He wore nothing underneath. She watched speechless as he climbed up onto the bed and positioned himself, propped up on one elbow, legs lolling apart.

Mrs Sidhu felt the warmth spread across her face. 'So,

not fruit. Well, not in a bowl, anyway.' She was aware of babbling. She cast her eyes almost anywhere else she could.

Ben clapped his hands. 'Please, our model is ready, take your places.' He ushered Mrs Sidhu to an easel.

Other people were arriving, rushing to their places, and some had already started sketching broad strokes in charcoal.

Mrs Sidhu scuttled to her easel and hid herself behind it, hands over eyes. What was she going to do? She opened her fingers a crack and noticed that Ben was leaving. She grabbed her bag and hurried along behind him. 'You're not staying? Perhaps I'll come with you.'

'I'm actually just getting this one started. I'm teaching two classes today.' He grinned. 'Don't you want to get going on your life picture?'

'I'm having second thoughts. You know, I'm not sure the human figure is my thing. Bowls of fruit, I can really get to grips with that. Plums, satsumas, grapes, nectarines, prunes.' Mrs Sidhu realised she was reeling off the names of testicular fruits. She jumped. 'Bananas.' Her hand flew to her mouth. 'No! Not bananas. Kumquats!' No one could misinterpret a kumquat.

'There's no still-life class this term. I just thought with your interest in *La Scaletta*, you'd be into the human nude.' Ben smiled that knowing smile, and Mrs Sidhu blushed ever more deeply.

Curse him, he knew exactly what he was doing. She thrust her chin forward and pointed at the model. 'Well, I'm not spending the next hour looking at that.' A giggle rose up across the class. Mrs Sidhu stopped pointing at what she realised she was pointing at and quickly drew her arm to her side.

Ben was clutching his stomach in silent laughter. 'Maybe landscape would suit you better. This way.'

The cool air outside the Pump House did something to calm the lava-hot blush across her face and neck. There was, however, the possibility that the blood would never drain away and would leave her permanently red-faced. 'Are you having fun?' she fumed.

Ben moved up the hill in easy strides. He was still chuckling. 'Me? Always. Are you?'

She scurried to keep up with him. 'I didn't appreciate being humiliated in there. In front of everyone.'

They were leaving the gallery behind and as they turned the corner they stepped out onto the green, the broad grassy square at the centre of Bowler's Green.

'You care what they think of you? Perfect strangers?'

'No. I've never cared what people think of me.'

'Relax.'

She bunched her fists. 'I am perfectly relaxed, Mr Trimble.'

'Call me Ben, please.' When Mrs Sidhu's shoulders remained hoisted up to her ears, he stopped and made a formal little bow. 'Forgive me. I was having a bit of fun, true, but there was something else. I wanted to shake you up a little, get your creative juices flowing. Surprise will do that. I haven't seen you since the big heist. Quite a night. Me and my harem talked about nothing else.'

She chose to ignore the barb. 'That's just the thing. I'm not entirely sure everything went exactly as the police think.'

They were halfway across the green. To her left, Mrs Sidhu could see the girl with the ginger hair. She was scowling and wiping down tables outside the Greenview. The caterer in Mrs Sidhu earmarked her as a good worker. This thought, though, only gave rise to dismal memories of Daisy Carr, and the mauve bruise of guilt that went with her death. The waitress looked up as they passed, saw Ben, then smirked at Mrs Sidhu. Mrs Sidhu pulled her hat down tighter and looked away.

Up ahead there was a cluster of people in a semicircle. They turned and waved as Ben approached.

'You have a theory?' Ben asked.

Mrs Sidhu scratched her head. 'Not exactly, only some pieces that don't fit.'

'So you thought, sign up for old Ben's art class and maybe snoop around the village a little, did you?'

Mrs Sidhu started to feel the heat rising in her face, until she saw the lopsided grin on Ben's face again. 'You're sending me up, or worse, humouring me.'

'Not at all. I like people who think differently. It's what art's all about.' Ben produced a contactless card machine. 'Now, Introduction to Landscape, that's five hundred pounds.'

The air seemed to leave her lungs. 'Oh.' The smile on Mrs Sidhu's face remained propped up in place while the rest of her face dropped around it. 'Um, do you have a special offer?' she asked hopefully.

'I do – the fifth class is free.' He winked. 'I know, I haven't put up my prices in years. Don't tell anyone, I am almost double subscribed, and you've leapfrogged the waiting list. But I have a good feeling about you.'

Mrs Sidhu pushed her card in. She could feel the money being sucked from her account.

Ben clapped his hands and his voice rose.

'We've got a new student joining us today. This is Mrs Sidhu.' There were murmured 'hello's and 'hi's. 'What about next to Gertie?' Mrs Sidhu recognised the woman who gave the tour on her first visit to the Pump House. 'If you and Ludo can shuffle along,' Ben continued. The man next to her, Ludo evidently, grumbled at having to move his easel before falling into a malevolent silence.

Ben positioned an easel for her and whispered in her ear. 'We're drawing a tree. Unless that's too suggestive for you.'

'I'm fine with trees,' Mrs Sidhu snapped back.

'Good.' Ben offered her watercolour paints, pencils, charcoal. 'Just start with whatever feels natural to you.' He held out his hand. 'It doesn't matter if you like paint or pencil or pastel or charcoal. Express yourself.'

Mrs Sidhu felt lighter, though her head was still reeling from the expense. No matter, she was here for Daisy. She wouldn't regret the money if it helped solve her murder.

This was more like her idea of an art class. They were outdoors, what the artists call 'en plein air'. Oh, yes, she had done her reading and researching.

A breeze ruffled her hair, sunlight twinkled between the leaves of a broad-trunked oak. There was no sign of naked men anywhere. And in any case, her canvas wasn't the white empty one in front of her. Her canvas was people.

She took a pencil from Ben's outstretched palm. The faceted faces felt familiar to her fingers.

Ben had chosen well for her by seating her next to Gertie.

'Gertie Dalrymple,' she said as an introduction, extending a large hand. The tour guide was exactly the woman she wanted to see. It wasn't hard to get her talking about the theft of *La Scaletta*. Everyone was gossiping about it. 'Such a tragedy,' said Mrs Sidhu, bending her head to one side and putting a hand to her heart. 'Daisy, the girl who died, was my waitress.'

Gertie sympathised with a wry turn of the lips. 'I'm so sorry. The whole thing is so awful. And I mean losing *La Scaletta*, it's a masterpiece.' She was working in watercolour. 'I love the way it finds the paper, the way it changes when you dab it on. It's not really in your control, you just guide it.' Gertie washed a green swathe over her paper with a minimum of guidance.

Ben stepped in with encouragement. 'Good, Gertie,' he enthused. 'Don't let yourself get tied down by notions of form or figure. That can come later.' He raised his voice. 'Everyone, what's rule number one of art class?'

The class droned the answer like schoolchildren, while Ben pretended to conduct them like a symphony conductor. 'Enjoy yourselves!'

Ben grinned. 'Well, off you go, it's your time.' He wandered away to the far corner to help one of the hot grannies from the cafe the other day.

Mrs Sidhu had to build up to the question that was on her mind. 'Is that what *La Scaletta* is like? Full of self-expression? You sounded so knowledgeable about it when you were giving your tour.'

Gertie clasped a hand to her chest. 'Oh, you heard my tour? I'm flattered, my dear.'

'And I saw you at the gallery opening too.'

'Oh, yes, I mean, who could resist? I must say I was looking forward to a peep at *La Scaletta* wasn't I, Ludo?' A superior smile spread across her lips. 'Of course, I saw it many times in their home, but there's something special about seeing it in a gallery. Alas, it was stolen before anyone had the pleasure. Poor Hector and Tani.'

Ludo growled. He was working in charcoal, drawing a profusion of angry, black branches shooting from a twisting trunk. She recognised him. He had also been there on her first visit to the Pump House. He was the rude man, with one eye larger than the other. Now the hostile familiarity between him and Gertie made some kind of sense. They were married, and had been for too long a time.

As if sensing Mrs Sidhu's thoughts Gertie continued. 'Ludo and I own the Breeze Gallery, just around the corner. We were so thrilled when the Keyses made Bowler's Green their new base, weren't we, Ludo?' She nudged him with her elbow, sending his charcoal spiralling into a bush.

He glowered. 'Absolutely bloody thrilled,' he said, picking up a fresh piece of charcoal from his tray.

'A new gallery, right here, in Bowler's,' Gertie continued. 'We have such an active art scene. Ludo runs the gallery and I run the Berkshire Arts Society.'

This raised a gleeful smile from Ludo. 'The Art Berks, as I call them.'

Now it was Gertie's turn to scowl. 'You know I hate that term.' She washed more colours across her paper, mauves and yellows, with no regard for anything she was looking at. She tilted her head. 'And I recruited the Keyses, which was a huge feather in my cap. They had us all round for a cup of tea.'

'I bet the Berks loved that.' Ludo gave a dry chuckle.

Gertie thrust out her large chin. 'Ludo, darling, do go and stick your head where the sun doesn't shine, won't you?' she bellowed. 'I'm trying to have a decent conversation here.'

Ludo grumbled, but quieted down.

Now Mrs Sidhu dropped in her question, as lightly as a feather on the surface of a pond. 'Is that where you found out about the attempted theft?'

Gertie's smile stayed frozen on her round face, while her brush remained in mid-swash, dripping watercolour onto the grass. 'Oh, you heard that. Of course, you said you were on my little tour.' She resumed her random brushwork. 'It was just a bit of local colour for the tourists. No one would mind, I'm sure.'

'So, it wasn't true? There was no attempt to steal the painting?'

In Mrs Sidhu's long experience, there was a dam in the hearts of women like Gertie, where the weight of holding a secret was always at conflict with the joy of sharing some juicy gossip. Mrs Sidhu knew that feeling herself. It was like a bird trapped inside her chest, flapping around, bouncing off the bars of her ribcage. Let it out, Gertie, let it be free.

Gertie paused to wash her brush. 'I cannot betray a confidence, my dear.' She crossed her heart with her free hand. 'I gave my word to Tani Keys herself.'

'Oh,' said Mrs Sidhu. Now that was a surprise; she must be losing her touch.

'Yes, they're art royalty, you know,' she said. 'Such a shame their painting was stolen.'

For some reason Ludo's chin trembled for a moment, his eyes falling sadly on his canvas. It was no more than a flicker, then he stiffened. 'Serve them right for moving here.'

Whatever this moment was, Gertie felt compelled to reach over and press her hand on Ludo's.

'Dear God, woman, I've dropped my charcoal again, my last bit! Can't you just leave me alone?'

Gertie pulled her hand away, a cat scalded. 'Have no fear, ignorant fool, I won't touch you with any other part of my anatomy.' Ludo walked away, nose in the air, to fetch more charcoal. Gertie swallowed, covering her embarrassment with a wan smile. 'Marriage, very over-rated,' she said.

After that they painted in silence. Mrs Sidhu kept herself busy and an hour later she put her pencil down and admired her work. It wasn't bad.

When the class finished, Gertie got her things together. She had a stack of pamphlets in her bag. 'I'm doing some leafleting for my art tours. Care to join me?'

Mrs Sidhu took a shiny pamphlet: 'Private studio tours – meet the artists.' There were listings of local artists, biographies and a map of the village marking out their studios. She slipped it into her bag.

'Not today. I have another appointment,' she said. Her eyes followed Ludo Dalrymple as he ambled back up the hill, his own drawing tucked under his arm.

29

The Breeze Gallery was set back from the main village street, on a small winding road. It had a bay window that breached onto the street like a pregnant belly, its three sides made up of palm-sized panes of glass contained in a lattice of lead. The display was of a dark-looking modern painting, randomly clumped with some dark furniture of lacquered wood, and some china plates.

An old-fashioned brass bell chimed as Mrs Sidhu pushed through the door. Ludo looked up from the newspaper, his large eye falling on her with a quick flicker of hope. A flicker that was dashed all too quickly. 'Oh, it's you,' he said, his gaze returning to the counter, where the *Chronicle*'s double-page feature on the art heist was spread out.

The Breeze hadn't had a breeze through it in a century. It smelled of furniture wax, dust motes hung in the air, and there was a clutter of objects some old and some new, as if the owner was in many minds about what approach to go for. Over an old-fashioned fireplace hung another dark oil painting. Mrs Sidhu thought it must be the same artist as the one in the window. Even she could see that the shop lacked direction, caught in a struggle between style and commercial success.

Mrs Sidhu had some burning questions to ask Ludo Dalrymple, but it doesn't do to rush things. She picked up a china plate and examined it closely.

'That's a very exciting piece. It's Turkish, Iznik,' Ludo said.

It was blue and white, with flowers and leaves in intricate patterns which beguiled the eye with movement and colour. 'I collect interesting plates.' Mrs Sidhu turned it in the light, apparently mesmerised. 'How much is something like that?'

Ludo had as much an eye for customers as he had for artefacts. The one big eye was on her like a jewel lens, taking her in, while she twisted and squirmed in her cheap, practical Marks & Spencer's top, her navy slacks and flat sandals. He had her valued in seconds. 'This one is fifteenth century. Costs thousands,' he said, scanning distant shores. The words unspoken that he doubted Mrs Sidhu had such sums at her disposal.

He took the plate gently from her hands and placed it carefully in its display cradle. Ludo Dalrymple turned his gaze back to Mrs Sidhu, his big eye like a lighthouse beam, while the small one wandered in another direction entirely, seeking an unknown solace among the dusty objects on the shelves.

'Out of my budget range.' Mrs Sidhu smiled. 'I'll leave it here for your more discerning customers.'

The small eye, the secret eye that Ludo kept for himself, cast around the empty shop and for the first time she saw the sadness in Ludo Dalrymple. Where were the discerning customers? All down at the flashy new gallery.

Without knowing exactly why, she decided to take a risk. She stepped forward to him and placed her small hand on his forearm. 'I wasn't just at the art class, I saw you at the opening night of the Pump House. You were there, weren't you? Because I think I saw you the week before and you were talking about the gallery pumping sewage.' Mrs Sidhu looked up at him, her head twisting in birdlike fascination. 'I took that to mean you weren't going. Why did you change your mind?'

Ludo drew himself tall. 'I was merely expressing an honest critique. I went to see if my worst fears were confirmed. They were.' He removed her hand from his arm.

'You see, I like beautiful plates, but my speciality is what goes on the plates.' She extended a hand. 'Mrs Sidhu's Fine Catering, Slough and environs. You may have tasted some of my work – I catered the opening. Did you try the food there? Perhaps you had something off my trolley? A glass of wine, perhaps.'

'No, I don't think I did.'

'Or perhaps you saw someone take it from my trolley just before the door opened on Gallery 2?'

'I'm afraid I left early. As I said, the collection was not to my liking.' A look of affront as sour as lemon juice spread across Ludo's features. 'If you'll excuse me I'll be upstairs.' He shuffled towards the stairs at the back of the shop. 'Do let yourself out.' Then after a thought added, 'The downstairs is covered by cameras.'

Mrs Sidhu clenched her jaw; he was going and she would miss her chance. She called after him. 'Oh, please wait.'

Ludo cast an arm to the air, stomping away to the stairs.

She was losing him and her one chance to find out what happened to Gertie at the Keyses' house. What could she do?

Ludo was as cold and hard as a frozen chicken. The only way to defrost him was to turn the heat up. Except this was a kitchen she didn't understand, with a whole new range of appliances. 'I . . . um . . . really like your gallery,' she babbled. 'And . . . I love the layout, I really do, and the artworks . . .' She was into a stream of jibber-jabber now, just allowing her subconscious to supply the next word. '. . . And it's just much more my taste than the Pump House.'

'You think so?' He stopped and turned back, eyeing the gallery with a sad look. 'One has tried to build a reputation, a certain sense of style.'

Thank you, subconscious; it had led her unfailingly to her true target. She had found Ludo Dalrymple's defrost cycle. 'Oh, yes, I far prefer this kind of thing to all that nonsense at the Pump House.'

His large eye found her, looking with a new curiosity. 'Me too. I had imagined curating something individual and exceptional here when we first opened.' His chin fell. 'However, the exigencies of crass commercialism mean we now sell almost anything.' He shuddered. 'I fear we are running more of a shop than a gallery.'

'Oh, I think it's wonderfully varied. And maybe with a little help I could find something more in my budget range.'

With a potential sale in the balance, Ludo defrosted a little further. He promenaded Mrs Sidhu around the dusty arena.

'It can't help, that huge gallery opening down the hill.

Is that what you meant when you said it served the Keyses right for moving here?'

Ludo shifted uncomfortably. 'I may have overstated.' He took a pace away, adjusting one of the displays. 'We're not really in competition as such. This is just a modest gallery, local artists, a few bigger names.' He waved his arms in a mock gesture of 'being impressed'. 'Not exactly the Keys collection.'

'I agree. You don't know where you are with all that modern stuff. Giant metal statues, rocks and everything like that. And, though I don't like to speak ill of my clients, I have to say Mr Keys is a bit of an odd one, isn't he?'

'He's a bit theatrical for Bowler's Green.' Ludo stroked his bow tie. 'It's all about "him", if you know what I mean. The famous Hector Keys eye.' Ludo's own large eye opened just a fraction wider, while the small one shrank.

Ludo led Mrs Sidhu to an even dustier and darker part of the gallery. 'There are some very interesting new painters we're representing.' He stopped with a flourish by an alcove where a painting hung. 'Here's one, fresh in.' He discreetly wiped the dust and a cobweb from the frame.

The painting was a portrait of an old woman, glaring in an ill-favoured way out of the frame. Her eyes were lopsided and her teeth were bared in either a smile or an animal snarl, it was hard to tell which.

Mrs Sidhu almost jumped back before recovering herself. 'Oh, my,' she said. 'It's very interesting.'

Ludo smiled. 'And quite inexpensive.'

Mrs Sidhu gulped, dry-throated. 'I am very intrigued. You know, it reminds me of something your wife said at the art class, about overhearing something at the Arts Society event at the Keyses' house. An argument, I think.'

Ludo drew back and sniffed. 'How does this painting remind you of my wife?' He pursed his lips, waiting for an explanation.

'Because –' Mrs Sidhu's mind raced for possibilities – 'the woman in the painting is feeling . . .' Feeling what? Anger, shame, joy? '. . . Feeling so many conflicting emotions . . .' Ludo was glaring at her, still waiting for an explanation. '. . . And I wondered what your wife was feeling at the time,' she finished finally and waited.

'It's true, the painting of the old woman is rich with emotional content.' Ludo smiled.

Mrs Sidhu breathed again, but her relief was brief.

'And it's only five hundred pounds,' Ludo added.

'Only five hundred?' Her voice was weak.

'Yes, you're in luck, we're having a sale.' Ludo produced a card machine.

Did everyone in this place have a credit card machine hidden on their person? Mrs Sidhu cursed the remarkable rise in point-of-sale technology. She produced her bank card, her heart sinking. She still had no answers. As her hand hesitated over the machine, she tried one last gambit. 'I always like a painting to mean something to me, a memory or a story. So can you tell me what your wife heard that night?'

Ludo sniffed. 'The woman overhears things, then prattles on at me all the time. I can't remember everything she says.'

'If you could search your memory, it would make all the difference. A story to tell about my wonderful new artwork.'

With the bank card hovering so close to the machine, Ludo wavered. He scratched at his head. 'Let me see. She went to the Keyses and she "somehow" overheard an argument that Hector was having with his wife. He said something along the lines that his assistant wasn't working out.'

'Ivor?' Mrs Sidhu's brow furrowed. 'You're sure they were talking about Ivor Langtree?'

'I'm sure that's the one because Hector called him useless, which he is. And said it was his fault that the painting was almost stolen the week before.'

'So it *was* almost stolen.' She tried to keep her voice calm.

'Oh, yes. Stupid boy forgot to turn the alarm system and cameras on.' Ludo nodded in grim satisfaction. 'They're all a bit away with the fairies up there. Anyway, Hector told Tani that she should disinherit Ivor. He's her nephew, you see, she's the money. Hector's "the Eye". That's how it works in these partnerships.'

Surely it was a marriage, not a partnership. This was, though, no moment to interrupt Ludo now he was in the flow. Besides, Indian marriages had for generations been brokered on practical values so why not artistic marriages?

Ludo continued. 'But then it turned out Ivor had also overheard and all hell broke loose. Words were exchanged, threats were made.' He smiled thinly. 'Wish I'd been there.'

'Where does Ivor live? He said he took a room in the village.'

'Oh, yes, heard about that too. Uncle Hector kicked him out. He lodges with Ben, Ben Trimble our art teacher.' Ludo scrawled the address for her.

The little brass bell on the door chimed as she left the Breeze. She had a gift-wrapped painting wedged under her arm and her bank account was five hundred pounds lighter, but she had some very intriguing information.

'Tez?' she said. Silence hung in the downstairs of 21 Jubilee Drive. Maybe Tez had gone out. The only sound was the thrumming of the dishwasher. She had been hard on him earlier and felt bad. He was a good boy.

Her heart thrummed along with the machine. She placed her new purchase square on the dining room table. It looked mysterious still in its paper wrapping. She had never bought a painting before. First a gallery opening and now an actual art purchase. This was indeed an exciting time. There was the matter of where to hang it, but first she must unwrap it.

She carefully cut the tape on the wrapping paper, noting its high quality and the logo of the Breeze Gallery picked out in gold. Not being one to throw away anything which could be reused, she smoothed it, folded it and stowed it away in a drawer set aside for just this purpose.

Now she returned to her new artwork, and with Hector's technique in mind, she addressed it. She closed her eyes and then opened them again. She jumped back a half-step. With the wrapping off, the old woman glared back with a yellow-eyed snarl. Appreciating art, she concluded, was harder than she had thought. Nonetheless, she had paid a lot of money for it.

She spent the next few minutes holding it up to the walls in various locations. The kitchen, of course. Then the living room, the vestibule, even the laundry room and the space under the stairs had the pleasure of its company. None of them did anything to dim the old woman's ferocious look. Then she had an idea.

She climbed the stairs in nimble strides. In the upstairs bathroom, tucked high up on top of the mirror cabinet, was a perfect location for the old lady to glare down on the world. The mist from her morning shower would do enough to take the sting out of her bad-odoured look.

She propped it up on the toilet cistern while she went to get a hammer and a nail. That was when she heard him.

'I'm sorry, I can't make it today.' Tez's voice was soft, almost tender in its apology. She crept closer to his bedroom door, listening intently. 'Yeah, I was looking forward to it too. No, no, I'm definitely into it.'

She edged closer still. It wasn't an intrusion, she told herself, she had been meaning to check the soundproofing on the bedroom doors for a while.

'We should reschedule,' Tez said. 'For a time when Mum's not around.'

Just as she had suspected, the soundproofing on Tez's door was terrible. She could hear everything with crystal clarity. At least, she was sure she would if she edged a little closer.

She edged a little closer. There, her theory was correct, she could hear everything.

'I'll call you. Bye,' Tez said, ending his call.

Mrs Sidhu decided it was time to cut short her sound check and scuttled away as fast as she could. When Tez's bedroom door opened, she was rummaging in the airing cupboard. 'Oh, Tez, have you seen the clean tea towels?'

He eyed her suspiciously. 'Yeah, downstairs in the kitchen where they always are.' Tez eased past her on his way to the bathroom. 'You all right? You're out of breath.'

Mrs Sidhu calmed her breathing. 'Just been doing a

morning workout.' Tez made for the bathroom. She waited for him to close the door and she pumped a clenched fist. There was no doubt about it, Tez was talking to a woman. He finally had a girlfriend. There was no mistaking the tender, almost grateful, tone in his voice. Gratitude was exactly what he should be feeling; she certainly was.

Her celebrations were interrupted by a yell of blood-boiling horror from the bathroom. Tez appeared, wrapped in a towel, soaking wet. 'What is THIS?' He held out the old woman painting. It leered evilly at Mrs Sidhu.

'I bought some art,' Mrs Sidhu said. 'Isn't it wonderful? Thought it would cheer up the place.'

'I'm not showering while that is staring down at me.' Tez thrust the painting into her hands.

'Oh. I'll find somewhere else for it, then.' She ruffled his hair. 'I don't tell you this often enough, but you're a very good boy.'

Tez's brow crumpled. 'What?'

'Nothing. Just wanted you to know that I'm rooting for you.'

'You're very weird today,' he said. 'Weirder than normal.'

She left Tez with a bemused look on his face and took the painting into her bedroom.

30

Burton found Jenny Leblanc at the Pump House. 'Ms Leblanc!' he called out, his voice echoing across the empty space covering the distance between them with long, spidery strides. His voice was too loud, his smile too broad. He nodded to the uniformed officer guarding the crime scene. Davis? Davids? Davidson? He really needed to keep track of all the new arrivals.

Jenny looked up from her phone, and Burton's heart did a jig. She looked so pale, so worried. 'Bad news?' he asked.

She shook her head, sending her dark hair bobbing like a shimmering ocean. Her colour returned a little. 'Nothing at all. Just texting with someone from Paris.' She slid her phone away quickly and tucked some of that distracting hair behind her ear. 'I'm glad to see you again. You were so kind last night. And can't I convince you to call me Jenny?' She gave the lightest of touches to his arm.

How do you order your heart to stop doing somersaults?

'I'm here to ask some questions.' Now his voice was a touch too formal, and the disappointment in her face nearly killed him. 'But it's nice to see you too, Jenny.' The resulting coy smile was enough to light him up again. He saw PC Davis or Davids flicker a look at him. He cleared his throat and detached Jenny's arm from his. 'Davids, see if you can find Ivor Langtree.'

Jenny interrupted. 'Ivor's not here,' she said. 'He might be up with the Keyses.'

Burton thumbed his cheek. 'I've just come from there.'

Jenny seemed to think for a moment before brightening. 'Well, of course. It's Sunday, his day off.' She bounced to his side, pressing against him. 'Do you need to look around the gallery again? I'd be happy to show you.'

Davids was still rooted to the spot. 'Davids, go and check outside.'

'For what, sir?'

Burton motioned his arms vaguely. 'Any evidence we might have missed last night.'

'But—'

'Because it was dark.'

'Yes, sir,' Davids said. He turned, muttering as he left, 'It's actually Peterson, sir.'

Burton grimaced for Jenny's sake. 'New recruits,' he said.

Jenny followed with her eyes. 'What's all this about? Am I being interrogated?' Her eyes opened wide, with a hint of excitement.

'Not exactly.' This was the awkward bit. Burton was on a limb, he should have brought Dove or kept Peterson in the room if he was questioning someone. 'We think Mr Keys may not have been assaulted, but was actually drugged in his food. The bump on his head was probably from his fall to the ground. Tani Keys tells me she passed the message to you to get Hector's food. Is that true?'

'Yes.' Jenny's mouth opened and she put her hands to her face. 'I didn't know about the drugs, but I would never hurt my boss.'

Burton moved to calm her. 'I'm not suggesting you did. But did anyone else know that Hector was having food delivered to him? Did you mention it to someone else?'

'I texted Mrs Sidhu, of course. I was with a group of people when I got the message from Tani. I excused myself. I think I might have mentioned it to them. But Chief Inspector, if someone drugged him, they must have planned it in advance. How could they know Hector would ask for food?'

'I don't know, it's a good question. Maybe they had a backup plan and then this came along. Maybe they knew his habits and were able to predict it. Does he have fixed habits about things like that? Does he always eat before a speech?'

'I haven't been here long enough to know.' She turned away to face the windows and the tension in her shoulders told him she was about to broach a difficult subject. 'There is something while you're here, Chief Inspector. How long do you think it'll be before you release the crime scene? It's just that a number of these works are on loan and need to be returned. People are a little anxious.'

'We're done with the main gallery. But Gallery 2 will have to remain under wraps for now.' Burton grimaced again. 'To be honest, we've probably had everything we can get from it, but you know how it is. Procedure.'

Burton looked up at the hanging sculpture, the inverted

figure of a medieval knight, barrel chested, sword pointing down. 'How on earth do you move them?'

Jenny followed his gaze. 'That one came direct from the artist's studio. It's not far from here, I moved it myself.' She caught him eyeing her. 'I don't mean I lifted it. It weighs a tonne, and that's without the liquid inside. It needs a special hoist at either end. Ned Barrow has one, naturally, and we've invested in one too.' Jenny pointed through the windows to the far end of the car park where a red vehicle growled. It looked like a forklift truck but with a hook at the front. It was loading a large bronze onto the back of a lorry.

'Impressive,' said Burton. 'And also impressive you've got your forklift licence.'

Jenny laughed. 'I can drive a truck too. Gallery director is a varied job. At times I have to travel with the artwork all over the world.' Jenny lingered for a while, looking intently at the dangling sculpture as if some new depth to its mystery had been revealed to her. She broke from the daydream, turning her focus on Burton.

She tapped a finger to her lips. 'You know, Chief Inspector Burton, I get the feeling that you're not that experienced in this world. I would be happy to help fill in the gaps.'

'How do they fence a painting like *La Scaletta*, that kind of thing?'

'That kind of thing exactly, but it's dinner time and I'm famished. Would you like to grab a bite to eat?'

'That would be lovely. I mean useful. I'm hungry, you're hungry, what could be more natural and useful.' His neck blushed and he rubbed at it.

'Good. I'm staying at the Digbourne Hotel, it's across

the bridge. Still living out of a suitcase,' she laughed, her hands covering white teeth. 'It's so embarrassing.'

'No, not at all.'

'I think it is. But the food there isn't bad, for English food.' She winked. 'Join me for dinner?' She bent a slender wrist to look at her watch. 'In an hour?'

It was Sunday evening already. He hadn't had a break since Saturday night. Twenty-four hours with no sleep and just the breakfast that he had long ago digested. Even DCIs are allowed a break.

'Give me a minute, just a word to my sergeant.' Burton held the phone up to his face. It unlocked with a ding. 'Real time saver, that feature.'

'Isn't it?' She had a curious look in her eye.

'Dove?' Burton stepped away to take the call. 'I'm going to grab a bite to eat.' He paused for Dove's reply. 'That's right. Peterson's here at the gallery watching the crime scene. Don't call unless you need to.' He ended the call. She watched him slip the phone into his jacket pocket. 'Great,' said Jenny. 'Let me freshen up and meet me there.'

31

Mrs Sidhu found Ben at the education centre. He was clearing up after the life class, putting away easels. Mercifully both the students and the model had left. The bed was still there. They stood either side of it.

He smiled when he saw her. 'Never thought you'd set foot in here again. The danger of seeing uncloaked fruit is far too high.'

Mrs Sidhu explained the reason she had come.

'You're still doing this?' he said. 'This Miss Marple thing?' Ben's moustache twitched and his smile crawled up his face. 'You are endlessly fascinating. Would you have dinner with me some time? I'd love to get inside that mind of yours.'

She bit down on the smile that wanted to form in her face. 'Really? What would an artist want with a chef from Slough?'

'You're not like anyone I've ever met.'

Her stomach muscles tightened. 'Oh.' She couldn't keep the disappointment out of her voice. So she was like a subject to him, something to view from all angles. She stared at the bed between them, the vast empty expanse of white sheets and crumpled duvet. She had read about artists and their models, their 'muses'. She could feel the blood rising to her face again and turned away. 'Does no one ever make that bed?' She must have shouted this because Ben took a step back and a passing student stopped and needed Ben's assurance that everything was all right.

Ben turned back to Mrs Sidhu. 'You see? I have no idea what you're going to say next. It's exhilarating.'

She took a breath and gathered herself. 'I'm sorry, habit of a lifetime. I have a son and he never makes his bed. And he keeps me busy in the evenings, cooking and looking after him.'

'Oh, I had no idea. It must be challenging having a young child.'

'He's twenty-five.'

Ben raised an eyebrow.

She put her hand up, palm out. 'Before you say what an unusual life I lead again, I'll consider dinner if you tell me everything you know about Ivor Langtree.'

'That's a deal.' Ben patiently gave her a potted biography of Ivor. He was one of those kids who was born with a rich aunt who spoiled him. He grew up well educated with refined tastes, but had no idea what to do with himself. What he did know was that Aunty Tani would pay for everything as long as he was learning, and learning most of all about art. 'So Ivor drifted from one course to another. He studied at Yale, at Oxford, at the Sorbonne.'

'So why did he come back?'

'Good question. He told me that Aunty Tani had decided

it was time to put all that learning to good use and to work for the family art foundation. So she got him a job as Hector's assistant.'

'Only Uncle Hector wasn't such an easy touch as Aunty Tani?'

'Right. Hector wasn't born with money. He started life in Bristol, drifted around small antique shops and galleries, buying and selling.'

'How did he get into the big-time art world?'

'He uncovered *La Scaletta* and overnight a masterpiece lost for over half a century is back. People scoffed at first – most discoveries turn out to be fakes or copies painted in the same style. But this one passed every test, convinced every expert. Including Tani's father. Hector charmed Tani and married her. Art's biggest power couple was born, and the rest is history.'

'It's Ivor's story I'm more interested in. Hector wasn't exactly happy with Ivor as an assistant, I understand.'

'There was a lot of tension. Then one day, they threw Ivor out of the big house. He came and took a room with me.'

'That's quite a comedown. He must have been furious.'

'It got worse. There was some kind of argument and suddenly Tani was threatening to sack him, even disinherit him. Don't know why.'

'I do.' Mrs Sidhu tried and failed to bury a smirk.

Ben shook his head, smiling. 'Of course you do.'

'Apparently someone tried to steal *La Scaletta* two weeks ago. Hector blamed Ivor; he forgot to set the alarms and switch the security cameras on.'

'You were holding that back on me? And here I am, sharing all my secrets.'

Mrs Sidhu toyed with the top button of her cardigan. 'Do you have any more?'

'Ivor said he needed money, his own money that his uncle didn't control.'

'Why?'

'Don't know.' Ben shrugged. 'Made it sound like he needed it now.'

Mrs Sidhu cast her mind back to Jenny's office. She scratched her brow, trying to remember something at the edge of her consciousness. Something at the gallery but not from the previous night, from this morning.

'One last question. Did you see Ivor last night?'

'He was at the private view, of course.'

'I mean at home. What time did he come back?'

'I don't keep tabs on my lodgers. There's a separate entrance. But come to mention it, I didn't see him this morning.

'So dinner.' Ben handed her a brightly coloured flyer. 'The Greenview are opening in the evenings and they're throwing a party to launch it.'

Ben placed his hands behind his head and closed his eyes in simulated bliss. 'Good food, some music and some dancing. Whole village will be there.' No reply came. When he opened his eyes again, the place was deserted. He was standing next to the empty bed. He shrugged and slowly started to tuck in the sheets.

32

The shining black oblong lit up, sending its vibration along the table into Burton's elbow and through his hand into his chin. The face on the screen was known to him, and the name 'Mrs Sidhu' was accompanied by the haunting whistle of music (his own choice of ringtone): the theme to *The X-Files*.

It was an old-fashioned hotel restaurant, with high ceilings, starched tablecloths and polished cutlery. For once in his life, Burton had a reason to regret being pulled away from something. For once in his life, he had a night off that he wouldn't rather be working. For once in his life, he had a reason to turn his phone off.

Of course, he shouldn't do that in the middle of an active investigation. He had never done it before. But where had that got him? He thought of all the times he could have turned it off, like his ex-wife's birthday.

He could still remember the glow of candlelight on her chin, as she blew hard and all the little lights spluttered out. He could still remember the hurt look in her eyes as he left. He still remembered the sad weight of a slice of cake in his pocket, and eating it at a crime scene.

Jenny appeared, wearing a little black dress. She had brushed her hair, or whatever it was women did these days to make it straight and shiny. Burton hesitated for only a fraction of a second before sliding the switch on his phone to off. He sighed. Just one hour, was it so much to ask?

'Have you picked the wine yet?' she asked.

He half-stood to greet her. 'I can't, I'm technically on duty.' Burton pulled a sad face, ironic he hoped.

'I can't drink alone!' She smiled again, pouring sunshine into his clouded world. 'And today, I feel like I really need a drink. I imagine you feel the same.'

'One glass can't hurt.' He glanced at the waiter. 'But you're French so I don't dare order in front of you. You choose.'

'I'm only half French,' she insisted. She picked out an expensive bottle of Chablis. 'Don't worry,' she whispered, 'the gallery are covering my expenses until I'm settled.'

They ate, and not the sort of food Burton normally had; small plates with intense flavours. The sort of food Mrs Sidhu was always pushing him to try. And Burton allowed himself a glass of wine. Or was it two? He lost count somewhere while looking at that hair, those white teeth, listening to that lilting voice. It seemed as if it had been so long since he'd enjoyed himself. Since the divorce, he reckoned.

In what seemed like no time, they were on desserts and she poured another glass of wine for each of them. 'I have a confession,' she said.

'Don't tell me you did it.'

'Don't, you're too funny!' More tinkling laughter followed before she filled his glass. 'Actually, I have an ulterior motive in getting you alone. I wanted to share something with you. Something I've kept private.' Her finger stroked the rim of her glass.

Burton took another glug of wine. It was good, the sort of taste you don't get from the wine he normally got his hands on. 'Sounds intriguing.' He held his glass out for more and she dutifully filled it with a smile.

'Have I ever told you about the process of radio-carbon-dating in twentieth-century paintings?' she was saying. 'Normal carbon-dating is imprecise and only useful for centuries-old artefacts. But this technique is brand new and it can detect to the year when a painting was created. I learned about it at a conference in Paris earlier this year. Do you know how that's done?'

Burton stifled a yawn. He wished he didn't feel so tired. 'I'm so sorry. It must be the wine. It's definitely not the conversation.' Burton's poker face was good, but Jenny hardly needed the encouragement. She seemed excited, giddy almost. 'You were talking about carbon-dating.'

'All the nuclear bomb tests that took place in the twentieth century have left their trace on every living thing by taking in radioactive carbon.'

His eyelids were drooping. He pinched his leg, hoping the pain would relieve some of the lethargy. He berated himself. You're with a beautiful, intelligent woman; if ever you should keep your eyes open, Burton my lad, now is the time. Jenny's choice of subject, however, wasn't helping.

'And you've kept that private?'

'No, I'm going off topic. You have that effect on me. Those policeman's eyes make me nervous.' She laughed again, and it sounded far off, a siren's laugh. She paused to pat her lips on a napkin. 'The thing I've been keeping from you – and you'll find this out sooner or later – is about me and Ivor. We've met before, when I was in Paris. He was at that conference too. We were involved. That ended when Hector called him away. I was hurt. I came here to talk to him, but he wouldn't listen. He said he had this plan, you see, to get even with Hector. It was dangerous and he wanted to keep me away from the danger. He made me swear to leave him alone and not tell anyone about us.'

Burton lifted a heavy hand. 'Sorry, I should really be taking this down in a statement.' He fumbled for his notebook, thick fingers not quite finding the pocket.

Her voice choked up here. 'I think I know what happened, and all I want is justice.'

'We want the same things.'

'No, you're not going to get it, Chief Inspector. Which is why I have to go it alone. I'm very sorry.' Here she pressed Burton's hand and looked deep into his eyes. 'I just wanted you to know.'

He yawned again. 'I'm so sorry, I feel like I need to sleep for a day. It's been one of those cases.'

She smiled wryly. 'Well,' she said coyly, 'you can sleep after.'

'After?' Burton raised an eyebrow.

She pressed herself forward, and her arm curved under her breasts, accentuating her . . . what was the word? . . . Décolletage, isn't that what the French called it? She leaned across the table and whispered. 'I thought you might like to come up to my room for a nightcap.' Her breath was warm in his ear. 'Or something. I have the feeling that you have so much on your mind, about this case, that you need to unburden yourself.'

After that, Burton had no memory of leaving the table, or even getting in the lift. He just found himself pressed against the steel doors, Jenny tugging at his clothes, her hot breath inside his mouth. A small and distant part of him wondered where all this passion had come from, what could have loosened her art curator stiffness. It was ultimately only a small and distant part of his brain. Could be it was his reputation – Berkshire's top detective. The main part was listening to the siren song, responding to the rush of hormones pumping through his body, to her tongue, to her body on his.

She stopped suddenly, pulling back. 'First, tell me everything about the case you've discovered so far.'

And Burton found himself talking. He knew he shouldn't, that it was against procedure. Screw procedure. He had to talk to someone. All up the lift and along the corridor, he burbled through the evidence he had from beginning to end.

The next thing he knew, he was on his back. They were in bed. It was dark and she was straddling him. He was wearing very little. Had they done it already? The smaller part of his brain laughed. My God. First sex since your divorce and you can't even remember it.

'I'm so sorry about this,' she whispered, her eyes tearing up, her face an apology.

'Don't be,' Burton said, and to himself he sounded drunk and slurred. 'I'm the one who's sorry. It's been such a long time, you see.'

'When's your birthday?' she asked, slipping his mobile phone from his pocket.

He told her. 'Am I getting a present?' he asked.

She didn't answer. She tried a few combinations and then seemed to remember something. 'Smile,' she said, holding the phone up. Burton opened his eyes, and he heard the phone ding.

He felt so heavy. He tried to move his arms but they were restricted. He heard the rattle of steel on steel. His hands were cuffed to the bedstead. He raised a leery eyebrow. 'It's like that, is it?' His head was spinning, but he'd only had a few glasses of wine. His phone was ringing and he had no urge to answer it at all. This was the nicest evening he had spent in such a long time. Such a looooooong time. He giggled.

She climbed off him and started tapping into his phone. 'Whatayadoing?' he slurred. 'Ordering pizza. Minesahawaiin.'

She switched the phone off and dropped it on the bedside table. 'I'm so sorry, but I just have to have that sculpture. And I have a boyfriend.'

His vision flickered and everything went dark.

33

Mrs Sidhu's Nissan Micra whined and complained into gear and jogged forward onto the road. Mrs Sidhu pounded the steering wheel. 'Move!' she shouted.

A moment later, she wrenched up the handbrake, stinging the palm of her hand and sending a wave of pain to her elbow. The car skidded the last couple of feet into the parking spot. Mrs Sidhu was out and running before it had stopped.

The glass entrance of the Pump House loomed up. Her trainers slapped out a rhythm on the ground. She was puffing as she got to the door, where she was relieved to see the lights on. The doors were open, there were people inside. She burst through and made for a knot of technicians, meticulously packing and crating a painting. The reverse of the procedure that Jenny had shown her a week ago. 'Have you seen Jenny Leblanc?' Her question was met with shrugs.

'She was just here, loading artwork into the truck,' said the closest technician. 'She might still be out the back.'

She raced to the back of the gallery, found Jenny's office.

It was empty. The folder was on her desk: 'Advances in Restoration and Valuation, Conference Schedule, Summer, The Sorbonne'. She flipped through to the back: 'Attendance List'. Her finger traced down the names to the L's: 'Leblanc, J.' 'Langtree, I.' They were there, together at the same time.

Daisy Carr wasn't the only one looking forward to starting a new life. Who starts a new life? A man in love. Ivor Langtree met someone on his course in Paris. He met Jenny Leblanc.

It took two people working together to commit this crime. Ivor drugged Hector's food. When Ivor calculated Hector was out cold, he went to Gallery 2. As Hector's assistant, he had the code to the side door.

Mrs Sidhu felt a pang of relief. It wasn't her who had left the side door open; it must have been Ivor. Daisy used that moment to get in. But Ivor hadn't reckoned on Daisy so he killed her. He stole the painting and left it for Jenny to collect. How, was still not clear. For some reason he took a glass of wine and a plate of food with him. They broke, and he hid the pieces in the service corridor. That part still didn't make sense. Why would he do that? Had he realised that the pieces could identify him? Why not just take them with him?

No matter, she moved to the second conspirator, Jenny Leblanc. They knew each other from Paris. They planned this whole thing together. Why else would they pretend to be strangers? On the night, Jenny remained the dutiful gallery manager; making sure she was seen when the double doors opened, expressing shock. Though perhaps the shock was genuine; no one, after all, had expected to see Daisy lying on the floor.

That would explain the delay in picking up the painting.

When the doors opened, Jenny was standing next to Hector and Tani. But afterwards, she could have changed into the strange costume and stolen the painting.

There were two questions that were stewing and bubbling in Mrs Sidhu's mind. The woman in the skull mask; if that was Jenny, then why the dancing and the bizarre outfit?

The second question had plagued her and Burton from the start. How did they get the painting out of the gallery? There was an answer that could explain both. It was so fantastical that she could hardly believe it.

The woman was dancing because it was an eye-catching distraction. She wasn't carrying *La Scaletta*, she was carrying a prop. There was no way of getting *La Scaletta* out of the gallery that night but they needed to make sure everyone thought it was gone. Which meant only one thing. *La Scaletta* was still here in the gallery, hidden and waiting to be liberated. Mrs Sidhu knew exactly where it was.

She was jogging again, on feet that hurt from twelve-hour days. She burst out into the gallery main space again. 'Where's the officer guarding the crime scene?' Again shrugs from the technicians. Her shoes slapped across the polished concrete to the Gallery 2 entrance and her face crumpled. The crime scene tape was gone, the officer on guard was gone. Burton must have ordered the crime scene to be released. She let out a sob of frustration. There was *Art Rocks*, there was the gap where *La Scaletta* once hung and there was another gap. *The Knight* was gone.

Somewhere in the distance a truck growled away.

That was how they planned to get it out of the gallery. It was hidden inside *The Knight*, and Jenny Leblanc had just taken it.

34

Dove checked his watch for the eleventh time. Where was he? Two hours had passed since Burton had last been in touch. Dove had every detective and uniform he could muster here waiting for a briefing and still no sign of the boss. He called Burton's phone for the eleventh time. It went straight to voicemail, just like the other ten times. He didn't bother leaving another message. For the eleventh time, he read the last exchange of text messages from his DCI.

> BURTON: Busy, can't talk. Release the crime scene at the gallery.
> DOVE: You sure?
> BURTON: We've got everything we need. Do it now. New evidence. Bring officers back to base. Urgent meeting.
> DOVE: OK

Urgent meeting, it said, and everyone was here. Everyone except the boss. For the eleventh time, he stared at the desk, the empty chair. A small whine crept from his throat. He had come in here like an abandoned dog, hoping that his master would return home.

He got an alert on his phone. He snatched it up. This would be him, delayed by bloody traffic. Dove was almost looking forward to Burton's growling voice, his demand for progress, but one look at the screen had him groaning again. This one was from the tech team and it was bad news.

'Device tracking on DCI Burton's phone failed. Must be switched off. Last location, Digbourne High Street.' Dove balled his pudgy fist in frustration.

The meeting space was full, and a few of the officers were starting to fidget.

He had no choice. He marched out in front of the gathered officers. 'I'm afraid we're going to have to reconvene. DCI Burton has been held up.' Officers filed away in a line of dark blue, returning to their duties or the canteen.

There would be no tea breaks for Dove. He rubbed at the queasy feeling in his stomach. He had eaten enough bad sandwiches to know the difference between tummy upset and a hunch. Something was very wrong. This was his boss, his responsibility; he had to find him.

Where could he be? That last location could have been recorded five, even ten, minutes before he switched off. A glimmer of thought flashed up in Dove's mind. What would the boss do? Dove sat in Burton's seat. He swivelled in the chair, then spun round to face the computer. For a while he stared at the screen, rubbing the back of his neck. On an instinct he pulled up a maps app. He entered Digbourne High Street. There it was, across the river from

Bowler's Green. He zoomed in on the high street and names of businesses popped up obediently. A flower shop, a newsagent, a hotel, a mini supermarket. A hotel. He clicked: the Digbourne Hotel had four stars on the reviews. The Digbourne Hotel rang a bell in his memory.

He grabbed the thick pile of statements from the gallery opening and began pulling them off and tossing them on the floor. It took him a wild few minutes to find the one he wanted. Jenny Leblanc, address (temporary): The Digbourne Hotel, Digbourne High Street, Digbourne.

Burton was still asleep when Dove got there, his arms dangling from the headboard, his head lolling. He had vomited down himself. Dove rushed to the bathroom and came back with a glass of water. He tried to get Burton to drink it. He quickly gave up and threw the glass of water over him instead.

Burton jerked awake, sucking in air. 'What's going on?' he gasped. He tugged his arms, rattling at the cuffs. Dove searched around and found the keys on the bedside table. Two clicks and they were off. While Burton rubbed the red rings from his wrists, Dove asked him what happened.

Burton shook his head. 'She must have drugged me.' He patted where his pockets should have been. His hands only found puckered flesh. He looked down, wide-eyed. 'I'm in my underpants, Dove.' He turned to Dove, child-like confusion in his eyes. 'Why am I in my underpants?'

Dove looked away while Burton, still shaky on his feet, washed himself in the bathroom, found his trousers and thrust his legs in. Scrambling into his shirt he said, 'Phone, where's my phone?'

'It's all right, sir.' Dove snatched it from the bedside

table and gave it to Burton, who listened intently to a long message, growing paler by the second. When he finished, Dove cleared his throat. 'When you didn't turn up, I knew something was wrong. I figured out where you were, sir.'

Burton clapped Dove on the shoulder. 'Well done, Dove. I've been a bit of a fool. But you did good.'

Dove beamed for a moment, then, like a cloud covering the sun, a frown gathered on his face. 'What exactly happened here, sir?'

Burton rubbed his temple. 'No time for that just now, Dove. We need to get to the gallery, I've just had a tip-off from Mrs S— an informant. The painting is hidden inside one of the sculptures. *The Knight.* Is Peterson or whatever his name is still on duty?'

A seam of confusion crumpled Dove's forehead. 'Well, no, he won't be. I followed your instructions, sir.'

A new cold wave of worry pulled at Burton's chest. 'What instructions?' he asked warily.

'The ones you texted.'

Burton scrambled to open his phone again, pulling it up to his face and reading the last few messages. 'Oh, no.' He whispered an obscenity.

PART III

Failure is part of life. Dealing with it is the problem.

Life With a Knife, Mrs Sidhu's Memoirs

35

They found the truck in the early hours of the morning. A lorry driver who pulled into a dirt farm road spotted the back door of the trailer open and reported it to the police.

Blue lights were on the scene when Burton crunched his car to a halt. He took a moment to take in external details. The livery on the side and back, 'Keys Foundation', the number plate which matched the one they were looking for, and the back door swinging in the breeze. 'Anyone been in?' he asked.

Dove shook his head. 'Told them to wait for you, sir.' Both of them slipped on gloves and while Dove held the rear door open, Burton grabbed the trailer floor, hooked a long leg up and hauled his heavy frame in. He dusted his hands on the sides of his trousers. His head spun a little, still groggy from the sedative. A moment later he heard a steady, mechanical whine. He turned to see Dove rising steadily. 'There's a tail lift, sir,' his sergeant said cheerfully.

Burton muttered something unrepeatable. The first thing that hit him was how dark it was. What little light leaked in from the car headlights was eaten up as the trailer extended away from him. The second thing was the same choking chemical cocktail from the gallery. His stomach lurched and he took a step to steady himself. 'This is the right truck,' he said. 'You can't mistake that smell. Light, please.'

Dove switched on his torch and shone it around the interior. At the far end of the container a couple of rusty chains creaked under the load of *The Knight*. It was too large to hang from the roof. It had been suspended horizontally with the sword end aimed to the front of the trailer. From this angle, he could see that the lower end was one piece, instead of two legs, resembling a sarcophagus. Where the feet would have been was a thick metal baseplate.

Burton gripped the chains, stilling their crazy swaying in the torchlight, and the swaying in his head. He stooped on the floor. A pool of liquid soaked the deck. He sniffed. 'What's this doing here?'

Dove frowned. 'She opened the baseplate, probably to get the painting out. It's what she did, isn't it, sir? It's how she got the painting out of the gallery.'

'Must have wrapped it in plastic to keep the fluid from damaging it.' Burton worked his heavy jaw, as if he'd taken a sucker punch. 'It's been hanging there in front of my eyes all along. I should have seen it.'

'You were distracted, sir. I mean, by all that business with the dancing woman in the mask.'

Burton took the lift down to the roadside. He strode round to the front and opened the cab door. It was clean, tidy, unpersonalised. Again it was the smell that gave him what he needed. The smell of Channel No 5. He slammed the door shut.

'Was it her, sir?'

Burton ran a hand over the back of his neck. 'Smells that way.'

On an instinct he flipped his phone torch on and took a walk around the truck, shining the light around until it fell on something that didn't fit. It was a rock, roughly pyramidal, and a rusty colour. It was nothing like the rocks around it, which were mud-coloured. It had marks on it that looked like blood. 'Dove! Found the murder weapon from the gallery,' he called out. Dove marked the spot and called in the photographer.

Burton's head still felt fuzzy. The doctor said that despite being unconscious, the position he was left in and the sedatives pumped through his system meant he hadn't got anything as useful or restorative as sleep: he was running on empty. At least he didn't have the kind of hangover Hector Keys had. He got a lower dose. Burton tapped his chin. 'Do we know what the sedative she used on me was?'

Dove shook his head. 'Only just sent off your blood sample. But –' Dove pulled an official report out of his pocket – 'we've got the results back on Hector Keys's blood and the food.'

Burton took the report and read. The pages were crumpled, and the light poor but he got enough. He blew a soft sigh. 'Looks like Hector Keys dodged a bullet.'

Burton folded the forensics report into his jacket pocket. Burton's stomach burned, and he stroked it. Dove, an undisputed expert on intestinal disfunction, clearly sympathised.

'And you too, sir. You upchucked most of the dose,'

Dove chirped. 'We've all been there. Except for me it wasn't drugs. Bad kebab – I barfed for days.'

'Could you please shut up, Dove?' For some reason Dove actually smiled.

'Welcome back, sir. I was so worried about you.'

For a moment, Burton was terrified that Dove would wrap him in a malodorous hug, and he'd 'upchuck' all over again. Instead the sergeant settled for a sweaty handshake and wandered away to direct the crime scene techs.

There would be an internal investigation, Superintendent Cara Hunter had assured him of that. Her voice patient and weary, as if she had been woken by a crying child, rather than a senior police officer. 'You're lucky you're on a decent run of form, Burton, I can shield you from most of it. Your man Dove said you must have been overpowered, and she used your own cuffs against you.'

Burton agreed that's what had happened and forbore to mention dinner, or what he was doing in Jenny Leblanc's room at the time. 'I was using her as a source on the case.' That was all he said in answer to the unasked question. Hunter rang off with one last piece of advice. 'Keep your mouth shut to the press. And solve the bloody case, fast.'

'Sir?' Dove broke in on his thoughts.

White-suited crime scene technicians were waiting to go in. Something was troubling Burton.

'Show me that again.' The bloodstained rock crinkled in its evidence bag as Dove handed it over. 'There's a lot of dried blood, and it's in more than one place. Like there's been more than one impact.'

'Daisy Carr was struck once,' Dove said.

'I just want a look inside again.' They both climbed into the back of the truck. Their footsteps echoed back from the steel walls of the container. His phone sang the theme to *The X-Files*. 'Mrs Sidhu,' he said.

The line crackled. 'Oh good, you're there. We've got some catching up to do. I expect you could do with some breakfast. Sergeant Dove told me you "upchucked" everything.'

Burton took the torch from Dove and shone it into the faceplate of *The Knight*. Misted cat's eyes reflected back, pale blue eyes, washed out like an old jumper. 'I could use something to fortify me. I've just found Ivor Langtree.'

36

'What can I get you?'

Poppy the waitress was wearing aggressively bright tie-dye trousers, her red hair coiled on top of her head.

'You do a full English breakfast.' It wasn't a question from Burton, it was an order backed up by a flash of his warrant card.

Mrs Sidhu had taken one look at DCI Burton's grey face and hustled him straight over to the Greenview Cafe. It was thankfully open. However, things were not straightforward.

A rebellious frown formed on Poppy's face. 'I'm vegan. I don't handle meat and the other worker isn't in yet.' She smiled acidly. 'Why not try our vegan breakfast? It's tofu done three ways.'

Burton blinked slowly, a soldier with a thousand-yard stare. 'Full English is on the menu,' he said flatly.

Mrs Sidhu glanced between the combatants. She had to have Burton's full attention. The last thing she needed right now was him in a bad mood. She took Poppy's arm and led her to one side. 'He's had a very, very bad night. Please can you make an exception this once?' Mrs Sidhu grabbed the sign-up form from the counter. 'And I'll sign your petition against . . .' Her eyes scanned what seemed to be a comprehensive document decrying a multitude of things. '. . . Everything,' she concluded and sketched her signature on the form.

Poppy's frown melted. 'Just this once. But if you don't challenge the system it'll never change.' With that she sloped into the kitchen.

Mrs Sidhu led Burton over to a table overlooking the green. The other customers were too absorbed in their phones and their newspapers to care or notice what an odd little pairing they made. 'Full English on the way. If she asks, just tell her I challenged the patriarchy and I didn't go down without a fight.'

'Agreed,' Burton said. 'As long as I've got sausages, I'm prepared to question the whole edifice.'

Mrs Sidhu toyed with the top button on her cardigan. 'How are you feeling?'

Burton narrowed his eyes. 'How much exactly did Sergeant Dove tell you?' he asked.

'Sergeant Dove is a professional officer, he would hardly reveal details of an ongoing case to a member of the public.'

Burton was relieved but his air maintained an element of caution. 'Glad to hear it.' He shifted in his chair. 'Have you seen the *Chronicle* this morning?'

She twisted at her cardigan buttons. 'I haven't bought a copy today.'

'Yes, you have.' With surprising speed he plucked it out of her bag.

Burton skimmed the front page. His cow eyes seemed to dull over as he scanned the story. '"Top Cop Flops",' he read out loud. 'Very funny.'

'You don't want to pay any attention to that.' Fortunately the food arrived not long after and Mrs Sidhu was quick to use Burton's plate to cover the newspaper. It was brimming with his favourite food groups: beans, sausages, eggs and toast. She mouthed a silent thanks to Poppy. Mrs Sidhu suppressed a smirk; she enjoyed watching Burton refuelling himself. Her husband had always had an appetite. For herself, she had settled for beans on toast. 'Beans on toast is the Western equivalent of dhal and rice. Protein and carbohydrate.'

Burton only grunted.

'Did you get my message?' she asked.

Burton nodded. 'I did, but I was tied up at the time.' He smiled, thin-lipped. 'You see, I can already laugh about it. So you wanted to talk.'

'I thought we could exchange theories,' she said. As Burton narrowed his eyes she hurried along. 'Or I could tell you what I think happened and you could just listen and maybe nod.'

With growing enthusiasm, she outlined exactly how the crime took place. Ivor's part was to drug Hector, cut the security feed and hide the painting inside *The Knight*. '*The Knight* is big enough to take the whole thing.'

Burton's fork stopped half way to his mouth. 'It's big enough, but wouldn't that horrible fluid inside damage the painting?'

'He must have wrapped it in a sealed package,' Mrs Sidhu countered.

Burton gave her a dubious look. 'Taking a big risk with

a twelve-million-pound artwork. One tiny puncture in the package and it's gone.'

She snorted. 'There's no other way they could have got the painting out. Unless you have a better idea?'

Burton's fork completed its journey and he ate in silence. Mrs Sidhu took up her tale once more. She didn't dwell on Daisy's death, as it seemed obvious that she walked in on him and he improvised, using a rock from a sculpture to kill her. Jenny's part was waiting outside for a witness (Mrs Sidhu) before performing her escape. No one would suspect the painting was still in the gallery. 'How am I doing?' she asked.

Burton chewed on a sausage, gulped down some tea and gave the barest hint of a nod.

She nodded back. 'Good. After that . . .' Here she slowed down, after a sharp glance from Burton. She hesitated to say what she had to say next. 'After that, all she had to do was convince the officer in charge to release the crime scene before anyone figured it out.'

Burton didn't need to hear that part of the theory. 'When that didn't work,' he said, 'she found a washed-up old cop, so desperate for female company that he allowed himself to be wined, dined and drugged.'

Mrs Sidhu made reassuring noises and kept up the pace of the conversation. This was no moment for Burton to start spiralling or go storming off. 'Then she stole *The Knight* with the painting inside and met up with her accomplice and lover.' Mrs Sidhu raised a questioning eyebrow and Burton gave another imperceptible nod.

'So far we're on the same page, then.' The only reply she received was the sound of cutlery scooping up beans, egg and sausage. Her chest tightened. Now came the hard part. 'Except I have two problems. Problem number 1. I don't believe Jenny Leblanc is capable of that.'

Burton's fork paused on the way to his open mouth. 'To my mind she's shown herself capable of manipulation and deception, and has a consistent MO. Let's remember Hector Keys was drugged too. In profiling terms she's a psychopath.'

'But am I right in thinking she and Ivor were in love? That he left her, that she came running after him?'

Burton assented once more.

'So why kill him?'

Burton's forkful had time to make it to his mouth. He chewed for a while. 'Because she was still upset he'd dumped her. So it's a two-for-one deal. Revenge and a twelve-million-pound payoff.'

She flexed her fingers. Her beans on toast, untouched, was going cold but she had no appetite. 'Well, I still don't see it. Then there's my second problem.' She pulled her Evidence Tupperware from her bag and gave it a rattle. 'The plate and glass.'

For a moment it looked as if Burton was about to splutter a mouthful of egg and sausage across the table. He managed to hold back. 'Not the broken crockery again, Mrs Sidhu. I've got two dead bodies, one of them preserved in embalming fluid like a Damien bloody Hirst.'

'Just hear me out,' she insisted, and kept talking before Burton could object again. 'I have narrowed it down. I know for a fact that Ivor Langtree is the only person who could have taken the rogue plate and glass into the gallery.' She turned the palm of her hand up. She thought again. 'But, on the other hand, why would he do that if he was about to steal a painting? He needed his hands free.' She turned her palm down again. 'On the other, other hand, maybe it had more of the sedative in, just in case Hector hadn't eaten the first dose.' Her hand faced up once more. 'But on the other, other, other hand how did they break? And why hide the pieces?' Her palm faced down again. 'On the other, other, other, oth—'

She felt Burton's hand on her wrist. He was staring at her, red-faced.

'Or,' he said, 'maybe it's just some broken crockery.'

He released her hand. She rubbed at the wrist. 'It has to be explained, Chief Inspector.' Burton appeared to disagree.

She changed the subject. 'Did Jenny say anything unusual? Over dinner, I mean?'

Burton flexed his jaw and looked to the distance. A pale beam of sunlight found its way through the window of the Greenview. 'A load of faff to throw me off. That she was worried about Ivor, that he was in danger and so was she. He kept their relationship a secret to protect her.'

Mrs Sidhu's pulse increased. 'She said that? That's odd, don't you think?'

'It was a distraction. And she went on about carbon-dating artworks.'

She felt that extra beat to her heart rate once again. 'That's hardly seduction talk. Maybe it means something.'

'I think that was just to put me to sleep.' He grunted. 'It worked.'

'What was Ivor protecting her from?'

'Like I said. It was a bunch of lies.' Burton insisted, leaning forward. He closed his eyes for an instant, twitching in a waking nightmare. 'She was playing the damsel in distress. It was all a distraction to get me to eat the food, drink the wine. To get me to trust her.' He pressed his fingers into his eyes, shaking his head. 'To get me up to her room, get my phone open and send those bloody texts to Dove. And I fell for it.'

Suddenly a pang of annoyance pricked her. Here she was trying to help him, and all Burton could do was throw her ideas back in her face and sink into misery. Her lower lip pushed forward. 'Well, what do you think happened? What's your great theory, then?'

Burton mopped up the last of the bean sauce with the last of his toast. 'I don't have a theory. Theories are for scientists, or for those art collectors down at the gallery. What I have is a suspect.' Poppy returned to clear Burton's plate. When she picked it up, the imprint had left a perfect ring of bean sauce right on the photo of Burton. He was leaving the Digbourne Hotel, his eyes wide and unfocused. To Mrs Sidhu he looked like a deer caught in the sights of a hunter's rifle. Burton pound his fist into it. 'And I'm going to find her.'

Mrs Sidhu jumped. She had never seen him this angry before. She toyed with her food and Burton pointed at her plate. 'You haven't touched your Western equivalent of dhal and rice,' he said.

She heard the hope in his voice. 'Take it.'

Burton dragged it over to his side of the table, then shifted uncomfortably in his chair. 'And before you go soft on the young lovers there's one more thing you might want to know.' He pulled Dove's forensics report from his pocket. 'The forensics team pulled an all-nighter. It was confirmed, they used your food to drug Hector Keys.'

She gasped. A rock seemed to have settled in her stomach. 'Maybe I should be relieved you've got a suspect.'

'There's more. We've identified the drug in Hector's food. Zolpidem, it's a sleeping aid, you can get it on prescription. All Langtree had to do was grind up the pills and scatter it over the food.' Burton grabbed the pepper mill and ground it over his beans. 'Easy as that.' He banged the pepper shaker down. 'And he wasn't messing around. If Hector Keys had eaten the whole thing, it would have killed him.'

'Oh, my word,' Mrs Sidhu said.

Burton swallowed and his eyes fell to the table, apparently studying some crumbs. 'Thanks for your theories but from here, leave it to me.' He sat back with his hands on his stomach, red sauce on his lips and a smile on his face. A minute later, the smile had faded and he wiped the sauce away with a napkin. 'Better get back to the station.'

'But there's so much more to talk about,' Mrs Sidhu moaned.

Burton clearly felt better after filling his stomach. He smiled indulgently. 'You know, there's only so much you can get out of me with one breakfast. Well, two breakfasts if we count yesterday.'

'Three.' She pointed at his now-empty plate of beans on toast.

'Three then, but my point stands. Leave this case alone.' Burton rose from the table and put his jacket on. 'And thanks for the pep talk. But we have to live with the price of our failures, Mrs Sidhu.'

37

Burton's office these days always seemed to have a woman waiting in it when he returned. This time it was Tani Keys, dark glasses eyeing him while a long leg dangled over her knee. He wondered if he should change aftershave.

'Chief Inspector, I'm catching up on the events of last night.' She carried a copy of the *Chronicle* tucked under her pale arm. Well, it was hardly going to make the pages of *Tatler*. 'There's a lot of speculation about my nephew.' She smiled without warmth. 'May I ask in what capacity you're treating Ivor?'

'He's being treated as the victim.' The chair creaked against his sudden weight as he threw himself into it.

Tani turned her head slightly. 'Good.'

'Victim of the murder, that is.' Burton heaved his heavy shoulders. 'However, he is a *suspect* in the theft of the painting. He went into the gallery, probably drugged your husband's food beforehand. We think he was the accomplice.'

Tani raised a finger and coughed ever so slightly. 'That's

where I can correct you. Ivor, my little Ivy, had no part in that sordid woman's plan. Are we completely clear on that?' She dropped her hands to her lap and brushed invisible dust from her skirt.

Burton leaned forward, elbows on his desk. 'Of course, ma'am. If you can tell me another reason he cut the security-feed wires and then went into Gallery 2?' Burton asked.

Tani's hands stopped brushing her dress. 'There are any number of reasons he would go in to see Hector. He was my husband's personal assistant. Perhaps he had a message for him. Or an edit for his speech. As for the security wires, surely anyone that night could have done that.'

'It's likely it was him as everyone else has been painstakingly eliminated by other witness statements.'

'Nonetheless, I'm sure that the final facts will bear out that my nephew was not a thief. He may have been a fool in love, he may have given that woman information, unwittingly, that aided her, but that is it. After all, he wasn't the only one taken in by her easy charms.'

Burton felt his face warm. 'We are searching for Jenny Leblanc as our top priority.'

Tani stood. 'Good. If I can be of any more help, please do call.' Her heels pressed tiny holes into the carpet as she walked away.

Burton sighed. 'Gawd save us from over-protective aunties.'

38

Mrs Sidhu stayed on in the Greenview Cafe after Burton left. It had been an eventful twenty-four hours and she needed to untangle her thoughts. The cafe was getting busier, and she had to wait to catch Poppy's eye, waving the menu. Poppy sashayed between tables with practised skill. A slender waist helped too, Mrs Sidhu reminded herself.

'Did you want anything else?' Poppy asked. Mrs Sidhu ordered more coffee, a strong one, she needed some rocket fuel in her. Poppy took her order efficiently onto a waiter's pad and returned with a cup of dark coffee. 'Triple shot,' she said.

'Thanks for making that breakfast, the Chief Inspector really needed it,' Mrs Sidhu said.

Poppy frowned. 'I did it for you, not for him.'

'Either way, I'm grateful. He had a hard night.' Mrs Sidhu added lightly, 'They found another body up there on the farm track, in the back of a truck. Ivor Langtree.'

She watched Poppy carefully. Her mouth formed an 'O'. 'I didn't know.'

'Did you notice anything either late last night or this morning?'

Poppy shook her head. 'We have truckers park up there sometimes. But you can't see the farm road from here – the hedgerow gets in the way. Poor Ivor.'

'What's up that track?'

Poppy paused, biting her lip. 'Nothing. Just some old farm, I think.' She tapped her pad. 'Can I get you anything else?'

Mrs Sidhu passed her a business card. 'You know, I work in catering and I've noticed you're a hard worker. If you ever want extra shifts, give me a call.'

Poppy thumbed the card. 'OK. But I don't plan on being a waitress all my life.'

Nor did my last one, Mrs Sidhu thought, and then thought it was too mournful. Here was a girl with her whole future ahead of her. She put on a bright face. 'What are your plans?' she asked.

It never ceased to fascinate Mrs Sidhu how simply taking an interest in someone could perk them up. For the first time, Poppy's permanent frown dropped. Her pink face glowed and she even produced a smile. 'Well, I can't say exactly yet. But when it happens you won't be able to miss it. The whole world will see me.'

Mrs Sidhu groaned inwardly. Another young person with dreams of becoming famous. It was called 'going viral' these days. She shouldn't be so hard. After all, Mrs Sidhu herself had spent a big chunk of her teenage years singing into a hairbrush and dancing in front of the mirror.

The image made her think of Daisy Carr. Burton's parting words echoed in her mind. 'We have to live with the price of our failures.' Mrs Sidhu was certainly paying for the price of her failures, and the guilt pressed down on her. Maybe it would go better for Poppy than Daisy. Mrs Sidhu played along.

'So mysterious. I can't wait. I'm sure it'll be brilliant.' The young needed nurture, encouragement. Poppy flapped away, hips swaying around chairs and tables.

Good deed done; now there was work to do. She turned over her conversation with Burton in her mind, prodding at her thoughts, tilling the rich soil of her irresistibly curious brain.

There were two things bothering her. The first was from Burton's conversation with Jenny over dinner. Ivor was protecting Jenny from someone.

This had the rich odour of truth to Mrs Sidhu's mind; it was too odd and too specific to place it as a lie. So the question was who he would be protecting her from by pretending he and she were strangers. It had to be someone in the village. Who else would care? Having satisfied herself on this point, she moved to the next.

The second point – and this one was so important that her finger clenched the biro tight, knuckles whitening – they had killed her waitress and used her food to poison her client. For that they would face justice, she was determined. Again the question it raised was a pointed finger. Who would want to kill Hector?

The simple answer was the one she had given to Burton: Ivor. Yet this answer felt flat and wrong on her tongue as soon as she had uttered it. It was a dish with a missing ingredient, a spice-less gruel. The more she thought about it the more adamant she was. Ivor simply wasn't a killer. Nor for that matter was Jenny.

Now poison, that was one thing. Killing a young woman, crushing her head with a rock, that was completely another. And as for braining your boyfriend and sticking him in a sculpture full of chemicals, it was the stuff of horror films. She had a growing sense that the answer lay elsewhere. But where? She pulled at a strand of her hair. She needed another way of thinking.

She tugged at the tangled-up contents of her bag until everything came out like a landslide. There among the junk of her life was what she was looking for: the smiling face of a cockerel.

It was stiff card, the back was plain and grey and had on it the words, 'Opening night menu for the Pump House Gallery. Everything will be orange.' They were in Ben Trimble's elegant handwriting, not her own scrawl. It was otherwise blank.

The card had given her inspiration once, maybe it would again. This time she would fill it, not with recipe ideas, but with a different kind of smorgasbord. She crossed out the title and made a new one underneath.

'Suspects in the Case of the Stolen Painting and the Murdered Waitress and the Attempted Murder of Hector Keys.' It wasn't exactly a snappy title. She double-underlined it nonetheless, to express the gravity of the charges. She chewed her pen for a while before coming to a decision.

This needed more flexibility than a single piece of paper would afford. She took up the cardboard and tore it into rough rectangles. Now she had to do this properly. On the first card she wrote:

IVOR LANGTREE
Nephew to Tani
Boyfriend to Jenny
Assistant to Hector
Argued with Hector
Helped Jenny steal 'La Scaletta'
Murdered
Why did he take a plate and glass to a robbery?

JENNY LEBLANC
Gallery director
Lover to Ivor
He dumped her
They stole 'La Scaletta' together
Claims Ivor was protecting her
Planning a new life together on the robbery proceeds?
So why kill him???

She shook her head and started a new card.

LUDO DALRYMPLE
Runs rival gallery
Hates the Keyses
Could have drugged the food
But he left the Pump House before the robbery

That's all she had on Ludo. It wasn't a great deal. Maybe there was another Bonnie and Clyde act here. She took up her pen again.

GERTIE DALRYMPLE
Watches the Keyses obsessively, knows their movements

Could have passed information on to Ludo inadvertently as gossip
But what sort of information?
Had ample opportunity to drug the food
But genuinely upset the painting was stolen

Given that Gertie and Ludo could barely get along while painting next to each other, it was hardly likely they planned a heist together. She pulled out another card.

THE ANGEL OF DEATH
Acrobatic and strong
Access to sequins and feathers???

The second of these things Mrs Sidhu quickly ascertained could be found online or through any decent art-and-craft suppliers. The first seemed to eliminate everyone on her list so far, except perhaps Jenny. Jenny looked fit and strong, she had good balance, could climb ladders while carrying artworks. It seemed a stretch, though, to imagine her pirouetting and somersaulting. That could only mean one thing:

The Angel is someone else, outside this list

She finished the cold dregs in her cup and started packing her things into her bag, reading each card again with a growing sense of depression. She had no answer to the simple question, who would want to kill Hector? Maybe DCI Burton was right after all: Jenny and Ivor. The cards were filled with writing but in reality she was back to square one, a blank canvas.

She suppressed a groan and cast her eye back to the torn-off and rejected part of the Cornflake box. The part where Ben's clear handwriting still stood, a lesson in creative thought. She checked her watch. It was nearly eleven and the art class was about to start on the green. She could do with a break. She had grown to enjoy her sketching, and she had paid good money for the classes.

A small panic rose up in her chest as she looked out of the Greenview Cafe window onto the green. After such a night as last night, people would be on their guard. They might even stay at home, windows locked and closed.

However, Mrs Sidhu need not have worried. They were gathering in the distance. The morning art class was a ritual that did not stop for death or disaster. Mrs Sidhu stacked her Cornflake cards, wrapped them in an elastic band, tossed them into her bag and made her way onto the grass.

39

The promise of an hour away from Burton, Tez, Varma and most of all the frustrations of the case was seductive. Gertie was already splashing colours onto paper when Mrs Sidhu took up her seat. As usual, she was in the mood to talk.

'Are you all alone in the world, Mrs Sidhu?' Gertie asked.

'I suppose I am. I have a son. But my husband departed me. He had a heart attack.'

'How sad,' Gertie said. Then added with a wink, 'Wish mine would.'

Mrs Sidhu wanted to say it wasn't sad, not really. She had found her feet, found a new life, a new career. But it didn't seem like the right moment. In the corner of her gaze, she watched Ben chatting up one of his harem at the far end of the group, a woman with high cheekbones and long white teeth. She reminded Mrs Sidhu of a thoroughbred racehorse.

The chairs were arranged once again in a semicircle

facing the Bowler's Oak. The wind whipped at the branches, tearing off a few leaves. 'Capture the motion,' was Ben's only mysterious instruction. Everyone set to work, scratching with pencils and brushes.

Mrs Sidhu pulled her own drawing out, and setting it up on the easel, pressed brittle lines into it with her pencil. It was coming along quite well.

'I like your scarf,' said Mrs Sidhu.

'Thank you.' Gertie preened. She was wearing a bright yellow silk scarf, decorated with ferns. She tilted her head back and gave everyone a good view of it. 'What do you think, dearies?' she bellowed. 'A genuine Suzy Cobb. That's right, the real thing and the Breeze is having her debut private view tonight. Quite a scoop.' If anyone had a clue who Suzy Cobb was they kept it to themselves.

Ludo sat on the other side of her as usual. She nudged him and hissed, 'Say something.'

'When did we become a clothes shop?' Ludo growled.

'It's textile art and Suzy Cobb is the hottest new thing. Well, she will be when people have heard of her. Tani Keys has graciously agreed to attend the private view. A word from her and Suzy Cobb will skyrocket. You really must come tonight, Mrs Sidhu. This colour would suit you.' She handed her an invitation.

Ludo spoke without looking up from his canvas. 'She doesn't have any money.'

'Oh,' said Gertie, pausing before continuing unabashed. 'Bring one of those Indian millionaires.'

Mrs Sidhu riffled her mental Rolodex for her Indian millionaires collection. Varma was the closest she could come up with. 'I'll try. It's hard to snag one at such short notice, they get booked up.'

Gertie stared at her, seemingly unsure of how seriously to take the remark.

'You said Tani Keys is coming, but what about Hector? Is he also going to be there? After all the tragedy with Ivor.'

Gertie clasped her hand to her heart. 'Poor man, still bedridden. It must be the shock after losing his nephew.'

A gleeful smile spread across Ludo's face. 'I suppose he can cuddle up to his millions.'

'Oh, Ludo, really.' Gertie slapped his arm.

'You know,' Mrs Sidhu said, looking severely at Ludo, 'I heard that if he had eaten the whole canapé, it would have killed him.'

'It'd be more convenient for *her* if he had died,' Ludo sniggered.

'What do you mean, her?' Mrs Sidhu asked.

'Ivor wasn't the only one who Hector had a row with. Oh, no, all is not well up at Castle Keys, so I hear.' Ludo turned his large eye to scan the other members of the class.

'Where did you hear that?' Mrs Sidhu asked sharply.

Gertie coughed. 'I'm sure my husband is mistaken.' She jabbed Ludo in the ribs. 'Aren't you, dearest?'

Ludo rubbed his side, grumbled, and turned back to his charcoal sketch. 'Perhaps.' He pulled a face. 'I sometimes mishear my wife gossiping about people.' He quickly moved out of elbow range.

Mrs Sidhu eyed Gertie, who blushed. 'I may have overheard Hector and Tani arguing. But I don't know what about. Husbands and wives fight like cats and dogs all the time, don't they?' Only if Gertie's own marriage was anything to go by. 'And poor Hector, he's still poorly.' She brightened. 'So I'm putting together a rota of people to keep him company.' She produced a piece of paper. 'Who wants first shift?'

'Help out a millionaire?' Ludo sneered. 'Can't he pay for his nursemaids?'

'It's not the same. The artistic community should pull together to show how much he means to us personally.'

'I'm telling you, divorce bells are ringing,' Ludo leered. 'Let's see what bloody Hector Keys makes of himself without all that money to back him. Let's see his precious bloody "golden eye" get him out of that one.' He made a final stroke to his drawing. 'I'm quite pleased with this,' he said lightly.

'Don't be a fool, Ludo,' Gertie said. 'Even if they did divorce, Hector would get half of everything, he'd be fine. It's Tani who'd lose out. It's all her family's money.'

Mrs Sidhu rubbed her lower lip before speaking. 'Gertie, I'd like to volunteer to help Hector.'

40

The gates to Peety Lodge opened obediently when Mrs Sidhu spoke her name and profession into the speaker and she drove her little Nissan in. She pulled up alongside a collection of smart-looking cars: a Lexus, a Mercedes, a couple of SUVs that she mentally started measuring up for boot space and then quickly reminded herself of the price tag. Nice to have the money.

She peeled the elastic band from her cards. She still had two blank ones left. She took one up and wrote:

TANI KEYS
Argument with Hector, is their marriage in trouble?
Could have drugged the food
Knew the food would be delivered
If Hector dies, she doesn't have to split the art collection

If that was true Tani had everything to gain from Hector's death and nothing to lose.

A new memory pushed up into Mrs Sidhu's mind. The

image of Tani Keys, at the gallery opening, dark glasses off, her red-rimmed eyes staring into the ladies' room mirror.

She scratched at her chin: red, tired eyes, and constant yawning. It gave Mrs Sidhu pause for thought. Tani was a woman who was not getting her eight hours. By the look of those eyes, Tani Keys had insomnia, and where there was insomnia there were sleeping pills.

She added one more line to her card.

Tani Keys has access to sedatives

Tani answered her knock, meeting her at the door, stepping outside onto the flagstones. Her dark glasses reflected the clouds skittering across the sky. Incongruously, she carried a sandwich on a plate. 'I'm so sorry, I have been somewhat busy with other things.' She glanced down at the sandwich with an arched eyebrow. 'Is this about your invoice? Please do send it and I'll pay it.' Tani hesitated, perhaps hoping that with that, the meeting was over.

Before Tani could turn and disappear back into the house, Mrs Sidhu cleared her throat. 'That's very kind, but it's not why I'm calling on you.'

A gust of wind caught Mrs Sidhu's hair, blowing it across her eyes for a moment. When she pulled the strands away she wondered how Tani's stayed so firmly in place. The butter-coloured styling formed a war helmet over her head, but the eyes that looked out were invisible, hidden behind those lenses. Mrs Sidhu knew what was behind there.

As if sensing her thoughts Tani yawned.

'Tired?' Mrs Sidhu asked.

Tani leaned back on the door frame. 'What is it I can do for you?' she said.

'I'm here to volunteer.' She pulled out Gertie's rota.

Tani read with an arched eyebrow. 'Who will save us from the kindness of our neighbours?' She gave a tight smile. 'I suppose you should come in.'

Mrs Sidhu stepped inside the house. Everything stood silent. 'Are there no staff here?'

Tani waved her hand. 'Hector sent them all home.' She walked through the house to the kitchen, where she poured a glass of milk.

'So you're here all alone, doing everything for him,' Mrs Sidhu said.

'I was.' Tani smiled thinly. 'Now it appears you're here.' She put the milk on a tray along with the sandwich. A glance at the packaging lying on the kitchen counter confirmed Mrs Sidhu fears. It was a supermarket special: grey-looking bread, two tired slices of cheese and a dry tomato. There was more nutritional value in the wrapping than the ingredients. And if it didn't kill Hector from sheer lack of flavour it was the perfect vehicle for another dose of sleeping pills. Except this would be a slumber he would never wake from. 'Is that for Mr Keys? Why don't I make him a fresh one instead?' She made a grab for the plate. 'Best leave these things to a chef.'

'It's only a sandwich. The sell-by date's still good.' Tani pulled it gracefully out of reach of Mrs Sidhu's flailing arm. 'I'm sure it won't kill him.'

Motive, means and opportunity. Tani was the first full house she had in her collection of Cornflake cards. It would surely only be a matter of time before she tried to kill Hector again. Fear grabbed at Mrs Sidhu's throat. It was happening right here, right now.

41

Eyes locked on that sandwich, Mrs Sidhu followed Tani upstairs to where Hector lay, like a child, slumbering in soft grunts and moans.

'Is he all right?' Mrs Sidhu leaned in closer. There was a small bump on his forehead, his complexion seemed grey and pale. 'He doesn't look well if you ask me.'

'He drifts in and out of sleep.' Tani seemed unconcerned. 'Wakey time, Hector, I've made you some food.' Tani spoke slowly.

Hector might have mumbled something in response, but Mrs Sidhu didn't catch any words she could understand. 'He sounds like he's drugged,' she said.

Tani put the sandwich plate down on the bedside table to give Hector's shoulder a shake. 'He was drugged, don't you remember?' she drawled. 'With *your* food.'

Mrs Sidhu's eyes narrowed. 'Shouldn't that have worn off by now?' She peered at the sandwich as closely as she could. Was that white powder on the surface, or was she imagining it?

Tani shook Hector again. He flopped around like a rag doll. 'He's always been a heavy sleeper.' There was some heat in Tani's voice, a hint of jealousy perhaps. 'Lucky man. Wake up, time for some lunch.'

'You know, DCI Burton said that there was enough sedative in that canapé to kill him. It's called Zolpidem. Ever come across it?'

Tani looked blankly at Mrs Sidhu, her dark glasses holding on her for some time. 'Lucky for him he didn't eat it all,' she growled. Even Tani's cool reserve was starting to show some cracks. She shook him again, more firmly.

Hector's eyes flickered open. 'Ah, he's awake. Come on, time to get some food down you.' Tani sat Hector up in his bed. He was dull-eyed, barely conscious.

Tani reached for the sandwich on the bedside table. It would soon be thrust down Hector's throat. Mrs Sidhu couldn't take the risk that Hector was about to take his last bite. Seemingly out of options, she threw panicked glances around the room until her eye fell on the window beside the bed. 'The problem is that it's so stuffy in here,' she said. 'I'll open a window, get some fresh air.'

In one fast move, Mrs Sidhu wrestled the window open, grabbed the plate and the sandwich and flung it out into the garden below.

Tani gaped. 'What on earth did you do that for?'

'Do what?'

'Throw that sandwich out of the window.'

'Because . . .' Mrs Sidhu stuttered, searching for something to say. 'Because it just wasn't good enough.' That was it, stick to the truth. 'Look at your husband here, he's at death's door and in my professional experience a poor-quality sandwich could easily push him through it.'

'Really?' Tani stroked her chin and lifted an eyebrow. 'You've had experience of death by sandwich?'

'Not exactly. But . . .' Mrs Sidhu raised a finger. 'But it's a scientific fact that good nutrition is the key to good health.' She swivelled the raised finger round to tap her own chest. 'Right here you've got an expert in nutrition. Use my skills, I beg you.'

The room stood silent. Tani fixed Mrs Sidhu with her dark glasses. 'If it's that important to you,' she shrugged, 'go ahead.'

Mrs Sidhu breathed out slowly. 'Good. Leave the food preparation to me. At least until I've figured out if—' Mrs Sidhu broke off.

A cold tension settled on the room. Tani waited for the end of the sentence. 'Figured out what?'

What indeed? She couldn't exactly say, until I've figured out if you're poisoning your husband. 'Until I've figured out if anyone else around here can make a sandwich properly.'

'Why don't I come with you,' said Tani, 'and you can show me how it's done?'

42

Mrs Sidhu cut razor-thin cucumber slices, trimmed crusts and made perfect triangular sandwiches. At her elbow, the kettle bubbled to a standstill. She poured steaming water into a pre-warmed teapot. China clinked, sugar tongs shone in the light from the window on a perfectly laid-out tea tray.

The sight seemed to soften Tani's face. 'It was kind of you to volunteer,' she said. 'You're not even part of Bowler's Green, and I can't imagine you have much money.'

'I have enough.'

'You don't hear that very often. I would like to pay you.'

'There's really no need.'

'The need is mine. I don't like to be in debt.' Tani left the kitchen in lazy strides. A few moments later she returned, and this time her walk was accompanied by a rhythmic rattle. She slapped a jar of pills on the counter. 'Here's part-payment. It was these you came looking for, wasn't it? It's what you're implying, that I'm trying to kill Hector.'

Mrs Sidhu read the label. 'Zolpidem. That's what was in Hector's food.' She raised a finger in Tani's face. 'Which only incriminates you more.'

'Except that two weeks ago most of them went missing.' Tani took off her dark glasses, revealing the same red-rimmed eyes, shot through with blood. The swelling around them was even more bruised and swollen-looking. 'I can't sleep without them and what with the gallery opening, I haven't had time to get more prescribed. I've had to ration them,' Tani slumped. 'Now Ivor's dead and I'm so very tired.'

Mrs Sidhu examined Tani's face, the tension, the greyed skin under the artfully applied make-up. Her hand went to her chest and she felt a wave of guilt. The poor woman was exhausted and bereaved and here she was accusing her of murder. 'Have you eaten?' Mrs Sidhu asked.

Tani shook her head. 'With everything that's happened, I haven't had much appetite.'

'I think Hector's still sleeping. Come with me.' And with the teacups clinking off one another on the tray, she led the way out into the garden.

'What about Hector?' Tani said.

'We can sit here, under his bedroom window. It's still open so we'll hear him if he needs anything.' While she spoke, she took the opportunity to kick the remains of the sandwich she had thrown out of the window into a flower bed.

No more words were said, until they were sitting at a wrought-iron table. A tree threw dappled shade over them. With the sun playing across the china, and the tea having steeped long enough to pour, they munched on cucumber sandwiches and talked like friends.

'What on earth made you think I'd want to kill Hector?' Tani asked.

'People. I mean, people in the village. They seem to think you're on the brink of a divorce. Aren't you?'

'Villages,' Tani breathed. 'Full of empty gossip. Yes, we argue – what married couple doesn't? You were married. Didn't you ever argue with your husband?'

Her chin dropped. 'We argued about holiday destinations. I always wanted to travel and learn things. He liked to save money. Back in those days, he made the money and he had the sway.'

'And now?'

Mrs Sidhu's chest swelled. 'I make my own money.' She told Tani how she had been left penniless and bereaved and how she had turned her life around. 'But I still can't decide on a holiday.' She tapped her head with a forefinger. 'He's still in my head, you see.'

'Hector and I have considered divorce in the past. But we have the collection, and we have our work promoting new artists, and it's enough. We're tied together by that: Hector's talent and my money. It's not a perfect marriage, but it works. Take one of those away and it would collapse. And there's one other reason. I don't actually have to kill Hector to keep my family's property. My father approved of Hector's eye, but he was cautious enough to make sure there was a pre-nup.'

'Oh. That does rather decide your innocence.'

Tani smiled, not her usual sardonic smile, but a warm smile. Mrs Sidhu had the feeling she didn't smile that way very often. She felt a small swell of confidence, enough to broach a difficult subject. 'I'm sorry about your loss – Ivor, I mean.'

Tani twisted her hands together. 'He was my sister's child. She died of leukaemia. Her husband ran away from it all. Went to pieces. I was Ivor's godmother. We never had children, so I made myself his fairy godmother. I made it my job to grant him every wish he ever wanted. And that boy wanted to learn. And when my sister died, it was my job to protect him. Right until . . .' She sobbed and though her head remained unmoved and unbowed, a tear escaped from under the rim of her sunglasses and ran down her cheek. Her face tilted up in appeal. 'Everyone thinks he was involved in the theft, the murder of that waitress. I know he didn't do it. He didn't have it in him. He loved art, and he loved it for itself, not the money behind it. He was not greedy.' Tani caught herself before she said more, perhaps embarrassed at her sudden outpouring.

At the mention of the waitress Mrs Sidhu's chest throbbed. 'It was my job to protect Daisy Carr. She was an innocent caught up in all this. Now it's my duty to find out what happened.' She licked her lips. 'Mrs Keys, Tani if I may, can't you please tell me, is there another reason you think Ivor didn't steal that painting?'

At first it seemed as though Tani wouldn't answer the question, that she was changing the subject. 'They always fought. Hector and I never had children – this work, these are our babies. So when Ivor came, there were sparks.'

Mrs Sidhu nodded. 'You can't win as a mother. The first one takes everything from you and takes you away from your husband. They resent it, however hard they try not to.'

'It was like that with Hector. In the end, I sent Ivor away to school. We've been sending him away ever since.'

'Until a month ago.'

Tani flexed her long hands. 'I spoiled Ivor. But I made sure he had the education in art that he needed as a Keys. So it was time for him to come home, learn the ropes, develop his own eye. Where better than at Hector's side? But it was doomed. They started arguing again. It all came to a head one night. Ivor went into Hector's study. He had something with him, an envelope. I assumed it was his resignation. There were raised voices. I was with Gertie Dalrymple at the time so I closed the doors so we couldn't hear. After they were done I went and saw Hector. He was incandescent.'

'What was the argument about?'

'Never found out. Neither of them would talk about it. But things seemed to settle down.'

'And the envelope?' Mrs Sidhu asked.

'I never saw it again. But I did find the remains of a burned one in the fire grate in Hector's office. All I could make out was a Paris postmark. It looked official.' She blushed. 'I shouldn't have looked, sneaking around like that.'

Mrs Sidhu laughed. 'It's the aunty in you. Own it.'

Tani put her tea down and took a more serious tone. 'Now Ivor's dead. I can't imagine for one moment he stole that painting. I even instructed DCI Burton to stop considering him a suspect.'

'I doubt that went well.'

'Not really. I feel a bit embarrassed about it now.'

'You can see his point of view. Here's Ivor, on paper at least, thinks he's about to be disinherited, desperately wants money to start his own life. He can see a way of doing so, while also striking at his hated uncle. He's got access and knows all the security arrangements. He even went into Gallery 2, I know that. So how can you be so sure he didn't steal *La Scaletta*?'

Tani turned her gaze away to the distance for a while, in silent consideration. She seemed to come to a decision. 'Because he tried to steal it once before.'

Mrs Sidhu's mouth fell open. 'You're talking about the break-in, here at Peety Lodge?'

'I never told anyone, but I witnessed more than I said.'

Tani examined the back of her hand, placing all her attention on one fingernail.

'It was the week before the argument between them. I was having trouble sleeping – I always do in the run-up to a private view. It's why I take the pills.' Tani rattled the little bottle of sedatives. 'But I couldn't find them in the bathroom so I went downstairs to see if I'd left them in the kitchen. That was when I realised there was someone in the house. I could see him.'

Mrs Sidhu's pulse speeded up, just a beat. She pressed forward in her seat. 'Who did you see?'

At first, Tani seemed unwilling to answer the question. 'I wanted to look at it again, you see. I couldn't sleep and I wanted to see *La Scaletta*. It's a painting that takes different lights and in moonlight it's something else. Then I saw someone.'

Tani told her tale and in Mrs Sidhu's mind it was as clear as a motion picture.

'It was Ivor, yes. I saw him standing there, with a knife ready to cut it out of the frame. But he didn't. He put the knife up to the canvas, and then he stopped.' Tani shook her head slowly. 'I swear he didn't see me. He changed his mind of his own free will. I decided not to call the police, but when I told Hector he was naturally very upset. He wanted to fire Ivor, even disinherit him, but I persuaded him otherwise.'

Mrs Sidhu's skin prickled. Ivor had every chance to steal the painting with ease and yet he didn't. Then two weeks later he stood accused of executing a complex and well-planned heist. Her head tilted to one side, birdlike. 'Why don't you tell the police now?'

'What would they say? They'd say, there you are, he tried to steal it once before. He lost his nerve or something.'

'Perhaps that's it. He lost his nerve on his own, so he turned to Jenny to help with the theft.'

'Whatever that woman could talk him into, it wasn't that. I knew my nephew, Mrs Sidhu, just like you know all yours.'

She had to accept this. Aunties know their young charges, what they're capable of, what they're not. 'So why did he break in?' she asked.

Tani folded her hands away. 'I don't know. Temptation? He must have been very close to cutting it out. There was some minor damage to the painting, a scratch by the frame, where you wouldn't notice it.'

A new strand of thought spun in Mrs Sidhu's mind. 'You said you couldn't find your pills. When did they go missing?'

'I . . . I don't know. It could have been that night, it could have been later. You see, earlier that evening we had the Arts Society over. Gertie and her bunch. The place was an absolute thoroughfare for the local arts community. Not much help, I'm afraid.'

Hector's voice could be heard from the room above.

'Tani? I'm up! And I've had the most wonderful idea.' This was followed by the clump-thump of his walking frame.

'He always was the ideas man.' She smiled, then shouted up towards the open window. 'I'm coming, Hector. Just give me a minute.'

Mrs Sidhu and Tani shook hands at the front door. Tani paused and Mrs Sidhu sensed she had more to say. 'I hope you get justice for your waitress.' Her voice choked up, her fingers tightening around Mrs Sidhu's. 'And I hope you get the bastard who killed my nephew.'

43

Just the facts, Burton told himself for the hundredth time.

In search of those facts, he counted off the number of leads he had. On Jenny Leblanc's whereabouts: zero. On the boat's whereabouts: zero. On the woman in the mask: zero.

With nowhere to go he had become exactly the kind of armchair detective that he had sworn to Mrs Sidhu he never would. He wondered if it was too late to learn the violin or if there was any opium in the evidence room. Burton had spent the day in his office chair, his back stuck once more to the faux leather.

A call to the FBI had finally been answered by a Special Agent Dryden whose voice crackled over the phone. 'If you catch this woman and get that painting back you'll go down in history,' was all he had to say. 'I looked you up, you know. You've got quite a reputation. Some kind of super cop.'

Burton was quick to downplay any such talk. 'It's really

about Jenny Leblanc. She's our top suspect, but she can't pull this off alone and she can't fence it easily.'

'She's not a name that's coming up on our system, Agent Burton.' He wasn't an agent, should he explain that? Probably not worth it, and he quite liked the sound of it. Agent Burton, super cop. 'So far there's no chatter with any of our known dealers in stolen art,' Dryden continued. 'Not this side of the pond, Agent.'

Lieutenant Colonel Francesca Bruni of the Carbinieri's Command for the Protection of Cultural Heritage was equally forceful. 'This woman is not known to us. *La Scaletta*, of course, is a famous painting. Yes, it is worth twelve million pounds at auction. In addition, if Jenny Leblanc has the painting she has to sell it.'

'That's what I wanted to ask. Would she have the contacts to do that, as an art curator?'

'I think it's unlikely. I asked around, and she seems to be a well-qualified gallery curator. She would know some private collectors, but the number of people who would be in the market for this are a handful only. And some of those are in Russia, and in South America. Criminal gangs, heads of drug cartels. They use art as escrow in big trades. Jenny Leblanc is not in that world. Unless she has used an alias.'

By mid-morning, the words he'd scrawled on the whiteboard were blurring, while hand-scrawled notes littered his desk. He moved them around, reordering them to make better sense as he clamped his phone handset between jaw and collarbone.

On the subject of Jenny Leblanc's identity, Jos Vansteen, head curator at the Rijksmuseum, was vehement. 'I've worked with her many times. She is a well-known curator and now a director of galleries,' he spluttered. 'No indications of criminality, extremely knowledgeable on twentieth-century impressionism.' His voice sharpened, reminding Burton of his old headmaster. 'She has single-mindedly devoted her life to art.' He coughed. 'It's something that's probably beyond your comprehension.'

Insulting, but fair, Burton thought.

By lunchtime, Burton finally laid down his phone, to the relief of his overheated left ear. He peeled his back from the chair and went out into the open-plan office where a handful of officers were standing around. 'Good afternoon,' he said conversationally. He might as well have fired a gun in the air. They scattered like frightened birds, dispersing to all corners of the room. Only Dove remained, hands folded behind his back.

'No red flags on her,' Burton said. 'Not with Interpol, the Carabinieri's Art Crimes Squad, the FBI – and Miami Vice for all I know. Jenny Leblanc is exactly what it says on the tin: an art expert, a professional curator with standing in her field.'

'And two days ago she steals a painting, kills her ex, and drugs a police officer,' said Dove. 'Seems a change of pace, sir.'

'Now there's an understatement.' It struck him that Dove was standing awkwardly. Awkwardness was not a new look on Dove but something about his posture was especially awkward. 'What's that behind your back, Dove?' he asked.

'Nothing, sir. Just some old rubbish to throw away.'

'You don't hide rubbish behind your back.'

'Hiding, sir? I'm not hiding anything.' In a swift move, Dove pushed something into a nearby waste paper basket, then stamped his foot down on it. 'There, it's gone, sir.' Dove's foot, however, remained stuck in the bin. He tried to shake it clear, but it just rattled sadly at the end of his leg.

Burton held out his hand. 'Let me see it.'

Dove, head bowed, stooped, tugged the bin free and pulled something from the inside. Burton snatched it from him and turned it over. 'The *Slough and District Chronicle*, today's issue.' He unfolded it. 'I think I've read this one.' He smiled, and it was not a happy smile but a gleaming smile with a flash of anger in his eyes. He raised his voice loud enough for the entire room to hear. 'I'm not made of glass. This is just a temporary setback. We are going to get these thieves.'

'You hear that, everyone?' Dove then lowered his voice. 'One thing, could we call them "heisters", sir?'

One of the desk phones in the office rang. It bleated out its call, unanswered.

'Heisters?'

'It's just that's what the press are calling them, art heisters, and we've all been calling them that. Maybe if we just standardise on that it'll be easier. More exciting too.'

'They're thieves, Dove, clear? And murderers.'

Dove's back straightened. 'Yessir. Crystal, sir.'

With irritation, Burton noticed the desk phone was still ringing. 'I can't think with that noise.' He stepped over to it, lifted the receiver and put it down again, cutting short the ringing.

Dove waved his computer tablet. 'We've got a time of death on Ivor Langtree, sir. He wasn't killed in that truck. He died about two days before. It's hard to tell exactly when because of the embalming fluid.'

'Elementary, dear Dove. There's only one other moment when she could have got his body into the sculpture.' Burton snapped his fingers. 'She killed him in the gallery during the theft. Stands to reason, she wanted to pin the blame on him. Another reason for her to get *The Knight* out of there.'

'There's a problem with that, sir,' continued Dove. 'We've got more on Ms Leblanc's phone. It's been dead since last night, but during yesterday she got a call from Ivor Langtree. If he's been dead for two days how did he make a phone call to his girlfriend?'

Burton stopped chewing the cud. 'And if she killed him and stuck him inside *The Knight* during the raid, why would she take his phone just to call herself?' Burton nodded. 'So someone else killed him, took his phone and called her for some reason.' He slapped his fist into the palm of his hand. 'Which means someone else is involved. Someone who posed as Ivor on the phone to her.'

'A third heister.'

'Thief, Dove. They're just thieves. This isn't *Ocean's Eleven*.' Burton stroked his chin. 'What about the woman in the mask? Are we assuming that's Jen—' He broke off – using her first name was a reminder of his shame. What should he call her now? 'The Leblanc woman.'

'Could have been, sir. The papers are calling her the "Angel of Death", sir. Should we standardise on that?'

'Masked woman will do,' Burton snapped. 'She was quite a gymnast.'

'We don't know much about Ms Leblanc's physical abilities, sir. Unless you . . . would you say . . . was she athletic?' Dove faltered under Burton's stern, cow-like gaze. 'We don't know enough about her.'

'It's a different woman.' Burton rubbed at his neck, where a hot flush was blossoming. 'The timeline doesn't work. We were both talking to Jenny Leblanc minutes before this "Masked Woman" appeared.' Why hadn't he spotted that before? Was he too determined to find Jenny guilty? Just as before he'd been too determined to find her innocent? Burton, my lad, you've lost your way twice. 'There's a third person involved.'

The desk phone started ringing again, accompanied by another at the far end of the room. Burton rubbed his face. He took shelter in his office, Dove following obediently.

Burton went over to the window. The man was walking his dog, but the woman with her coffee must have missed her bus or something. The man tugged at the lead, while his dog sniffed at a bush. Both of them seemed lost, pulling in different directions.

Burton had wondered about getting a dog when his wife had left him. Something had put him off the idea. He turned to find Dove looking up at him, waiting patiently for his orders. 'Sit, Dove.' Dove did as he was told.

'What about the boat she stole, anything there?' Burton asked.

Out in the open office, three phones were ringing. No, make that four. Five. Six.

'No one's reported it, sir. It must be hidden away somewhere. I've sent every spare officer out to look for it.'

'It's the Thames, Dove, not Frenchman's Creek. How many places are there to hide a motor launch of that size?'

Burton shook the pea that was rattling round in his head. He was getting a bad feeling about all of this. 'Why not just dump the boat? It's incriminating. Why keep it?'

He put his head out into the office space. Every single phone was ringing. 'What's going on?' Burton asked. 'Why are all the phones ringing? And why is there no one here to answer them?'

'I just said, sir. They're all out looking for the boat.'

'Right, yes.' Behind him he heard his own phone joining in. In two long strides he was back at his desk. 'Chief Inspector Burton,' he said. His face turned pale as he listened.

44

Mrs Sidhu crunched the handbrake on her Nissan Micra as she rolled to a stop outside 21 Jubilee Drive. After all she had seen and learned, home was a welcome sight. Her crumpled old armchair awaited her in front of the TV.

The lights were on. Tez must be home and she was looking forward to seeing him, cooking him dinner, hugging him and having him wriggling out of her arms, pink-eared with embarrassment. Maybe even worming some details out of him about this girl he was seeing. Sometimes it took someone else's loss to appreciate what you had.

Her seat belt whined into its holder, after a few yanks to engage the recoil mechanism. Even so, yearning as she did for the cosy comforts of home, she didn't move for a while. The street was quiet and her mind was busy.

She pulled out her deck of cards, rolling the rubber band onto her forearm like an old-fashioned bank cashier counting pound notes. She pulled out Tani Keys's one first, and slashed a line through the existing writing, before she added some new material. Now it looked like this.

TANI KEYS
~~Argument with Hector, is their marriage in trouble?~~
~~Could have drugged the food~~
~~Knew the food would be delivered~~
~~If Hector dies, she doesn't have to split the art collection.~~
~~Tani Keys has access to sedatives.~~

Pre-nup: has no motive for poisoning Hector
Sedatives went missing, but almost anyone from the Arts Society could have taken them
Saw Ivor with a knife about to steal the painting

Then she found Ivor's and Jenny's cards and laid them on each of her thighs. Taking her pen she modified, adding and crossing out until she was satisfied. She sat back to admire her work which looked like this:

IVOR LANGTREE
Nephew to Tani
Boyfriend to Jenny
Assistant to Hector
Argued with Hector
~~Helped Jenny steal 'La Scaletta'~~
Murdered
Broke into Peety Lodge but didn't steal 'La Scaletta'. Why?
Why did he take a plate and glass to a robbery?
Because he didn't go in there to steal the painting
Had an envelope from Paris – Hector burned it

JENNY LEBLANC
Gallery director
Lover to Ivor
He dumped her
They stole 'La Scaletta' together
Claims Ivor was protecting her
Planning a new life together on the robbery proceeds?
So why kill him???
Who was Ivor protecting her from?

That was what she had. She was now convinced, more than ever, that whatever Jenny Leblanc was up to, she was not a murderer or a thief. Nor was Ivor.

So why did Ivor go into the Keyses' house that night? Did he really go to steal *La Scaletta* only to have a change of heart? And why did he go into Gallery 2 on the night of the theft? More questions instead of answers. But she did have one new clue to play with. The envelope. It had to have some relevance. What could it have contained? Tani thought a resignation, in which case why would Hector burn it? He would be glad to see the back of his troublesome nephew.

She blew through compressed lips. None of this got her any closer to the identity of Daisy's killer, nor who stole the painting.

She rolled the rubber band down her wrist, snapped it around the cards and tossed them back into her bag.

Cool air and the distant scent of vanilla tantalised Mrs Sidhu's nose as she put the key in the front door. Someone on the row was baking a cake. She jiggled and cajoled the key in the lock. The front door once again lost the latest battle in its lifelong war to keep her out and yielded with a plastic squeal.

She dumped her keys into the bowl, swung her coat onto a hook. With a sigh she eased her feet out of her sticky shoes and thrust them into a pair of mules.

'Tez, I'm home,' she called out into ringing silence. Maybe he was out after all. She felt a twinge of disappointment. He was out all the time these days, doing who knows what and with whom.

From somewhere within a noise followed, and again that whiff of vanilla, and now with notes of cinnamon. Her fixed fantasy up to now had been defrosting a container of frozen spinach dhal and consuming it in her favourite armchair. How her backside longed for the perfect fit of her chair. Now, taking faltering steps towards the kitchen, she indulged herself in a new dream. What if Tez had actually made dinner for her? A gentle smile threatened on her lips, but it never fully materialised.

A few yards closer and her dream was dashed when she heard the voice. It was a woman's voice, and she was crushed by a new worry. She remembered Tez's phone call from the previous day. His girlfriend was here! She could not make out the words, yet there was something disturbing about the woman's voice. It was oddly familiar. That should not be a surprise. The tension in her shoulders eased a smidgen. In fact, it was good news.

The voices of all her unofficial nieces were known to her. She had always turned her nose up at heavy-handed Asian matchmaking. She liked to move in more subtle ways. On the other hand, there was something comforting in Tez meeting someone from the local community, a known quantity.

Her fingers scrabbled on the kitchen door knob with all the excitement of a child unwrapping a birthday present. Who could it be? Priti from the vape shop? She smelled of vanilla. Gudi from the petrol station? But no, Gudi smelled of diesel. On the other hand she was assistant manager so she had prospects. There were so many girls out there, and just the idea that any of them could be interested in Tez was making her dizzy.

She should stop this. This was no state of mind to meet her future daughter-in-law. Maybe there was time for her to breathe into a paper bag. There wasn't. She just took a deep breath and by force of will took herself in hand.

After all, she was the grown-up here. What was needed was a bit of dignity. She prepared herself and made a little speech in her mind. 'Oh, hi.' This would be accompanied with a casual hand wave. 'You kids just carry on as though I'm not here.' And she would defrost her sabzee, make some light chit-chat and breeze right back out to the living room. She would even put the telly volume right up, to make the point that she couldn't hear them.

With this plan in mind, she drew her spine straight, brushed herself down and pushed open the door to the kitchen in full casual mode.

Casual mode lasted about three seconds. This was the time it took for the shock to travel up the optic nerve, and rattle around her brain before lodging itself deep inside the rage centre of her mind. She gasped, and the decorous speech, the airy dismissal, the oh-so-casual exit went up in flames. They were incinerated by the anger rising up in her belly.

When it comes to swearing the Punjabi language is far better equipped than the English. And on this occasion, Mrs Sidhu could thank her luck that she was bilingual. She unleashed a storm of insults in her parents' language that had no equal in the tongue of Shakespeare. This took in curses ranging from flicking one's fore-teeth all the way up to brother-in-law's dog (a deadly insult). When she was done in Punjabi, still fighting for words, she stuttered before letting loose with the only English words she could find. 'Get your filthy hands off my son, you . . . you . . .' For the second time in three days Mrs Sidhu's mouth formed around unfamiliar words. 'You . . . dirty slag!'

45

'A million pounds?' Burton spluttered.

Tani stared at him blankly from behind her dark glasses. 'It's a fraction of the value of *La Scaletta*, so why not?' She tapped the ash from her cigarette into an overloaded ashtray.

'I wish you had come to me first.' Burton had gratefully accepted the offer of a cup of tea when he arrived at Peety Lodge and was now wishing he hadn't. The temptation to throw it across the room was too great. 'Before offering a reward, especially as large a one as a million pounds.'

Tani pouted. 'Didn't you just say your phones were ringing off the hook? Well, there you go, then.'

Burton put the tea down and rubbed his eyes. The Keyses' living room did little to soothe his mood. The pure white walls and furniture dazzled his eyes, while the collection of modern artworks simply bewildered and confused him. Everywhere he turned were contorted shapes, angled lines, body parts dissociated from their usual locations. One small sculpture he had inadvertently put his hand on had turned out to be a pair of iron buttocks on a pair of legs. Meanwhile the hardness and angle on the Italian sofa were making him wish his own backside was made of the same stuff. It was tough to focus on the matter at hand. 'We have received a huge number of tip-offs,' he said.

'Then it's only a matter of time before you find the woman who stole our painting and killed my nephew.'

Burton swallowed back the biting response forming in his mind. 'Not all the tip-offs are helpful. And we can't be sure that she did kill your nephew, Mrs Keys.'

'Of course she did.' She blew a geyser of smoke across the room at Burton. 'And she's got our painting.'

Burton ground his teeth. 'Yes, well, I've had to call off most of my search officers just to handle the phone lines.'

The doorbell rang.

'Perhaps you should get that and I should handle this, my dear.' Hector Keys had sat silently up to now. He was propped up at the far end of the same rock-hard and steeply sloping sofa. He had a multitude of cushions to help, and Burton would have given his right arm for just one of them.

Tani crushed out her cigarette and strode from the room, leaving the two men together.

Hector cleared his throat, and spoke in weak voice. 'The reward was my idea, I'm afraid, Chief Inspector. It was supposed to help you.'

Burton regretted his peevishness. The poor man was clearly still feeling the effects of being doped. Burton took the edge off his voice. 'That's a kind thought, sir. Maybe we'll get lucky and a decent tip-off will come through.' He cleared his throat. 'Maybe you've remembered something yourself, sir, as the drug slowly wears off.'

Hector chuckled. 'Sadly not. It's still a great clash of lines and colour. Now, Tani tells me that poor Ivor is dead.' Hector's silver eyebrows appeared above the frame of his pink spectacles. 'All the important stuff happens while I'm zonked out.'

'Yes, sir. We found his body. It looks like he was working with Jenny Leblanc, but she decided not to split the proceeds.'

'Remarkable. He got in with the wrong crowd. Don't tell my wife this, she doted on him, but I predicted it. He was always given too much free rein in my opinion. These things never end well.'

Tani returned to the room. 'Look, Hector, Gertie's here to keep you company.'

Gertie Dalrymple waved a large hand from the corridor. 'Hector, how are you feeling, dearest?'

'How lovely,' Hector said.

Gertie raised a large canvas bag. 'And look, I've some *objets* for you to take a look at. An expert valuation would be so helpful.'

'Surely your husband would be just as well placed,' Hector said hopefully.

'Ludo's fine, but he's hardly Mr Golden Eye, is he?' Gertie chuckled hoarsely. Poor hubby, thought Burton. Out-'eyed' by Hector, that must sting a bit.

Hector, with a little help from Tani, got himself up to his walking frame. My word, he was frail, you would have expected him to have bounced back by now. As he clanked out of the room he threw Burton a wide-eyed look and hissed, 'Now, if you can save me from Gertie Dalrymple, you can have the reward yourself.'

Burton stifled a chuckle.

46

It was so quiet in Mrs Sidhu's kitchen that you could hear three individual hearts beating. Mrs Sidhu might have been exaggerating to herself, but only just.

The first of the three hearts in question was Tez's, which was probably thumping like a washing machine with a pair of trainers in it. This was most likely because his mother had just burst through the door and let loose with a series of obscenities in guttural Punjabi. Obscenities that he had only heard when he'd run his dirty trainers through the washing machine.

The second heart belonged to Mrs Sidhu and, she would recount later, was not actually making any sound at all. This was because she believed it had stopped.

The third heart might have missed a beat or two as well, because it belonged to the cause of all this heart-thumping, heart-stopping and heart-breaking. It belonged to Mrs Sidhu's long-term catering rival Mrs Prakesh.

'Of all the people I imagined my son with, this is the

lowest, the worst. the . . . the pits of hell!' Her stomach was doing revolutions.

Mrs Sidhu was an observant woman; she had made a lifetime's habit of picking up on details that others so often missed. Anger, though, lays a veil so thick on the senses that even the sharpest eyes are blinded. Thus it was that in her blood-pumping rage, she missed several details that could have given her pause.

Instead she flung a finger in the direction of the front door and shouted, 'Out!' She couldn't bear to think of it. Her son, Tez, poor innocent young Tez, twisted to the evil will of that wrinkled old prune.

Tez finally found his voice. 'Mum, I know it's bad but I didn't think you'd be this upset. We wanted to include you, we really did.'

She felt as though her feet were detaching from the ground, as though she was a balloon. All she could think of was Mrs Prakesh's victorious smirk. She had taken her son's innocence, possibly even his virginity. Tez was twenty-five, true, but he was not exactly a fast developer. Now he was developing too fast, and in a very unsavoury way.

'Get out!' she repeated. And the kitchen of all places. She would need to disinfect every surface. It was unforgivable, unfathomable.

Mrs Prakesh threw something down on the counter. 'Come on, Tez, we'll come back when she's calmed down.' Tez too threw something down and made for the door.

Mrs Prakesh lingered a moment before she departed. 'If it's any consolation, I wanted to tell you. It was Mr Varma who stopped me.'

Her stomach lurched. 'Varma knows as well?' Her legs

were feeling weak. How many people were in on this . . . disgusting liaison?

'Of course he does.' Mrs Prakesh snorted. 'It's *his* birthday.' With that she and Tez left.

As the feeling of unreality slowly seeped away, like air from a puckered balloon after the party was over, as her heart rate returned to normal small details, the ones she had missed before, were starting to impinge on Mrs Sidhu.

There was the conversation itself. The fact that Tez and Mrs Prakesh were so calm, even though they had been caught in flagrante delicto. Then she stumbled over to the kitchen counter and picked up the white cotton items the two of them had thrown down. They were aprons. They had been wearing aprons. Why would they be wearing aprons? What new twisted perversion was this?

She moved along the counter, and as she did so a cylindrical shape loomed up at the far end.

Then there was that last comment that Mrs Prakesh had made. The comment about Mr Varma.

She reached the end of the counter, the smell of vanilla and sugar drifting up to her nose. The cylindrical object came into clear focus. Dumbfounded, Mrs Sidhu read the writing on top, picked out in crimson. 'Happy 60th Birthday Mr Varma.'

A wave of relief swept over and around Mrs Sidhu. Tez and Mrs Prakesh weren't having sex. They were baking a cake. A cake for Mr Varma's birthday.

Mrs Sidhu stood still. Time passed. A fly buzzed against the window, gave up and tried its luck against the light bulb.

A new wave was forming out in the ocean of uncertainty

that was Mrs Sidhu's life. A wave of doubt, a wave of betrayal. Mr Varma was having a birthday party and she had not been invited.

Mrs Sidhu had quite a lot to think about. Her home, occupied as it was by an alien, and highly passive-aggressive birthday cake, didn't feel like a safe haven any more. Not only had she been banished from the birthday party of her husband's closest friend, but the manner of her finding out had been a rollercoaster of emotion. The anticipation of meeting Tez's girlfriend, the sheer horror of thinking he was seeing Mrs Prakesh, and the final mixed emotion of relief that he wasn't and cold rejection that not only had she been excluded, but Tez, Varma and Mrs Prakesh had kept it from her.

She did what she sometimes did when she was upset. She found an Eighties channel on the radio and drove without any destination, slowly letting the steam out of the pressure cooker that was her mind.

Motorway lights shone horizontal bars of light in a regular beat, like some hospital patient being rushed to the operating theatre. That was fitting, a social life so terminal that it needed open heart surgery.

Her oldest friend was turning sixty and he had kept it a secret from her because he didn't want her at his party. She was an embarrassment. She was an outcast. That was the flat line.

Without thinking, she took the exit towards Digbourne and the current of her thoughts changed direction, allowing her impressions of the day to stream past.

The music on the radio was from her heyday and that heyday was a long time ago. Mark Almond was singing about his tainted love. She had come from a world of jukeboxes and stereos, words that no one even understood any more.

She squealed to a halt just before the Digbourne bridge and walked out, standing eventually halfway across the water. She was like the bathing woman in 'La Scaletta': half-in, half-out. It's where she lived her life, halfway between this and that. Halfway between home in Slough and the greener realms of Berkshire, halfway between her dwindling older friendships, and these people she didn't understand, and their intrigues and their dead bodies. Was that why she did it?

On the other side was Bowler's Hill and halfway up it the village of Bowler's Green, with lights in all the pretty houses. At the foot of the hill sat the Pump House, also with some lights left on inside and around the marina. It was closed by now, but one of the lights twinkled as if someone had walked in front of it.

And suddenly Mrs Sidhu felt very tired: tired of her work, tired of her suspicions, tired of her complicated secret-cake-baking son.

Everything important that had happened to her had happened decades ago. Half her friends were dead and the ones that weren't had stopped talking to her long ago. The only one who hadn't was Varma and now he too had turned his back on her.

She wanted to forget about all of this, she wanted to forget about the case, forget that she had no idea who killed Daisy Carr, forget about Varma's birthday and where he could stick that. She needed a new direction and she deserved some fun. She needed to be 'all-in'.

Acting on impulse she rooted around in her bag and

pulled out a business card and her phone. 'Hi, it's me, Mrs Sidhu. That dinner you talked about, I've changed my mind. Let's do it.' She paused. 'And can I ask you to bring something with you?'

47

Ben waved her down as soon as she walked in. 'I grabbed us a table. Lucky thing, it's a popular night. Half the village is here.'

He helped her with her chair. 'Half?' she said. They laughed. The Greenview was packed out. She watched with interest many of the same faces that had been at the Pump House opening. The feeling was mutual; she could feel a hundred pairs of eyes on her.

Poppy took their order with her usual freckled frown. Poppy who'd called Mrs Sidhu a biddy two days ago. No amount of youthful glowering could hide her intrigue that she was with Ben. Mrs Sidhu could see from the snatched glances from other tables that this appeared to be an opinion shared by most of the other diners.

Poppy returned with drinks. Mrs Sidhu was driving so she had opted for a glass of red wine – 'just one, mind' – and Ben followed suit. 'I've got to drive too, making a delivery later.' When asked what he was delivering, he remained coy and would say no more.

So it was awkward at first. Mrs Sidhu was never comfortable in the spotlight. She knew that of herself; it had dictated her life and career choices, as a wife and mother supporting a husband and son. Then a caterer, dwelling in the background, letting her food speak for her. Ben, however, was good at making her feel at home, and instinctively broached the subject of crime.

'I'm a little surprised,' he said. 'I mean, two murders and a stolen artwork. You'd think people would stay at home with the doors locked. Especially this crowd, they've all got expensive art on their walls.'

Mrs Sidhu took a sip and rejoined the subject. 'Lucky you came to a chef. Never underestimate the power of food to bring people together, and to heal them.' A grin crept across her face. 'Or the power of a good gossip.'

He swirled his glass. 'I had a feeling I was dealing with an expert in both those areas.' He appraised the wine, but he was looking at her. 'Excellent body, good legs, and notes of sophistication.'

She blushed. It was the cheesiest line in the history of fromage-laden date-night openers, but he was grinning with mirth. She was starting to enjoy having some attention. As long as it was Ben's personal spotlight she was in, she felt like she could dance and not care. Ben, though, was always going to attract attention.

She was one of the women who had fluttered around him the first time she met him in the Greenview. One of those women with too many overly large teeth, stuffed into high cheekbones and shiny hair and gym-trimmed bodies. On her way to the ladies, her eyes snagged on Ben. On her way back she contrived to look surprised. 'Ben! Oh my, you're here,' she shrieked. He rose and gave her a hug and she turned him, putting herself between Mrs Sidhu and Ben. Mrs Sidhu was treated to a close-up view of her expensively clad and expertly toned backside. When she had done with him she returned him to his chair, leaving a trailing hand on his shoulder. 'Ben, it's so nice to see you here.' She glanced at Mrs Sidhu and put her hand to her mouth. 'I'm so sorry to interrupt. Ben, I had no idea you had an Indian aunty.' She shot Mrs Sidhu a vicious, toothy smile before swaying away to join her husband at their table. The husband raised a glass and toasted Ben, who returned it. The husband, silk-tied and fitted-suited, returned to scrolling his phone, probably for stock quotes.

Mrs Sidhu sat open-mouthed for a moment. 'What have you done to the women around here? And when I say "done", that's what the rumour is.' She winked.

Ben chuckled. 'I swear, nothing more than the appropriate level of charm to get them to sign up for art classes.' He spread his fingers on the tablecloth. 'But what can I say. There's something about the teacher, the instructor, that reaches them in places where their bored, and frankly boring, husbands can't.'

'And don't forget the allure of the artist.'

'Who can forget that? Artists are like priests. We are in contact with mysteries that mortals can barely comprehend.'

'Priests are celibate. But none of the husbands seem to hate you.'

'I keep their demanding wives occupied at what is actually an incredibly low cost compared to a luxury spa day or a weekend shopping in New York. Honestly, that's my business model – if I can keep my price point slightly lower than Tiffany's, I'll have business for ever. We should team up. You teach cooking, I teach painting.'

'It'll be like a middle-aged finishing school. All we're lacking is deportment and a "How to be the perfect wife" class.'

'Excellent, let's take this place back to the nineteenth century. It sounds bad, I know but after all . . .' They said it together, clinking glasses. 'It's a gig economy.'

Ben remembered something and disappeared under the table for a moment. 'I brought that thing you asked for.' He placed a cardboard box on the table. 'What's left of Ivor Langtree. This is mostly work stuff, I think.'

'What did he study?'

Ben gave his opinion that Ivor had studied far too much and done far too little. 'And that's coming from a teacher. His last course was art restoration. Those are the tools of the trade.'

Mrs Sidhu pulled out an odd-looking torch, a hand magnifier, and a strange headset. The torch she'd seen before – it was called a blacklight, and used ultraviolet light to reveal DNA. She put the headset on and blinked, looking at her hands.

'It's a Mag optivisor. Magnifies stuff and leaves you free to work with your hands,' Ben said helpfully.

There was the binder from the technical conference. It was Ben's copy of the same conference binder which Jenny had open on her desk. Open on her desk, the echo sounded in her head, why open? The thought passed as she handled the rest of the items in the box.

There was a printout of a graph – it rose and fell with jagged lines, but she could make no sense of it – and was marked with hand-scrawled lines and notes, all illegible except for the number '94'. Apart from that there were a couple of old books – one was a biography of Oppenheimer. It was bookmarked with a scrap of paper. On the page, Ivor had underlined that famous quote from the scientist, the one pulled from the Bhagavad Gita. 'I am become death, destroyer of worlds.' Mrs Sidhu shuddered.

'Are you all right?' Ben asked.

'Nothing, just a memory.' She had heard the same words not long ago, uttered by a very disturbed young man. The words seem to be following her around.

'Was Ivor interested in the nuclear bomb?' she asked.

Ben shrugged. 'He thought the bomb tests were important for some reason. "The sixteenth of July 1945. The whole world changed that day. And so did the art world." That's what he said.'

Again she heard that echo of something someone had said, something she couldn't place for now. She looked at the scrap of paper he had used to bookmark the page. It had some letters and numbers written on it, she read them out loud. 'F14C1.08, what's that?' she asked.

Ben had no answer.

There was one last item, gleaming from the bottom of the box. Flecks of paint marked the blade, unmistakably the colours of *La Scaletta*. Just as Tani had said, Ivor had put his blade up to the painting, even damaged it slightly, but had stopped short of cutting it out of the frame. 'A surgeon's scalpel?' Mrs Sidhu asked. 'Why would he own one of those?'

'Not just for surgeons,' Ben said. 'Restorers use them too.'

The food arrived, and Mrs Sidhu returned the box to Ben. 'I'll stick it back under my bed until there's a bring-and-buy sale.'

'Or hand it over to the police – there might be evidence in there.'

Ben shrugged. 'Let them come and ask for it, then.'

A lasagne and chips came for Mrs Sidhu and a fish and chips for Ben. He apologised again. 'I should never have brought a chef here. It's basic stuff, but honestly this is all there is in the village. All the fancy stuff is over the river in Digbourne.'

'I don't mind a bit of humble home-cooked fare. And you don't need to apologise.' It was a half-truth. He didn't need to, but she was starting to enjoy how sorry he was about everything. It was another side to him, to see him as nervous as she was.

'What about your own work? Here you are helping the upper middle class churn out pictures of trees. Isn't your own art suffering?'

'To be frank, yes. You won't believe this but I was once a very successful young artist. I did a lot of still life, and then life painting. I had a talent for the human figure. Had a London gallery on Cork Street representing me. That's a good street to have a gallery on, for those who don't know, or it was back then. Who knows now. Sorry, you probably knew that – I'm being patronising.'

'Not at all. When it comes to art, if you assume I know nothing you'd be overestimating me. So what happened?'

'I started just churning it out. My work began to sell, so I started making more of the same thing, over and over and over. You become like an art forger, except you're forging your own work. Do you know what that feels like?'

'Replace Cork Street with Slough, and paintings with aubergine bhaji, and I have a very good idea. You become a victim of your own success.'

'That's exactly it. I fell out of love with painting. I found another way of making money from art, and that's where I am now.' He sipped on his wine.

'And you make enough from teaching to keep you in mediocre wine.'

Ben coughed nervously. 'More or less. Along with a side hustle or two.' He swallowed his wine and poured more. 'You know, this is ironic, given Lefevre's own thoughts on his most celebrated painting. Oh, you don't know?' Ben beckoned Mrs Sidhu in and whispered, 'He hated *La Scaletta*. He felt it had come too early in his career. It caused such a stir that it stopped him making more work for years. He once broke into a gallery where it was hanging and tried to set fire to it.' His hand bumped hers. She didn't move it away. 'Can you believe it? Now it's worth millions.'

When they'd finished dinner, a four-piece band started up, bashing out covers from the Eighties. 'May I have the pleasure?' Ben took her hand and they danced, danced like she hadn't since she was a teenager. In those days she would sneak out with her best friend to a daytime disco. Tonight they danced ironically – there was no other way to this soundtrack – until it was closing time. Which given this was the sticks, was only eight o'clock. Nonetheless, Poppy stood at the door with her broom, and a stern look threatening to sweep everyone out onto the green.

48

'Thank you for a very nice evening.' Outside, a gusty wind picked up, bouncing the branches of the Bowler's Oak, stirring up the grass around it, stripping it of leaves. Not too many, she hoped; her drawing was only halfway through. A bubble of surprise popped – was she actually starting to care about this artist lark? She suppressed a smile and checked her watch. 'Oh, look at the time. My son will be wondering where I am.'

Ben took a deep breath. 'And Mr Sidhu?' He scanned the skies where clouds were skating across the moon. 'Is he waiting up too?'

Her heart was beating too strongly, like a badly timed drumbeat, working against the flow of the music. 'Mr Sidhu?' She was suddenly aware of his closeness.

She was carrying Ivor's box. Ben glanced at it. 'Why the curiosity about Ivor?'

'I don't know, he seems such a sad, lonely young man. Maybe I feel the same sometimes. Apart from being a woman. And old.'

'You're not old, but I am disturbed to hear you're lonely. Is that something I can help with?' Eye contact, and far too much of it, was making Mrs Sidhu feel nervous.

'You know, you're very clever,' he said. 'I've spent a whole evening with you, you know everything about me, you got my best stories out of me, and I barely know a thing about you. I haven't even got your first name out of you.'

Everyone was leaving the Greenview. 'Mr Sidhu has passed on. It's OK, it was two and a half years ago.' Through the permanently fogged-up windows she could just make out Poppy stacking tables on chairs. With energetic movements she was making light work of it. She could use someone like that in her business, some new energy.

Catering staff, always the last ones to leave, still sweeping up on your own when the party was long over. It was the loneliest of jobs. Maybe that's why she had chosen it, an automatic answer to all the questions. 'I'm sorry I have to be up early' or 'I can't tonight, I'm working.' A conversational chastity belt.

'And your first name?' Ben persisted.

'Slough rules. We don't do first names until the second date, and until our parents have met and approved the bond.' She laughed and somehow the sound was unfamiliar to her. Was that really the first time she'd laughed since her husband's death? 'But thanks for telling me so much, and sharing your stories.'

That story about Lefevre had struck a chord. There was something there that was chiming with something else. Something that was drawing the rhythm of Mrs Sidhu's thoughts back to baseline normal. There was something destructive at work in this village. Despite the warmth and the good times vibe tonight, she could feel it.

'Thank you for sharing about your husband. I'm sorry, it must have been terrible for you. I've never been married, I can only imagine.' He chuckled. 'There. You've found out something else about me. You are good.'

Lefevre hated his own work, his best work, he hated *La Scaletta* so much that he was prepared to burn it. She was sinking into a familiar feeling that could make her feel alone even when she was standing inches from a man. Close enough to smell his aftershave. While her heart beat out a new message, and her mind raced away in another direction, she was dimly aware that he was watching her, that she needed to reply.

She jerked up her head. 'Don't beat yourself up. It's something I could have guessed.' Is that why she was, despite herself, starting to like him? Because he'd never been shackled to anything, never suffered the arguments, the love, the loss? Maybe that's why all the women around here liked him. They could tantalise themselves with the idea of an available man, fresh out of the bottle, no baggage.

'Then I hope I've earned a second date, and maybe another piece of your biography, beyond that you're a widow from Slough with one son, who seems strangely immature for a twenty-five-year-old.'

She couldn't hold back a laugh. 'Ha! Well, Asian men mature very late. And die young. But in that short sweet spot they're—'

'Amazing?'

'You wouldn't believe it if I told you.'

Somewhere behind her she heard the key turn in the

lock. 'Goodnight, Ben.' Poppy hopped onto a cute little electric scooter, and whined away, smirking. The place was in complete darkness now. They were alone. Ben's lips were parted, his eyes looking into hers. A shadow flitted across her. Something brushed her mouth. Her lips tingled in a strange, unfamiliar way. The shadow moved and Ben pulled his head back. He was looking at her, his pupils wide. She felt something she hadn't felt in years. A moment passed. She blinked. 'Did you just kiss me?'

Ben nodded. 'What did you think? Up to Asian standards?' He grinned. 'Or am I about to get a police record?'

She should feel enraged, or shocked, or embarrassed, but none of those feelings were there. There was a warmth, a heat she hadn't felt for a long time. A breeze picked up, ruffling Ben's hair.

Mrs Sidhu tried to bury a smirk. 'No, I wouldn't say that. It was quite good.' Ivor's box rattled as she held it out to him. 'But if you don't hand this in to the police, you might get that record. It should really be in evidence.'

'You know far too much about police stuff. But I'll try and remember to do it tomorrow.' He opened the boot of his car and leaned over to put the box in. The warm breeze rustled a plastic sheet lying on the floor of the car boot, lifting a corner before Ben caught it and tucked it back under the thing it was protecting.

Mrs Sidhu froze. 'What's that? Your delivery?' she asked.

'Yeah. Just something I'm working on. Delivering it tonight.'

'An original? Can I see?'

He scratched his nose, hesitating. 'It's not for public consumption. Kind of a private commission.' He coughed and closed the boot.

Ben's car ground away into the night. The warm breeze dropped, and the swelling she'd felt in her chest collapsed, a punctured balloon. She unlocked her car, and threw herself into the seat with a groan. She had just seen something and she wished she hadn't. She pulled out one of her Cornflake packet suspect cards, the last blank one left. She clicked her pen open and wrote:

BEN TRIMBLE
Penniless artist
Handsome
Wonderful
Great kisser
Has 'La Scaletta' in the boot of his car

49

Ben Trimble drove, following the river for a mile or so before the road cut inland. Traffic was light at this time of night as he climbed Bowler's Hill. At one point he passed a police car and a sweat broke out on his back. It kept on going and the sweat cooled. No need to worry. No one knew what he was doing, he was just another soul out for a drive on a lovely evening.

He let that grin crawl up one side of his face. That was a close call with Mrs Sidhu. She had bought the line about the commission. The best lies are close to the truth. This was his commission and it was a good little earner for him.

He saw the turn and took the fork to the left. The traffic thinned here, and the treeline thickened. He checked the rear-view mirror. The lights from the river were far behind, swallowed up by the thicket of branches, criss-crossing. One set of car lights, dim but visible, hung behind, weaving like fireflies as the road curved one way and the other. They were far behind, though.

He slowed when he saw the lay-by and the flowers by the tree. That was the marker, this was the spot. The car bumped and ground as he pulled off the tarmac road and onto mud. He checked the rear-view mirror again, for the yellow headlights. He stroked his moustache and waited. No one overtook him. Funny, there were no turn-offs on this road. He waited a while more. No one came and he was getting tired of waiting. It wasn't unusual for people to get lost looking for the village. They usually realised at some point they had taken the wrong fork and turned back round.

He left his own lights on, so he could see what he was doing, and the twin beams cut through the evening mist. His boots snapped and snagged on twigs as he carried his load. He put the painting down and for a moment couldn't help admiring it, what a genius Lefevre was. He carefully wrapped it again, and leaned it against the tree trunk, on the other side from the flowers. He found the nook in the tree, his hand wriggled inside for a moment, scared at what it might touch in there. He was soon grinning again as it closed on something soft. He pulled it out, and counted. The money was all there.

Sometimes he thought about his secret patron, but sometimes it was also better not to ask questions. That was Ben's way, live and let live, as long as you get to live too. So why did he shiver, though the night was still warm? The mist was thickening to a grey soup and it was dark and lonely out here.

He shrugged off the feeling and hurried back to the car. He patted the money bulging his pocket. He had done nothing wrong. He was living by his wits, like all the artists before him. Just a job, just a commission. He deserved his payout, he'd worked for it. Even so, he locked the car door from the inside.

The engine gunned up, and the noise gave him bravado and drowned out his doubts. He needed a drink somewhere warm and cheerful. Maybe one of the pubs over in Digbourne. No, better, he had a bottle of wine at home. It was a shame Mrs Sidhu wasn't there to share it. He hated lying to her, but she would never know. Anyway, it wasn't a complete lie. He just didn't say what he had been commissioned to do.

The tyres spat stones up as he pulled away from the tree and the flowers and the canvas propped against the trunk, and from the unmistakable feeling that he was being watched.

50

Mrs Sidhu wanted to believe the best. It was in her nature to believe the worst. Circumstances would have to agree, the world was full of devious men.

She watched and asked herself once again what she was doing here. It was the time of night she should be in bed, or making Tez a cup of hot milk and almonds. 'Almonds are good for the brain,' her mother had always told her, and she had filled Tez's little stomach with them in that hope. It must have worked, because despite appearances he was more devious than she could have imagined. Tez's lies and what he had told her about Varma were an injury, a bruise whose extent and depth she was not yet ready to feel out and explore. Maybe that's what she was doing here, avoiding that conversation. And here was another devious man.

Or was she looking for reassurance? Reassurance that Ben's kiss was not a lie and that someone on this earth actually was telling her the truth.

She had seen *La Scaletta*, revealed for a single moment.

The thrall of colour was instantly recognisable. So why not just call the police? The answer was that she needed to be sure. In fact she needed, more than anything, to be wrong. Otherwise the first man she had kissed since her husband passed away was a thief and a murderer. That said a lot about the choices she was making these days.

She had followed Ben's car at a distance, and to begin with all seemed normal. Ben was heading up the hill into Bowler's Green, back home. When he passed the turning for his home and took the other direction into the dense woodland, her heart sank.

She kept pace, and with no other traffic to shield her she shrank back, dropping away, terrified that he might stop, turn round and ask her what she was doing following him.

When he pulled over, she thanked her lucky stars she had an old car. Modern cars have lights that come on automatically when the engine starts. Her old Nissan had a twist knob below the steering wheel, and she turned the headlamps off, then let the engine carry her along until she rolled to a stop about a hundred yards back from him. Cloaked by darkness, she killed the engine and waited.

When he started unpacking the boot of his car, that's when all hope was lost. She watched and watched as his guilt unfolded before her up until the moment he drove away. The rubber band twanged as she pulled the newly minted suspect card from her bunch.

BEN TRIMBLE
Penniless artist
Handsome

Wonderful
Great kisser
Has 'La Scaletta' in the boot of his car

The biro made a sad click as she popped the button. She added:

Could have drugged Hector's food
Needs the money
Delivered the painting to woods
Has an accomplice?

As she waited the car grew colder and colder and the mist outside became thicker. She shivered and thought about the sorts of film where dark creatures emerge from misted woodlands. She thought about turning the engine on. That idea she scotched straight away, as it would draw immediate attention and undo all her good work so far; following Ben, seeing through his lies, understanding that he was not working alone. Someone was coming for that painting and she could not risk scaring them off.

Of course, if it was too cold for her, she could call Burton. He was paid to spend entire nights sitting in freezing-cold cars waiting for something to happen. He probably had flasks of hot coffee and sandwiches. No, she could not call Burton yet. While there were very few innocent explanations for a man leaving a painting by a tree at – and here she checked her phone clock – ten o'clock at night, she wanted more than anything to give Ben the maximum benefit of the doubt.

Her phone buzzed and she scooped it up. 'Varma' read

the alert and she silenced it immediately, joining the fifteen or so unanswered calls from him. She was not ready to talk to him, not yet, maybe never.

Instead, she tapped out a text to Burton. 'Ben Trimble has stolen La Scaletta. Arrest him. Will explain later.' Instead of sending it, she left it open, ready to send if the moment was right.

So she blew on her fingers, pulled her thin coat around her tightly and wiped the condensation from the window with a tissue. Another product of her overstuffed bag.

It was an hour later, when she was down to her last tissues and at the point of wondering what frostbite felt like, that she saw the movement.

For a moment, she thought the wind had picked up again, catching the branches of the tree with the flowers. But the other trees stood still, like silent witnesses to the crime. It had to be a person pushing through the woods. She squinted and finally saw them. Hard to tell if it was a man or a woman, they were so wrapped up in a great big coat. Something yellow pulled up over their face, and head tucked into a hat.

She watched as they found their way round to the back of the tree.

Her forehead furrowed. They had arrived here somehow, but there was no evidence of a car, no one had passed her since Ben left, and she would have seen headlights coming the other way.

The figure stumbled around the back of the tree and disappeared from view.

Mrs Sidhu woke up her phone. There was very little time. The figure was already gone from sight, heading back into the woods. She decided to add one more line to her text: 'I'm going after the accomplice.' She pressed send. No time to linger.

She slid the door catch up. The car door couldn't help its creak, being old and partly rusted, but still she cursed it for its betrayal. Fast strides took her towards the tree, some hundred yards. She had cut a hundred to fifty before she trod on a branch. She almost fell, and forced her mouth shut against the yelp. She froze. A moment passed, then two. A slow rustle followed and slower footsteps after that. There was no hurry, she hadn't been heard. The movement was away from the road, deeper into the woods.

The figure was ahead, stooped and weighed on one side with the flat parcel wrapped in plastic. They were hastening into the mist. Following was not easy, picking her way through trees until finally she found the path. That was how they had got through the woods. She wondered where it would lead to. They were a long way from Bowler's Green now, a fifteen-minute drive down the hill.

Her careful paces fell into a rhythm and she had closed the gap to twenty yards when the phone buzzed. Hardly a loud sound, but in the silence of the woods it could have been a pneumatic drill. Burton! She spat curses at herself. She should have known he would call after a text like that. She slapped her hand to it, crushing its hum with one stroke, and turned the whole thing off. Not soon enough. The figure ahead threw backward glances. There was that flash of bright yellow again, and they moved off at a run.

She had to see the face of Daisy Carr's killer. Daisy whose finger still pointed directly at Mrs Sidhu's heart. At the end of the path was light, and the other broke cover of the treeline into whatever lay beyond. She ran without caution, her feet plunged into ivy and moss, tearing at her shoes. She lost one and then the other. Sharp thorns tore at the flats of her soles, and between her toes. She kept going, running out of breath. The phantom ahead disappeared, more light and the sound of thunder. Yet there was no storm.

Mrs Sidhu broke into open space and as she did there was a blinding light and a dragon's roar. She fell back, covering her eyes until it passed. She stood up, her eyes following a pair of red eyes as they dwindled into the distance.

The sound of the car diminished as it sped down the hill. That was how they had arrived without her noticing. There was another road. Dejected, she walked back through the woods picking up one of her shoes, and it was clear from the angle of the road that the woodland was shaped like a triangle, bordered by two roads that met at the peak of the angle. Which meant that the other road ran back down the hill into the village. Her jaw clenched tight. That didn't narrow her suspects down at all.

Her feet were marked with scratches and flecks of blood from her barefoot chase and there were a few more before she found her other shoe. As she bent down she saw in the corner of her eye a flash of bright yellow. She reached down and lifted up a silk scarf, bright yellow, and decorated with a pattern of ferns. Maybe she had narrowed her suspects down after all.

51

The Breeze Gallery looked the same. The window still poked into the street like a pregnant belly and from it spilled a warm light. The door was as stiff as before and Mrs Sidhu had to put her shoulder to it. The little bell announced her.

'You're too late for the private view, dearest. I'm about to shut up shop.' The room was empty of people and Gertie's voice boomed from somewhere in the back. A moment later she emerged, wiping her hands on a tissue. 'Oh, Mrs Sidhu, it's you. As I say I'm about to close up.'

The door Gertie had emerged from was still open and Mrs Sidhu craned her neck to look inside. 'Putting things away?'

'Yes, we can't keep all the stock out, it clutters things up.'

Gertie's neck was bare but for a silver necklace. Mrs Sidhu's eyes narrowed. 'Have you lost your scarf, the yellow one I saw you in this morning?'

Gertie ran her hand to her collarbone. 'Oh, no, not at

all.' She reached behind her counter and plucked it out. 'I put it away while I was cleaning up. Didn't want to get it dirty. It's one hundred per cent silk, if you're interested.'

'Have you sold many?' Mrs Sidhu asked, trying to keep the desperation out of her tone.

Gertie looked closely at Mrs Sidhu as if for the first time since she had entered the shop. 'Are you all right? You look terrible.'

Mrs Sidhu waved away the enquiry. 'I'm fine. I fell over in some things.' She flicked a lump of something that she fervently hoped was mud from her elbow.

Gertie watched in consternation. 'Dear woman, you look all in. Let me get you some tea or something stronger.'

Mrs Sidhu balled her fists. 'No need.' She soothed her voice and prayed that Gertie's evening had not been too successful. All she needed right now was a dozen more suspects. 'You were saying about the scarf sales.'

'Not great, I'm afraid. Just three sales including mine.'

Mrs Sidhu squealed. 'That's wonderful.' She did a dance of joy on the spot.

Gertie's heavy jaw dropped. 'I'm glad you think so. Poor Suzy Cobb came all the way from Bristol.'

'I'm sorry, that was insensitive. Bristol is a long way to come. Tell me, who bought the other scarves?'

'Tani bought one, she's such a great supporter. She stayed all night – she's only just left.'

That counted her out. 'And the other sale?'

Gertie's head dropped. 'That wasn't an actual sale if you know what I mean.' She spoke with a lowered voice though there was no one around to hear them. 'Poor Suzy, she was doing so badly and looking so terrible, Ludo stepped in and bought one too.'

'Ludo, your husband Ludo?'

'Who else, dear girl?'

An act of kindness from Ludo, now there was an oddity.

She must have read her thoughts. 'I had to give him a nudge,' Gertie admitted.

Mrs Sidhu's eyes scoured the room. 'And is he here now?'

'Oh, no, he left.' Gertie smiled enthusiastically. 'He's taken tonight's place on the Hector rota. Isn't that wonderful?' She clapped her hands three times. 'I mean, him and dear Hector finally becoming friendly.'

Once again, a tremor of disquiet was passing through her mind. Something she was missing. 'So Ludo has gone to see Hector just now?'

'No, he went out much earlier. Had something to pick up, he said. A new work and he was going to ask Hector's advice, get a valuation.' Gertie laced her fingers and raised her eyes to heaven. 'It's only a matter of time before we're all round there, me and Ludo, Hector and Tani.'

Mrs Sidhu very much doubted that. The thought that was solidifying in her mind was that Ludo had to be the figure she had chased in the woods. He had *La Scaletta* and he was taking it to Hector. That made no sense. Why steal a painting just to return it?

That disquieted feeling stalked her all the way to the door. She had her fingers on the brass knob – it was cold to the touch and tingled the nerve ends – when a new thought broke on her. 'How do you come to know an artist based in Bristol? It must be a hundred miles away.'

'We used to live in Bristol. Before we bought this place. I used to run an arts society and Ludo bought and sold. Mainly art fairs. He started off selling junk in car boot sales. Glad to say we've improved ourselves since then. Anyway, we got to know artists from the local area.'

A car boot sale in Bristol. Mrs Sidhu's heart beat faster. Oh, my God, a car boot sale in Bristol. 'We have to go to Hector's house right now.'

Gertie put a large hand to her bosom. 'It's a little soon, I'll probably wait another week.'

'Not for your double date.' She spoke harshly, cutting her words sharply. 'We have to stop Ludo doing something terrible. He's heisted *La Scaletta*.'

Mrs Sidhu ran onto the street on her bruised and scratched feet. She could hear Gertie's flat-footed stride behind her and her puffing voice. 'I . . . don't . . . understand.' She panted. 'Ludo . . . couldn't . . . heist . . . anything.'

The distance between the Breeze and Peety House was short; the elaborate chimneys could easily be made out as they rounded the corner from the high street.

'Ben helped him.' Mrs Sidhu said. 'Don't ask me how, but I saw it with my own eyes.'

Gravel crunched underfoot as they passed the tall black gates of Peety House. In the distance she could hear sirens singing their discordant song.

Gertie gasped again. If she was trying to say something it was lost in asthmatic aspiration. 'Why would he do such a thing?'

They were at the front door, pushing it open. 'You really don't know?' Mrs Sidhu asked.

52

'Hello?' Hector called out into the darkness.

It was tiresome of Gertie Dalrymple to have all these people dropping in on him. He had left instructions that they should go straight to his collecting room.

Oh, yes, they were a nosy lot, these villagers, and he had his own privacy to think of. He dragged the walking frame ahead of him, with dry palms. This was no moment to . . . no, he pushed those thoughts to one side. Future plans had to wait until the chaos ended.

The collecting room was on the upstairs floor, and Hector made the journey there from his bedroom across finely woven Persian carpets. He was feeling impatient, ready for this to be over. To be rid of the walking frame. Yet Hector knew the value of theatre. Yes, the drugs overdose had taken a toll but again, the value of sympathy was not to be underestimated. Not only that, it was of course very useful that his investors, his customers, his circle, thought him an injured animal. Such an animal could strike with more surprise, could sell more art.

His shuffling perambulation brought him finally to the door of the collecting room. The sight of a muddy footprint on the threshold had him cursing Gertie Dalrymple once again. Who were these people she was sending up here? He shoved the door open with his frame.

Inside, it was blackness. He tried the light switch. Nothing. His jaw tightened. He tried it again, still nothing. These old English houses looked grand enough, but they were appalling to live in. He would have the fuseboard checked later.

For now, there was a window at the far end of the room, throwing what little light the night had to offer across the floor. More muddy footprints led towards the back of the room.

He heard a sound somewhere back there. Suddenly fearful, he held his breath a moment. The moment passed in silence. Shadows splayed from steel sculptures, looking down on him with hollow eyes. He told himself off for being silly.

A footstep broke the silence. 'Hello?' he repeated. 'Don't be shy.' Better turn on the charm for the locals. 'Very kind of you to come up and see me.' He shuffled his frame further into the room. The sound seemed to come from the direction of *Spaceman*, a life-sized sculpture. It was one of Barrow's, blending the costumes of knights, astronauts and superheroes. It was the one piece in his collection that, if he was being honest, Hector didn't really like. He was not a comic-book fan: superheroes, knights and astronauts were such childish fantasies. Of course though, popular themes, and it had suited his purpose to promote the work of Ned Barrow at the time.

Silence spread through the room like a blanket. That

twinge of fear pricked at his innards once more. Was someone playing games with him? Now he wished one of them were here now. Batman, Spider-Man, Catwoman. Such ridiculous pairings of animals and people. Still, superhuman strength would be so useful. He clenched his hands into pudgy fists. 'I'll call the police.' That's what heroes did, wasn't it? They gave the bad guy a fair warning. 'Make yourself seen,' he warbled, calling out into the darkness.

Every pair of eyes in the room seemed to be looking directly at him. One pair moved. The body they belonged to stepped forward. It was silhouetted and in its hand, it held something. Hector let go of the walking frame. In terror he took a step back while his hand groped for any kind of weapon. The slick of sweat on his back lubricated his gentle slide to the floor where he slumped, head in hands, stifling tears.

Nothing seemed to happen for a long time. When he opened his eyes, the figure was standing over him. He gasped. 'Oh, it's you. Thank God it's you. I was so scared.' He pulled himself up to standing, vainly trying to regain his dignity. 'I thought it was . . . I don't know what I thought.'

'You don't remember me, do you?' The figure loomed forward.

'Of course I do,' Hector snapped, wiping away the moisture from his face. He really had been a stupid fool, behaving so cravenly. Now he looked like an idiot. He adjusted his pink glasses, which had fallen skew-whiff across his nose in his panic. 'You run the gallery in town, we've bought several of your pieces.' His voice cracked. He put a stop to that straight away. He spoke louder, clearer; he was the one in charge. 'Listen here. I don't know what you want but we've been very supportive, I'd say.'

Ludo leered. 'Thank you, such charity from the great, the marvellous Hector Keys. The man with the golden eye. But you've bought one of my pieces before, many years ago.'

The man produced a knife and with one decisive slice he cut open the bindings on the bundle under his arm. The tarpaulin landed on the floor, the plastic crackling.

Hector's mouth opened and closed again, his pupils almost disappearing to pinpricks behind those neon-pink glasses. 'What on earth are you doing with that?' he gasped.

'Coming back, is it? Car boot sale, Bristol, ten or so years ago.' Ludo hefted the knife from one hand to the other. 'Starting to remember me now, are we?'

The sweat that had barely cooled on Hector's face from his earlier panic broke out on his face with renewed vigour.

'How about an expert valuation?' The hand was around him. The knife came up fast, a blur. 'What's a fair price? Four hundred quid, wasn't it?'

The lunatic was going to kill him. 'Steady on,' Hector said. His voice was cracking and he gave up trying to control it.

'You swindled me. You're going to pay,' Ludo breathed in his ear, clutching his knife with one arm and the painting with the other.

A moment of hope sounded as Hector heard voices. 'Up here!' he shouted.

Ludo grinned. 'They won't get here in time.' The knife point pressed, dimpling pink skin.

Hector's world moved in slow time. Banging footsteps

were rushing up the stairs. Faces Hector recognised came bursting through the door. Mrs Sidhu shouting, Gertie screaming.

It was too late.

Ludo drove the knife in hard and yanked it sideways, tearing a jagged line across bare flesh.

PART IV

Reputation is everything, in catering as in life.

Life With a Knife, Mrs Sidhu's Memoirs

53

'Well, Mr Dalrymple, you've been busy with your knife.'

DCI Burton had seen a lot of weird things in his career, but the sight that had met him in Hector Keys's collecting room was in the top ten.

Not for the first time, Burton reflected that Mrs Sidhu was like a cat. She had the habit of proudly dumping dead mice and birds at his feet. That left him the job of clearing up the mess and making sense of it all.

He had hoped it would make more sense in the sparse white interview room at Newton police station.

'Bring in the body, Dove,' Burton said.

A wave from Dove and officers in gloves carried in the sad remains of *The Bathing Pool* or *La Scaletta*. Dalrymple's first cut had torn a line through the unfortunate bather's neck, poor girl. He hadn't stopped there, and now the shredded canvas flapped like a flock of brightly coloured birds.

Dalrymple sat, back upright, stroking his belly through his frayed waistcoat, his mouth clamped shut.

'Mr Dalrymple, you've been caught red-handed with a stolen painting. Not only that, you've destroyed it. The only thing going your way is that you didn't hurt Mr Keys.' Burton smiled in a friendly way and sat on the edge of the table. 'It'd be better to just own up and then we can make this all as painless as possible.'

'Painless?' Ludo's large eye revolved, rolling to the ceiling. The smaller watched Burton with stink-eyed malevolence. 'Do you have any idea of how much pain that man has caused me?'

Mrs Sidhu had filled Burton in on Ludo's background, how he had sold *La Scaletta* for a few hundred pounds, how he had watched in shame and anger as the painting made Hector a rich and famous man, exalted for his 'golden eye'. How the other character in the legend of Hector's acquisition became the butt of art dealers' jokes the world over. He was the man who turned down the Beatles. How he had fled from Bristol, started a new life. And how that anger had burned ever brighter when the Keyses had moved in. The only saving grace was that the fool in the story remained anonymous. Only Ludo knew it was him, and that knowledge burned.

'Is that why you did it, then?' Burton asked. 'Was that the plan? To get even by extorting money from Hector Keys for the return of his painting? Then why destroy it?'

Dalrymple smiled, lips disappearing. 'I just wanted him to know what it felt like to have your heart torn out.' He stroked his bow tie. 'Now, if you want to know about the painting talk to Ben. I'd like to go home now.' He refused to say any more.

Burton ground his teeth. He sent Ludo to a holding cell

and summoned Ben Trimble. He was to get very little more out of the art teacher.

'Come on, let's get this over with, Trimble.' By this time it was the early hours. Burton circled the interview room like a weary vulture. 'We've got a witness who saw you with *La Scaletta* in your car, and saw you leave it in a remote piece of woodland.'

He stopped to lean over the table. Burton was a big man, and towering over the seated suspect usually had an impact. Trimble seemed not to notice, wrapped up in his own thoughts. 'She followed me up there?' Ben's eyes softened. He was like a child who's just found out Santa is only a man in a padded suit. 'You think you know people, trust them, and you think they trust you.' He nodded and for a moment Burton thought he was going to get a confession.

'What are you going to do with her?' Ben asked. 'Arrest her?'

Burton's neck blushed red at this point. 'Arrest *her*? What for?' He kept an icy calm in his voice.

'Invasion of privacy or something? Stalking? I mean, she followed me.'

Burton's icy calm shattered. He smashed his fist on the table. 'What was the plan? Steal the painting, then extort Mr Keys for the return? How long have you and Dalrymple been working together?'

Ben started. 'Hey, I haven't done anything wrong.'

'What do you call this, then?' He pointed to the slashed painting. In reply, Ben simply pointed to the bottom-right corner. 'That's my signature.'

A ripple of disquiet spread through Burton's chest. He looked closely, indeed there were the initials 'B.T.' Burton sent a uniform out for a printout of the original painting. He squinted his eyes. It was there, in the corner, the flamboyant signature of Gaston Lefevre. Burton stroked his neck, pacing before turning back to Ben. 'OK. You didn't steal the painting, you forged it. You still conspired to extort Hector Keys. That's two crimes.'

'I didn't conspire with anyone.' Ben leaned back in his chair, that slow smile creeping up under his moustache. 'And it's not a forgery if I signed it. It's a replica, an homage to the great artist. It was painted to order for a client.'

'Mr Ludo Dalrymple.'

'Apparently. I never knew who the client was until tonight. I just got a message from an anonymous email address with instructions. Half payment in advance and half cash on delivery. I held up my end of the bargain, and the client theirs.' Ben chuckled. 'Don't worry, I'll declare it on my tax return.'

In the end, Ludo confirmed that he'd commissioned Ben, and he hid his identity as so many art buyers do. Ludo had even invited Burton to an auction so he could see for himself. Burton had declined sharply. As for the performance at the Keyses' house, he had simply destroyed his own property. He couldn't even get him for breaking and entering. He was on his bloody wife's help rota; technically the Keyses had invited them in.

'What now, sir?' Dove asked when they got back to Burton's office.

Burton swivelled on his chair for a while, breathing softly. 'We don't have any choice.'

54

The doors opened and Mrs Sidhu was relieved to see Burton. 'What's going to happen?' she asked. 'Have you charged them?'

Newton police station waiting area had two sets of doors. The outer doors onto the street and the inner doors into the station. It was like an airlock, packed with the worst smells imaginable.

She seemed to have lost her privileges as far as going past the inner door was concerned. So she had been waiting in the cold silence and the bad smells, among the drunk people and the injured people, and the shouting mad people, until the sun bulged over the horizon. Now, seeing Burton approaching the doors, she stood.

Burton's face was cold, suffused with a strain of frustration and tiredness. 'We're letting them all go. That painting you tipped us off about was a copy painted by Trimble. Dalrymple paid for it legally,' he said without ceremony and held the door open.

'It was? He did?' Before Mrs Sidhu could ask any more

questions, Ludo shuffled out of the doors, a blanket draped over his shoulders. His eyes were on the floor, searching perhaps for the scraps of the dignity he had clearly dropped somewhere.

Gertie followed in his wake. 'Ludo, speak to me, please. Are you all right? Say something?' But Ludo marched on, seemingly mute from a mixture of cold shock and red-hot rage.

As they passed Mrs Sidhu, Ludo continued sleepwalking out through the door of the police station. Gertie stopped beside her; her eyes followed her husband's steady progress. 'Why didn't he tell me over all these years?'

Mrs Sidhu wanted to say that it had been the same with her own late husband. Why don't they tell their wives the important stuff? That over time the habits of marriage set like concrete, and we become frozen statues of our dynamic younger selves.

For the first time Mrs Sidhu saw herself in Gertie Dalrymple. Not in the heavy jaw or the over-use of chiffon and perfume to soften her naturally gruff personality. Had she spoken too often in her marriage, had she become set in concrete? Had she and her departed man become like the Dalrymples? A pair of dogs barking at each other. 'I'm sorry,' she said. 'At least you know.'

'A lot of good that does,' Gertie hissed at her. 'You had to go digging. Why can't people leave things alone?' She marched out of the door

'But –' Mrs Sidhu's voice faltered – 'I was just trying to help. Inspector, please tell them.'

Burton's face was impassive. 'People don't always want help, Mrs Sidhu.'

Mrs Sidhu was left with the words stinging her but had

very little time as Burton held the inner door open once more. This time Ben sidled through, making for the exit with long strides.

'Oh, Ben, I'm so glad to see you're all right.' Mrs Sidhu tugged at his elbow, hastening to keep up with him. 'You are all right, aren't you?'

'Never felt better.' His voice was stiff. 'I've been accused of everything from forgery to murder via theft.'

'It's been such a series of misunderstandings.' Mrs Sidhu got to the outer door first and held it open for Ben. 'I wish you'd let me explain.'

'Explain, what's to explain?' He pressed his fingers to his temples, caging them. 'You saw something, put one and one together and came up with twelve million. Then you followed me to the woods.' He was spluttering now. It was the first time she'd seen him angry. It was the first time she'd seen him anything but good-natured and having fun. 'Then you called the police to arrest me. Then chased a man through the same woods and followed him to Hector's house and had him arrested too. All makes perfect sense to me.' The length of his speech left him breathless.

Mrs Sidhu swallowed, then raised a hopeful smile. 'I thought you liked the different way my mind worked.'

He ground his jaw. 'Just stay away from me.'

He was ten feet from her, walking into the sunrise, before Mrs Sidhu found her words. 'I suppose the misunderstanding was mine. I couldn't imagine that someone with an extraordinary gift like yours, a gift for making things out of thin air, would want to copy something. It never crossed my mind. The first artwork you've produced in years, I expected something else, something out of this world.'

Ben stopped, and she walked to him. He was side on to her now, refusing to turn. Traffic was starting to pick up and in the distance two dogs played in the park and sniffed each other.

'You know what I think?' Mrs Sidhu said. 'I think you have talent but you're so busy not taking anything seriously, you don't take yourself seriously. Maybe you should.' She stood on tiptoe and planted a kiss on his cheek. 'I'm sorry for everything. Have a nice life.'

Ben walked on. If she could have seen his face, she would have seen a thoughtful look on it; she would have seen him touch his cheek and look at his hands.

Mrs Sidhu, however, never stood still for too long. She was back in her little green car and heading towards home and her bed.

All through the drive back asking herself questions, asking herself what she was doing in a place of such madness of iron monsters, and rock art and stolen paintings and forgeries and skull-masked women. It was only when she passed the 'Welcome to Slough' sign that she put all that behind her. Good old Slough, where life was simple.

She heaved the front door open and shucked off her coat and shoes. More than anything she wanted to sleep. She made for the kitchen, where a cup of hot milk had her name on it. Waiting for her was the very last person she wanted to see.

55

'I've solved all your problems,' Tez said.

It was raining, a gentle, almost soporific rain that fizzled against Mrs Sidhu's kitchen window in Slough. She was fading into Aloneness. In these moments, her skin would prickle and she would lose contact with the outside world. This could last minutes or hours.

'Mum, I've done it.' Tez, who had been waiting patiently for her to notice his triumphant attitude, decided he could wait no longer. He gripped the air and did a little dance. 'It's all going to be OK.'

She mumbled something that might have been a 'good morning' and wandered over to the fridge. She had no time for him. Tez was a distant voice right now, like the sound of surf in a seashell. Her own thoughts ran like an index finger racing along the line to find out what happened next.

She found the grey cards, torn and frayed at the edges. She secured each one to the fridge door with a magnet. They looked back at her. If old pieces of Cornflake packet could laugh, these were having a laugh riot. She wrenched at the cap of a marker pen. The lid pulled away with a pop and she spat it into the bin. It was time for an update. First she found Ludo's card, and made her changes.

LUDO DALRYMPLE
Runs rival gallery
Hates the Keyses
Could have drugged the food
But he left the Pump House before the robbery

Well, she had got to the root of that. Here she added:

Ludo was the man who sold 'La Scaletta' for peanuts

It was a solid motive, she thought, even though the police had released him. Except Ludo had a different plan: to dismember a fake version of *La Scaletta* in front of Hector and to watch him suffer. Not a sane plan, by any means, but why do that if he had the original?

'Listen to me, Mum, I've put both things right,' Tez continued, his excited voice muffled to her senses. 'First the Mrs Prakesh thing.'

She was oblivious, focused on the point of the marker as it hovered over the next card before she slashed a line through it all.

BEN TRIMBLE
~~Penniless artist~~
~~Handsome~~
~~Wonderful~~
~~Great kisser~~

> ~~Has 'La Scaletta' in the boot of his car~~
> ~~Could have drugged Hector's food~~
> ~~Needs the money~~
> ~~Delivered the painting to woods~~
> ~~Has an accomplice?~~

Then she wrote at the bottom.

> *Made a copy of 'La Scaletta' to sell to Ludo*

She threw the marker pen into the bin. She had no answers. The other cards were unchanged. Daisy's killer was still out there. No answers, just questions.

Swiping her hands across the fridge door, she knocked all the fridge magnets onto the floor. Daisy Carr deserved a proper tombstone. She took up a new marker pen, writing directly onto the silver metalwork.

> *How was 'La Scaletta' taken from the gallery?*
> *Why was the painting stolen in such a spectacular way?*
> *Why was Ivor killed?*
> *Where is Jenny Leblanc?*

'I'm sorry, I should have told you that I was working for her.' He manoeuvred himself around until he blocked her path.

Her son's face fuzzed into focus. Mrs Sidhu said, 'You did the right thing, you got yourself a job.' Even if it was with that grimacing hussy, she thought. 'Tez, that's not what I was upset about.' She slipped past him to stare at the fridge door once more.

'Oh. So what was it?'

'Um. What?'

Tez's face drifted into view again, his features pulled to the centre of his face, interrupting her view. 'What was it that upset you if it wasn't me frosting Mrs Prakesh's cake?'

Her fingers tightened on the marker pen. More than anything she wanted to continue her chain of thought. 'Is it important?' she asked, trying to dodge around him.

Tez blocked her path, arms crossed.

There was going to be no getting around him, avoiding what she was avoiding. The horror of Mrs Prakesh in her kitchen with her son leeched into her. What could she say? That her mind had leapt to the conclusion that they were frosting each other, on her kitchen counter? Mrs Sidhu tried to start a sentence three times, but each time she only got as far as taking in a breath and raising a single finger. Until, finally, a way out presented itself. 'What was the other thing?'

'Other thing?' Tez raised an eyebrow.

'You said you had two things to tell me.'

He beamed a wide smile. 'Oh, yeah, Varma's party.'

The chill of Mrs Sidhu's guilt melted by the flame of sudden indignation. She seized on it. 'That's what I was upset about! You, Mrs Prakesh, Mr Varma, all lying about his party.' It was true. It was humiliating to learn that the whole town had been sneaking around, whispering behind her back, planning and plotting. Her beady eyes drilled into Tez's.

'It was bad,' he said. 'We should have told you. Varma asked me about hiring you, and I told him you were going on holiday. He had to hire Mrs Prakesh. We all know how you feel about her, so we agreed it was better not to tell you.'

'Huh. I didn't even get an invitation!'

'That's why I sorted it out, talked to Varma. I got you an invite.' Tez gave a shrug. 'I just want to make everything right, Mum'

Some of the fire in her died down. That was actually quite thoughtful of him. She pouted. 'Well, I suppose that's something.' She shouldered past Tez. At least she could get back to her fridge door.

Tez let out a deep breath. 'I'm so glad you forgive me. And that's not all. I've got another surprise. It's not just an invitation to the party. I got us the gig. The biggest job in Slough. We're catering Varma's birthday.' He babbled happily. 'Isn't that great? You're working for Varma again!'

She wheeled back round to face Tez, his grinning teeth, his wide eyes. 'I'm doing what?' It was the shock spreading across Tez that told her she was shouting.

'Varma wants you back, Mum. Isn't that great?'

This was turning into a nightmare. 'But I stopped . . . I was free.' The anger leapt up in her again. 'And you went behind my back? Again?' Her balled-up fists banged on the fridge door. 'Who told you to interfere?'

Tez was unmoved. 'Mum, you need something normal in your life.' He cast a glance at the scribbles on the fridge, at the scattered pieces of cardboard on the floor. 'What's this supposed to be?'

'This,' she said firmly, 'is a crime fridge.'

Tez sighed and Mrs Sidhu had the reeling feeling that at the age of twenty-five her son had decided to become a grown-up. Well, too late – she was the grown-up around here.

With the sound of slippers crunching on fridge magnets she left the kitchen and stomped up to her bedroom. Once inside, she slammed the door, drew the curtains, crawled under her duvet and burst into tears. After which she finally fell into a restless sleep.

To Mrs Sidhu it seemed as though she danced in a stream of light, and that stream tumbled her through dizzying rapids and over waterfalls. It tore every part of her into pieces, into a blinding pool of sunlight that shook her bones with awe and tore the breath from her lungs until she was drowning.

She was broken into dots, tiny gleaming shards of colour, falling with one arm reaching up to try to break the surface, to hold on to that which could not be held.

The dots reassembled, pulling themselves into shapes that blurred like frosted glass until there was a hand, from nowhere, a hand reaching down to her. If only she could reach it, but she just kept falling, falling into the light, falling for ever into such a beautiful light. It would be so easy to give in. The light could take her. She woke up.

She was lying on her back, and even with a stiff breeze billowing the curtains she was drenched in sweat, her skin burning like a forest fire. Her mouth was wet, a trail of saliva trickled down her cheek onto the pillow. The swirls on the ceiling were like giant sequins and their swirling threatened to drag her back down. She tried to rearrange her thoughts, force herself away from the realm of sleep into the land of the living.

She slipped quietly out of bed and took a shower, letting the water gush over her until she felt normal again while the dream faded.

She dressed, padded downstairs, and grabbed her car keys and coat. She had business on her mind. Tez might have dodged her anger, but she had every intention of giving Varma a piece of her mind.

56

There was to be no sleep for DCI Burton. Returning to his desk he found Sergeant Dove waiting for him. On his desk was an evidence bag, inside it a red rock.

'We've got the test results back from the rock, sir, the murder weapon. You want to know what, sir?' Dove stood with his fingers interlaced, his two forefingers pressed against his lips.

Of course he wanted to know what. Burton waited for the answer. He was beginning to detest these dramatic silences from Dove, but he gave in with an uneasy sigh. 'Yes, Dove, please do tell me, Dove. I want to know, Dove,' he said with biting sarcasm.

Burton's tone was, as usual, wasted on Dove. He continued unabashed. 'The blood and hair on the rock belong to Ivor Langtree and Daisy Carr – it's a DNA match.' He slapped his hands on his thighs to emphasise the importance of the news, a shining look of joy on his wobbling cheeks.

Burton picked up the evidence bag; it crinkled in his

hands as he turned it over. 'That's good,' he said. 'Not exactly a surprise, but it ties things up.' His back straightened. 'All this has been a distraction. Ivor Langtree and Daisy Carr were both killed at the gallery on Saturday night. Jenny Leblanc remains our primary suspect. She used Ivor Langtree to help her steal the painting, then killed him. We need to find her.' As Dove said nothing and as Burton continued to wait for him to say something a new thought occurred to Burton. He sighed. 'Have I interrupted your flow, Dove?'

'There is actually more, sir, and I thought it was worth pausing because it's weird and without a decent pause it might just get swallowed up.'

With a wave of his arm Burton indicated that Dove had the floor. 'Please.'

Dove cleared his throat and walked to the door. Once there he whirled round. It was what the crime fans called 'a Columbo turn'. However, when executed by a tubby British sergeant who had to recover from a bout of giddiness afterwards, it lacked the panache of the original. 'Ivor Langtree's and Daisy Carr's blood and hair are not the only blood and hair on the rock.'

Burton ground his jaw. 'You could have mentioned that before, Dove.'

'Yes, sir. I'm doing all this for emphasis, sir.'

'So Leblanc has killed or hurt someone else. Someone is either dead or walking around with a serious head wound. Hospitals?'

'Checked them, sir. Lots of head wounds, but no one in the last forty-eight hours.'

Burton screwed his eyes shut tight, fighting the urge to scream. Maybe he had got this wrong. Maybe Mrs Sidhu had got this right. There was another possibility. Now, the grim truth was dawning that he had to front up to what he had been avoiding for the last day. He picked up his car keys and threw them to Dove. 'Come on, Dove, you'd better drive.'

It took twenty minutes for them to fetch up at the doors to the Digbourne Hotel.

'You sure about this, sir?' Dove asked.

He was sure, at least, of one thing. It was going to hurt.

At the Digbourne Hotel lobby he showed his warrant card, but it hardly seemed necessary. The receptionist's hand covered a smirk. She recognised him.

In the restaurant, he conjured up his dinner with Jenny Leblanc. It was like poking a sore tooth, checking that the pain was still there, recoiling at the soreness of the touch. 'He wanted to keep me away from the danger,' she had said.

Then poking where the pain was deeper, they took the elevator. Burton suffered disjointed flashbacks. The drugs had been kicking in hard by then, but the memory of passion and kisses flooded over him.

Then finally, in a silent ritual, they put on white jumpsuits and plastic overshoes and snapped on latex gloves. Burton tugged down the police tape on the door and entered. They stood over the bed in her hotel room. Dove had his hands folded together, like a mourner at a funeral. Burton winced to see the handcuffs still dangling from the headboard.

He blinked. He had to see it dispassionately, block off his humiliation and anger. Just the facts. Her straddling him fully clothed, him half-awake and half-asleep, undressed. He had looked into her eyes. The look of her was desperate, not triumphant. 'I'm so sorry about this,' she had whispered, her eyes tearing up, her face an apology.

When Burton finally spoke his voice was quiet.

'All right, Dove, get anything you can. We need her DNA. Hair, body fluids, anything. Then get the lab to check it against the third trace on the rock.'

'Why would she bonk herself on the head, sir?'

'She wouldn't, Dove. That's what I'm worried about.'

And they got to work.

Burton was striding through the doors of Newton police station when he got the phone call. A mechanical voice, heavily filtered, told him he should check his inbox. His desk computer pinged and there it was, marked as urgent. No salutation, no message, just a video attachment. He watched it twice, unblinking.

57

Mrs Sidhu pulled up into Varma's cash-and-carry car park. Brown leaves scattered the ground, and now that rain had given way to sunshine once more, steam was rising from the asphalt like smoke over the river. Mrs Sidhu crossed the black, misted expanse and felt like a ghost. A few of Varma's burly lads were emptying pallets of boxes in through the wide-open warehouse door. They stopped to respectfully greet their 'aunty' as she passed into the building. She received their respect with a curt nod. She was in no mood to chat.

She made her way past the bulk discount opportunities declaimed in large multicoloured letters. The smell of disinfectant, mingled with the aroma and spices, advertised in one sniff the width and breadth of Varma's stock. She climbed a flight of steps, her flat heels clanging on the painted metal stairs. At the top she pushed through a doorway marked 'Private'.

Once inside, the atmosphere changed completely. Linoleum gave way to garish carpet and the jarring smells outside were replaced with lavender and sandalwood. Light music was playing, something with a bossa nova rhythm.

'Mrs Sidhu, I want you.' Varma was smiling and swaying at the hips. He clicked his fingers to the beat. 'Actually, I need you.' He strode dramatically across the floor and took her hand. 'Do you dance?'

'Actually, no,' she said as Varma dragged her across the room regardless. 'Mr Varma, what are you doing?'

'This is just a bit of morning aerobics.' Varma stopped, spun and with a twirl dumped Mrs Sidhu onto an easy chair, while he made his way round his desk. While Mrs Sidhu pulled her hair out of her eyes and tried to arrange herself with dignity, he spoke. 'I'm so glad you've come.'

That was a state of mind Mrs Sidhu would be happy to change. 'Mr Varma, how could you? You kept your birthday a secret from me. I demand an explanation.' And she got one.

Varma wrung his hands and explained how it had seemed best at the time. How when he heard about her holiday he genuinely – genuinely, mind – had not wanted her to cancel it, being genuinely (that word again) concerned for her health.

By then Mrs Prakesh's services had been engaged, otherwise he assured Mrs Sidhu that she would have been first on his invitation list, and first choice to cater. 'The thing is, Mrs Sidhu, I was embarrassed. By the time you came to me for advice, it was all too late. We thought it was best to keep it from you. I can see now that was a mistake.'

During this long speech, Mrs Sidhu had built up a tension in her body that longed for release. She had a long speech planned too and was in the mood to take the stage.

As if sensing this, Varma gave her no chance. He stepped to his next point, as nimble with his mind as with his feet.

'But now I feel like I have this completely undeserved opportunity. An opportunity to engage your catering brain. I am so glad you came back to me.'

Again, Mrs Sidhu had some choice, finely chosen words to say on the subject of coming back to work for Varma. Again, Varma was ahead of her.

'The thing is, Mrs Sidhu, it's not often that someone like me gets a chance like this.' Here he took the opportunity to bow his head to her undoubted greatness. 'A chance to employ someone who has catered an ART GALLERY opening.'

He looked at Mrs Sidhu's head as if he could eat it. It was very off-putting. 'I want you to cater my birthday. Before you say anything, please remember that when you started off as a caterer, I was there for you. I funded you. I supported you. I gave you employment.'

The anger that she had built up throughout Varma's frankly self-serving speech suddenly ebbed away, and speech over, Mrs Sidhu took a moment to calmly collect herself, to reflect on Varma's words before saying what she had on her mind.

'Phooey!' was what she had on her mind. 'You wanted me out of the way so that I wouldn't embarrass you at your party.'

'How could you possibly do that?'

'By being me, that's how. It's what I do, I alienate people.' Her gaze fell to the floor. 'It's my speciality. For your own sake, stick with Mrs Prakesh – everyone seems to like her.' She finished glumly. 'Even my own son.'

Mr Varma grimaced and then continued, with a greasy

smile. 'Mrs Prakesh makes excellent food, hearty food, wholesome food but it's traditional, budget stuff. I need someone who can make expensive food, fancy food, with strange names that no one can pronounce. I want people to associate me with fine cuisine.'

'Mr Varma, there are lots of restaurants opening up in Slough with exciting food. Just ask any one of them to cater.'

Varma seemed to struggle with what he wanted to say. His head dropped and with it all the pretence, all the cheap charm and bluster. He played with the end of his tie. 'The truth is, I need this to be from me, from a personal connection. So people will see me in a different light, see me as a new man, not some old relic. I'm turning sixty, Mrs Sidhu.' His voice was small and low. 'Suddenly I feel old.'

Mrs Sidhu felt a tug at her heart. She had never seen Varma this vulnerable before and it was cutting against her instincts. Maybe he was a changed man. How could she say no? 'Very well.' She raised a warning finger. 'But only as a one-off, mind.'

'Excellent,' said Varma. 'Now, when I say expensive food, I don't want you to take that too literally.' It took five minutes of Varma scratching out his plan with a pencil on a pad of paper for him to prove he had changed very little. He outlined Mrs Sidhu's budget, which in the final analysis was laughably small, and his ambitions, which were grandiosely large.

He had even used terms like 'locally sourced', and when Mrs Sidhu explained to him that didn't mean sourced from his cash-and-carry warehouse, his eyes opened in wonder. 'I'm learning so much.'

Mrs Sidhu left Varma's cash-and-carry with the piece of paper curled in her hands. 'I just want it to go perfectly, Mrs Sidhu.'

Outside, she turned the key and pumped the accelerator on her car. The engine whinnied into life like a tired horse. As she drove away, new thoughts were playing new tunes in her mind.

Varma wanted his event to be perfect. She had catered weddings, funerals, birthdays and everything in between. It was hardly an unusual request. This time, though, it turned her mind in an entirely new direction. There was a question she had not asked herself, not on the Cornflake cards and not on her crime fridge.

Important events have to go perfectly. Every caterer knows that.

Mrs Sidhu worked, and worked hard, for three days. She worked as she had for the Pump House opening. She chopped, she cooked, she fried, boiled and roasted until sweat soaked her hair, and damped her whites. In between she schooled Tez on food preparation, presentation and most of all on how to deport himself as a waiter. There was no reason why the people of Slough should not be treated to the highest standards.

She had to find a gift, of course. Something appropriate for an important birthday. Varma, like her late husband, was a difficult man to shop for. He had everything, and a new tie or a pair of slippers hardly seemed appropriate for a big birthday. She had to think of something.

At the same time, she could not entirely still her new line of thought.

On the morning of the party she stood in front of her

fridge. It was stocked up, all the food chilled and ready to transport. It was when the door slapped closed that a doubt tugged at her mind.

The fridge door was as she had left it: tall, grey, covered in black writing. It was Daisy Carr's tombstone and a reminder of Mrs Sidhu's failure to bring her killer to justice. Maybe that's why she had blanked it out of her mind the last few days.

The final questions surrounding her death were still unanswered. Today, there was another question.

She scrambled around in her drawer until her fingers closed over cold plastic. She pulled the lid off the marker pen with her teeth and spat it out into a bin.

Important events have to go perfectly. Every caterer knows that. That's when you turn to the ones you can trust.

This question was so simple she had never even thought of it up to now, but it was the key to the whole thing. With the chiselled point of her marker she wrote it up, squeezing it in above the others.

Why did the Keyses hire ME?

58

Blue-white light flickered on Burton's face. 'Play it again, Dove.'

The digital team had hustled Burton out of his office as soon as he told them about the email attachment. While they picked over his computer for any clues as to the attachment's sender, they were using Dove's desk.

Burton plucked at a Twix wrapper and dropped it in the bin. Dove failed to take the hint, and Burton sighed and decided he might as well just rest his elbows on the piles of chocolate and sweet wrappers and discarded fast food cartons.

Dove rewound and they sat through the message once again.

Burton leaned back in his chair. The video followed the format of kidnappers and hostage-takers the world over with one exception. The hostage, placed on a chair, dead square of camera, was not a wide-eyed, gagged human being, but a painting. The rest of the script ran as per normal. 'I have the painting. I want two million pounds in cash in exchange for it. Used notes in a briefcase.' This came from the Angel, the woman in the sequinned skull mask. The background was disguised with a bedsheet strung across it, the lighting was harsh and stark. 'The exchange will take place tonight, at eight o'clock, at this location.' She held up a map with a red X mark on it and the video stopped abruptly.

'She matches the description, sir,' Dove said. 'She's been smart, we can't trace the IP.' Dove leaned in. 'Do you think it's Jenny Leblanc, sir?'

Burton didn't answer directly. 'Did the DNA results come back from her hotel room?' he asked.

'Just in, sir. It's Jenny Leblanc's blood on the rock.'

He grunted. He had no idea what he had been hoping for, positive match or negative.

He looked again at the frozen frame on the screen. One thing was certain. The woman on screen wasn't Jenny Leblanc, he just knew it from the way she moved. There was something familiar about her but it wasn't Jenny.

Burton shut the computer window down, blinking out the carefully arranged hostage tableau. He checked his watch and stretched. 'Eight o'clock, she says. She hasn't given us much time.'

'So we can't plan a sting, sir.'

'Let's see about that. First, we've got a house call to make.'

'That's the end of the recording,' Burton said. His large frame was perched once again on the edge of the white sofa in the Keyses' living room. It was too low for a man of his height, and his long legs folded almost in half. He clutched his knees to keep himself upright. Hector and

Tani sat either side of him while his laptop lay on the coffee table in front of them. 'What do you think?'

'Hmmmm. Fascinating. Visceral. Raw.' Hector rubbed his thumb against his cheek. 'It's so stark, so dark.'

'He's not asking for a review of the video piece, Hector.' Tani lit a cigarette, the smoke curled around her fingers. 'Two million pounds.' Her other hand was wound around a gin and tonic, ice rattling against the edges. 'It's a fraction of the painting's value. Why are they asking for so little?'

'We think they're desperate.' The smoke from the cigarette stung his eyes. 'They steal the painting and they're out of their depth. They realise how hard it is to sell with the police looking for it. So they make an offer. You've already put up a million for the reward, so why not ask for two?'

Tani had to lean forward past Burton's body to get Hector's attention. 'Is it our painting?'

Hector pushed his face up to the laptop, his nose almost touching the screen. 'Undoubtedly.'

'I recommend that you accept.' Burton coughed, waving cigarette smoke away. 'The woman's outfit matches the description of the woman who stole your boat and made off with the painting. It's either Jenny Leblanc or another accomplice.'

'Nonetheless, two million pounds is quite an outlay,' Tani said.

'You'll get it back. The plan is to seize the painting, the thieves, the whole gang. If you want those responsible for Ivor's death to be punished, we need to catch these people.'

'I do.' She crushed her cigarette into the ashtray. 'Then it looks like we have little choice. What do we do now?'

Burton shifted uncomfortably. 'The drop is tonight. It's short notice to get hold of two million pounds in cash. If you can't raise it in time, we can try to negotiate another drop, but we don't know how that will go down.'

'The money isn't a problem,' Hector said quickly. 'As you say, I already have a million for the reward money. And we always keep some cash in the safe.'

Tani scoffed. 'I don't know if we have another million in the safe, Hector.'

'I'm sure we do,' Hector said. 'We were talking about that small Cézanne, remember? In the end we decided against.'

Tani seemed to search her memory. 'Yes, I must have forgotten.' She drained her gin and stood, coming round to stand behind Hector. He was still entranced by the video.

Burton let forth a sigh of wonder. These people had two million pounds in cash around the house.

Tani seemed to sense his thoughts. 'When Hector sees something he wants, I get it for him.' She stroked Hector's silver hair. 'It's always a good return on my investment. I hope that's the case here, Chief Inspector.' She spoke casually. 'Do you want the cash now?'

'I'll send a car for it, with a security detail and a receipt for you to sign.'

As Burton unfolded himself from the sofa, his knees cracked, complaining about their long captivity. 'I'll be taking personal charge of the operation,' he said.

59

From the beginning she'd had doubts about the Pump House job. Not that it would lead to double murder or a multi-million-pound art theft. She could not have expected that. Doubts, rather, that this was not a job meant for her.

First there was her creative block. Why was it so hard to think up food for a catering job? She had done it hundreds of times in the last few years. It was for the same reason that Varma had found such a new respect for her. But this job, catering a gallery opening, felt like a sudden, dizzying step up. Anyone could see that. Yet the Keyses had hired her anyway.

Mrs Sidhu's pulse was picking up pace. There was a name in her mind, a name that Tani had mentioned the first time she went to the Keyses' house for that catering trial, a name Tani had mentioned. What was it?

Mrs Sidhu rubbed her brow, trying to force the memory to the surface. She was certain that it began with an M. Mike? No, it was longer, two syllables. Michael? Martin? Too ordinary, there was something more exotic about it, something European, something French. Marcel? Mathieu? No, it could be French but it could be English too. She had it.

'What about Maurice?' That's what Tani had said.

Good. She stilled her mind from racing ahead too fast. Enough for now that on the subject of catering, there existed a Maurice. She moved on, because there was another puzzling element to the job: the fee.

At the time she worried that it was too good to be true. Perhaps she should have listened to her instincts. But they had made her an offer she couldn't refuse.

The art class was coming to an end when Mrs Sidhu arrived. Ben was packing up his easels, paints and pencils. She approached, swallowing back her nerves. It was just a few short hours ago that Ben had left the police station after a night's questioning. She quelled her dread, tried to concentrate only on the answer she needed. She tried to concentrate on Daisy, whose killer still walked free.

As she approached, he stopped packing and looked at his paint-stained fingers. 'I'm afraid you've missed the class.'

'I wasn't sure, after last night, if you'd want me here. I still haven't finished my picture.' She pulled it out of her bag, with a struggle that only added to her embarrassment. 'You see.'

He picked at his fingernails. 'You've paid, the space is yours,' he said coldly and added, 'there's one class left in the series.'

She nodded and put the picture away again. Once again the struggle to wedge it back into the bag giving her a hot flush. 'I really did enjoy dinner last night,' she said.

A snort came out of his mouth. It might have been

surprise or disgust. 'Well, you're not here about dinner and you've missed the class, so what can I do for you?' He drew himself up, and she could see his eyes were clouded, his face creased and cold. Even his moustache had lost all its cheeky intrigue. She wondered if she'd ever see that slow smile again. Thinking that only made her realise how much she wanted to.

Mrs Sidhu's head pulled back into her neck. She felt numb, unable to process Ben's speech for a pause. She fumbled with her top cardigan button. 'The Keyses, do they have a regular caterer they use?'

Ben looked surprised at the question. 'I don't know exactly.' Paintbrushes clattered as he threw them into a jar. 'I seem to remember some snooty-looking man at one gathering of theirs. A lot of dry fish stuff.'

'You don't remember the name?'

He snapped another easel closed. 'Gertie will know – ask her. She'd love to talk to you, I'm sure. Gertie!' Before she could stop him, he had beckoned her over. 'I have to pack up so if you'll excuse me . . .' Ben turned his back to her and continued his work in pained silence.

Gertie came over, sketchpad clutched under her arm. She eyed Mrs Sidhu with more suspicion than hurt. 'Surprised to see you here.'

'I can't apologise enough for what happened last night,' Mrs Sidhu stuttered. 'It was a misunderstanding.' She glanced at the space behind Gertie, a space absent and empty.

'Ludo is taking the day in bed. If that's any wonder.'

'I just happened to wonder if you know the name of the caterer the Keyses normally use. They do have a regular one, don't they?'

'They certainly do.' Her fingers closed on her heavy

chin. 'It's Dent's of Windsor. They're very grand.' Her eyes narrowed. 'Mr Dent is very discreet.'

Mrs Sidhu's mouth was dry. 'Dent's of Windsor. Would that be *Maurice* Dent?' On Gertie's curt nod Mrs Sidhu licked her lips. This was exactly the information she had been expecting. 'Tell me, when the Keyses hired me, were you surprised at all?'

'At the time, I just thought it was Hector being original and capricious. But if you ask me now – yes, frankly I don't know what they were thinking of.'

Note to self, thought Mrs Sidhu, don't ask Gertie for an online review.

'We've used them for Arts Society meetings too.' Gertie smiled thinly, and offered up more, perhaps as an attempt at injury rather than supplying information. 'Maurice Dent's not just a caterer, he happens to be very knowledgeable about art. Everyone likes him. But suddenly the Keyses dropped him. For you.' Gertie's thoughts on that needed no online review.

It was only when Mrs Sidhu was leaving the little group, when she was deep in thought, that she heard Ben speak. 'Don't know why I'm telling you this but I'm going to start painting originals again.' When she turned to look, he was walking away, an easel under his arm, his head uncharacteristically bowed.

'Hello, Dent's of Windsor.' The voice at the end of the phone was nasal and high-pitched. 'Maurice Dent speaking.'

Mrs Sidhu knew of Dent's. High class, high end – in fact, it was just the sort of operation she aspired to be.

She had weighed up her options. To go in person would give her a chance to read him, the nuances of face and body that a person can't hide. Then again that would give him the same opportunity with her. Mrs Sidhu had a decent poker face, but she hardly looked like one of his typical clients. Her appearance, and any lack of confidence on her part, would raise questions from the start.

To call on the phone would give her less chance to watch, but she could be more direct and by tone of voice she could command more respect. That was what she had chosen. 'Mr Dent, I have a question. Am I right in thinking that the Keyses at Bowler's Green are clients of yours?' Her tone was musing and warm. Despite not being there in person she had taken care to stage things meticulously. She went to her bedroom, so as not to be disturbed by a chance knock at the door. She blocked out the wood-chip wallpaper, the Artex ceiling, the tired curtains and sagging bed, by blinkering her eyes with her hands.

On the dresser, her old-woman painting glowered at her, red-eyed. It was her only piece of original art so it was there to get her into the part, a talisman to help channel her persona.

'Oh, yes, we hold the Keyses as valued customers.' His voice dropped. 'Such a tragedy about *La Scaletta*. A great painting, one of the most important pointillist pieces of all time.'

'Indeed, a painting you know well, I expect.'

'It hung in their house and, as I say, I regularly cater there. I'd know it anywhere.'

'I thought so. I was very surprised you didn't cater the opening of their gallery. We were talking about it at the last meeting. We all thought it must be because you were already booked up.'

There was a cold silence, and an awkward cough. 'What meeting would that be?'

'Oh, I should have said. The Berkshire Arts Society. I've just joined. I'm a collector, moved to Bowler's recently.' She was careful to shorten the name, knocking the 'Green' off, as she'd heard the locals do. 'My name is Mrs Sidhu—Sidhuson. We're a very old family, and everyone in the society says you're such fine caterers.'

'Oh, thank you. The little gathering the society had on the early impressionists made a huge *impression* on me.' He laughed at his own joke.

Mrs Sidhu followed suit. 'So very droll. That's why we like to use you – you combine food with such a deep knowledge of art.'

'I don't like to brag, but we do all the art events at Windsor Castle. The Keeper of the Royal Paintings is a valued client.'

For a man who didn't like to brag, he did a lot of bragging.

'And the Keyses,' Maurice said. 'They have been customers of ours since they moved to Berkshire. Such a pleasure to be in their house.'

This was the moment she had been waiting for, the moment to drop in the question and to do it casually. 'I know, and talking of pointillism, have you seen the Seurat in their hallway?'

Maurice Dent leapt on it. 'You mean the Pissarro? It's a Pissarro in his pointillist phase.'

Mrs Sidhu paused for so long that Maurice Dent thought the line had gone dead. 'Hello?'

Mrs Sidhu jerked back to the present. 'Do you know, I did wonder, it's just that someone else mistook it for a Seurat.'

He laughed uproariously. 'Oh, that's a good one, it really is. I bet Hector had a good chuckle about that. I mean, what sort of people are they letting into the Arts Society these days?'

The ice was broken, she could try her question again. 'I know, that's why we were so surprised when you weren't at the Pump House.'

Maurice didn't miss a beat – they were old friends now. 'Not as surprised as I was.'

'Were you already booked up?'

'Not at all. Apparently it was entirely Hector's decision.'

That was all she needed to know, but Maurice continued.

'They say he went with some dreadful woman from Slough. Scraping the bottom of the barrel.'

Mrs Sidhu spoke through clenched teeth. 'I wouldn't say dreadful.'

'Oh, come on.' Maurice Dent chuckled. 'You're being too kind. I heard she tried to make everything look like a dessert. I mean, amateur hour. Thank goodness they regained their sanity.'

'What do you mean?'

'Hector called just this morning. They want me for the gallery reopening tonight. Short notice, but for Hector Keys, one moves mountains.'

'Of course.' Before she put the phone down, she had one last thing to ask. 'Just so I have the information, what would you charge for an event like that?'

Maurice Dent mentioned a figure. It was half what the Keyses had offered her.

Downstairs, back in her kitchen, thoughts were turning in Mrs Sidhu's fertile mind.

On the biggest night of their lives the Keys abandoned their trusted, snooty Cordon Bleu, by Royal Appointment caterers and instead gave her, a chef from Slough, a trial and picked her without hesitation. She was a good cook, she was under no illusions about that, and a decent caterer, whatever Maurice Dent thought. She also knew that people like the Keyses would never take a risk on her after eating only one pudding.

Then there was the matter of the mistake.

She recalled the night that they had hired her, the trial, and then Hector taking her through the house, stopping to adjust the painting before announcing that it was a Seurat. Maurice would not have chuckled so much if he'd known that it was Hector Keys who had mixed up his own Pissarro for a Seurat. Now why would a man of Hector Keys's obvious art knowledge and sophistication make such a mistake? The answer to that was simple. He wouldn't.

Mrs Sidhu sensed another cog turning in the plan and another little lever kicked into place.

The crime fridge loomed up.

Why did the Keyses hire ME?

Her jaw clenched tight. The marker squealed across the fridge door.

Because I know nothing about art

Not only that, but they gave her a fee twice that which Dent would have charged: an offer she couldn't refuse.

She capped her marker. That was it, the chain of thought

came to an end, there was nothing else. She searched her insides: they were cold and empty. She still didn't have anything to tie this altogether. For some reason, the Keyses needed a caterer who was ignorant about art and would do anything to get her. That was all she had. There seemed no reason for it.

That was one down. She moved to the next question on the fridge.

How was 'La Scaletta' taken from the gallery?

It was in *The Knight*. She knew that. There was no other explanation. Yet her marker stopped short of the fridge. She took her Evidence Tupperware from her bag, looked again at the pieces. She still had no explanation for them. Something seemed off.

'You ready, Mum?' Tez was at her side. When she looked up at him, confused to see him in waiter's black and white, he raised an eyebrow. 'Varma's party. It's time.'

Her hand flew to her mouth. 'Oh my, have you got him a gift, Tez?'

Tez froze. 'I never thought of that.' He looked at his phone. 'We have to be there in twenty minutes. We'll stop at the petrol station on the way.'

'We can't give him something from the petrol station. It's his sixtieth.'

Mrs Sidhu chewed her fingers in thought. Tez circled the kitchen, head down. 'There is one thing,' he said eventually. When he explained his idea, Mrs Sidhu hastily agreed. They wrapped the gift together.

60

It was, in the end, a far cry from the Pump House opening.

Varma had gone the extra mile hiring the entire bar area of the Heathrow Holiday Inn. He could have gone a mile further up the road and hired the Hilton, but he must have run out of petrol.

If Mrs Sidhu was bracing herself for open hostility on the hotel floor, she did not meet it. She was almost disappointed. The occasion was pleasant and low key. She received hugs and Tez gave out dishes. She had gone with her old crowd-pleaser favourites – Indian dishes with a fusion twist – while keeping the menu within Varma's restricted budget.

The birthday boy himself was holding centre stage among a younger band of up-and-coming Asian retail entrepreneurs. He greeted Mrs Sidhu warmly. 'This food is excellent, Mrs Sidhu. I never knew high-class cuisine could be so frugal.' He slapped her back, while his young guns nodded their approval. 'Every one of you should take note – Mrs Sidhu is a top caterer and a top businesswoman.

If you need someone to whip up an affordable menu for your event, she is your go-to gal. She is living proof that if you work hard, you get what you deserve.'

Mrs Sidhu's heart swelled and she covered her blush. 'Mr Varma is too kind. Don't listen to him.'

Varma laughed. 'You see, what a saleswoman!' He slapped her back again, causing her to choke.

Only Mrs Prakesh brought her bitchy 'A' game. 'Oh, Mrs Sidhu, how delightful to see you here.' She smiled her lizard smile. 'These saag-meat bites are so different. So slimy, so bitter, I mean, you can really taste the cooking oil. How do you do it?'

Mrs Sidhu wanted to say that slimy, bitter and oily should be Mrs Prakesh's strapline, but she bit her tongue for Varma's sake. The last thing he wanted was a scene at his big birthday.

Mrs Prakesh was not to be held back, though. 'I thought with your art gallery job you'd be too big for Slough these days. Oh, I completely forgot, you managed to kill your client. Let's hope nothing goes wrong today.' Mrs Prakesh drifted away to spread evil and discord elsewhere, leaving Mrs Sidhu fuming. Here she was, back in Slough, getting static shocks from synthetic carpets, and being pouted at by the likes of Mrs Prakesh.

Her thoughts were interrupted by Tez. 'Mum, the slide show is starting. Come quickly.' He led her by the hand as everyone gravitated to a big screen. Varma was fiddling around with a digital projector, while rejecting help from a young nephew. 'I can do it, just give me a minute.' Varma waggled a wire and the screen lit up.

Male pride. Her mind rewound to Burton's slide show on day one of the police investigation. The demonstration had proved that the crime was virtually impossible. The disappearance of *La Scaletta* in such a short time frame had to be something of a miracle. That was before they knew how it was done, hidden in *The Knight* along with poor Ivor's body. There was no other way of getting it out.

Varma, meanwhile, had got the first slide up. It was a picture of him and Mrs Sidhu's husband long before they were married. It must have been the Seventies – they were boys more than men, and very groovily attired in matching cowboy jackets. She smiled, despite herself, to see her husband again, so young, posturing. So much of him in Tez.

Another picture clicked up. 'Bilhar Bhatti!' The cry came from Mrs Sidhu's mouth with a soft smile of remembrance of those soft lips. The fact that it was echoed by several other women in the room almost made her laugh.

Bilhar Bhatti had been the wild boy of Slough when Mrs Sidhu was a teenager. Bilhar could build an entire bicycle out of stuff he found on the dump.

Across the room eyes met hers, mirthful, sharing a joke that the men couldn't.

There followed more laughter, more memories, stretching from the Seventies up to the present day. She had asked Tez to give her a signal when the show was coming towards the end. He did so now, jerking his wrist up and tapping his watch.

Mrs Sidhu busied herself lighting the candles on the cake, barely finishing as Varma called out, 'Last slide!'

Before Varma could bring the last picture up, the projection winked out again. Mrs Sidhu blinked and held very still. Something new was stirring at the back of her mind.

Meanwhile, there was a groan from around the room. Varma swore and started waggling the wire, his nephew begging his uncle to let him help.

When the image leapt up again, Mrs Sidhu felt as though the electric current was wired directly into her brain. 'Do it again!' she cried out. Blood drained from her face, her eyes locked on the projection. She lurched forward like a zombie, in doing so knocking into the trestle table and sending onion bhajis frisbeeing across the room. The birthday cake teetered, wobbled and seemed about to settle. Oblivious, Mrs Sidhu took her second step, giving it an extra bump and sending it careening. It hit the floor, shattering into lumps of sponge and globs of icing. Burning candles scattered in all directions.

Varma hopped from foot to foot. 'Mrs Sidhu! What have you done?' Small fires were starting around the hotel lounge.

Mrs Sidhu, though, barely saw it. She was in another place and another time. She clutched the projector wire and waggled it. On, off, on, off went the photograph.

She left the party without so much as glancing back. If she had, she would have seen Varma trying to stomp out the flames around his pile of gifts.

Her mind was occupied with only one thought. There was another way of getting the painting out of the gallery.

Mrs Sidhu was back in her kitchen, in front of the fridge door again. Her mind whirled as she stood, hand stroking the small of her back. She had so much she had to get straight, but this was so confusing. So unbelievable, so crazy.

There was a plan at work here. She sensed it clicking

and whirring away like so many intricate cogs and levers. She had just been ignoring it all along.

Pressing her head against the metal door she closed her eyes. She had felt like this before, not so long ago, overwhelmed by possibilities. 'Creative constraints,' she muttered. 'Everything must be orange.'

She stood back and looked at the next question on her list.

How was 'La Scaletta' taken from the gallery?

She recalled three incidents, the first of which was Burton's re-enactment using an overhead projector. The second was the slide show at Varma's party, when the projector broke down. The last was her private audience with the great painting. How full of light it had been, so much so it had plagued her dreams. So . . .

How was 'La Scaletta' taken from the gallery?

She just needed a starting point, a constraint that once made, everything else would flow from. What if it wasn't inside *The Knight*? What was the alternative? Once again the marker scraped across the fridge.

It was never in the gallery.

Then, hardly daring to think she had written what she had been trying to avoid thinking since Varma's party, she took up her marker pen once more.

It was a projection

That was why the Keyses had abandoned their usual art snob caterer and chosen one from humble old Slough. They needed someone who wouldn't know a projection from the real thing. Now that crazy idea was out, she didn't miss a beat and went straight to the next question.

Why was the painting stolen in such a spectacular way?

And the answer to that one flowed easily from the marker pen.

So no one would think to check if it had ever been there

It made sense. She herself had served as witness that the painting was in the gallery. She and Burton were both witnesses that it had been stolen by the mysterious Angel of Death. In a sense it had – it must have been left for her already to pick up. It was never in the gallery at all.

This plan was like a piece of pure theatre from the beginning. No, it was like a magic act, full of noise and distraction and sleight of hand.

Her eyes turned to the next two questions.

Why was Ivor killed?

Next to this she wrote what came into her head.

He knew someone's secret

And the final one.

Where is 'La Scaletta' now?

Her train of thought bumped up against the buffers. It bounced and something bounced in her brain too.

Pacing across the kitchen she grabbed her bag. Papers, loose change, make-up, hairbrushes clattered and slid around as her hand roamed its depth. Finally she clutched a slick-coated piece of paper. She pulled it out. It was Gertie's tour brochure and her eyes raced down to the relevant passage. 'Visit the artists' studios at King's Farm barns (prearranged tours only).' On the back was a map. Not exactly Ordnance Survey but a serviceable enough map of Bowler's Green. Slowly she orientated herself around, her finger running from the river, up the contour lines of the hill. Then she found the little roads that made up the village, the high street leading to the green itself. There was the side of the green that the Greenview Cafe sat on. Her nail scraped along and found the lay-by where the truck had been found, the truck that cradled Ivor Langtree's pale body, in part preserved by the fluid from *The Knight*. Next to the lay-by was a thin track and next to that a label that said 'King's Farm Barns'. And next to that were a group of greyed-in rectangles marked 'Studios'.

61

Burton spoke into his radio. 'What's the situation?' He stomped around a soggy farm field on the outskirts of Bowler's Green.

'I've found the drop spot.' It was Dove who spoke. 'No one here yet, no sign of the painting. What do I do?'

'The arrangement is to wait for the signal, so hold your men back. Make the money drop and back off. I want them caught, all right, so stay ready.'

'Yes, sir.'

This time of year there was no crop, so Burton had an uncluttered view. That was the only favour providence was doing him tonight. There was a full moon up there, but thick cloud was hiding any light that might have helped them see what was going on. The soil was waterlogged and he had neglected to bring wellington boots. He was wearing his customary loafers and his socks were already sopping wet.

Burton got back into his car, and wound down the window. He used the ledge to steady his elbows before scanning the scene through night-vision binoculars. All he saw was darkness.

Rain drummed on the roof of the car. Burton rubbed his temples. He'd been awake now for as long as he could remember. The night-vision binoculars slipped from his hand and his eyes rolled up into his head.

62

Mrs Sidhu had never been in an artist's studio before and had no idea what to expect. The flyer wasn't joking when it described it as a barn. It was night, and the big doors were open spilling dim light onto the broken concrete track. Inside there was darkness, metal carcasses and old farm machinery everywhere. Somewhere off in the corner, a machine screamed and a shower of sparks rained onto the floor. There was music too; industrial, aggressive and thumping. Over the drumbeat, a voice ranted, spitting poetry like a mad prophet.

She moved towards the sparks, making out a human form among the semi-human ones. He came into focus as she got closer. It was his eyes she saw first. Hard and bright they shone out from the darkness. Uncertainty assailed her, coming all this way alone. To overcome it she waved in a friendly way, walking towards him. He did not wave back.

The sparking stopped. Ned Barrow shouted something unintelligible over the music. He was in his twenties and walked with a swagger. The top half of his overalls were pulled down, strapped around his waist, leaving him bare-chested. Despite the cold air pouring in through the double doors he was oiled with sweat. His chest and arms were tattooed.

Hurriedly he pulled the overalls up, buttoning them to the top. He shouted again, this time close enough for her to hear over the bass thump pressing into Mrs Sidhu's ears. 'Hey, this is private!'

'I'm here for the studio visit.' Mrs Sidhu waved Gertie's leaflet. 'Gertie's supposed to meet me here. Is she here yet?'

His eye fell on the booklet Mrs Sidhu was carrying. He grimaced and made an X with his forearms and shouted, 'Not today, no studio visits today.' His voice was drowned out by the music.

Mrs Sidhu found the sound system on a workbench, half-buried by tools. It was a portable stereo with an old-fashioned CD player, covered in flecks of paint, dented from being dropped or having things dropped on it. The music snapped to a stop at her touch and Ned's next words were far too loud. 'I'm not doing studio visits today!' he roared into unexpected silence, then repeated his words more softly. 'I'm not doing studio visits today. Gertie didn't tell me anything about this,' he added. 'So if you don't mind . . .' He reached for the play button, half-turning away.

The stench of chemicals rose up to her nose. Nearby was an open tank, thick with black liquid. The same liquid that was in all of his sculptures.

If he started the music again he would walk away, swallowed up in the depths of the huge barn. Her meeting would be over before it had started. Questions burned inside her, but it would not do to launch in too quickly. 'What a shame,' she said. She clawed at her hair. Searching in desperation for an idea, any idea, to capture his attention, she rambled on. 'Isn't that Gertie all over? She's such a scatterbrain. Or maybe it's me and I got the day wrong.'

What inner forces drove an artist? Then a half-idea came to her. According to Varma there was one thing that united all men: the urge to sell their wares. 'It's the biggest racket in the book,' he had said. So, pulling on her spectacles, she began looking around the place as if searching for something. 'I knew I should have gone through Hector and Tani.'

'You know the Keyses?' Barrow's hand hovered silently over the play button. His glass-chip eyes cut jagged lines in Mrs Sidhu's countenance.

'And Hector said you had some available work tucked away that might be for sale. I'm an art collector, you see. I buy art.'

This was also not strictly a lie, as she had just bought the painting of a sour-faced old woman. That had set her back five hundred quid.

Hands on hips, he swayed, eyeing her closely. 'Hector and Tani? They could have told me.' He compressed his lips then jerked his head back towards the piece he was working on. 'I suppose he'll want his commission. But all right. Come with me.'

Before she knew it, Ned was walking away into the murky depths of the studio and she was rushing to catch up, the acrid smell of death all around them.

'It's so awful for Hector, *La Scaletta* being stolen.' She glanced up. Above them, dangling on chains, his latest creation was coming together. Mrs Sidhu shuddered. A human shape, as yet unformed, a monstrous embryo. 'Your work is about death, isn't it? Poor Ivor was found quite close to here. He was inside your sculpture.'

'Yeah.' He shouted over his shoulder. 'Just up at the end of the farm track. What a week. First Hector gets knocked out, the painting is stolen. Now they're saying Ivor's been killed by the gallery manager. What a mess.' He gave her a smirk.

Mrs Sidhu controlled a flush of anger. 'And of course a poor young woman was killed. She was murdered, quite deliberately. Murdered.' She repeated the word with gravity and Ned's step missed a beat.

'Yeah, that was a shame. She was in the wrong place at the wrong time.' He stopped to pore over his workbench, as if he had misplaced something in the mess. 'At least that's what the police tell me.'

'I imagine you would know.' Mrs Sidhu swallowed and decided to press on. 'Those were prison tattoos on your chest, the ones you quickly covered up when I walked in.'

'Observant.' He cackled. 'And you know a prison tattoo when you see one. Not many art collectors do.'

'I have nephews,' she said. 'Not all of them are good boys.'

'So you thought, maybe, that an ex-convict would know something about it. Maybe he's involved.' He found what he was looking for among his tools, wrenched at a wooden handle and pulled free an old hammer. The head was smashed around and worn.

Mrs Sidhu swallowed. 'Oh, I didn't mean it like that.'

His eyes rolled to the rafters. 'Of course you did. Gives the little old ladies a bit of a flutter when they buy a Ned

Barrow piece. They can tell their friends that a criminal made it.' There was a soft pat-pat-pat as he tapped the head of the hammer into the palm of his hand. 'Brings a little danger into their lives.'

Mrs Sidhu took a half-step back, watching the hammer. 'So why didn't the police arrest you?' she asked.

He waited, circling in the shadows, hammer rising and dropping. 'Two reasons. First, I have no reason at all to steal from Hector. He saved me, he saw the art I was making in prison and he gave me a new life. Now instead of mayhem I make art. Or maybe a little bit of both.'

She tried to keep her voice light and conversational, though it was hard to keep out the tremor. 'What's the second reason?'

'That I've got a watertight alibi, at least for Ivor's body being dumped. I was away at a private view in London on the night that happened. Hundreds of witnesses. In fact, I only got back today. It should have been tomorrow but the last night got cancelled.'

Mrs Sidhu stopped retreating. 'Let me stop you there.' Suddenly her neck was tingling. 'You say you've been away? You're supposed to be away until tomorrow.'

The thud of the hammer stopped. 'That's what I just said.'

She spoke urgently now, with an aunty's command in her voice. 'Who arranged this trip? It's important.'

Perhaps surprised by the change in Mrs Sidhu's demeanour, Ned stuttered. 'Hector, of course. He arranges everything.'

'And he doesn't know you're back?' Mrs Sidhu took the hammer from Ned's hand and placed it on the workbench. She stepped past him and plunged further into the barn.

Ned called after her. 'I haven't seen him. Only got back a couple of hours ago. What's going on?'

Mrs Sidhu cast sharp glances around her as she scuttled. 'Do you know Jenny Leblanc? They say she's the one who's behind it all.'

'I met her once,' Ned said. She seemed nice. 'Posh, French. Not exactly my first choice for a criminal mastermind.'

'I'd have to agree,' Mrs Sidhu said.

She was at the back of the barn now, where more dusty farm machinery lay in wait for a time when it could be used to tear food out of the ground. 'Do you have any work back here?'

Ned raced to catch up with her. 'Hey, that's off limits. It's not safe back there. Just a bunch of machinery falling to bits.'

'Have you been in this area since you got back?'

Ned brushed away a cobweb from his face. 'I never come down here much.'

'That looks new.' She pointed to a digger at the end, its arm hoisted in the air like a salute. 'That one has no cobwebs on it.'

'I use that as a hoist. My work can weigh over a tonne when it's finished, so I use that to load and unload from the trucks.'

'Like the truck the Keys use to transport work.'

'Yeah.'

'Like the truck that was found at the end of the farm track just yesterday.'

Ned's eyes widened. 'What are you implying? I already said, I've been away.'

'What's your work about, Mr Barrow?' she asked.

'Death.' He grinned.

He seemed so young, what did he know about death? 'What were you inside for?'

He looked away. 'Got into trouble when I was young. Stole stuff, small stuff.'

He looked too young to have done all that, Mrs Sidhu thought. 'So not murder.'

'Like I say, Hector's a salesman, and he knows how to spin a tale.'

She squinted her eyes into the darkness. Something hung there from the forks. 'Do you have a light back here?'

Ned hit the lights. Another of his sculptures hung there, monstrous and swaying gently as though it was alive. Ned's jaw opened and closed on empty air. 'What's that doing there?' he spluttered. 'It's an old piece, a study I did for *The Knight*.'

Its giant head hung at eye height. The visor opened with a snap. Mrs Sidhu looked into a face frozen in a scream. 'Congratulations, Mr Barrow, your work really is about death.'

Mrs Sidhu swung round and walked out of the double doors. Ned stood swaying for a moment. Tentatively he approached his sculpture and peered inside, then reeled away, gagging.

63

Burton woke up with a jerk. His lap was vibrating. He didn't know how long he'd been asleep. He clutched for his phone, ramming big fingers onto the answer button without looking who was calling. 'Report. What's going on?'

A woman's voice answered. 'Chief Inspector?'

'Jenny?' His voice was thick and drowsy.

'It's Mrs Sidhu, Chief Inspector. Did I wake you? I'm so sorry.'

Burton cleared the grit from his eyes. 'No. I mean, yes. I mean, no. Look, I'm very busy.' He was flustered. Why had he said her name? Had he been dreaming about her?

'What are you doing?' she asked.

Burton clenched his jaw. 'I can't tell you.'

'Well, if you're in bed with a woman called Jenny, you obviously can't tell me what you're doing. Quite a co-incidence, you being in bed with a woman called Jenny twice in one week.'

'What do you mean?' Burton reddened. 'I am not in bed! I'm on a stakeout.'

He had that familiar feeling of being tricked by Mrs Sidhu.

She continued. 'There, you see, I knew you'd tell me what you were doing. Anyway, you really wouldn't want to be in bed with Jenny Leblanc right now.'

Burton grunted. 'We found her blood on the stone that killed Ivor Langtree and Daisy Carr. She might be hurt.'

'I can go one better than that. She's dead. I've just found her decaying corpse in an artist's studio.'

He scratched at his neck. 'You've done what?' Maybe he was still dreaming.

'Jenny Leblanc is not the Angel of Death. But you'll want to send some uniforms and a forensics team to Ned Barrow's studio. No, he's not the one who did it.'

'Mrs Sidhu, I don't have time for jokes.' Burton wanted to smash the phone to death on the dashboard, but he couldn't muster the energy. He took a deep breath. 'I shouldn't tell you this, but I'll have the painting back very soon, and this Angel of Death woman too. Whoever she is.'

The radio crackled. 'Hang on,' he said to Mrs Sidhu and picked up the radio receiver. 'What's happening, Dove?'

Dove's voice was fuzzy with static. 'Movement, sir.'

Burton saw the sweep of headlights in the distance. 'I see it.' He snapped off the radio and picked up his phone again. 'I have to go, Mrs Sidhu, it's happening.' He ended the call, cutting short her squeal of protest.

He dumped the phone and the radio and picked up the night-vision binoculars. It was a grubby white van, probably a VW Transporter, too dark to make out a number plate. A jolt of adrenaline and the tiredness was gone. He picked up his radio. 'Standby.' His eyes followed the van until it pulled up, wheeling round to turn the headlights straight at him, flaring the sensors on the night scope.

He winced and pulled the binoculars away, shielding his eyes, the after-image still glowing on his retinas. The lights blinked twice. 'It's them. Wait for my signal.' The driver left the van lights undipped. Clever – Burton couldn't watch through the binocs. He smiled. It didn't matter. He had officers ready to pounce the second the painting was in his hands. There was no way they could get away.

He checked his watch, waited two minutes. The lights flashed three times. 'OK, that's the signal. Everyone move now!' Burton jumped from his car and started running across the field, loafers sinking into the mud.

64

Outside Ned's studio Mrs Sidhu slid her phone away into her bag. A breeze plucked at her hair. Burton thought he was about to get the painting and the Angel. It was going on right now. Something sparkled on the floor. She crouched.

'Was that the police?' Ned staggered out of the double doors. 'You know I didn't kill her, you told them I didn't kill her.'

'They're busy.' She licked her finger and placed it on the little star. When it came up, her finger had a sequin stuck to the end. 'Use sequins in your work, Mr Barrow?'

'Not mine,' Ned said. 'Might have come from the studio next door.'

'Who's in the studio next door?'

'Girl who works by the name of Petra.'

'Petra the other artist in Gallery 1?' Mrs Sidhu fished around in her bag, pulled out her gallery guide and read.

Artist's statement
Petra: Art Rocks

Petra made her debut in 2023 at the Grange Gallery in Reading, a member of the now defunct Dutch Master Collective. Since then she has shown throughout Berkshire and beyond. Her latest work explores the relationship between tactile and visual. By using rocks traced with words and drawings she references rock art seen throughout the world and challenges the stereotyped value placed on art in Western art norms.

Well, she was none the wiser after that. She pocketed the guide and walked along the farm track to the next studio along, her shoes crunching on grit and splitting concrete.

Ned followed her. 'I don't understand.'

'You're being set up, Mr Barrow, or to put it in terms that an artist can understand, "framed".' She smiled thinly, and he didn't appreciate the joke.

She pulled at the big double doors. A padlock rattled in the hasp.

'Who has keys to this?'

'Petra.' Ned shifted his feet. 'And the landlord.'

'Mr Barrow, there's a dead body in your studio. In a hour or so's time the police are going to burst in there and you will be accused of murder. You, with the help of Hector, have carefully crafted a history of trouble and violence into your story. You will go back to prison, and this time to a much bigger and worse one.'

Barrow wiped the sweat from his face. 'OK. It's the same key for both locks.' Barrow fished a set of keys out of his pocket and unlocked the padlock. The big doors swung open. Mrs Sidhu stepped inside.

This one was another repurposed farm building. She tripped on an old nitrogen fertiliser bag as she pushed through the door. It spilled a handful of its contents from a rip in the plastic. More were stacked up, unused, covered in dirt alongside grime-covered bottles of bleach and pesticide. She recovered her balance before she fell.

The room was full of rocks, some single, some in piles, some in display cabinets and some on tables. Somewhere, muffled by distance, a steady rhythm banged out.

Ned Barrow followed her in. 'She doesn't much like people coming in here uninvited, you know. We artists are very private about our spaces, our processes.' He spoke softly, as if Petra might jump out at any minute, but of Petra herself there was no sign. 'And she's got a very angry energy.'

'I feel the same way in the kitchen,' said Mrs Sidhu. Ned threw her an odd look and she coughed. 'I like to cook, in between the art collecting.'

Mrs Sidhu picked up one of the rocks. It had writing on it: '£10,000'. She looked deep into the porous grain of the stone. 'What point is she making?'

Ned gestured to a screen on the wall. 'Hector got her to make a video about her work. She plays it on there when she has a group in.' He thumbed a control and the screen leapt into colour and light.

As soon as it did, Mrs Sidhu's heart jolted. Petra wore harem trousers and a loose top, and emphasised her words with languid movements more like a dancer's than an artist's. It was her: the body, the movement were the same. This was the woman in the skull mask. There was no doubt. This was the woman who had pushed her into the river. Who had left her to die. She shuddered, remembering the death's-head mask, the eyes and the smile inside the smile. The final things that shouted out to Mrs Sidhu were the red hair and the freckled frown.

65

'It's Poppy, the girl from the cafe.' The same cafe that was less than a mile away down the track, where the body of Ivor Langtree had been found in the back of a truck.

The video continued. It must have been shot during a studio visit; she was speaking to a group of people. It was less of a tour and more of a diatribe.

'We've got so used to this sanctity we place around art,' Poppy said. 'In galleries we're told, "Don't touch, stand well back, no photography."' She spread her arms wide. 'The *Mona Lisa* is protected by bulletproof glass. How mad is that? Everything is off limits!'

'Waitress, eh? A lot of artists have a day job,' Ned said. 'Keeps the wolf from the door, and stops you going mad, stops you getting inside your own head too much.'

'Gig economy.' Mrs Sidhu laughed mirthlessly.

Onscreen, Poppy continued her speech. 'Art has become something outside, alien, commoditised, we've allowed that to happen.' Poppy grimaced. Mrs Sidhu tried to imagine those lips inside the rictus of a skull mask. 'It's our responsibility as artists to comment on it.' She swept her arms around. 'So please, touch, pick up, feel.'

The video continued and Mrs Sidhu took Petra at her word. She clutched one of the rocks scattered around the room, held it in the palm of her hand. The answers were here, she knew it, she just wasn't asking the right questions. 'They say she's not ready for the big time,' she asked Ned. 'Do you agree?'

'She's a developing artist.' He shrugged. 'But yeah. The work isn't there yet, simple as that. It's interesting, it's got some social commentary but no more. She says as much herself. Keeps saying her next project will put her on the map.'

'And what is her next project?'

'Wouldn't say. Something spectacular.'

'Something spectacular.' Mrs Sidhu absent-mindedly hefted the rock. It was rough in the palm of her hand. 'There's a rock like this in police evidence. It was used to kill Ivor Langtree and my waitress Daisy Carr, and probably Jenny Leblanc too.'

'Well, she has got an angry energy,' Ned said.

Something glittered as she moved. She squatted, licked her fingertip and put it to the concrete floor.

'What have you got there?' Ned asked.

When it came up, on the end of it was a second perfectly round, ivory-coloured sequin. 'Another one.' There were no masks or outfits in the room.

A moment or two of rummaging in her bag produced her torch. Then she got down on her haunches. In the oblique light there was a veritable trail of shining points. Little sequins lighting up, leading her on.

'*Your* waitress.' Ned was somewhere behind her, his

words fading as she walked on. He scrambled to catch up with her, physically and mentally. 'Who are you? I mean, you don't know enough to be an art collector.'

'I'm Batman. But I've got a day job too. I'm also a caterer.' The door was set into a wall that spanned the width of the barn. 'What's in there?'

'I think she's got a darkroom. She does some photography with an old-fashioned SLR. You know, proper film.'

Photography. There had been a camera tripod on the jetty when Poppy escaped with *La Scaletta*.

'Hey, don't open that! She could have exposed film out.'

It was a reflex with Mrs Sidhu: the word 'don't' always brought out the worst, always triggered the little fire, and like a reflex the flame moved faster than thought. The door opened with a satisfying creak into darkness.

Her hand found a light switch and black walls were flooded in red light. The room was more like a corridor, long and thin, not the sort of space you wanted to spend a lot of time in. She wondered why it was so small; there must be acres of space. Her main studio took up barely half the barn.

To one side was a small kitchen: two rings and a pot half-filled with goo. She sniffed and her nose wrinkled. For a girl who ran the cafe, she was not much of a cook. Next, there was a sink and a long bench. Plastic trays sloshed various chemicals, no doubt developing fluid. Above them, strung out on a washing line, were photographs, glinting and wet.

'Never heard of privacy?' Ned entered and pulled the door closed behind him.

The photographs on the washing line made a sequence, like a film strip stopped in frozen frames by an unseen remote control. Mrs Sidhu caught the shiny paper of each one by the corner. Click: there was the white-faced angel of death. Click: there was the white-clothed chef in a half-crouch. Click: there was the moment she hit the river, caught as the foam splashed up into an arc. Click: there was the skull face close up with *La Scaletta* on display.

Ned gulped. 'I don't understand. Why would Petra be involved with all that?'

'Because she can't help herself. People tell her not to do something, and she goes right ahead and does it. Same as Daisy. Same as . . .' She didn't want to finish that sentence. 'Some people are like that.'

Ned plucked the last photo from the wire and let out a slow breath. 'She had the damn painting all along.'

She cast her eyes around in the dim red light. There was no sign of *La Scaletta*. You couldn't miss it in a space this tight.

'So what you were saying about me being set up?' asked Ned. 'You think Petra killed Jenny Leblanc?'

'No.' Mrs Sidhu gave a weary shake of her head. 'I don't think she's a killer and she couldn't plan all of this. She's being used like you.'

'So who?' Ned's face flushed. He was angry now.

Mrs Sidhu felt for the crumpled ball of paper in her cardigan pocket, and uncurled it once more and read it again.

DEAR RESIDENT,
'LA SCALETTA' WILL BE STOLEN AT PRECISELY 7PM, FROM THE PUMP HOUSE GALLERY ON OPENING NIGHT.
YOU HAVE BEEN WARNED.

'You said the landlord has the keys to the studios,' she said quietly. 'Who is the landlord, please?' She knew the answer before it dropped from his lips.

'My patron, Hector Keys. But that's crazy. Why would Hector want to steal his own painting?'

Goosebumps prickled her forearms. 'He wrote the threats. Don't you see? He was the only one who took them seriously.'

'If he wrote them, then why would he take them seriously?'

'Because they gave him the excuse to lock himself in Gallery 2 alone.'

The weight lifted from her entire body as the single chime of a feeling she knew only as Aloneness plucked the string of her heart. In this state, she lost track of all time.

If Hector stole his own painting, then he killed Daisy and Jenny. Yet, burn as she did to catch Daisy's killer, the first murder was the one that mattered the most. Hector killed Ivor.

Why didn't Ivor take the painting when he had the chance the first time? Obviously because Ivor never had any intention of stealing the painting. Something shifted, a grain of sand in the mountain of all this evidence.

If Ivor never intended to steal the painting, what was he doing in the middle of the night in the Keyses' house with a knife? Tani Keys was sure it was him, that he had stood in front of *La Scaletta* with his blade before changing his mind and leaving.

Not quite, he must have done something because Tani said there was minor damage. 'A scratch by the frame, where you wouldn't notice it.'

The grain of sand struck another, and another; now the whole world was shifting under Mrs Sidhu's feet in a landslide of new ideas.

Ivor Langtree had a reason to be there. He had a knife in his hand. Her mind now working faster, she remembered three things in quick succession.

First, Ben had shown her a box of Ivor's things over dinner; the scalpel was in the box and the blade had paint on it. Next, she recalled the folder that was on Jenny's desk, the conference that both she and Ivor had attended, the one where they met. She couldn't remember the exact name of the conference, but she didn't need to. She recalled the final thing. DCI Burton had told her just yesterday morning over breakfast the conversation he had with Jenny Leblanc. 'She thought Ivor was in danger and was trying to protect her. And some stuff about radio-carbon-dating artworks.'

The floor of Mrs Sidhu's world stopped moving. Everything stood still. The moment of Aloneness faded slowly, and she found herself in a darkroom full of blood-red light, a sense of hard reality returning. 'A letter from Paris,' she said.

This was the explanation for everything. She came round from her reverie. Ned stared at her.

'Hector Keys has a secret,' she said. 'He killed his nephew and stole his own painting to hide it. He killed Jenny because she suspected him, and then pinned it all on her. He killed Daisy because she saw him kill Ivor.'

'Why?'

'Because *La Scaletta* is a fake.'

'Impossible.' Ned threw his hands in the air. 'It passed every test when Hector first discovered it. Infrared, X-ray, it was in all the arts press. The painting was checked out.'

'There's a new test. Someone in Paris at the –' she struggled to remember the name, a set of initials – 'the OCBC,' she said finally. 'They've made a new test, using carbon-dating from nuclear tests, and Ivor sent a sample to them.'

'But what's Petra got to do with it?'

That was a good question. Mrs Sidhu swept her eyes across the darkroom once again. In the dim red light she saw why the room was like a corridor: there was an outline in the black-painted walls. At the far end of the darkroom was another door.

She put her hand to the handle and pushed. White light flooded into the room from the space beyond. They stepped out into it.

A low whistle escaped from Ned's lips. 'She's got a whole second studio in here.'

This was a photographic and video studio. There was a monitor and a computer rig attached with leads to a digital camera. The lens was pointing at a chair. Behind it hung an old bedsheet. Mrs Sidhu touched the mouse and blue light fell from the screen. Petra appeared, disguised by her mask, and issued a ransom demand.

So the painting had been here.

'Sounds like she's in it for the money,' said Ned. 'But I don't believe that. She never wanted to be rich. In fact, quite the opposite.'

He was right, Petra wasn't in it for money. Mrs Sidhu was already moving on, looking at more black-and-white photographs pinned to the walls. These were older and she appeared unmasked in many of them. Some were taken at marches where she appeared in other strange outfits, or just covered in paint. She held up banners and placards with slogans like 'Art is not an inve$tment'.

Ned pointed. 'You see. She was a protest artist, I know that much from her artist's statement. She was part of the Dutch Master Collective.' Seeing Mrs Sidhu's look of confusion he carried on. 'You haven't heard of them? Look, here it is.' He led her along the line of photos. 'Their finest hour.'

The photograph Ned tapped on was confusing, a blur of light and movement. She cocked her head, trying to get an angle that made sense. Details came through: a dark shape torn apart by an explosion at the centre of the frame, pieces of paper scattered like confetti at the edges.

'They blew up a million quid.'

'Oh, my word,' she whispered. That was it, it was as clear in her head as pure sunlight. Hector had a fake painting and two problems. The first problem was that his nephew knew about it. So Hector found a sculptor and a protest artist. He had a double use for both of them. He liked his value for money, our Hector. Ned Barrow provided the means to hide Ivor's body and as a patsy for Jenny's murder. Petra too, he had a double use for. First to provide the murder weapon and second a means of disposal for his other problem: his fake painting.

'What happened to this Dutch Master Collective?'

'They split up. How do you top that?' He pointed at the exploding money photo.

Images from the moment she entered Petra's studio flickered through her mind: nitrogen fertiliser, a small kitchen smelling of chemicals, a photograph of an explosion.

'There is one way. Blow up twelve million pounds of art.'

66

Mrs Sidhu was about to hit redial to call Burton when the rhythmic banging struck up again. Air played on her face, night air tinged with farm smells. Walking into the flow she found the source.

There was one more door in Petra's studio. It was at the back of the barn. It slapped open and closed in the wind; a slow handclap, a mocking celebration of all her connections and deductions. Mocking because she was too late. Petra and the painting had been just here, possibly moments before.

She caught the door in mid-swing, silencing the banging. As she stepped outside, the wind caught at her hair, straggling it across her lips. In the distance she could make out an electric whine and a pair of white wings, gliding over the fields like a giant bird. Poppy was on her scooter heading down the hill, down towards the village, towards the river, and with an inevitable sense of déjà vu, Mrs Sidhu had to go down with her.

Mrs Sidhu still had the newspaper in her bag. She flipped

through and found the photo of Daisy on page two. After a few days in her bag it was looking a bit wrinkled and chewed up. She straightened it out, carefully flattening it with the edge of her hand. She looked so young, so completely at peace. She had her whole life ahead of her, and still would if Mrs Sidhu had paid attention, stopped her at the right moment.

Poppy was planning to destroy that painting in a spectacular explosion which she saw as an artwork, and that Hector had pushed and encouraged her into. She clapped her hand to her head. It was obvious now. The last part of Hector's plan had to be that. It had to be to destroy the evidence that revealed his motive, and to do so in a public fashion with witnesses so that the insurance company could not deny the claim. Which meant one last thing. That the final loose end for Hector was Poppy.

She couldn't bring Daisy back, but she could stop it happening again. She could save Poppy. She stuffed the paper into her bag.

It ends as it started; she knew exactly where Poppy was heading. The electric scooter had a head start. She had to get there first – it was her only chance to stop this madness. She jumped into her Nissan Micra, gunned the engine and slipped it into gear. The gearbox rattled complaints but the car obeyed her foot as she pressed it to the accelerator pedal.

67

Burton, Dove and half a dozen officers converged on the drop spot at the same time, torch beams criss-crossing on the white van. Slowly, an armed officer opened the driver's side door. Simultaneously, two others opened the passenger door and the sliding side panel door. 'Come out very slowly with your hands up,' Burton said, stepping forward. A man emerged, hands in the air. He was in his late teens or early twenties. His greasy hair was under an old baseball cap, his chin covered in patches by a straggly beard. He quivered, swallowed and found his voice. 'Delivery for a Chief Inspector Burton.' He nodded towards the cab where a styrofoam box sat on the passenger seat.

One of the armed officers eased it open. After a tense moment he nodded curtly and stepped away. 'All clear.'

Burton had barely moved forward when he felt a hand on his chest.

'Allow me, sir.' Dove strode up to the van and, bustling past the armed officers, took charge of the package.

'What is it?' Burton asked.

'Looks like a vegan full English breakfast, sir.' He held the carton up. Inside nestled two tofu sausages, a rasher of seitan bacon, and some scrambled tofu.

Burton froze. 'That bloody waitress from the cafe. It has to be.'

'We've secured the ransom money, sir, hasn't been touched. She didn't come for the money. I don't get it, sir,' said Dove.

'It's not about the money.'

'Then what's it about?'

Burton's chest sank. 'I don't know, but this is a distraction. She wanted us all up here so she could be elsewhere.'

'So where is she?'

Burton strode away a few yards, feet squelching into mud. He needed to think. Something missing from the picture. He turned again. This seemed to be his life these days, going round in circles while being immersed in water. He rubbed his neck. Water, there was something about water. 'Why did she keep the boat, Dove? We never found it, and you said it yourself, why not just abandon it?'

Dove's chest swelled. 'I did say that, sir. What does it mean, though?'

'Maybe she kept it because she means to use it again.' A star shot across the sky, popped and scattered into hundreds of smaller stars. 'What's going on tonight?'

'The gallery are having a reopening,' Dove said. 'They're putting on some fireworks.'

Burton's feet went numb. It wasn't just the cold water and mud. 'I know where she's going.' He took a lungful of air and cupped his hands to his mouth. 'To the river! Everyone to the river!'

68

Tonight she was Petra. Poppy the waitress was gone. This was her final transformation. She would spread her wings and fly.

Each breath she took was hard and sharp, angled and carved by the night air. Only her lips felt the cold; the mask absorbed the breeze on her face. Under her feet, the electric motor whined. She pictured herself, a stately progress on her scooter, with her wings unfurled behind her. Except that she had *La Scaletta* clutched between her thighs. Not the perfect choice, aesthetically, but it was the final effect that would be important.

A joy was in her, a triumph. She twisted the throttle. The scooter gave a low whine. She resisted the temptation to twist the throttle any further. Easy does it, she thought. In the crease between her gorgeous wings, she could feel the backpack bumping gently against her. Inside was the package she had cooked up earlier, strung with curling wires connected up to the mobile phone.

She had done it before, learned it from the older guys

in the Dutch Master Collective. They did a lot of 'pyrotechnics' as they liked to call it, back in the day. One of the older hands had shown her the recipe. She slowed the scooter, it was delicate stuff, wouldn't do for it to go off early. There was time, the police would be running around for ages.

Soon she could smell the dankness of the river.

The best place to hide a boat is the exact place it was taken from. Hide it by the riverbank, or leave it abandoned somewhere it would be found as sure as sure can be. Repaint the name, take off a few fittings, add a few more – change the silhouette – and if you throttled it quietly back to the same marina at night, covered it over with tarps, it looked like it was stored away for the winter. No one would pay any attention at all, especially the police. Of course it helped that her patron had made the arrangements, her patron had paid the mooring fees in the new name, her patron had done everything for her.

Patron, she liked the word. It made a reality of her art, and with a hint of pride, giving her a sense of recognition. Not that she needed that, she told herself. It was about the work, the final product. She reddened under the mask, she was protesting too much. This was her moment.

That was the best bit, that and sending that cop a vegan breakfast. She wished she'd been there for that, to see his face. How long had it taken him to remember her? she wondered. After tonight, he would never forget her. No one would forget her.

Even better, there was no crime. If Hector Keys wanted to commission performance artist Petra to blow up his own painting, and his own boat, that was his business. When she fretted that she had no permit, had to clear it with the police, her patron, Hector, was there. 'Leave that to me,' he had said. 'My lawyers will see to that. This is your act of rebellion, your moment to express what you're trying to say.'

When asked about the twelve million he was losing, he smiled. 'With the name you're about to make for yourself, we'll clear twice that on your first exhibition.' She had duly signed a representation agreement, and a non-disclosure clause. 'You must share this with no one until we're ready.'

She smiled to remember it. It was time, she was ready. She dumped the scooter outside the gallery and carried the painting to the back of the building. The boat was there, just as Hector had promised.

There were selfies and selfies to die for. This one was to die for. She was setting the camera down on the marina boardwalk when she heard the decking creak and a voice emerged from the dark.

'Here we are again.'

69

'Here we are again,' Mrs Sidhu said. The boards under her feet wobbled, ripples fanned out across the water towards the expensive yachts moored in the enclosure. Nightwater, how she hated it. A week ago, she had been in that water. She shivered at the memory of it. Truth be told there had been no swimming lessons in between. It would be best not to go in again. Mrs Sidhu grounded herself, standing with her legs apart, flinging her arms out like wings. 'This time I know who you are, Poppy.'

Poppy stopped in mid-stride, perhaps stuck between two personas, surprised to hear her real name. She hesitated on the riverbank. The skull-faced grin on the mask now looked like an uncertain smile. The white wings quivered. The painting was clutched in her arms, canvas facing out to Mrs Sidhu. Reflections of the gallery lights, caught by the river, played across the colours, rippling the whole thing to life.

A gasp escaped Mrs Sidhu's mouth. Fake or real, it was stunning. This, though, was no time for art appreciation.

The skin across her neck tightened. 'I'm going to need that painting.'

Poppy's fingers tightened on the painting. Almost imperceptibly, the skull head shook from side to side. 'Get out of my way, you're in the middle of my performance piece.' She placed a foot onto the boardwalk.

The movement travelled from board to board until Mrs Sidhu felt it swell under the arches of her feet. She teetered and her feet shuffled, finding a new balance. She put up her palm. 'Wait. You've been manipulated, Poppy.'

Poppy peeled her mask off. 'Yeah. Your whole generation thinks that we're so dumb, we're so easy. Maybe you're the ones being manipulated. Maybe you all go out and spend millions on art, when it's free. Art's not a commodity, it's not an investment.'

Mrs Sidhu didn't spend millions on art, but that didn't seem worth mentioning at this moment. 'I agree with you. I spent five hundred pounds on a painting. I hate it. I did it just to impress someone.' She swallowed back the fear. 'I know what you're going to do, Poppy. You're going to blow it up. I've seen your studio. If you do, you'll only be helping the art investors, men like Hector Keys.'

Poppy seemed confused here. 'No, Hector's the one who's supported me. He wants me to do it.'

'Why would he want that? He represents everything you hate. You want to do this so much, to be seen, to be loved, to make an entrance into this world. You've stopped asking questions.'

Poppy snorted. 'Well, why then?'

'Because the painting you're holding is a fake. He wants it destroyed right here in front of everyone. That way he gets the insurance, and most of all he built his reputation on that painting.'

Poppy swivelled the painting, holding it with one hand against her side. 'It doesn't matter what he wants. When the painting blows up, this will go down as the greatest statement in the whole of art protest history. This will be a defining act.'

A burst of tiny explosions scattered across the night sky above.

'Stand aside, unless you want a second bath.' She put another foot forward, with purpose this time.

'I know about your past. I've seen your work in your studio, your other studio. It's good, even Ned Barrow thinks it's good.' She was relieved to see Poppy stop once more. Flattery will get you everywhere, every time. However hard we rebel, we want even harder the approval of those we respect. 'You have the explosives with you, haven't you?'

Poppy nodded. She jerked a thumb over her shoulder, towards her rucksack. 'Home-made and very sensitive. I'm all ready to go. The only thing in my way is you.'

'You aren't going to survive, Poppy. That's Hector's plan. You know too much. You're the last link to him. Ivor's dead, Jenny's dead.'

She saw the seed of doubt in Poppy's mind grow and she spoke fast. 'Tell me how this is supposed to go down.' She hoped 'go down' was youth-speak enough to bridge the gap.

It clearly wasn't. Poppy groaned impatiently, reminding her of Tez trying to explain how her mobile phone worked. 'I'm in control. I get on the boat, I set up the painting and the charges, and I swim back to the riverbank.'

'So how do you set off the bomb?'

Poppy waggled a red mobile phone and its doppelgänger attached to the rucksack. 'Two burner phones. I send a four-digit text from one to the other, the numbers one to four.'

So anyone who knew the phone number and the code could send the trigger text. 'Who got you those phones?' Mrs Sidhu asked.

'Hector.'

Now she heard the falter in the young woman's voice. 'He arranged everything.'

'Let me guess, Hector chose the four-digit code. He knows the code and he knows the burner phone number. He can set it off any time.' Mrs Sidhu nodded over at the gallery lawn. A growing crowd was gathering to watch the fireworks display. 'He'll have a grandstand view.'

Another firework burst overhead. An age seemed to pass before Poppy's face twitched, her eyes opened in panic. 'Get it off me!'

Mrs Sidhu thanked the stars. She rushed over to Poppy and they both scrabbled at the straps.

70

Hector Keys surveyed the scene. The gallery looked good, better than ever. He breathed in the air, the rich air that he had long ago got used to. The smell of it, what was it? Oil paint, suffused with expensive perfume, and the best white wine. He sipped his own glass of Sancerre and threw a quick glance at the group Tani was chatting to. An earl, a hedge-fund manager, a senior civil servant and a consultant surgeon. His people. It had not always been so. When he was dragging himself around the junk stores and car boot sales of the early Eighties, his people were the tracksuit-wearing brigade he now despised. Then came his discovery, and it had changed his life: the man who discovered *La Scaletta*. He had left the tracksuits and cold mornings behind, along with them the fingerless gloves and the constant roaming among the stalls and junk shops for a living. A living? He laughed, he was barely breaking even. Then came his transformation. He had replaced his West Country twang with an Etonian burr and his threadbare jumper with a silk suit.

Hector checked his watch. Time to put these childish things to one side, for a moment anyway. He stepped up to Tani, put his hand on the small of her back. 'It's all about to start,' he said. 'Why don't we step outside?'

The cool night air soothed his skin and some of the tension eased from his neck. He had seen it, he was the one who had *La Scaletta*'s true worth. No one could take that away. It didn't matter now that it was a fake, not really, because it had fooled everyone and not just him. He looked back through the huge glass window. He allowed himself a moment to take in what he had achieved. The buyers were standing with their backs towards him. Tani threw him an understated smile. That was what he loved about her. That was what money did for you, when you had it from such a young age. You had no need to overstate yourself. It was called refinement and she had conferred it on him. It's why he had taken her surname. To be a Keys, to stand at the peak of an artistic Olympian dynasty. Now even she danced attendance on his 'eye'. His golden eye.

A thunderclap and a shower of gold exploded above.

For all that refinement, it was his instincts that had really changed the game. 'Put on a show,' his father had said, shifting the cards from hand to tea-crate to hand again. 'Put on a show and they won't see the trick.' The one gift his father had given him. When he had breathed his last halitosis-laden breath, a skeletal shadow in his hospital bed, Hector told himself it was for the best. He was not the sort of father suitable to bring into his new world. Nonetheless, he would have been proud.

Hector had put on a show, all right; an all-singing all-dancing light show, a magic show. And tonight he was putting on an even bigger one, the final turn of the card. He smiled. The only proof that his golden eye might just be fool's gold was about to go up with a big bang. His jaw clenched to think of it, that of all the people who might have discovered his mistake it was Ivor. Little Ivy, who had never spent a morning in a freezing-cold car park. Little Ivy, who was born with a silver spoon stuffed into his mouth, and every other orifice. Little Ivy, with his doting aunt. Well, he had dealt with that little problem, and with his girlfriend too. Dealt with them both rather elegantly, he thought. However far he had come, his hands had not lost their wiry strength. Another gift from his father.

Their group stepped around the building, heading towards the marina. That was when he heard the oohs and aahs. These weren't the sounds of wonder from the enjoyment of fireworks. This was a rising hubbub. He pushed his way up through the crowd, quite forgetting his lame-dog act. 'What's going on?' he demanded.

His stomach turned cold when he saw what they were all pointing at. Mrs Sidhu and Poppy together on the boardwalk. They were wrestling. No, she was trying to get the pack off the girl's back. His skin burned again, and the cool air did nothing to soothe it.

Behind him someone spoke up.

'They've got *La Scaletta*. Look!'

From somewhere came police sirens, and blue lights flashed, rivalling the fireworks.

Hector's legs trembled, as if the frailty that he had been feigning for days was real. He reached for a handkerchief and patted his brow.

'Are you all right, Hector?' Tani was looking at him. They all were.

'Yes,' he croaked. 'Would you excuse me? I have to send a quick text.'

He stepped away from the group. His skin was aflame. He resisted the temptation to claw at his forearms and neck.

The sirens and blue lights were close now, but there was time to finish this. He slipped the phone from his suit pocket. The red one, the killer one. Four digits, that's all it would take.

71

The distance between Mrs Sidhu and the riverbank was maybe fifty yards. More people were coming out of the gallery to look at the fireworks and the curious display on the boardwalk. She saw Hector pull away from the crowd. Their eyes locked across the water. He pulled out a red mobile phone. Poppy saw it too. 'He's putting the code in!' she shrieked.

Mrs Sidhu scrambled, hands and mind moving fast. Poppy's jaw dropped; her eyes expanded in shock, she seemed to freeze. Mrs Sidhu leapt forward, tugging harder at the straps keeping the bag on. It was a four-digit code, that was what she had said. The numbers 1 to 4 and send.

By the time Mrs Sidhu got a good grip on the backpack, Hector had already hit **1**.

Mrs Sidhu tugged hard. The nylon straps were tight and cut at her fingers. However hard she pulled, the bag wouldn't slip over Poppy's shoulders, not past the wings on her back. She reached for the zip.

'Don't open the bag!' Poppy shouted. 'If you take the bomb out it'll go off.'

Mrs Sidhu turned her attention back to the wings and started tearing at the feathers.

Hector tapped again. 2.

Another handful of feathers flew. It was no good, the wings were well attached. 'How were you planning on getting the bag off, Poppy?'

'I . . . I was going to cut the straps off. Wait—' She pulled a knife from her pocket. Her hands, numb from shock or fear, flapped, her fingers slack. The knife fell to the boardwalk with a clatter, bouncing twice – and in seeming slow motion, as Mrs Sidhu swiped a hand for it but missed, it spun and splashed into the river, sinking silently into the depths.

On the bank Hector tapped again. 3.

There had to be a way. And now again in slow time, Hector's thumb was arching over the keypad. Poppy's legs were giving way, collapsing to her knees, and as she did so her hands flew to her tear-streaked face, waiting for the coup de grace. *La Scaletta*, released from her arm, was teetering on its edge. That was it and with the instincts of a mother, used to catching anything and everything her child dropped, Mrs Sidhu saw her own hand grabbing it.

The second her fingers felt the touch of the frame she had the answer.

Everything moved fast again. She caught the painting. In one movement she had it in her arms. She jumped up nimbly and took two, then three, then half a dozen, steps back and just hoped she had calculated right.

Hector's thumb froze.

Poppy snivelled, wiping the drool from her nose with

her sleeve, looking up with surprise at a world that should have ended by now in the shockwave of fire.

The cold around Mrs Sidhu's heart warmed a little, one tiny drop of meltwater seemed to fall. She was still on a knife edge, a skater on thin blades on very, very thin ice. She cleared her throat. 'You need both, don't you? It's not enough to kill Poppy, you have to destroy this painting too.' The meltwater turned to a trickle and soon to a river. She was right.

Hector laid cold eyes on her. His thumb still hung over the phone. He smiled, raised his thumb again.

He was going to do it anyway, she could see it.

Mrs Sidhu wasn't going to save this girl. There were only seconds left. She could jump clear now.

'Please don't leave me,' Poppy sobbed. 'Please don't leave me alone.'

Every maternal instinct in Mrs Sidhu's body told her to hold the girl. It would be the hug of death. The last hug she would ever give. Both of them sobbing now, tears streaming, she took Poppy, and her ticking bomb, into her arms. This girl wasn't dying alone. There was one chance still.

Hector punched the keypad once more. **4.**

Events on the bank hit fast wind. Hector held the phone aloft, the last digit in. All he had to do was send.

Burton sprinted around the corner of the building. Eyes bulging, scanning, too slow to take in and interpret the facts.

Hector's thumb came down.

Mrs Sidhu kicked the painting as far up the boardwalk as she could. She grabbed Poppy by the waist and rolled them over the edge, into the black.

Hector hit the button, and Mrs Sidhu and Poppy disappeared under the water with hardly a ripple.

72

Ice-cold water froze Mrs Sidhu's lungs and washed away the hot tears on her cheeks. She was back in the liquid crypt and there was a sense of déjà vu about it. Again, her impact with the water expelled the air from her lungs. This time she had company. They were alive. The bomb didn't go off, but it was not the end of their troubles.

She saw them as if from above. They were turning and falling together, folded in each other's embrace, wrapped in white angel's wings.

This was no rescue, just a reprieve. She had swapped a fast, fiery death for a creeping, cold one. The tension in her lungs was already building up, oxygen levels plummeting, carbon dioxide climbing. The water hammered at her, demanding to come in. Her own traitor of a body wanted to unlock the door. She clamped her mouth shut.

If Poppy knew how to swim she seemed to have lost the will. She clung to Mrs Sidhu like a wet rag. It was all on her, and she wasn't losing this one, there would be no repeat of Daisy Carr, not on her watch.

They fell another yard, and the light was going. She shook Poppy hard by the shoulders. We have to work together, she thought. She pointed up, to where dim fireworks were breaking silently across the skies. Poppy jerked her thumb at the rucksack. She was right, if they surfaced with that on her back, if there was any chance the phone was still working, that would be it.

The pressure to breathe in was becoming irresistible. The water monster hammered again against her clenched teeth, demanding to come in. But that way lay death, and they both knew it.

Mrs Sidhu flipped Poppy round and tore at the wings. The glue holding them together was starting to dissolve and big chunks flew into the water. One came away cleanly, aeroplaning down into the depths. She worked desperately on the other one. Poppy was going slack, bubbles escaping her mouth.

She tore at it again and with relief it started to disintegrate. She was down to the stub attached to the shoulder when a new danger crushed her heart. She fumbled, losing grip.

The cold was making her fingers numb, they were switching off. Worse, both of them were vertical in the water, tombstoning making them sink even faster. What was it she had read somewhere? They were supposed to get horizontal, kick with their legs. Though that was impossible until the rucksack was off Poppy.

She had to open her mouth – it was the only way. Her growl of defiance was the last bubble of air escaping her lungs. Doors open, the unwelcome guest came gushing in. Ice-cold water slammed into her lungs, but she knew what she had to do. She bit down hard on the wing stub and wrenched her head back. She sobbed with relief as it came away. She ripped the straps free and, as her feet hit the river bottom, she pushed Poppy hard upwards. Poppy reacted, she found some life, kicking her legs, achieving that life-saving horizontal position. Hands reached down from the surface grasping for her.

It was all an ocean away for Mrs Sidhu. She gave up her last resistance and the water took every corner of her chest in its paralysing embrace.

She was in the dream again, the dream with all the dots. She was a stream of coloured points bursting across the sky like a firework. One by one each point of light flared bright and then fizzed out.

It was over.

73

In the darkness, there was a light and it seemed as though the light was getting closer. It streamed around her, broken into dots, torn apart and shifting and changing and moving. Her lungs burned, she could hold on no longer. The light was getting closer and closer. It was telling her to move towards it. Her arms reached up to it. She ached to touch the light.

The dots whirled and swirled and reassembled. The distant dull thuds and thumps in her ears transformed into screams and splashes. The sounds bouncing off white tiles, the smell of chlorine in her nose.

Mrs Sidhu broke the surface. Warm water ran off her hair and slicked off her back. She sucked in a life-sustaining breath. The world was so full of the stuff, and you hardly ever appreciated it until it was taken away from you.

Footsteps followed her halting progress across the pool. 'Well done,' the feet said. 'Putting your face in the water is hard the first time. Now, do it again and blow bubbles.' The feet were attached to bare pink legs and then to a body clad in a neon-yellow T-shirt, declaring its occupant as 'Leanne, Qualified Swim Instructor, All Ages'.

Mrs Sidhu grimaced and glanced across the chopping water at the rest of the class. One of them was picking her nose, and two of the boys were more interested in splashing each other than blowing bubbles. She grunted and clutched her styrofoam kickboard, kicked her legs and plunged her face back in. All sound ceased except for the rhythm of bubbles bursting from her mouth.

A bump on her palms and she surfaced again. Her hands flapped, body sinking under her until mercifully she clutched the edge of the pool.

'A whole length. That's really good, Mrs Sidhu. Top of the class.' Leanne beamed at her, then turned her attention to her other charges, clapping her hands. 'Hey, stop messing around, you two, or I'll tell your mums.'

'I'm not sure about this.' She coughed. 'It still feels suspiciously like I'm just avoiding drowning.'

Another face loomed and she looked into steady, cow-like eyes. Burton crouched by the pool. 'That's the trick with swimming. It's the art of not dying.'

She snorted, and water came out of her nose. 'I think I actually hate water. I might never bathe again.'

'That I'll deal with, but I'm not pulling you out of a freezing-cold river for a third time. Twice is enough. Time you learned.'

Half an hour later she managed another entire length of the pool and had broken up a fight between the two splashers. This earned her a gold star from Leanne and a hot coffee from Burton in his car.

She took a slurp. 'Thanks for bringing me,' she said. 'But you didn't have to threaten me with handcuffs.'

'Oh, yes, I did,' he said and slipped the car into gear.

Two weeks had passed since her last dive into the Thames. Two weeks and she had resisted asking, resisted even looking in the newspaper or the online news sites. 'So,' she said. 'What news?'

'Thought you'd never ask.' The car accelerated, and soon green fields were unfolding before them. 'All the tests are back.'

She held her breath.

'You were right,' Burton said.

She mashed her fist into her palm. 'Yes!'

Burton caught her up on the case. After she'd gone into the water, Burton and his officers had quickly secured *La Scaletta*. 'It's a fake. A very good one, fooled everyone for years, but now this new test comes along and proves it. Ivor Langtree took samples of the paint and canvas and got them tested.'

'Ivor finally had some leverage over his uncle,' she said. 'And a chance to start a new life with Jenny.'

Burton took up the story again. 'Hector confessed under questioning. He lured Ivor into the gallery on the promise of a briefcase of cash. Even got him to cut the security camera wires so they wouldn't be caught on camera making the exchange.'

Mrs Sidhu pulled the Evidence Tupperware from her bag. 'Ivor walked into the gallery in celebratory mood, a new life ahead of him, wine and canapé in hand. That's when Hector hit him, before he even knew what was happening.' She rattled the box. 'Ivor dropped these. Hector had to hide the shattered pieces.'

'If they were found in the gallery,' Burton said, 'it would

suggest violence was done to Ivor. Hector couldn't have that. He was pinning the whole thing on him.'

She grinned. 'So Hector got the pieces out into the service corridor.'

'But he still had to get Ivor's body into *The Knight*.'

'That's when Daisy walked in.' Her smile faded. She had no appetite to relive that moment.

Burton paused briefly, then said, 'Sounds about right.'

That was as much of a compliment as she could expect from Burton. Mrs Sidhu felt a warm glow; she had been right. 'But Hector already had it all planned out. He couldn't risk Ivor changing his mind, or someone else testing the painting. So he curated his own gallery. He made sure he had the murder weapon to hand.'

Burton nodded. 'Rocks.'

'And the means to dispose of the body,' she said.

Burton smiled mirthlessly. 'A sculpture full of embalming fluid. Brilliant.'

'Hector even gave himself an alibi.' Mrs Sidhu wagged her finger. 'He stole Tani's pills and had them crushed up in his pocket. While I was marvelling like a fool at all the light in his projected painting, he put it on the canapé.'

Fields gave way to townscape as they entered Slough.

'No one suspects a man that's just narrowly escaped death himself,' Burton said. 'He was careful to only eat half, mind. He must have taken Ivor's phone from the body, and he sent texts posing as Ivor, promising her a new life. He manipulated Jenny into getting the sculpture out of there.'

'Killing her too and pinning Ivor's murder on her at the same time.'

'And for the finale, he has Poppy blow up the painting right in front of the whole village. Fake painting gone, reputation intact, and collects on the insurance claim.'

Mrs Sidhu exhaled slowly. 'That's what it was all about. His reputation.'

'Talking of which, mine seems to be restored.' The *Chronicle* lay in the footwell. She plucked it up and read aloud. '"Top cop solves the case and saves old woman for second time".' She clicked her tongue.

Burton shifted in his seat. 'Full disclosure. I had a bit of help with the case.'

Mrs Sidhu raised her eyebrows in mock shock. 'Do tell.'

'Sergeant Dove has really stepped up this week.'

She slapped his arm with the paper and laughed. 'Has he indeed?'

Burton chuckled. 'But seriously. You did all right. Not that I approve. For future reference leave it to the professionals – we get there in the end.'

'Well, at least you saved this old woman on your own, whoever she is.'

'And you saved a young life.'

'Yes, I wish I could have done that twice.'

'You can lay Daisy to rest. Poppy has her whole life ahead of her because of you. Once we've got her through some charges of intent to cause an explosion.'

'Go easy on her.'

'I'm doing everything I can. She won't get a custodial sentence.'

'Thanks again, and for taking me swimming.'

'Same time next week,' he said. 'And so on until you can do it without floatation aids.' Burton eased the car to a halt outside her house.

'You're really enjoying this.'

Burton turned to face her. 'When you were down there, what went through your mind?'

Mrs Sidhu was at a loss. She adjusted her bag strap nervously. 'Don't know. Staying alive, I suppose. Why?'

'When I was in that hotel room, with Jenny Leblanc, just before I passed out –' he sighed – 'I thought I was dead, but the strange thing was that dying wasn't the worst part of it. It was that I didn't actually have anything to live for. All the missed opportunities to meet people, women, all wasted because . . . I don't know why. It's just what happens to men like me, in the job I'm in. It's always difficult to get back on the bike, as it were. Do you know that feeling?'

Mrs Sidhu said nothing.

'Then I think about Jenny Leblanc. She was so hung up on one bloke that she let it drive her mad, she let it destroy her life.'

74

Mrs Sidhu unlocked her front door in thoughtful mood. Tez was at the kitchen table, where she had left him doing her accounts. Thinking about Ivor had given her an idea. Stop thinking of Tez as a series of half-finished courses and start thinking of him as a series of half-completed courses. One of which was basic bookkeeping. 'How are you getting on with the accounts?'

'I'm a bit rusty on this spreadsheet stuff, but I think I've got the hang of it.' He tapped some keys. 'As far as I can tell, you're bankrupt.'

'What?' She stamped her foot. 'But how?'

'Like I say, I'm no accountant, but I think it's because you've got no money in your account.' He tapped the screen in a businesslike way while she paced nervously behind him. 'You spent all that outlay on the gallery job. Then you bought art classes and a painting.'

'I can afford it. I have savings. And the Keyses owe me the fee for the gallery opening. That was a lot of money, Tez.'

'Which would be fine if you had actually invoiced them.'

The bottom fell out of her stomach. 'I forgot to invoice,' she said, her voice small. 'But hang on, I can do that now.'

'They're bankrupt too. The entire fortune is based on the art collection which is based on Hector Keys's reputation. You destroyed that.' He snapped the laptop shut, more than a little smugly. She was starting to detest this new grown-up Tez. 'Do you know why this happened, Mum?' Tez uncrinkled the husk of a Post-it note and thumped it down on the table in front of her. It read, 'CRIME DOESN'T PAY'. 'It happened because you forgot some important advice from yourself.'

She fumbled at her top cardigan button. 'I couldn't let him get away with murder, could I?'

Tez groaned and rubbed his forehead. 'It doesn't matter. My work here is done. You owe me for the accounts and for waiting at Varma's party. Cash is preferred.' He held out his hand.

'You just said I have no money in my account.' Mrs Sidhu crossed her arms. 'I don't get paid, you don't get paid.'

Tez clutched the table. 'What? I did all that for nothing? No way.' Tez's finger waved accusingly at her. 'You have to do something. Or . . .' He hesitated before landing the threat that cut through Mrs Sidhu's heart. 'I'll go and work for Mrs Prakesh.'

Her jaw hung loose. 'You wouldn't.'

'Watch me.' The next sound was that of the front door slamming. She stood stroking her chin for some time afterwards, clicking through her options. Her heart sank. It didn't take her long to calculate that she had only one: baking up an old-fashioned dish called humble pie.

75

'Mrs Sidhu.' Varma's nylon trousers crackled with electric energy, and it was an angry energy. It had been built up over much time pacing his office carpet in a state of rage and shock. 'You have a nerve.' He aimed a finger at her face. 'I'm not paying you a thing. My birthday was a complete disaster.'

'Mr Varma—' she started.

He put up his palm, abruptly silencing her. 'First you nearly ruin my cook-chill business with your toilet food.'

Varma was referring to a trifling incident in which Mrs Sidhu had been forced to cook food in a perfectly clean bathroom because she was fed up to her teeth with a visiting relative from India. Was that really going to follow her around for the rest of her catering career? She threw up her hands. 'Mr Varma—'

Again he stopped her with a raised hand. 'Then, I allow you back into the bosom of my heart, and you ruin my birthday by destroying my cake and setting fire to all my gifts. The only one that survived was this.' Varma held up the visage of a snarling old woman. He looked at it with horror on his face. 'Who would give me something like this?'

'I don't know. But, Mr Varma—'

Once more he raised his hand. 'No, Mrs Sidhu, to cap it all, I have experienced a disaster that I have never before experienced in my entire sixty years. I lost my deposit!' He gasped at the wonderment of it. 'I've actually made a loss on my own birthday!'

A silence fell in the room. Varma dumped himself into his office chair, arms crossed.

Mrs Sidhu placed her hands on his desk, leaning over him like a small but fierce bird. 'Mr Varma, please listen to me,' she said in a small voice.

Varma's eyebrows rose. For a moment he seemed to be about to say more. Then he looked away.

Mrs Sidhu quelled her hurt, and all the unfairness of everything he had said. She had come here to be the bigger person, she had come here to cook and eat humble pie. 'Mr Varma, I am here to apologise.'

This seemed to go some way to assuaging him. 'I'm listening.'

'Even though I was completely right about everything, and was only doing my best for everyone concerned, I am prepared to offer this apology.'

Varma waited a while. 'Is that the apology?' His eyes widened. 'I don't think you know how apologies work, Mrs Sidhu.'

'Then let me go one better. I'm here to offer you a business deal.'

The alertness in Varma's eyes, the stiffening of his posture, told her she had his attention. 'The problem we've had in the past is that you require someone to cook, shall we say, traditional dishes for you. Whereas I have ambitions to cook more imaginative fare. You have focused your efforts solely in Slough, and you have Mrs Prakesh's help on that front. Meanwhile I've had great success outside Slough in the rich, well-moneyed, high-wealth areas of Berkshire.' She was laying it on now, inch-thick frosted icing with cherries and all, and it was working. Varma was licking his lips. Now it was time. 'As it happens, I am in need of some inward investment at this time. Mr Varma, have you considered the possibilities that investment in a high-end catering business might offer you?' She thrust out her hand. 'Partners?' She held her breath.

Varma looked at her outstretched hand. 'Why would I take this risk?'

'Because you were my husband's best friend. You're my friend, and I don't have many of them these days.'

Varma stiffened. 'In business, one should never let sentiments rule.'

Mrs Sidhu's heart sank. She had lost. It was over. Sidhu's fine catering was just one more on the pile of bankrupt businesses. She was so lost in regret that it took a moment for her to feel the pressure of Varma's hand in hers.

'Don't make me regret this,' said Varma. 'We can talk numbers later.'

76

It was evening by the time Mrs Sidhu found herself knocking on Ben Trimble's door.

It swung open. Ben was in the doorway, half-turned and looking back down his hallway. 'Hey, look, I've got some pasta on so—'

Then he saw who was at his door. He threw his hands up in surrender, eyes wide. 'If this is a second date, forget I ever asked. I'm terrified about how it would turn out.' Then a line of anger creased his brow. 'Not to mention the manipulation. You went to my art classes for information. You went to dinner with me for information. You came to my house for information. You followed me. You used me. I hope you've had your money's worth.' He started to close the door.

'Wait,' she said. 'It's true, and I'm here to say I'm sorry. I never wanted to go out with you.'

Ben's face crumpled. 'Ouch,' he said.

She cursed herself. 'I'm not very good at apologies. It's one of the problems with being right all the time.'

He smiled despite himself. 'You're certainly right about that.'

She buried her face in her hands. 'I've done it again.'

'Actually, the weird thing is that when you've got your nose stuck into a crime, you connect with people. It's just the rest of the time you're unavailable.' He looked back into the house. 'That pasta is boiling over so—'

'I'll get to the point. I actually came to show you this.' Mrs Sidhu carried a folder under her arm. Inside was a single piece of cartridge paper.

'Your drawing of the Bowler's Oak.' Ben scanned it with expert eyes. 'It's quite promising. But it's not finished.'

She took it gently from him. 'Yes, that's exactly it. I'd like to finish it but perhaps in the spring.' She cast a glance around, at the bare branches of the trees all about. 'When things are growing, instead of dying.' She took his arm. He didn't resist. 'And I came to tell you my first name.'

Ben's moustache crinkled into a smile. 'Isn't that breaking the Slough rules?'

She pushed him gently backwards into the house. 'Not necessarily. We could get more acquainted.' She kicked the front door closed behind her. Two minutes later, a pot of pasta boiled over. Both Ben and Mrs Sidhu were too preoccupied to care.

ACKNOWLEDGEMENTS

Huge thanks to my publisher HarperCollins, Julia Wisdom at Hemlock Press, commissioning editor Kathryn Cheshire, and my agent, Adam Gauntlett, for making this book possible. Special thanks to my editors, Kathryn Cheshire and Jo Thompson for their guidance, encouragement and eternal good humour. Thanks also to Felicity Denham (publicity) and Toby James for another delicious cover design.

Just Desserts has Mrs Sidhu delve in to the world of art, which I find as beguiling, confusing, and inspirational as she does. So thanks to my guides through this world. First of all, thanks to my wife Tess Recordon who is a working artist. She has taken me to galleries and exhibitions around the world, educated me and drip fed my curiosity. I'd also like to thank Mary Kempski, who provided expertise on the process of art restoration and transportation. I'm only sad I could not use more of her immense knowledge in the plot. Also, thanks to Susan Sciama for debating and helping with the Italian nickname for the stolen painting in the novel.

My wife gets double mention. Not only is she a busy artist, she faces the uphill task of marshalling a very needy Border Terrier and an even needier writer into an effective household. This is something she does with grace and without complaint. Thanks also to my family and friends for the support, the conversations, the cups of tea and drinks in the pub.

A massive thanks to my fellow crime novelists who have been so welcoming and endlessly helpful and a big thanks to Cara Hunter for giving up her name.

Most of my thanks go to the readers, fans, bloggers, booksellers and book lovers. Meeting you all has been a huge pleasure and your support is what makes this job worthwhile.